BY L.V. DITCHKUS

Crimes of the Sasquatch: Book I of The Sasquatch Series

Mission of the Sasquatch: Book II of The Sasquatch Series

SOON TO COME

Passage of the Sasquatch: Book IV of The Sasquatch Series

NEW SERIES

The Chrom Y Chronicles

Legacy
of the
Sasquatch

Book III of The Sasquatch Series

Legacy
of the
Sasquatch

Book III of The Sasquatch Series

L.V. Ditchkus

Pinon Press
Colorado

To Dylan Tracy,
A kind and exceptional man

Chapter 1

REVAL (SASQUATCH HOME WORLD)—OCTOBER 20
KALEV

The scent of burnt hair stung Kalev's nose. He rubbed the back of his fur-covered hands across his eyes. When his vision cleared, he saw the transfer had succeeded. The dense jungle of home, jammed with ancient trees towering over cram-packed flowering bushes, had replaced the shaggy juniper trees and scraggly undergrowth of Dylan's world.

The Sasquatch wriggled his toes on the spongy trail. To the right of his foot, he spotted a finger-sized vent that emitted a column of moist, fresh air. When the wind storms blew, the flow would decrease to a trickle, but now it ruffled his hair. Or at least it would if his fur was not so filthy from living in Porgu for the past months.

He breathed a sigh of relief. They had made it home.

Kalev stretched to inventory his condition. His arms and shoulders moved without pain. He flexed his toes and bent each knee. Everything seemed to work correctly.

He stood to inspect his surroundings. Where had they arrived?

A thirty-foot tree stood next to the trail. Kalev leaned over a waist-high bush and pushed fist-sized blossoms out of his way. He rubbed the tree, then smelled his hand. The scent seemed familiar. He knew this tree, but the location seemed wrong.

The trail should be straight, but it curved before it snaked out of view. Maybe someone had trimmed the plants along the path to divert its direction. Kalev had been away for six months. The change was possible.

He ignored the inconsistency, firmly confident about their location.

Kalev looked down at Dylan's naked, crumpled body—on its side in a fetal position. Kalev rolled him onto his back and pulled his legs and arms straight. No bones appeared out of alignment, and there were no apparent cuts or bruises.

The Sasquatch leaned close to watch the skin on Dylan's neck tremor with a pulse. Thankfully, the frail being had survived the transfer. If he had died, all of Kalev's work over the past months would have been for naught.

He rubbed a lock of Dylan's hair between a thumb and finger and sniffed. The burnt odor came from Dylan. Something on his hair must have reacted with the lightning when they transferred.

Kalev rolled his eyes, disgusted with how they added scents to their hair and skin to hide natural fragrances. Of course the aromas of Dylan's world were overwhelming and repugnant. Kalev snorted. Maybe they were right to try to cover them up.

Between the smell of Dylan's burnt hair and both of their body odors from living in Dylan's world, Kalev needed to act quickly to clean off the foreign scents. Someone might stumble across them on the trail, and he planned to keep Dylan a secret until the most auspicious moment.

His mission in Dylan's world was complete when Kalev successfully transferred them both to Reval. But his final use for Dylan lay ahead. Those objectives would take detailed plans and precise timing. He was up to the task and would not fail.

He hefted Dylan over his matted shoulder. The being did not awaken but made a subtle groan. Transporting him and cleaning him would be easier while he was unconscious. If he were awake, Dylan would pelt Kalev with a million questions about the transfer.

The Sasquatch had promised to introduce Dylan to other Sasquatches but neglected to mention they would travel to a different dimension before meeting them. Dylan was a curious little creature, but Kalev had the upper hand with a superior intellect. These primitive beings were stunted and motivated solely by survival instincts.

Kalev straightened and gripped his captive by the thighs. First, he looked in one direction and then the other. Kalev considered options. Unless the terrain had dramatically changed, a seldom-used bathing pool lay only a few minutes' walk down the trail.

Kalev held Dylan afloat and watched the solution dissolve Porgu's contaminants from their bodies until the pool could absorb no more dirt, insects, and the horrid food that had plagued Kalev's stomach for the last six months. The color of the pond changed from vivid blue to orange—a sign of toxins polluting beyond capacity. He hauled Dylan to another pool with the same results. At the third, Kalev watched threads of orange coagulate when they absorbed contaminants and then dissipated.

When he believed they smelled sufficiently neutral to avoid detection, Kalev sent a message to Tiina about his return. He expected her response to be instantaneous.

Minutes passed. *Where is she?* The Tiina he knew from before his journey would have rushed to see him. His gut gripped in nervous anticipation.

Others must have detained her from rushing to meet him. Why else would she postpone welcoming him home?

His second notification went to both Tiina and Alevide. While he waited for them to come, Kalev pulled the still unconscious Dylan into a secluded nook. He suspended the man's limp head on the lip of the pool and tucked leaves around his shoulders to prevent him from slipping under the surface. After all it took to bring him from Porgu to Reval, a drowned prize would be insurmountably unfortunate.

Kalev stood in the waist-deep fluid and seethed. They should be here to revel in his glory.

Chapter 2

TIINA

Tiina relaxed on the shore of the woodland pool and succumbed to hypnotic bubbling from the natural spring. The sounds dispelled her anxiety. She followed her daily exercise routine and extended her legs to hover above the surface. Tiina pursed her lips and breathed in staccato gasps in an attempt to dispel her anger. Let Kalev wait, she thought. She needed time to sort out how she felt.

She inched her heels downward. Her abs and thighs trembled from the strain. Seconds ticked by, and the pool glimmered in the fading sunlight. Tiina fluttered her feet and formed ripples that cascaded to the far end.

Earlier, when she was oblivious to his imminent return, Tiina had spent the day with the other Council members. They had considered the list of volunteers for transfer to Porgu—the land of hardship, disease, and ruthlessly cruel creatures. The members evaluated whether candidates had the skills and temperament to take on the arduous assignment. Typically, more than a dozen individuals petitioned to go. They were eager and desperately wanted to experience the dangerous and primitive conditions.

While she had never volunteered to make the journey, Tiina served on the selection committee and debriefed returning researchers. Many came back fulfilled, able to contribute to the group's knowledge of Porgu's crude society. Others returned weak and suffered from acute loneliness and malnutrition. All were unequivocally different. Kalev left months earlier, and she wondered how he had changed.

Exhausted from the day's discussions, she desperately needed this soak. Tiina held fast to the edge and slipped into the pool to submerge just above her waist. With elbows splayed, she hung on the lip with her abs taut. Toes pointed, Tiina scissored her legs and admired her long, toned thighs and hard belly, still as firm as anyone half her age. Despite being nearly a half-century old, she was the youngest member of the Council. Tiina contributed youth and optimism while the others offered caution and experience.

In the afternoon session, her colleagues had issued final decisions on two petitioners, a son and daughter of an eminently successful former transferee. The daughter was approved, and the son denied. Tiina suggested they separately notify the family for each application—perhaps with a day between each announcement to inform them about the rejection first. There was no need for the family to struggle between a celebration or acting quietly empathetic.

The decision to reject the brother took extensive deliberation. On the positive side, his mother had transferred with few ill effects and returned with breakthrough data on coastal habitat development. But the Council ruled her son's temperament erratic and his addiction to social engagement too strong. Ultimately, they suggested he could resubmit an application in five years.

If left exclusively up to Tiina, she would have approved his request. His enthusiasm for the trip felt infectious. But more seasoned, skeptical members prevailed. While disappointed for the petitioner, she recognized the value of decisions made by the committee. Different views and perspectives kept mishaps to a minimum. Tiina hoped her contributions helped find the best researchers, able to endure the rigors of the journey and the hardships of solitude.

Moments before her meeting ended, Kalev's transmission had crept into her thoughts, not a bold, trumpeted announcement for all to hear but a niggling whisper meant only for her. He had returned and wanted her to join him. She had glanced around and could see none of her peers were aware of the message. *He is only calling me.*

Inch by inch, Tiina submerged the rest of her body. She floated on her back and felt her silky hair spread like the tendrils of a plant dispersing their roots. First one flick of a leg to engage muscles from hip to toe, then the other. She bent her hands at the wrists and waved them to propel herself forward.

Low branches hovered overhead to filter the daylight, and leaves rustled in a faint breeze. Tiina reached the far end and spun to retrace her path. Eyes closed and ears below the surface, silence blanketed the outside world. Calm and quiet enveloped as her anger eroded. Yet she could not suppress her curiosity. Where did he go, and what had he learned?

Like a rock crashing through a window, the second notification blasted into her mind. *Now he is calling out to someone besides me.* But who? Was he injured? Why the urgency?

Tiina jammed her feet into the pool's soft bottom and stood upright. Moisture dripped from her hair to splatter the surface like a shower of rain. Perhaps she should disregard the message. Kalev had left suddenly—without warning or permission. Her lips drew into a line, eyes narrowed. Gone for nearly half a year, he had left her to cover his absence with lies.

Torn between anger and curiosity about his journey, she swam to the pool's edge. In one swift movement, Tiina placed her palms on the rim and lifted her body into a crouch. She straightened, thinking and deciding.

With complete disregard for her moist body, Tiina dashed into the forest to meet the returning adventurer.

Chapter 3

DYLAN COX

Eyes closed, Dylan floated on his back in a sea of warm, viscous liquid. Protected and womblike, consciousness came slowly. He felt neither fear nor pain, only the rising and lowering of his chest while he breathed. Several sets of steady hands supported his body. He could tell that a being stood near his head and held his shoulders.

Gently, a pair of hands shifted and moved from underneath to rest on his chest. Dylan jolted—someone pressed him under the surface. Others joined to hold him below.

He choked and thrashed to escape and resurface. His captors withdrew, and he wedged his feet into the mushy bottom. Dylan exploded to the surface to catch his breath and stood with his head and chest exposed.

Dylan dragged an arm across his face and struggled to clear his vision. He blinked and coughed. Dylan glanced down, grateful the opaque liquid obscured his nakedness.

Three beings stood with him in the waist-deep pool. At least it was waist deep for him. All were Sasquatches but defied the hulky, ape-like characterization from movies and myths. With high cheekbones, v-shaped swimmer physiques, and fine fur, short on their faces and long and wispy on their heads and bodies, they looked like hairy brunette versions of a Scandinavian volleyball team.

Dylan recognized Kalev, the Sasquatch he befriended at a backwoods cabin in Colorado. Except for Kalev's more chiseled facial features and sapphire-colored eyes, one could have been Kalev's twin. The other, obviously female with breasts, stood slightly shorter and with darker hair. But even that one stood nearly two feet taller than Dylan. The trio silently stared at him, Kalev with satisfaction and familiarity and the others in wide-eyed amazement as if he was the oddity.

"Are you trying to kill me?" Dylan sputtered, despite knowing Kalev only communicated telepathically.

Kalev quickly transmitted the words, "We attempted to awaken you. You are safe here."

Contrary to Kalev's calm response, Dylan watched his compatriots jolt at the sound of Dylan's voice. The taller grabbed Kalev by the arm while the shorter hunched. Her eyes darted as if she worried about being discovered. Had they ever heard a human speak?

They don't know how to communicate in a spoken language, but Kalev has probably transmitted information about me.

Dylan turned from the audience to inspect his hand while he lifted it from the pool. The oozing liquid had the consistency of maple syrup, but it was turquoise blue and did not stick to his fingers. It slithered off to evaporate instantly and left no residue. He raised and lowered his hand to be sure the results remained consistent. They did. The effervescent solution tingled as if millions of tiny fish chewed his skin.

Dylan raised an eyebrow and waved an open palm toward the forest that surrounded the pool. "Where are we?"

Kalev moved forward and laid a hand on Dylan's shoulder. The Sasquatch couple stayed back and hooked their arms to peer around Kalev in a synchronized lean. Kalev placed a finger against his lips, encouraging silence. He touched his forehead to announce an intended transmission. Dylan closed his eyes but knew the images would block his vision irrespective of whether he kept them open or shut.

For the past few days, he and Kalev had communicated with this method. Dylan knew to open his mind to accept Kalev's message and expected a mixture of images and words, which Kalev had picked up from Dylan's transmissions.

Dylan's ability to receive information remained slow, basically at a child's level in Kalev's society. Instead of a flurry of images to convey ideas, Kalev spoonfed concepts to Dylan, while his own flawless memory picked up hundreds of words and memories from Dylan. Despite their efforts, cultural differences rendered the transfer of knowledge to a snail's pace.

Dylan's vision filled with images of family. His parents distributed Christmas gifts, and, when he was younger, his mother held his hand in front of the polar bear enclosure at Brookfield Zoo. Dylan responded with the word *parents*, and Kalev shook his head. After some thought, Kalev added the transmitted words, "This is my brother and wife."

"Your wife?" Dylan said. The smaller Sasquatch had robin egg blue eyes, wide with curiosity mixed with fear, that shone from under a spray of dark brown fringe. Her narrow shoulders stood as straight as a runway model, and round breasts topped with tiny charcoal nipples poked through the fur cascading down her chest.

Kalev repeated his silent shush.

Dylan rolled his eyes and sent a message. "Okay, no words out loud, only thoughts."

Kalev nodded and transmitted, "Brother's wife."

Dylan knew names for people, locations, and things were rendered moot in a society with telepathic communication, particularly when their visions contained a frantic mixture of still images intermixed with video clips.

Dylan was hard-wired in verbal dialogue and needed names. He christened Kalev's brother Alevide and the wife Tiina. Kalev nodded and smiled at Dylan's naming conventions.

When Alevide put an arm around his wife's shoulders, they leaned their heads together as if they were transferring messages. Alevide held one hand up. Kalev snarled at the gesture—being excluded grated him. Could they accept Dylan's transmissions as Kalev did? Perhaps not. Even if they captured the transfer, they would not understand what Dylan meant. He and Kalev had spent days together to forge a bond and train each other how to communicate. If Kalev planned to stay longer than a few hours, Dylan would teach Tiina and Alevide a few words.

"Now that we know who's here, I'd like to understand where we are," Dylan said aloud. Kalev shot him an exasperated look and pressed a finger to his lips. "Okay," Dylan whispered. Kalev's head cocked in a nonverbal reprimand. *When you're in a telepathic society, I guess no talking means just that.*

Dylan tapped his forehead to warn Kalev of a transmission. Then he flipped through images of his last experiences in his world. Dylan focused on each vision to give Kalev a linear visual message. First, he streamed memories of the remote Colorado cabin. He pictured following Kalev up a dirt track to the summit of a mountain. A full moon illuminated their path. While Dylan expected Kalev to signal for other Sasquatches to join them on the mountaintop, that did not happen. So Dylan sent images from the summit of Kalev warming Dylan by holding his furry body against Dylan's naked one. His final transmitted image pictured Kalev with his arms raised to the heavens, right before an explosion and a cascade of fireworks. The message ended there because Dylan's memory had blanked until he woke in the pool.

Once his transmitted memories finished, Dylan offered Kalev a bewildered gaze and outstretched hands. Kalev smiled and moved forward to embrace his human friend. He held him gently and stroked Dylan's head like how a mother would comfort a stressed child.

Kalev leaned back enough to look Dylan in the eye. He touched his own brow, and Dylan closed his eyes to receive the transmission. He hoped for answers.

Kalev's vision included snippets of Sasquatches, some who walked in pairs and others in larger groups sitting on the ground. They laughed, responded to humor with playful shoves, and sat in communal pools. Dylan noticed they often leaned toward each other. They sometimes touched brows or the sides of their heads. Dylan sent a message with people talking. Kalev responded with a similar vision of the ever-silent Sasquatches, with the words, "Talking. Very fast."

Dylan smiled at Kalev's repeated tutoring. He already knew Sasquatches communicated at warp speed. Dylan's next message juxtaposed a vision of Church Mountain's summit and this pool, surrounded by lush plants that seemed to reach far into the pale pink sky. Dylan transferred the words, "Where are we?"

Kalev's transmission mirrored Dylan's vision of the pool and included, "You should call this place Reval. It is my home."

Chapter 4

KALEV

D ylan's childlike smile prompted Kalev to pull him into an embrace. Dylan transmitted, "You guys are very touchy-feely. That's a custom I'll need to get used to."

Without responding to Dylan, Kalev thought, he has no idea how different we are and how easily we can manipulate him. At that moment, Kalev decided the word *halvek* would be his newly invented term for a human. From penetrating Dylan's thoughts, Kalev knew spoken languages evolved. While his modification might never catch on in Porgu, Kalev was pleased with the change.

Kalev stroked Dylan's back but watched Alevide and Tiina. She started first. Her message exploded in Kalev's head with images of rebellious Sasquatches and the repercussions they suffered when the Council conferred justice.

"What have you done?" Her transmission did not include words, but her question was clear to him.

"I needed to go there," he responded telepathically with a flurry of images conveying the concepts of desire and Porgu to both Tiina and Alevide. In the Sasquatch vernacular, he transmitted, "I have learned more about their culture than dozens of others who transferred. For centuries, our researchers have brought back incremental information that added to our understanding, but my communications with this human will increase our awareness of their species a hundredfold."

Tiina crossed her arms, jaw clenched. "Your intentions sound noble now, but it has been years since the Council rejected your transfer application. That you went without permission will be tough enough for them to hear. Bringing this one back was unconscionable."

Dylan interrupted their transmissions with his own. "Can't you include me? I assume you are talking about me."

Kalev understood but knew it was lost on Tiina and Alevide. Kalev raised an open hand to them, the universal signal for a private conversation, and more polite than a raised fist, which meant *your input is not welcome.* Then he responded telepathically in Porgu words to Dylan, as the others would not have comprehended the halvek's language anyway. "You could not possibly understand our conversation. I will explain it to you later when we are alone." Dylan huffed and submerged up to his chin while his gaze shifted between the Sasquatches.

Kalev turned and transmitted with authority to Tiina and Alevide. "Don't tell me you are not tempted to hear what I have learned. We have been wrong about so many of their traits and behaviors. For example, you would be interested to know they have a hierarchy of how they treat lower animals."

Tiina responded with a smirk. "What is there to know? They enslave lower animals for food and sport. What more could you possibly discover about that?"

Kalev knew she would not be able to resist. "They have developed systems to rank animals. Many become food, but different groups of halveks eat only specific types. Others are raised exclusively for comfort or entertainment. No one would kill and eat one of these." Kalev included images of domestic dogs and cats to accompany his last transmission.

Tiina softened, apparently intrigued by the concept. "How do they establish this hierarchy?"

"It is completely arbitrary but widely understood and accepted. I believe the rules originated from first determining the extent of loyalty within the animal's temperament. The perceived attractiveness of these lower creatures may have also played a part in the original decisions."

"What is considered attractive?"

Kalev rubbed his chin. After some thought, he sent visions of puppies and kittens.

"The young ones are deemed attractive but not the old?"

Kalev reflected longer. He replayed Dylan's memories and tried to make sense of the halvek's irrational ranking. He transmitted images of petite poodles, schnauzers, and a Chihuahua.

"Only the small ones?" Alevide joined the silent discussion.

Kalev filed through images of Great Danes, horses, and giant pet pythons before he transmitted, "No, size is not the sole criteria."

"Just the healthy ones?" asked Tiina.

Visions of three-legged pets swarmed through Kalev's mind. "No." He shook his head. "It is not clear to me, but that is why I need to spend more time with him. Their culture is primitive but not as simple as we assumed.

Alevide waved a hand. "You are digressing and putting Tiina and me at considerable risk with the High Council. What are your intentions with him?"

Kalev glanced at Dylan. "I will keep him hidden until I have learned more. He is my discovery, and I do not plan to tell the Council about him until I learn all I can."

Kalev intercepted another transmission from Dylan. "I know you're talking with them, but I can't see what you transmit. Tell me what's going on."

With an exasperated eye roll, Kalev responded, "You must be patient. They did not know you were coming."

"I'm not an invited guest? I'll bet that went down well."

"Went down?"

Dylan smiled. "There are many interpretations, but I meant they must have been surprised."

Kalev nodded, knowing Dylan had no idea about his plans. The halvek would play a significant role in Kalev's final objective. "Please avoid talking aloud and enjoy your soak while I work on a plan with my family."

"I thought you brought me here to engage with them. If you intend to get me home soon, we'll need to start a conversation with Alevide and Tiina—and anyone else who might be interested in meeting me."

"You may have misunderstood the length of our visit. There will be plenty of time for you to know them."

Dylan straightened. "How long before we go home?"

"Transfer opportunities are regular but not on the same day. We will be in my homeland for some time."

"How long? Days? Years?"

Kalev placed a gentle hand on Dylan's shoulder and indicated toward Tiina and Alevide. "I will explain everything to you when we are alone. Right now, I need to create a strategy with my brother and his wife. They have influence in our society and will be important in your introduction to our High Council. But this will all take time. You are a curious being. Use your time here to learn about us. There will be much for you to absorb about the way we live."

"How much time?"

Dylan is refusing to give up, Kalev thought, but transmitted, "Longer than a day, but much less than a year. We will discuss everything later. Please, enjoy the pool and allow me to talk with Alevide and Tiina."

Dylan huffed. When Kalev nodded toward the length of the pool, Dylan leaned back and floated. Then he broke into a vigorous backstroke to the far end.

Kalev's eyes darted into the lush undergrowth. He looked for hints of approaching strangers. Should he physically retrieve him? At the far end of the pool, Dylan flip-turned and stroked back to the Sasquatches, where he grinned at Kalev and floated silently. The Sasquatch shook his head. Dylan's impulsive behavior could derail his plans. He would need to devise ways to keep him under control.

Tiina smacked Kalev's arm. "You have to tell the Council. They will know what to do. He should not be here."

Dylan was not the only one who would need to be constrained. Kalev smiled at Tiina. "You know how anything unconventional frightens the Council. They will decide Dylan is dangerous and vote to euthanize him."

Tiina and Alevide exchanged meaningful looks. Kalev knew they agreed with him. The society's processes evolved over the centuries through rituals and commonly understood pacts. Behaviors out of the norm were discouraged. Dylan's presence was not merely out of bounds—it would prompt swift action to restore order.

Kalev watched the pair while they nodded and exchanged thoughts. "Let me see your transmissions." Kalev insisted.

Alevide held up an open hand, and Kalev huffed at the rebuff but decided to wait.

Finally, Tiina sent a message to both Kalev and Alevide. "We agree with you. They might react with haste to eliminate him. We should take this opportunity to learn how he reacts to stimulus and what can trigger his survival instincts."

"I will keep him hidden until the time is right to present him."

Alevide transmitted, "Do not make us regret this decision. For *today*, we will help you keep Dylan a secret from the Council. It will not be easy. He is noisy, and someone could overhear him. Where will you take him for the night?"

"My sleep site is not far from yours. If no one has taken over that spot since I left, I could hide him there."

Alevide responded. "When you left, we told everyone you went to visit our mother and father. We never gave a reason for your visit. We let others believe Mother needed support with personal issues, and you went to comfort her. Since everyone expected you to return, your place remains unoccupied."

"No one knows I made the transfer?"

Tiina answered, "No one except the two of us."

Kalev looked at Tiina and then Alevide. Their secrecy worked well for his plans. Kalev could reveal Dylan on his terms without facing the consequences of the illegal transfer. He transmitted, "Thank you for keeping this a secret."

Tiina straightened. "It is a secret until tomorrow. I plan to tell the Transfer Section where you have been and you are back." Kalev knew her group would want to know about his transgression. They were the sole authority to approve who went to Porgu and when. Her section also debriefed those who returned. They would question Kalev about his experience.

Tiina continued. "After they talk with you, my section will notify the tribe's High Council."

"One day is not sufficient. If I promise to tell the Council soon, will you give me time to consider how to let them know about Dylan?"

"As a part of the Transfer Section, I *am* a Council Member. We decide who transfers and who does not. You disobeyed our decision. I am obligated to tell them you went without authorization."

"But you were not part of the Transfer Section when I applied and was denied. If you were, I probably would not have been denied."

She tilted her head. "I am familiar with all the applications that have ever been brought forward, including yours. You have made a big assumption when you say I would have contested their decision."

Kalev's shoulders tensed. Surely, she would have defended him in front of her section. Their rejection was arbitrary and spiteful. Tiina would have convinced them to authorize his transfer. If so, he would not have needed to resort to subversive means to retrieve Dylan and bring him to Reval. "Your anxiety over this situation is making you say things you do not mean."

"Do not tell me how I feel or what I think. You've been away for months, and my contributions to the Transfer Section are essential to their work."

Alevide placed his arm across his wife's shoulders. "My love, your commitment to the Council is resolute. But your devotion to our family should also play a part in this decision. Can we give him a couple of days to consider options?"

Her mate's justification of Kalev's proposal seemed to calm her. She looked toward Dylan. To Kalev and Alevide, she transmitted, "You should not question my commitment to our family. I have kept Kalev's illegal transfer a secret while he was away." Her shoulders slumped. "You know I cannot win with both of you against me. What you suggest runs against my better judgment, but I will give you a couple of days."

"I am forever grateful," Kalev responded.

The conspirators snapped to attention when they heard footfalls approach. Kalev grabbed a startled Dylan. In one bound, he leaped from the pool to hide in the bushes. He gripped the squirming halvek and wrestled him into a cocoon of soft leaves. Boughs of low trees and shrubs shielded them from those who might wander into the clearing.

Kalev placed a hand over Dylan's mouth and gestured to be silent before he sent a hasty vision of two walking Sasquatches and the words, "Someone is coming."

"Why can't I meet them?" Dylan immediately transmitted.

Kalev held him close. "It is too soon. Do not talk or send transmissions. They may overhear."

Dylan's eyes filled with concern. Then, he rested his head against

Kalev's chest and sniffed. "You smell better here than in Colorado," he whispered.

Kalev lifted Dylan's chin with a knuckle to look him in the eyes. He pressed a finger to Dylan's lips. "Silence." Discovery this soon after the transfer would be a disaster. There was much to do to prepare Dylan for his presentation.

Kalev recognized the visitors by their open transmissions to Tiina and Alevide. A mated pair, they came to the pool to relax. They seemed pleased to see their friends already soaking and moved near Alevide and Tiina, who maneuvered to ensure their guests faced away from the bushes hiding Kalev and Dylan. Kalev peeked around the leaves to gain a clear view of his brother and Tiina.

The group's communications were mundane—a typical exchange of views about the latest Council decisions and an update from Tiina about contenders for upcoming transfers. While Kalev listened to their transmissions, he rubbed Dylan's back to keep him calm and silent.

He knew the halvek was not able to capture their thoughts. While Dylan could understand Kalev, his messages were sent slowly and with only the bare minimum of information. The couple's rapid-fire transfers would be uninterpretable and could overload Dylan's underutilized brain.

Suddenly, the male stopped short. He stood and sniffed. "What is that smell?"

Kalev tightened his embrace on Dylan and hoped the male Sasquatch would not come to investigate. Tiina responded immediately. "I think this pond may be starting to turn. I noticed some orange threads on the surface when I started to soak. We have used this one quite a lot lately and may need to give it a break."

"It is not the same scent as a turning pool." The male lifted his arm and sniffed it. He scrunched his nose. "Smells bitter. Reminds me of a scent from when I did the transfer."

Alevide waved a dismissive hand. "A couple of days ago someone came back from Porgu. She may have overused this pool to do her first cleanse." His transmission included an image of the female who had recently returned.

The male nodded in recognition and resubmerged himself until his shoulders were covered.

To Dylan, Kalev transmitted the words, "You are doing well. Continue your silence." Dylan tucked an ear against Kalev's hairy chest.

In the pool, the male transmitted, "I guess that might be it. We will look for a refreshed pool tomorrow for our soak." His mate nodded agreement while he continued. "I heard about the recently returned transferee. We plan to sit in at tomorrow's Council meeting at the Amphitheater to hear about the situation. I understand there was controversy over her early return."

Tiina's shoulders slumped. "Something bad happened to her. I do not know the details yet, but she returned after being away only a few months. I will find out more at the meeting."

The female peppered her response with visions of faces creased with empathy. "I hope she will recover from her journey. Not everyone manages the transfer well."

"All I know is she endured tough conditions. We will hear more tomorrow." Tiina placed a hand on the female's shoulder.

The male nodded. "I would be interested to know what happened."

"I have an appointment to debrief her tomorrow afternoon sometime after the windstorms and the mists. Our Transfer Section will broadcast any public information after our discussions."

The male rubbed his chin. "The odors were the worst part of my experience."

Kalev sighed and wished they would abandon the odor topic. But the male continued. "Before I went there, I could not imagine how many different fragrances there would be. It was not only the horrific ones, like their excrement and rotten trash. Each flower and fruit had a different smell." He shook his head. "They added scents to their bodies, some were pleasant but many smelled dreadful."

His mate interjected. "It is hard to imagine some researchers have gone there solely to learn more about odors. A friend narrowed her observations to plants. Some flowers' scents are designed to attract insects for pollination purposes. Carnivorous vegetation uses its fragrance to attract prey."

Tiina grinned. "Can you believe their plants can eat meat? While it is understandable for animals, as their resources are limited, but plants?"

"Based on what we have observed, most plants take sustenance from the soil. The carnivorous ones grow in places where the soil is nutrient-deprived, like in the desert or bogs. They adapted this ability to survive. You almost need to experience the brutal conditions there to comprehend how evolution continually improves their survival objective."

The two couples mused about botany research and then reverted to views on local politics. Finally, the visiting pair bid farewell to Tiina and Alevide.

Long after the couple's footsteps faded, Kalev emerged with Dylan. Kalev smiled while he watched Dylan survey the perimeter. *This is good. He's learning to be cautious.* If Dylan helped to stay hidden, then they would have more time to prepare before introducing him to the High Council.

He indicated for Dylan to re-enter the pool.

They slipped in and stopped in front of Tiina and Alevide. The couple sat on the edge with their legs dangling.

Kalev watched Tiina stare at Dylan. What could she be thinking? Before he could ask her intentions, she leaned forward, the typical movement before someone would send a message.

A split second later, Dylan shrieked and grabbed both sides of his head before he plunged below the surface.

"Stop!" Kalev commanded and moved between Tiina and Dylan with his arms outstretched. But he knew full well his body could not block the assault of Tiina's transmission.

Tiina shrugged, and Dylan resurfaced. She must have stopped her transmission. Dylan emerged from his crouch. He still trembled from the mental attack.

"Are you okay?" Kalev pulled Dylan into an embrace and cradled the back of the halvek's neck with a massive hand.

Tiina tilted her head and stared at the pair as if she wondered how her message had derailed.

Kalev explained, "You do not understand how primitive these beings are. They communicate aloud with words to represent each person, thing, and action. Without an ability to transfer images, they create context one word at a time. Their unsophisticated brains cannot handle our communications."

Tiina looked at the halvek and drew her arms across her chest. "How will you learn anything from him?"

"He has already taught me quite a lot. The key to understanding him will be to learn his language. I have a good start, but I need to know more. This evening I will teach him to open his mind further, so I can retrieve what I can."

Alevide smiled. "Our parents used to trick us into opening our minds so they could see if we planned to misbehave. Is that your plan?"

"Exactly."

Chapter 5

As Alevide and Tiina looked on, Kalev smiled and rubbed the top of Dylan's head. This initial day in Reval had been a staggering success. He had convinced both Tiina and Alevide to give him much needed time. The foundation for meeting his objective was solid.

Dylan interrupted Kalev's musings with a transmission. "You guys seem to be making plans but are leaving me in the dark."

Kalev tilted his head and tried to make sense of the colloquialism. "Please repeat," he sent.

"Sorry. I thought we were supposed to learn about each other. But I'm standing here alone while you're exchanging messages without me. Are you planning to teach me how to communicate with Alevide and Tiina?"

"There will be time for an exchange at a later meeting." Kalev straightened to listen for any sign of other Sasquatches headed to the pool. "For this evening, I will take you to my sleep site. It will provide us with a place to rest, away from all others."

"I take it we're not headed back to the cabin in Colorado tonight?"

"It is not possible right now. Our journey to my sleep site will be short. But we will need to move quickly and would go faster if I carry you. I do not want to risk meeting any others along the way."

"I'm feeling like a decoration dog at this point." In response to Kalev's head tilt, he added, "Some people carry around a small dog as an accessory to their outfit."

When Kalev scrunched his brows in confusion, Dylan attempted to clarify with transmitted visions of women with either a toy poodle or Chihuahua draped over their arm. Dylan sent the words, "Not everyone does this—mostly wealthy women. But now is not the time for a lesson about behaviors of the top one percent. Will you let me walk on my own?"

Kalev had no idea what Dylan meant about *one percent* but wanted to convince the halvek that stealth was imperative. "When we were at the cabin, I sat in a chair, drank the nectar you made for me, and hid when you talked with visitors. I made accommodations to be with you, yet stayed concealed from others. It is your turn now. You must trust me."

Dylan pulled his lips into a line, clearly unhappy with Kalev's request. Eventually, he said, "Okay, you can carry me. But only this once. I may be two feet shorter than you, but I'm not a child."

Without agreeing to any future arrangements, Kalev cradled the naked man into his arms and hurried toward the familiar camp. Tiina and Alevide transmitted visions of farewell.

"You've got me by the short-hairs today, big fellow, but I plan to do some exploring tomorrow," Dylan transmitted, while Kalev knelt to widen the sleep site. Uncertain of why Dylan sent a vision of his sparse pubic hairs, Kalev shrugged and accepted the information.

Surprised at the amount of vegetation that had crept into his space, Kalev took each encroaching plant between his fingers and rubbed. Errant stems and leaves atrophied and slithered into the lush undergrowth.

"Let me try that," Dylan transmitted and sidled next to Kalev. Dylan mimicked the maneuver and watched the plants respond to his touch. "More people would take up gardening if they only had to touch plants to destroy weeds or prune shrubs. It seems like the vegetation responds to your instruction to retreat."

Kalev smiled while Dylan transmitted endless words without visual context. *I will grow to understand your ramblings soon,* Kalev thought, as he watched Dylan marvel at the submissive plants.

Once they cleared enough area to accommodate two inhabitants, Kalev laid on his side and rested his head on a bent arm. Kalev stretched out to enjoy the clean, soft surface—so different from the filthy hard surfaces of

Porgu. He patted the adjacent ground and motioned for Dylan to join him.

Dylan sat cross-legged before he rested a hand on Kalev's shaggy calf. While Dylan stroked the fur along Kalev's shin, he transmitted, "Your fur feels different than the matted mess you had on the mountain. I can tell from here, it smells better, too."

"In Porgu, there are no cleansing pools to keep our fur unsoiled and free from mats and infestations." Kalev lifted an arm. He blew against the fine long hairs to make them sway.

"People would pay a fortune to take a bath in one of your pools," transmitted Dylan. He ran a finger over his own, virtually hairless, arm. "It's better than a bubble bath."

Kalev received an image of one of Dylan's childhood baths complete with gray plastic submarines and a yellow duck.

The Sasquatch smiled. "Here, nature provides the pools. When they become polluted with excess waste, we allow them to rest and rejuvenate. In a few days, the ones we spoiled will be blue again and ready for other bathers."

Dylan lay down on his side and rested his head on the crook of an arm. "Don't judge us for how we value scarce resources. Maybe your society would have evolved differently if you had to work for a bath."

"Now who is judging?"

Dylan chuckled and moved closer. He patted Kalev's arm.

Kalev leaned forward until his forehead nearly touched Dylan's. Kalev sent a series of visions to showcase the terrain near their nest and beyond. Snippets captured walks through shadowy forests, lush meadows teeming with flowers, and vast lands inhabited by other families and tribes. He included a range of Sasquatch—some with lighter and others with darker fur. Each individual had a different eye color with every shade of brown, green, and blue.

While the visions continued, Dylan leaned forward to drape an arm across Kalev's shoulder. Eventually, Dylan pulled back and sent a transmission. "First, I want you to show me how to return, but your world holds so many mysteries I'd like to explore. Before I go home, I hope you take me to some of the places you've shown me."

Dylan's openness to embark on a journey could work to Kalev's advantage. He nodded and sent the words, "We will go when you are prepared."

Dylan sat upright. "Show me how to get ready."

"First, we need to rest. Lie down and let me teach you how to open your mind further. The more I know about you and your customs, the better I can prepare to show you my world."

Kalev explained how to relax and keep thoughts accessible. While the halvek slept, Kalev gained an expanded view on the world according to Dylan.

Chapter 6

OCTOBER 21
TIINA

Tiina woke with the morning light and spooned her back into Alevide's belly and chest to try to catch a few more minutes of sleep. Even though he slept, he drew her close and transmitted automatic messages of intimacy. Despite his soothing visions, her mind raced. She stewed over Kalev's reckless decision to retrieve Dylan.

What was he thinking? She sighed. Tiina knew the answer to that question—Kalev always chose paths to defy normal.

He had been wild since the day she met him at the annual festival held near his tribal home, a full day's walk from where her family lived. The festival served as a time to exchange stories between tribes, arrange matings, and celebrate the lives of the recently deceased.

While Tiina had seen Kalev and Alevide at previous festivals, the event of her twentieth year seemed different. Instead of joining gangs of youths to play games and cluster to splash in pools, Tiina stayed close to her parents and listened to their political discussions. But she glanced toward Kalev and Alevide, a handsome pair, cocky and young.

Mother nudged her, a clear sign to encourage Tiina. "You have played together every year. What is different today?"

Tiina shrugged. "It just is."

Her mother smiled knowingly and turned back to the older generation's discussion about who should assume the next role as High Council chair. Out of the corner of her eye, Tiina watched the boys' rough play. They teased the young females and vied for attention. They were obviously seeking mates.

She caught Kalev's attention first. He slapped Alevide's arm and nodded in her direction, and the pair came after her as a team. They both sent messages directed solely to her. At least she thought they were not sharing transmissions with one another. There was no way to be sure.

Kalev's communications spoke of shared adventures, travel to visit other tribes, and her flawless features, especially her dark brown hair. Alevide's approach featured his hopes for a life-commitment, children, and the intelligence he spotted in her gray-blue eyes. Each asked her to meet at a soaking pool. She replied to both and sent visions of a secluded pool not far away from the crowds.

The afternoon evaporated while the trio splashed and floated. They flirted and stroked each other's faces and arms. By the time the evening ceremonies started, they were inseparable, with each male on the lookout for something more than a day of fun.

Physically, she yearned for Kalev. Their magnetism made her giddy. Everything seemed possible in his perspective. On the other hand, Alevide seemed grounded in tradition and shared her values. By the end of the evening, she had not made any decision. Kalev made his disappointment known with a pout and aggressive pacing. Alevide seemed indifferent.

Days later, Alevide traveled to her family's tribe. He served in the Family Section of his local Council. The section approved mating choices and decisions to have children.

When Alevide asked for a transfer to her tribe's Family Section, the High Council had supported his request. While she had thought he might be after a dalliance, he made clear his intentions to mate and have a family. His persistence paid off as they mated soon after his relocation.

Tiina shook away memories of the past and turned to raise on one elbow. She looked at her sleeping mate and ran her fingers through the long hairs that had untucked from behind his ear while he slept.

Their relationship had suffered when they lost their son. *Could that have been over twenty-five years ago?* But they decided to stay together. She knew several couples who separated after catastrophic circumstances, and no one on the Council or in their families protested those separations. But Tiina and Alevide stayed together and remained childless—any attempt to have another baby was dangerous. Both found comfort in daily routines and contributions to their tribe.

Tiina leaned forward to kiss Alevide's cheek. His scent brought a flutter to her chest. She transmitted a series of visions depicting shared intimacy. Her hands groomed his fur while Alevide moaned, still half-asleep.

She gave him a final kiss before Tiina rose to take a morning bath and find breakfast.

Refreshed and fed, Tiina walked toward the Amphitheater, a cleared circle on a hilltop with vista views of their territory and the snow-covered peaks that reached far into the pink sky. On her way, she paused to address errant plants that had invaded the path in the night. She bent to rub arrow-shaped leaves between her thumb and finger. They responded and curled into a tight roll before they slipped into the underbrush beyond the pathway.

A strand of heart-shaped leaves tinged with purple veins crept forward and took the place of the plant she had pruned. Tiina smiled at the aggressive interloper. She waited until the vine inched forward by nearly a foot before she lifted it from the path to drape it over a low branch. The transfer might encourage growth toward the forest rather than to block the trail. She watched the tip sway as if it sniffed the air before the vine meandered into the undergrowth.

About halfway to the Amphitheater, Tiina approached the Auk—a dark, expansive hole. She crossed her arms and held on to her shoulders. While Tiina slowly rocked back-and-forth, she stared into the shrubbery-choked pit and imagined what might have been.

She took a breath and raised on tiptoe to pluck a snow-white flower hanging from a high branch. Tiina stood at the edge of the precipice and nodded before she tossed the blossom into the depths. Upward air currents kept the flower aloft until gravity prevailed and pulled the bloom into the darkness.

Tiina turned and continued her journey to the Amphitheater, where the Transfer Section met. Despite her commitment to giving Kalev a few days, she planned to report his transfer at the meeting. For the time being, she would keep his secret about the halvek.

Chapter 7

DYLAN COX

Dylan pushed the cover from his body to inspect his bedding in the morning light. Deep forest green and nearly as large as a bedsheet, the leaves were a half-inch thick with a texture like dense felt.

The previous evening, Kalev had plucked a half dozen of them from a tree hanging over their sleep site. He had saved three for himself and handed over the others. Dylan had copied Kalev's technique and placed one where he planned to lay, fluffed another into a makeshift pillow and saved the last to cover his body.

Dylan drew his blanket leaf to his chin and sniffed but found no fragrance. Their soft texture reminded Dylan of his tradition to change to flannel sheets on the first night of autumn—a soft switch from the crisp, cool cotton of summer.

He glanced at Kalev's sleeping body. Kalev had complete control over Dylan. Should he trust him or make a break for it while the Sasquatch slept? The forest was dense, and the trails riddled with unknowns. Would unfamiliar Sasquatches attack him? What other kinds of wild animals lived here? Without knowing how he got here, how could he get home?

Despite being bossy and condescending, Kalev seemed to be protective of him. Dylan reached out and touched Kalev's covered shoulder. The Sasquatch shrugged but his breath remained rhythmic and unaffected. He still slept. Kalev seemed to trust *him*. After all, Dylan could bolt or harm the Sasquatch while he slept. Kalev probably had good reasons for transporting Dylan here, or he wouldn't have risked their lives to come. At least Dylan suspected the transfer was dangerous. Any form of conveyance with lightning ought to be risky. But why were they here, and what could Dylan gain from the experience? Maybe he could learn from the Sasquatch or figure out a way to introduce them to humans. For the time being, he'd stick with Kalev.

Dylan ran his tongue over his sticky teeth. *I could sure use a toothbrush.* His stomach growled, and he recalled his last meal in Colorado. More than a day had passed. He did not want to wake Kalev but was nervous about wandering far on his own. Dylan rose to crouch at the edge of their site and explore the perimeter.

Flowers and green plants sprouted from every direction to form a dense border and lean into the space he and Kalev had cleared the previous night. Maybe the vegetation was waiting patiently until the moment they abandoned the area. Would they send out tendrils to reclaim their turf?

Dylan reached to touch a fern with crimped leaves. Did it inch backward, or had Dylan imagined the movement? He stuck his hand into the bottom layer. The lowest level retreated, but some of the heartier varieties did not. Dylan sat back. Why did only some react? He would ask Kalev about that once he woke up.

Mid-sized bushes dripped with blossoms of red and violet. Their variegated leaves had veins of white and yellow. Stunted trees with giant leaves, reminiscent of palms, shot from the undergrowth with delicate brown stems coated with tiny white flowers. Upon closer inspection, Dylan saw the blooms looked like popped corn threaded through a string for a holiday tree.

Dylan stood and stared at the cloudless sky visible between fanlike leaves at the top of the trees. He assumed the sun shone somewhere beyond the scope of his view, as he'd watched the nighttime heavens change slowly from a pale gray to the muted pink. The sky seemed without clarity or depth. At one point in the evening, he had caught sight of the waning moon. It glowed with an aura that maintained a haze for the entire night. He never spotted a single star and wondered if fog blocked the sky.

Dylan tracked the gigantic trees from their tops into the dense undergrowth and lost sight of the massive trunks when they dissolved into the camouflage of the lower layers. He wanted to avoid the path to the main trail and shoved aside a thicket of leaves and branches to enter the woods.

While he slithered between boughs, Dylan blindly reached into a mass of leaves with both hands until he touched a rough solid surface. He dug his fingers into knobby bark and pulled forward to within inches of the tree trunk. In the dim light, Dylan leaned in to inspect the tree. Mottled and creased, the massive trunk stood as stout as a telephone pole, only a dozen times wider.

The forest seemed to close in on all sides and stifle the air. A claustrophobic dread made Dylan's heart race. He needed to retrace his way back to the sleep site. He turned and leaned his back against the tree.

When he took a deep breath and started to move forward, something squirmed across the tops of his toes and encircled his ankle. Dylan shuddered and lifted his knee to shake free from whatever coiled around his foot. It held fast, then gave a sharp tug.

"Let me go!" Dylan tried to bend and identify what grasped him, but leaves blocked his view. What held him? A snake? Something worse?

A brutal yank propelled him to his butt. Without mercy, it dragged him toward the sleep site. Leaves whipped at Dylan's face and arms. He grabbed handfuls of grasses and vines to slow his momentum. But the assailant was too strong.

"Stop!" Dylan yelled when he broke into the clearing.

He sagged against the ground and broke into nervous laughter when he realized Kalev had curtailed his exploration.

Kalev released his grip on Dylan's ankle. The Sasquatch returned to his bed, shook his head with a tsk, and curled back under his blanket.

As the Sasquatch jerked the leaf cover tight across his shoulder, he transmitted, "Stay here and sleep."

Despite a few scratches, Dylan felt no worse for his adventure. He glanced at Kalev's still form and decided to ignore his advice. Dylan strode to the perimeter of their site to sit cross-legged next to the edge. He faced a bush heavy with blood-red blossoms, reminiscent of the dense dahlias that edged his front yard in Chicago. He touched the flower with the tip of a finger and expected it to recoil like the plants he and Kalev cleared the evening before. But the flower bobbed in response to his poke and did not wither or withdraw.

He plucked the bloom. Dylan cradled it in his palm and sniffed. No fragrance. He licked the petals and wondered how many toxic plants grew in Kalev's world. Hunger trumped curiosity, and Dylan took a bite. He chewed. The bitter flavor triggered a gag, and Dylan spat out petals and stamen on the ground. He swiped his tongue across his arm. *I'm starving. What do they eat here?*

Dylan spotted Kalev shaking with mirth under his leaf-blanket. With an exasperated huff, Kalev transmitted, "You are a curious child."

"Still, not a child." Dylan looked over his shoulder. "What's for breakfast?"

He did not rise or lift his cover. "Are you hoping for bacon and eggs? If so, you will not find them here."

"Seems like you've picked up a lot more about life on Earth since last night. Don't tell me twelve hours of letting you poke around in my head accomplished that."

Kalev's face emerged from under the leaf. He smiled. "You would be surprised at how much I can absorb in a night. There are some topics we will need to cover in more depth because I do not understand the rationale for your world's history and your personal choices."

Dylan laughed. "Join the club. There are things I do and say that I don't understand either." He moved toward Kalev. "I'm serious, what's there to eat?" He pointed to a crimson blossom. "Please don't tell me it's all about the flowers. I can't imagine developing a taste for them."

"Do not be concerned. You will not starve. Before I find sustenance for you, I have a question about something you said last night."

"Shoot."

Kalev paused as if considering his words. "When we cleared plants from the sleep site, you said the plants succumbed to my command to retreat."

"Seemed like it to me."

Kalev tilted his head. "This idea is strange to me. Your perspective is that we have power over the plants. That they bow to our desires. You are mistaken."

"Well, you needed more space and took it from them. Right?"

"Not really. I view it more like a compromise. We both wanted the area, and I only took what I needed to have a comfortable space for myself.

I would not force them to give up what they required for themselves."

Dylan smiled. "Sounds like you've rationalized your taking. You both wanted the space, and you decided your needs were more important." Dylan considered whether Sasquatches might be able to communicate with vegetation in the same manner they telepathically talked with each other. "Did the plants have an opportunity to weigh in on your decision?"

Kalev scoffed. "No, we do not communicate with them. You have an interesting view of our relationship with plants. I never thought about it that way." He paused. "I will find a place for you to eat. But before I go, you should know where we are."

"Finally. Tell me where we are and how we got here."

"Do you want all the information now, or are you hungry? I only intended to explain this place site in relation to other areas nearby."

Dylan felt his stomach growl. "Okay. Give me the short version. I can wait for the long story."

Kalev pointed over Dylan's shoulder. "The sun rises in the east."

Dylan raised an eyebrow. "You learned the names for compass directions from me. So, you should know I'm familiar with that concept."

Kalev shrugged and pointed. "The Amphitheater is on a hill to the south, and most close-by sleep sites are east of here. Alevide and I were not originally from this tribe. So, we made our private sites farther away from the cluster of Sasquatches who lived here before us."

"Where are Tiina and Alevide?"

"Close, but there is a small rise between us. They are nearer to the Amphitheater. The pools we visited yesterday were north of here. They are farther from the Amphitheater and Tiina's tribe's sites, which means we seldom use them. I will go now to see if there are Sasquatches around. We need to keep you undetected for a time."

Dylan gestured toward his naked body. "I hate to be immodest, but is there something we can do about my situation? You and all of your buddies have fur, and I feel a bit intimidated by excessive exposure."

"Are you cold?"

Dylan considered the question. Despite an afternoon, evening, and morning in Kalev's world, Dylan did not recall feeling either hot or cold. The temperature seemed neutral. "No, I feel fine, but I don't normally walk around buck-naked. I suspect tailors are in short supply. But are there any alternatives?"

Kalev looked at Dylan and nodded in agreement. The dense leaves from their beds still lay in a pile where they had tossed them off. Kalev draped one over Dylan's shoulder and stood back as if to consider the effect. Dylan tied the longest corner at his shoulder and wrapped the leaf around his body. Toga or sarong? Dylan wondered. No matter, the surface was soft and stuck to itself. Once clad, Dylan felt less vulnerable.

Kalev left with a warning to stay off the trails and out of the woods. Dylan obediently sat and hoped Kalev would return shortly with a tray of carryout for breakfast.

Dylan tried to rest, but sleep remained elusive. Every sound sent him into the forest edge to hide in the vegetation. While he huddled against the leaves, he wondered if poison ivy grew in Kalev's world. His skin tingled from the psychosomatic fear of plant toxins.

About an hour after Kalev left, Dylan felt nature call. He scratched his head. *I don't see an outhouse, and I forgot to ask Kalev about the peeing protocol.* When the urge strengthened, Dylan grew indifferent about how Kalev might respond to a breach in Sasquatch customs.

Dylan marched to the edge of the cleared site and urinated on the bushes. Most plants appeared impervious to the stream, but a knee-high shrub with delicate orange blooms blackened as if burned and withered into the undergrowth. The adjacent vegetation migrated to fill the void and left only a few charred sticks to memorialize the bush's demise.

Distinct footfalls triggered another leap into the brush. When Dylan received Kalev's familiar transmission, he sighed in relief and crawled out.

"Where the hell have you been?" Dylan transmitted.

With a sideways glance at the assassinated bush, Kalev replied, "Could you have waited until I returned before you desecrated our area?"

"Maybe you should have told me some basic etiquette before leaving me?"

"I thought you were hungry."

"Starved. What have you brought back?" Disappointed, Dylan could see Kalev's empty hands.

Kalev shook his head. "Nourishment here is not the same as what you consume back home. We need to use a pool."

"Like the one we were in yesterday? You didn't tell me to slurp up the bathwater."

"Not the same type of pool. We were in a bathing pool. It dissolves impurities outside and inside your body. The nutrient pools are different, but they are always close to each other."

"Wait a minute. So I was supposed to relieve myself in the pool we soaked in?"

Kalev nodded. "Yes. Once your diet has changed to what is available here, it won't be so disgusting."

Yuck. Dylan thought about shitting in his bath. "Okay. How can you tell the difference between the bathing and the dining pools?"

Kalev transmitted a vision of the blue pool from the previous evening with the words bath and soak. Then he switched to emerald green pools and the word "food."

Dylan replied, "I hope Sasquatches aren't colorblind. They might try to take dinner in the latrine."

Kalev tilted his head as if he considered Dylan's message. After a moment, his lip curled into a faint smile.

When Kalev glanced toward the treetops, Dylan followed his gaze. "What do you see?" Dylan asked.

"Can you detect the trees have started to sway?"

He strained to notice any difference and watched the uppermost leaves thrash into a frenzy. The highest branches whipped like a car's wiper blades in a downpour. Dylan nodded.

"Twice a day, we have wind storms. They can be violent, but usually they simply whip the tops of the trees. Most of us find comfort in the sound and take a nap, either in our sleep site or wherever we happen to be. Few Sasquatches travel during the windstorms, so the trails have less traffic. The sound will muffle our footsteps." He turned to Dylan and continued. "Especially yours, my clumsy friend."

"What are you talking about? I've been a jogger all my life. Awkward in social settings, perhaps. But not clumsy."

Kalev expression changed from flippant to empathy. "Perhaps I do not have the right words. You move loudly through my world and bump into plants while you look around instead of where you go. You also release unharnessed thoughts. We can hear these things."

The Sasquatch touched a wispy plant that reminded Dylan of the air fern his business partner, Tom, had nursed to health in the dining room of the house they shared in Chicago. Dylan wondered if Tom had grown concerned about his whereabouts. Before Dylan left with Kalev, he and Tom had agreed to give Dylan two days with the Sasquatch before Tom would expect a call by noon.

That's today. If Dylan failed to make contact, Tom would travel the eleven-hundred miles from Chicago to Salida, the tiny mountain town in rural Colorado.

Kalev interrupted his thoughts. "Tom will expect you to contact him tomorrow?"

Dylan folded his arms in front of his chest. "That was our plan, but unless you can locate a payphone, I won't be calling him."

"How long will it take for him to forget about you?"

Dylan frowned. "I hope you're not asking because you don't intend to show me how to get back there."

"You don't have to worry about it. I wonder about the nature of your relationship. Would he be inclined to disregard you if you do not contact him?"

"You don't understand human friendships. He will come to Salida to look for me and won't stop until we reconnect when I'm back there."

Kalev nodded before he responded. "Of course. You will have many stories to share with him when you are together again."

"He might even believe some of them." Dylan straightened. "Hey, how did you know I was thinking about Tom?"

"Remember when I showed you how to open your mind to me? Well, your thoughts are still available. I hear what you are thinking."

"All the time?"

"Not exactly. The intensity is greater when we're close. But even far away, I can hone in on your thoughts if I specifically seek your transmissions."

Dylan looked toward the trail out from the site, concerned about who might wander in. Kalev put his arm around Dylan's shoulder and continued. "Don't worry. No one is near enough to hear you. Your thoughts would be part of the consolidated noise that we hear all of the time."

"You mean every thought you have can be heard?"

Kalev shook his head. "It does not work like that. Last night you opened your mind for me to retrieve memories and ideas. We teach children this technique right after they are born. This process helps parents teach them how to live within nature and our culture. Once they are older, we show them how to close their minds in whole or in part."

"To keep secrets from their parents?"

Kalev smiled. "Yes. But also to operate within our society. There are times when we need to negotiate or persuade. You must be able to hold back information."

"So, let me get this straight. When I came here, I had the perfect ability to remain undetected, and you've opened the floodgates to allow anyone to hear my thoughts?"

"Straight ideas? Floodgates? Your meaning is clear this time, but forgive me if I don't always follow your point."

Dylan snickered. "Sorry about that. Metaphors and dialect slip into my speech more than I imagined. I'll try to keep them in check."

Kalev smiled and raised an eyebrow. "I appreciate what you can do to limit slang, but I cannot ask you to change your patterns—as you cannot expect me to modify my transmissions."

"Easier said than done."

After a moment to consider Dylan's message, Kalev agreed. He pointed at the swaying trees and transmitted, "The wind storm will help to muffle your transmissions to those who do not look for them. We should go to the pools I have located. Once we get there, I will show you how to suppress your thoughts. I sent a message to Alevide and Tiina with the location. They plan to join us."

"Can we trust them to keep me hidden until we have a strategy?"

"Alevide, absolutely." Kalev paused. "Tiina, hopefully, yes."

Chapter 8

TIINA

When Tiina arrived at the Amphitheater, most of the other twelve Transfer Section members were already there and seated in their traditional spots around the circle.

She could tell they communicated with each other, as they leaned forward to touch foreheads or occasionally moved apart to laugh or look directly at faces. The Sasquatches emphasized points with a slap across a shoulder or pat on the arm. Males and females engaged without discrimination. A sense of familiarity permeated the discourse.

Tiina detected their open discussions as a blur of images but did not want to focus on any specific conversation. She scanned the group to strategize whether to sit in her customary place between two junior members or two seniors. The younger ones might be more critical of Kalev's recent behavior, while the senior members may view Kalev's unapproved transfer as a forgivable foible of middle age.

Before she reached a decision, Tiina spotted her parents walking hand-in-hand. Tiina smiled at them and signaled a greeting. She needed to appear calm about Kalev's return and knew any mention of Dylan was off limits. Tiina took a wide track around the perimeter to approach them.

"Mother. Father. You look relaxed. Did you have a good soak this morning?"

Her mother embraced Tiina and rubbed her back and shoulders. Mother began her transmission with flashes of images from Tiina's youth to give context to their loving relationship. Then the message turned into an explanation of Tiina's parents' morning routines. "You know we enjoy our private time each day. It helps us prepare for these meetings. Since your father agreed to serve as High Council Leader, he needs time to calm his mind before he comes to the section assemblies."

While proud the High Council requested her father's service, Tiina knew the stress would take a toll on his health and good nature. Many years earlier, her mother served in this capacity. While she tried to keep a balanced perspective on the demands of the role, her mother grew thin from the pressures. Her father's time was long overdue when they nominated him.

The leader presided over the High Council as well as all four sections—Judicial, Family, Ranger, and Transfer. Judicial deliberated about members who violated social norms. Family handled questions related to mate selection or childbearing. Rangers patrolled the tribe's territory to inventory resources and collected news from members not on a Council. Tiina served on the Transfer Section, which handled selecting, training, and re-integrating those who made the transfer to Porgu.

Her father was at the midway point of his term. He led with calm authority, but Tiina knew he looked forward to assume a new, less rigorous position within the Council.

Tiina exchanged embraces with her parents and told them of Kalev's return.

"How is his mother?" Tiina's mother asked.

Tiina winced and wondered if she should tell them the truth. Better to wait until after she informed the section. Tiina did not want to stress her father. "His mother still suffers from the loneliness she has felt since Kalev and Alevide transferred to our tribe. But I know she always appreciates his visits." Not a lie but definitely avoiding the truth. "I will tell you about his journey soon. Or, Kalev may want to fill you in on the details himself."

Her mother nodded, but Tiina detected a tick at the side of her eye. She knew this tell. Her mother was growing suspicious. Tiina would need to be vigilant to keep her stories straight.

"When will we see him?" asked her father.

"Not for a couple of days or perhaps longer."

Her mother raised a brow, and Tiina continued. "He may need to leave again for a while. So you may not see him until the festival."

"But that is weeks from now," her mother transmitted.

"He is thinking about resuming his Ranger duties."

Her father jerked in surprise. "I thought he enjoyed his new responsibilities with the Transfer Section. He is very social. It seemed like a good fit to have him talk with returning members and summarize their experiences for the tribe."

Tiina tapped her foot while she considered Kalev's motives for his time spent with the Transfer Section. Initially, she assumed he wanted to spend time with her, but after everything he did, she suspected he joined to plot his illegal transfer. "He is a gifted communicator. Even when he was a Ranger, he excelled at connecting with the members who lived away from the Amphitheater and transmitting the details back to the other Rangers and the High Council. Everyone shares their stories with him. That made Kalev a natural to debrief transferees after their return."

Her father pressed further. "But he wants to resume his Ranger position?"

"He does not think of it as a step backward. Kalev enjoys both roles. He learned much while he was a de-briefer, and he will use those experiences to improve his Ranger responsibilities." Tiina grinned. "You know he is not the sedentary type. He may want to spend a few weeks exploring our territory."

Her father snorted in agreement. "You're right. If forced to stay in one place, he might get himself into trouble."

"You might not have heard, but Kalev continued to help the Rangers even while he worked with the Transfer Section. I heard the Rangers were shorthanded while Kalev went away. Remote visits are a low priority, and the other Rangers have not kept up their patrols over our entire territory. It will not surprise me if they have already contacted him to help. There must be fully spent pools that have faded and new ones sprouted at the perimeter of our territory. He could spend the next several weeks conducting reconnaissance and only return to inform us of any changes."

Tiina's mother interjected. "It is probably for the best, but I would like to catch up with him and hear about his trip."

"I can arrange for you to meet in a couple of days if you would like me to." Tiina hugged her father and then her mother.

When she released Mother, Tiina watched her raise an open hand to Tiina's father. After the signal, Tiina received a message directly from her mother. "I know there is more to Kalev's disappearance than a benevolent trip to see his parents. If his mother were unwell, Alevide would have been the one to go and not Kalev."

Of course her mother was right, but Tiina was in too deep to come clean. "You underestimate Kalev's relationship with his mother. He is devoted to her."

"You need not take up his cause with me. I know his type." She grasped Tiina's arm. "Be careful with your heart and head around him. You chose wisely with Alevide. Do not risk what you have with the lesser brother."

Tiina pressed her forehead against her mother's. "Do not worry about Kalev. He and Alevide are a package deal, and I need each relationship for different reasons. They are both good for me."

She turned toward the meeting and opted to slip between the most senior members. Each had supported her opinions in the past. Tiina nodded a greeting to her neighbors and settled into position with her legs crossed. She noticed her father and mother descend into the open area behind the Transfer Section members.

Tiina organized her approach on how to report Kalev's illegal transfer. She scanned the other members to anticipate their reactions to her announcement. Tiina wanted to be first on the agenda before she lost her nerve to report the transfer but lie about Kalev bringing a halvek back from Porgu. *Well, not really a lie—more like an omission.* While minor falsehoods were acceptable between family members, outright fabrications at a section meeting were unheard of.

She opened her mind to the bedlam of exchanged visions. Images of a female Sasquatch permeated the discussion. The nearly twenty-year-old Sasquatch seemed immeasurably distraught with vacant eyes and slumped shoulders. Other images showed her family members while they attempted to console her, to minimal avail. The female had been away for less than a full year, which was atypical for a transfer.

The young Sasquatch had returned with valuable information from a swampy region. The place was devoid of most humans but teemed with animal and plant life. While the larger animals obeyed her, smaller pests ignored her commands. Her frustration escalated from the intolerably hot climate and only sporadic digestible plants.

Once Tiina gleaned the magnitude of the female's condition, she realized her news about Kalev's return would be relegated to a later session. The female's all-consuming distress had led her to petition the Transfer Section for euthanasia.

Chapter 9

DYLAN COX

Dylan knelt at the edge and ran his fingers across the top. "This one is smaller than the pool we bathed in a few minutes ago." The pond's contents had the consistency of partially set lime green gelatin. Ripples bumped across the surface, and Dylan raised a tentative hand to his nose to sniff. The subtle fragrance bore a hint of spice, along the lines of cloves or cardamom.

Kalev nodded. "I looked for one that is not close to our tribe's sleep sites. So it is infrequently used. The longer it stays undisturbed, the darker the color and the more nutrients it holds. With use, it will fade to a pale yellow. It will remain abandoned until it has had time to heal and rejuvenate."

Dylan looked up. "The bathing pools are blue, and the ones for food are green?"

After he considered the questions for a moment, Kalev replied, "Your naming conventions for colors confuse me."

"Seems pretty simple to me."

Kalev promptly sent a vision with the word 'blue' and rapid flashes of a turquoise backpack, indigo beads, aquamarine sky, a navy jacket, and a sapphire ring.

Dylan laughed. "I get your point." He looked at the pond. "Are you sure this isn't green because someone peed in the blue one?"

Kalev raised an eyebrow. "We don't release waste into the green pools, only the blue ones."

"I was teasing, but that's good to know. I'll do my best to maintain your standards. What do we do? Drink from the side? Go for a swim?"

"Watch me." Kalev sat on the edge and slowly slipped into the pool until the trailing hairs of his head disappeared into the seemingly endless depths. Moments passed, and Dylan stared at the spot where Kalev had vanished. Finally, Dylan spotted him at the other end. Kalev gasped for air when he broke the surface. Kalev gave a quick nod, which Dylan assumed meant to follow Kalev's lead.

He dropped the leaf wrap, perched on the edge, and dipped his feet. The liquid reminded Dylan of what a tub full of warm motor oil might feel like—sludgy and slick. He grabbed fists full of grasses and held fast, while he submerged his knees, thighs, and waist. Dylan kept his eyes on Kalev and slowly released his grip to sink. Soon his shoulders were covered, and then his head.

Unsure of how to move forward, Dylan jackknifed to swim headfirst. He stroked down and expected to touch the bottom with his outstretched hands. Dylan opened his eyes and glanced over his shoulder. He watched the outside light fade away as if an anchor pulled him farther into the emerald deep.

Dylan froze. His heart pounded. Unable to feel whether he was sinking or floating to the surface, he thought, *there is no bottom. I'm going to drown in this soup.* Dylan gagged. His lungs spasmed and searched for air. *I should feel scared of dying, but I don't care what happens to me. What kind of drugs are in this stuff? I feel like I'm full of nitrous oxide gas.*

Fluid filled his mouth and nasal passages. He succumbed. When he again looked over his shoulder, he watched the surface grow lighter while he ascended. Like a discarded corpse, Dylan's body broke the surface. He rolled to float on his back.

Kalev's muscular grip pulled him to the edge with a stroke reminiscent of a sun-bronzed Jersey Shore lifeguard. He slipped an arm around Dylan's chest and tipped him forward to pound his back while he transmitted urgent words. "Breathe. Now. Breathe."

While he coughed to clear his lungs, Dylan swiped goo from his eyes with the back of a hand. Despite swimming for his life from the depths, Dylan laughed and looked up at Kalev. The Sasquatch held him afloat with concern stenciled across his shaggy brows.

"You could have told me what to expect. I could have died," Dylan said.

"You exaggerate. You would not have died. If you had gone unconscious, you would have floated to the surface, and I would have revived you."

"Some warning would have been nice."

"We believe new events are best experienced without preconceptions."

Dylan struggled to right himself and gripped the hair on Kalev's shoulder. He scissor-kicked to keep from sliding under again. "That's a load of crap. I'll bet you had weeks of instruction before you came to my world."

"Do not make assumptions about issues you know nothing about."

"Whatever."

"Do you feel the nourishment?" In addition to the question, Kalev transmitted a series of concerned-looking Sasquatch faces.

He must wonder if I can absorb their food. Dylan realized his ravenousness had dissipated. "I don't feel as hungry. What does this pool do?"

"Nutrients absorb into your body from what you ingested and through your skin. We will submerge several more times to take what we need."

"Based on my euphoric feelings, I'm guessing there's a narcotic floating around in here, too." He paused to lick his lips. "Before we take the second trip to the buffet, tell me where the hell we are. And don't give me a one-word explanation. You've learned hundreds of my words by now. Give me a better description than *home*."

"In time."

"Not later. Now."

"Conversation occurs in bathing pools. They are a place to socialize. Where we eat is reserved for reflection and to absorb what the body needs. After months in your world, my body is a shadow of my former physique. It will take several days to replace the body mass I've lost. Give me this time to recuperate. We will talk when we return to a private area."

Dylan acquiesced and managed a slow backstroke to the other side while Kalev repeated his routine to descend and resurface.

After Dylan propped his arms along the edge to keep from sinking into the bottomless chasm, he examined the plants next to the pool. Soft grasses of brilliant green dangled beyond the bank to dip their tips into the liquid like a drinking bird toy, an insatiable pendulum of perpetual motion.

To test their resilience, he rubbed a dozen blades between his fingers. The violated strands receded, like the ones encroaching into the sleep site from the night before. But they produced replacements. New shoots crept from under the sod patch and slithered into the pool, never farther than an inch from the bank.

While he continued his exploration, Dylan lapped his tongue along the surface and swallowed. He detected a hint of sweetness. Otherwise, the gummy liquid tasted flavorless.

"Where do you go for Indian or Thai food?" transmitted Dylan when Kalev resurfaced.

Kalev stroked toward Dylan. One hand gripped the side of the pool while he pinched Dylan's face between long brown fingers. "Give me a few minutes of silence, or I will drown you."

Dylan pried away Kalev's grip. "I don't buy your idle threat. Teaching me about this place gives you a woody."

Kalev narrowed his eyes at Dylan's statement. "An erection is not a physical reaction we associate with education. You mix the concepts of power and sexuality in ways unfamiliar to me. However interesting, this discussion will occur in our sleep site or a bathing pool but not here. If you plan to adapt to life in Reval, you must learn our customs."

"Why do you call this place Reval?"

"I took the liberty of naming our worlds. We are in Reval, and your home is Porgu."

"Sounds like you've started to appreciate the concept of names."

Kalev gave an authoritative sneer. "It is only necessary due to your limited ability to communicate telepathically. Visions do not have the potential for bias that words create."

"What sort of bias?" asked Dylan. He rose out of the pool and covered himself with his leaf wrap.

"In Porgu, an individual to be honored might have a dignified name while lesser beings could have names with lower status."

"First of all, most people are given names at birth. No one can predict whether they would become a success or failure. Besides, your society could create bias, too. For example, if you discuss Porgu, you might transfer images of the less pleasant areas."

"All are unpleasant."

"Hardly. Images of things like flowers, hillsides, or lakes carry vastly different impressions than mosquito-infested swamps or exhaust-choked cities."

Kalev crossed his arms. "I agree. We could bias communications. But we rarely do. We deal mainly with facts."

Dylan smiled. Point won.

"By the way, I place this trip in the 'vacation' category. When do you plan to show me the way back?"

"We will have that discussion at a later time, too," Kalev transmitted before he submerged.

Dylan frowned and considered the implications of Kalev's deferral.

Chapter 10

OCTOBER 22
TIINA

Tiina parted the fronds blocking the insufficiently maintained trail to reach the seldom used sleep site. After she muscled her way through a tight opening, Tiina could see a pale-haired Sasquatch curled in a fetal position in the center of the space. Vines with olive green arrowhead-shaped leaves fringed the perimeter.

Tiina trimmed the errant strands before she knelt behind the silent form. The female's shallow breath was barely detectable under the scant rise and fall of the blanket leaf. Tiina laid down behind her and wrapped an arm around her waist.

"How are you feeling?" Tiina transmitted with intermixed visions of mothers while they tenderly cuddled babies. The female snuggled against Tiina and released a soft moan, but did not otherwise respond.

She stroked the cover over the younger Sasquatch's arm. "I am here to understand what happened on your transfer. You requested something tragic and irrevocable. I want to be sure you have thought through your decision."

The Sasquatch inched her body away from Tiina in slow, jerky movements. When she turned over, Tiina saw her face streaked with sweat, tears, or both. Tiina traced a finger across the young female's prominent cheekbones and transmitted, "You are safe now. If you let me know what happened, I can arrange for time with others who will help you to overcome these feelings."

The younger Sasquatch slowly shook her head, closed chocolate brown eyes, and snuggled her face beneath the blanket. Tiina tried again. "Can you give me indications that what I've heard in the Transfer Section meeting is correct?"

She nodded and peeked from under the covers.

"You returned from your transfer in less than a year, much less time than most. In my experience, our tribe members tend to be away for nearly two years. They return exhausted and malnourished, but not inconsolable. I understand you arrived in a swampy area, filled with lush plants. That must have felt somewhat like home. Right?" The female's brows pinched in disagreement. But Tiina continued. "Well, maybe not too similar. There were probably loads of insects and reptiles. I would have found those annoying."

"And painful," transmitted the female. She sent visions of wasps and mosquitos, along with an alligator snapping its jaws.

"Are you hurt?"

The Sasquatch shook her head. "All of my external injuries healed after a series of soaks in the pools. I came back with bites and scrapes, but there are no remnants of those annoyances now."

Tiina rubbed her shoulder. "What then?"

"I could not eat."

"You found it difficult to eat? But were there plants like the ones we suggested in your instruction? What about nectar from flowers or berries?"

"I grew too upset to eat."

Tiina leaned back to gain a better view of her face. She had never seen such a vacant stare. Tiina tried to probe for thoughts, but the younger Sasquatch blocked any hint of what she had endured. Tiina sensed despair hiding a veiled emotion—perhaps frustration or anger.

She stroked the hollow of the young Sasquatch's cheek with the back of a finger. "What happened? You are younger than most transferees. Do you think you should have had more preparation?"

"My mother started my instruction when I turned four, much earlier than most," she transmitted with her chin tipped in self-assurance.

"I know your mother. Her transfer yielded a wealth of information about bird migrations and snow patterns. I am sure she taught you well. Something else then. Were you unable to control a large animal?"

"No. My animal management skills are superb. I met with a bear, wild pigs, and massive snakes. All of these responded easily to my direction. My skills are superb. But my reaction to certain experiences makes me unfit to go on living."

"Can you tell me a bit about what troubled you so much?"

She pulled away from Tiina to roll over and wrap the blanket tight around her shoulders. "I will not talk to anyone. You must understand I have not come to this decision lightly. Please, do not push me for answers. I will stay here until they give me a date for my extermination."

"Have you told your parents why you made this decision?"

"No. I am an adult. They trust my ability to reach an appropriate decision."

"I understand they have already started to mourn your passing, but I am surprised they agreed with your decision."

The young Sasquatch threw back the cover to glare at Tiina. "Do not assume they accepted without discussion and argument. This is my choice and not theirs. As far as they are concerned, I am no longer part of our family. Consistent with our traditions, they will accept my body once the Council finishes the ceremony.

"Will they take your body to prepare it for the Festival?"

"They have not decided whether to take my body to the Festival or ask the Council for anonymous disposal."

Tiina nodded. "This is our way and their right. But I wonder if they might be pleased to have a different choice. What if you changed your mind?"

She tightened the blanket. "Once I notified the Council, the decision became irrevocable."

"Others have recanted this decision."

The young Sasquatch glanced over her shoulder and transmitted with authority, her eyes creased with determination. "These cases are rare, and the petitioner does not return to their family. They are banished."

"Not banished. They become nomads or relocate to another tribe."

"But even in a new tribe, they are chastised for their lack of decisiveness. These outcasts are not able to serve on a Council. My parents did not raise me to live such a life. They intended for me to be a Council member, maybe even a leader. If I cannot fulfill my parents' dreams, then

I do not want to continue."

"What about your dreams?"

"They are consistent with my parents' expectations." She turned away and pulled the blanket over her shoulder.

Tiina spooned into her back and wrapped an arm around her slender waist. "How about you give yourself time to think about that?" Tiina stroked her shoulders. "My mate, Alevide, and I would like you to consider another alternative. Come and stay with us for a few days. You do not have to communicate with us—join us to bathe and feed. You faced a trauma alone when you were away. Now it is time to be with our kind, among those you can trust. If, after a couple of nights, you still want to be alone, I will accompany you back to this site where you can remain until the Council decides on your petition."

The young female writhed free and rolled to face Tiina. "I appreciate your persistence, but I will not change my mind. However, I will accompany you if that will make you feel better about your role in the Transfer Section.

Tiina smiled, pleased the younger Sasquatch agreed but skeptical she only accepted to appease Tiina.

Chapter 11

KALEV

Kalev watched Dylan cover his ears when the wind whipped the upper branches into a frenzy. Limbs collided and dropped leaves to wither and dissolve into the soft trail when they hit the ground. The howling escalated, and Dylan gritted his teeth.

Amused, Kalev nodded toward the path. Dylan hauled himself out and modestly wrapped a blanket leaf around his body. Each time a branch thwacked, Dylan cringed.

After they reached where the ancillary path merged with the main trail, Kalev paused. He scanned each direction to verify the route was vacant as the wind's roar obscured approaching footfalls. Kalev motioned for Dylan to follow him to a bathing pond a short distance away.

He glanced over his shoulder to watch a distracted Dylan trip along the trail while he gawked at the mists swirl between the treetops and conceal the uppermost limbs. *The halvek must learn to focus, or someone will surely discover us. If not today, then soon.*

When they reached the edge of the turquoise pool, Kalev gave Dylan a definitive nod. They inched from the rim and sank feet first into the fluid. Dylan slipped below the surface. Kalev watched Dylan launch across the pool with freestyle strokes and flutter kicks through the thick liquid until he reached the far end. After he executed a flip turn, Dylan swam back to stop and stand in front of the Sasquatch.

Kalev dipped his shoulders under the surface and felt his fur spread out from his skin while the solution cleaned remnants from his hair, skin, and bowels.

When Dylan bent his knees to submerge up to his chin, Kalev reached forward to rub the halvek's stubbly chin between his thumb and finger. "Feels coarse."

"I'd shave, but I suspect you don't keep a spare razor."

Kalev laughed. "Perhaps you will look more presentable as your hair lengthens. The baths may provide nutrients for growth."

"My facial hair is coming in fast, but I'm not sure if the not-so-hairy parts will change." Dylan raised an arm to inspect it.

"No matter either way."

"Why aren't there other Sasquatches here?"

"We sleep when the winds are violent. It is dangerous to walk among the trees when the storms rage, especially when the afternoon mist comes. A tree could fall on you."

Dylan visually traced the tallest trunks from where they disappeared into the mist to the ground. Tiny rivulets creased the bark, like pearls threaded through the quills of a feathered fan. The beads of moisture ran down the bark and built momentum until a vertical stream disappeared into a mound of greenery. *What could the halvek be thinking?*

"Does it ever rain here?" asked Dylan.

"Not like in Porgu. We only have the mist."

"If everyone avoids the mist and wind, why isn't it dangerous for us to be out?"

Clever halvek. "Better to risk a falling tree than to bump into someone on the trail. We need to keep you a secret until the time is right. Besides, I know these trees well—both the weak and the strong. I have seen many come down, and none have surprised me."

"I'm sure your outdoor skills are unparalleled, but now that we've finished with silent breakfast, I want some answers."

The Sasquatch nodded. His long hair created tiny waves in the solution surrounding his neck and shoulders. "This is the right time for discussions. What do you want to know?" The halvek would want to understand his circumstances, and Kalev had prepared. Let him know enough to keep him interested in staying but not enough to prompt rebellion.

"First of all, on our way between the food pool and this one, we walked by a place with overgrown trees, all choked out with bushes and plants," Dylan began.

"Yes. I have chosen a word for this place—Auk."

"I'm not familiar."

"It's a place of reverence for us."

"When we passed, you walked on the far side of the path."

"Did I?" Kalev asked.

"Absolutely. What's in those woods?"

"You should not journey there. It is a place to be revered but not visited."

"Do you keep secret stuff there? A military base? Perhaps a brew-pub?"

Kalev crossed his arms in front of his chest. "There is nothing for you in the Auk. Respect our right to have a sacred place and leave it alone."

"No need to get snippy. I got it. Next, where are we? What planet are we on?"

Kalev paused to rub his chin. He hoped Dylan assumed he was considering his response. "It is difficult to explain in the words you have given me. We are still on Earth."

"Hardly." Dylan jabbed toward the woods. "*This* is nothing like Earth."

"We are here but not in the same space where halveks exist."

Dylan raised an eyebrow. "Halveks?"

"My word for you. Your term is *human*, but I think halvek is more appropriate."

"I don't know why you need to change it."

"Mine is more appropriate."

Dylan tsked and shook his head. "I'll take your word for that. So we're still on Earth, and we didn't transfer to a different planet?"

"You are correct. Both places exist here. We do not travel beyond the planet or to a different time. We capture energy when the moon's pull is strongest and fling our bodies into Porgu." Kalev gave a heavy sigh. *These simple creatures are not satisfied with straightforward answers.*

"Sounds like we are in a different dimension. How did I get here?"

"I brought you."

"You've brought others here?"

"No. You are the first, and based on your annoying questions, you may be the last."

Dylan scoffed. "You've been putting off my questions for nearly a day. You said you'd talk with me in this pool. I'm not leaving until I understand where I am and how I can get back."

"There is not sufficient time to answer all of your questions now. You will need to prioritize."

"That's not what I want to hear, but I'll do my best."

Kalev extended a hand to encourage another inquiry, and Dylan responded. "I'll want to know how to go home, but I'm surprised to hear I'm the first human to come here." Dylan combed his fingers through his hair. "You've never transferred with a person?"

"No Sasquatch has brought a halvek to Reval."

"How are you certain?"

"We transfer knowledge between tribes and have perfect memories. I can assure you no other halvek has been here before you."

"If you had no prior experience, how did you know I'd transfer alive? You could have killed me."

Kalev smirked. "Were you harmed?"

"No, but I could have been."

"I was confident you would be undamaged."

"How?" Dylan smacked a fist on the surface and prompted a rolling ripple across the top

"It would be difficult to explain. You must trust me."

"Here's another question. Porgu and Reval—how did you come up with these names?"

"When I accessed your languages, I made decisions about a few names."

Dylan considered the names. "I don't recall any places on earth with those names. What do they mean?"

"I have borrowed from words that remind me of these places. One is a place of perfection, and the other is a disaster."

"I don't need to guess which is which, but I'll have to live with your naming conventions." Dylan bit the inside of his lip. "More importantly, when will you teach me to transfer back to Porgu?"

Kalev smiled. "It takes preparation and extensive mind control. I doubt you would ever be able to manage a transfer on your own. Not all Sasquatches can attempt the transfer."

Dylan shrugged. "My acumen might surprise you, but we'll leave it at that for now. Next question—why did you bring me here?"

Kalev knew the question would come eventually, and he needed to deflect the discussion. "Our kind has always transferred to Porgu. We have observed the development of your society from the time you lived in caves and ran away from wild beasts."

"Well, that's a long time. What have the Sasquatches done while we evolved?"

"Things in Reval have remained much the same. We live in tribes where we work on the Council or contribute to our collective knowledge about Porgu by transferring."

"Does the Council keep order?"

"No. Each Sasquatch is personally responsible for keeping our traditions. But if someone strays, the Judicial Section may intervene.

Dylan cleared his throat. "Give me more. What does Judicial do?"

"They have the worst job. The Judicial Section deals with Sasquatches who have acted contrary to our beliefs." Kalev turned his back in hopes the questions would soon end.

"Criminals?"

"Your word is too strong. Our infractions are not like in Porgu. We fulfill our needs without stealing or imposing power over one another. Examples of infractions might include a Sasquatch who neglects to report a turned bathing pond or who walks on disheveled trails without trimming them."

"Seems fairly minor. What would happen to someone like that?"

"The Judiciary would convince the individual that the actions or inactions do not serve society as a whole."

"And if they refused to comply?"

"Refusals are rare, but the Council might ask them to leave the tribe. Anyone can survive away from the group, but we are social beings. The banished individual might take time to travel to other tribes and exchange views. If they came back in a few years, perhaps more matured, the Judiciary would allow them to return."

"Is that as bad as it gets?"

"Once, a long time ago, a member was euthanized for bad behavior."

"That's worse." Dylan straightened. "What happened?"

"I would rather not say."

Dylan scoffed. "Big secret? Who am I going to tell?"

"I want you to experience the best parts of Reval before you judge the aspects you will not understand."

Dylan shrugged. "Feels like the pot calling the kettle black, but we can have the discussion later. Don't assume I'll forget."

Kalev raised an eyebrow. "I would never make that assumption."

"Now tell me what you do."

"I have served many vital roles both back at my original tribe, where my parents live, and in this tribe."

Kalev straightened and stepped closer to Dylan before he continued. "I have mainly served as a Ranger. We travel to check on families who live farther away from the center of our territory and monitor the pool status. That is why I know the location of unused pools. With you here, I will avoid giving updates on some pools and take you there without fear of detection. My Ranger role allows me to survey our territory. I much prefer these tasks than to sit around a section circle and consider petitions."

"I can relate. I'm not much of an office guy either. My detective work lets me walk around outside. To help me prepare for when I meet your leaders, maybe you'll take me on one of your circuits. How long are you away?"

"Usually a couple of weeks. I could take you with me so you can see more of our terrain."

"You mentioned transfers connect to moon cycles. Jen told me tides are highest at both the full and new moons. May I assume your transfer cycles are timed like tides? Am I stuck here for two weeks? Or can you harness the energy at any time?"

"Only when the moon is at its fullest."

"In a month?" Dylan continued to transmit, but Kalev had enough questions. He blocked transmissions and nodded at the halvek as if he were still listening.

Dylan's ability to relate the moon's energy and the lunar cycle surprised Kalev. Before he had engaged with the halvek, Kalev believed this type of higher-level thought was beyond their grasp. He would need to monitor Dylan closely and provide information on a limited basis. He did not want Dylan to gain independence—perceived or otherwise.

Kalev glanced at the gently swaying treetops. The mists had nearly disappeared but left a trickle of moisture to run down tree trunks and plop from leaf to leaf. "The windstorms have passed. I will leave you here, in this pool, alone. Try to rest and do not wander away."

Dylan stood. "Wait. Where are you going? Can't I come along?"

"No. Many Sasquatches travel immediately after the storms. It is not safe to be on the trails. This pool is secluded and remote. Alevide told me it was spoiled. But it has rejuvenated. No one will come here."

Dylan reached for Kalev's arm. "I thought reporting pools inappropriately was a criminal offense here?"

"Really, more questions? I told you *not* reporting a changed pool is inappropriate."

"You're arguing semantics. Between bringing me here and lying about resources, I feel like I've hooked up with a Sasquatch criminal."

Kalev rubbed Dylan's shoulder and gave a slow smile. "Do not be concerned. I only have your best interests in mind. You must prepare before I introduce you to the High Council. When you meet them with a fuller sense of our traditions, they will appreciate my delays."

The halvek bit his lip as if thinking. Kalev gave him a confident pat on the head before he transmitted, "I need to meet Tiina. I will return soon."

When Dylan lowered until his shoulders were submerged, Kalev smiled, pleased that Dylan accepted his suggestion without argument or further queries. He climbed from the pool to firm up his plans for Tiina.

Chapter 12

TIINA

Tiina floated on her back and breathed deeply while she tried to drown out the young female's anger and frustration. She scissored her legs to work her muscles against the sludgy liquid until she reached the far side of the pool. Then she flipped to return.

Her head torpedoed into a body. He groaned at the collision and pulled her from the fluid by her shoulders. Then he planted a passionate kiss on her lips. Eyes closed, she surrendered to him. His lips fluttered over her ears and neck to escalate her desire. "Alevide, I've missed our midday soaks."

"Have I been away for so long that you have forgotten the taste of my kiss?" Kalev's transmission disarmed her. She opened her eyes and smiled.

"That is what happens when you run off on an adventure and abandon your lover." She returned his kiss.

He pulled her close and stroked the long hairs around her face. "I thought about you continually while I was away. Dreams of your body kept me from going insane in Porgu's miserable conditions. Each night I longed to hold you. Tell me you missed me as well."

She traced his lips. His body responded, and his embrace tightened. She grasped his face in both hands and hoped he could read the apology in her eyes. "I missed you, but this is a bad time for me. I could conceive. We both know I reserve those days for Alevide."

He grasped the back of her head in his palm and brushed his lips across hers. She felt him tremble with longing. Tiina entwined her fingers behind his neck and submitted to his embrace.

He pulled away slowly and scanned her face. "You have asked the Family Section for permission to have another child? You are a bit old for that, right?"

Tiina shoved his chest with both hands before he tugged her closer and laughed. "I was teasing you. I thought you and Alevide decided not to have another child after what happened with your first."

She sighed and rested her forehead in the space between Kalev's chin and chest. "We have blanket authorization from the Council. He and I can decide." She pulled away and cocked her head. "But when I say my fertile days are reserved, it means I would couple with Alevide if he wanted to. Our intimacy has been sporadic and never in my conceiving time since my pregnancy over twenty-five years ago."

"But you still take lovers?"

"Of course, as does Alevide." She paused, a flirtatious smile crossing her lips. "But you will always be my favorite." Tiina wrapped her legs around his waist and leaned backward to float without releasing him. He took hold of the flesh and fur on her slender hips to slowly spin her in a circle.

"Give me a few days, and I'll be available for you," she transmitted.

Kalev bent his knees and sunk to submerge his shoulders. His hands slid under her backside. The movement forced her upright, and she could feel his desire between her legs. Tiina squirmed out of his grasp and laughed. "I know you were away for months, but you will have to wait."

She pressed his chin between her thumb and forefinger and leaned inches from his face. "I want you, too, but find someone else for a day or two until I am ready." Tiina released her grasp and dug her toes into the mucky bottom to crouch and face him. Her knees touched his, and she clasped his hands below the surface.

Tiina stroked a thumb across the back of his hand. "Tell me about your naked friend. What did you learn from him today?"

"He is eager to understand our customs. I am concerned the High Council will be nervous about his curiosity. We may need to send him back before he meets anyone from the sections or the Council."

"I think the Council would be intrigued. He could fill gaps in our research and help us to understand halvek behaviors. They are such strange and violent creatures—always fighting with each other and spending time to create shelters, material goods, and food. They have nearly destroyed their environment with all of their inventions. And for what? They seem no happier than when our ancestors observed them." Tiina straightened. "Once you teach us his language, we can transfer that ability to the Council before they meet him."

"I believe you overestimate the curiosity and benevolence of the High Council. Research in Porgu is distant and on our terms. A halvek in Reval spells chaos. These primitive beings do not know our customs and can be prone to violence. If the High Council discovers him before we tell them, they would certainly vote to extinguish him."

Tiina raised a skeptical eyebrow. "We do not even know if our euthanasia ceremony would work on him."

Kalev scoffed. "They might try it if only to find out."

"Good point. But as long as he is already here, I would rather believe the Council would want to know more about him." She paused her transmission. "You should know my mother has asked about you. They do not know the truth. Alevide and I told them your mother was unwell and you went to visit her. Do your parents know you are back?"

"They did not know I had left."

"You were away for three months, and they did not know?"

Kalev shrugged. "They typically do not hear from me for months at a time. Alevide is continually in touch with them, and he did not tell them about my transfer."

"I am certain they have asked about you. My tribe believes you were with them. You should visit your parents before their inquiries filter to my village. If your family speaks directly to my parents, they will ask me why we said you were there. Getting these stories crossed will not bode well for you."

"You are right, but the Festival is only a few weeks from now. I will see them then."

Tiina thought he should be proactive but resisted transmitting her views. She held tight to one of his hands and leaned backward to float. While she succumbed to the bath's soothing effects, Kalev slowly pulled her in a circle. She realized Kalev's decision and any consequences from that decision should be his alone. "Alevide can send word that we plan to attend and will see them there." Tiina paused before she continued. "I have an idea to share with you. I mentioned my plan to Alevide, but he is reluctant to agree."

"Now I am intrigued. Tell me what you are thinking."

Before Tiina responded, she closed her eyes and enjoyed how he moved her body over the surface. After she carefully organized her next transmission, she opened her eyes and locked on to Kalev's. "I spoke with a young Sasquatch who returned early from her recent transfer. She was traumatized by something that happened in Porgu but is not willing to say anything except she hated the insects and could not eat."

Kalev tugged her closer and slid his palms under her shoulder blades. He transmitted, "That is not enough to cause undue distress. Everyone faces those challenges. What about a large animal attack or an encounter with a halvek?"

Her brow creased. "I asked about the animals. No problem there. I encouraged her to open her memories, but she has buried something deep in her conscience and will not share."

Kalev moved her sideways and tracked his finger across her abdomen. He traced the lines of her taut muscles from a lower rib to below the navel. She giggled and flutter-kicked away. As Kalev lunged forward to catch her foot, he transmitted, "Okay. What do you want to do?"

"I would like to introduce her to Dylan."

"What?" Kalev released his grip. "I understand why Alevide was opposed, as am I."

Tiina sprung upright to stand, her feet wide apart and hands on hips. "Are you taking his side?"

Kalev paused for a moment before he responded. Slowly, he stood. The pool's transformative liquid dripped from his body hair and evaporated before the drops could break the surface. He drew her into his arms before he transmitted, "Of course not. Your idea caught me off guard. I only want to know why you plan to introduce them."

Tiina lowered into the liquid. "I have two theories to test. First, if she had a bad experience with a halvek in Porgu, then meeting Dylan may bring those memories to the surface where I can access them and understand what happened to her."

"And the second reason?"

"If she has no fear response to him, she may decide to befriend him."

Kalev rubbed his chin. "Why would she warm to him?"

"They are similar ages, and he poses no risk of her story becoming part of our collective knowledge. She could confide in him, and no one need ever discover what happened to her in Porgu."

Tiina assumed his nodding head meant he agreed with her. She did not care why he took her side, as long as he agreed and would help her to convince Alevide.

Kalev transmitted, "Now that I think about it, I believe having them meet is a logical suggestion. I can work on Alevide. You know how stubborn he can be. I will get him to agree and let Dylan know."

Tiina tilted her head, pleased to gain an ally and unconcerned about any price to pay for his support.

He stroked her cheek. "When do you want to make the introduction?"

"Soon. Maybe in the next day or two. I need to prepare her to meet him. Will you teach me how to communicate with him?" Kalev did not respond. She continued. "Do not be so selfish with your halvek."

Kalev winced. "Dividing his loyalty could challenge my ability to control him."

"I will not distract your prize." Tiina reached between his legs. "Besides, I can offer you something in return for your instruction. While we have to delay pleasuring each other, I can ensure your satisfaction now."

Chapter 13

OCTOBER 23

The Transfer Section meeting convened immediately after the afternoon wind storm and mist. Members filtered into the Amphitheater and took their seats in the circle. Transmissions flew among the Sasquatches, mainly to share views about the traumatized Sasquatch.

Tiina's father quieted the group by sending a message to ask for order and deference. They ceased independent transmissions and opened their minds to accept only his visions. "Our first order of business is to consider the euthanasia petition of the young Sasquatch who recently returned from Porgu. She claims irreparable trauma from the transfer. The young transferee proclaims her extermination is the best course of action for herself, family, our tribe, and society. Before we vote, I would like to hear your ideas about her petition."

Tiina straightened and rubbed her hands over her thighs. She directed an open message to her father while a few others did the same. Tiina indicated she wanted to contribute. Her father gave her the floor.

The members leaned toward her and opened their minds to accept her transmission. Before she started, Tiina organized the arguments she had polished on her way to the meeting. To be persuasive, she needed to be logical and focus on the long-term benefit to the tribe.

She took a breath. "I communicated with this member at length yesterday. She is indeed severely distressed by events that occurred while away. While her petition claims her condition came from annoyances such as insects and a lack of nutrition, I believe there is an underlying factor she is not currently sharing."

A fellow section member started to interrupt but retracted his vision. Tiina continued. "I urge the section to delay acting on her petition for a few weeks. Additional time will allow her to recover from the shock and, perhaps, divulge the real reason for her distress."

Tiina paused for emphasis. "You should know her family has already accepted her decision for euthanasia. They began the mourning process and are unable to take her back into their unit. Therefore, I propose Alevide and I will care for her these next weeks and encourage her to explain what happened. Her death would prevent us from understanding what caused her distress. Thus, these important events, however horrific, would never join our consolidated knowledge. A short reprieve for our final decision could provide information vital to our research and comprehension of Porgu."

Tiina's father thanked her for her view and asked for others. An older male Sasquatch, with stray gray hairs sticking out from his chin, asked to contribute.

After her father yielded to him, the older Sasquatch began. "While I respect Tiina's suggestion, I must stress that we have a responsibility to follow our traditions on these petitions. Before any euthanasia request comes to the section, the petitioner's family spends time with the individual to discuss the ramifications. Her family undoubtedly counseled her before they started their mourning period. They already consider her dead. We cannot allow tribe members to make weighty requests only to recant them later. The Council will end up with dozens of petitions from immature Sasquatches who want attention or pity. I believe the Council should follow our traditions and vote on her request today and, if approved, schedule the euthanasia for tomorrow."

Other opinions followed. Without similar recent requests to guide them, the members struggled to know how to proceed. Some aligned with Tiina and others with the elderly section member. When no others volunteered to contribute to the debate, Tiina's father summarized the discussion. "There is value to all of the opinions stated today. While I generally do not condone efforts to thwart our customs, I understand the importance of adding to our collective knowledge of Porgu and its inhabitants. But before we render a decision on whether to accept her petition, we should delay our determination for four weeks. This timeframe should be sufficient for Tiina and Alevide to coax information from the petitioner. Irrespective of whether they succeed or fail, the vote would still go forward in four weeks. Please transmit your view on this matter."

The proposal passed by a narrow margin, and Tiina breathed a sigh of relief. The young Sasquatch had won the gift of time. Tiina would find a way to convince her to withdraw the petition. Tiina had lived through tragedy and knew any vile experience could be overcome.

Once Father concluded the meeting, Tiina approached her parents. Her mother smiled. "You did well today. Your position was logical and well supported." Tiina beamed at her mother's compliments but raised a brow at her next statement. "So, what is our Kalev up to?"

Tiina chastised her. "Why do you ask about Kalev more than you do about Alevide?"

A slow smile spread across her mother's face. "That is because Alevide's days are predictable, while Kalev is always up to something extraordinary. Did he enjoy his visit with his parents?"

Tiina sighed. "Yes. But he still might take a Ranger journey, once he has rebuilt his strength."

"Was he ill?" Her mother's head tilted, and Tiina spotted that familiar questioning tick at the side of her eye.

Tiina realized her error and backpedaled. "No, of course not. He is merely tired from being out of his routines and looking after his mother."

Tiina turned to her father and transmitted, "Thank you for framing the final motion to include my stance."

Her mother laid a hand on Tiina's arm, a sign that she intended to send a personal transmission. But Tiina closed her mind to any incoming visions from her mother.

Seemingly unaware of the clash between his wife and daughter, her father smiled and kissed the top of Tiina's head. "Your idea was the right course of action. The collective should benefit from her experience. I hope you can convince her to share her story."

"I do, as well," Tiina transmitted to both her parents. When she leaned her head toward her father's, she added, "I have an innovative idea to get her to open up."

"Do you plan to share your intentions?" asked her father.

"Not at this time. If it works, I will tell you everything."

Her mother narrowed her eyes and drew her lips into a firm line. Tiina knew the expression. She was warning her daughter to think carefully before proceeding.

Chapter 14

OCTOBER 24
DYLAN COX

While Dylan and Kalev lounged in a relaxation pool not far from their sleep site, Dylan asked, "You're sure Tiina can be trusted to stick to your *hidden until ready* plan? Not that I wouldn't mind meeting a few new folks around here."

Kalev rubbed the top of Dylan's head and inspected a lock of hair. "The coarseness of your hair has diminished. Your body has responded well to the cleansing and the regenerative powers of our pools." He dropped the lock and submerged to cover his shoulders. "The young Sasquatch will not talk with her family or the Council about you if that is what you mean."

Dylan combed his growing mane with the fingers of both hands. He smoothed silky waves and tucked strands behind his ears. "How are you so sure?"

"She is already dead to her family, and the Transfer Section does not want to hear from her for the next four weeks. They have given her a stay on their decision."

"You sound a bit dismissive. You're talking about killing a child."

"She is not a child. She is your age."

"Okay, but it's still murder."

"It is *not*. The transferee requested to be extinguished. You must have something similar in Porgu."

Dylan considered the question. "It's complicated. Many religions and governments prohibit suicide. Some believe life is too precious to give anyone the right to take their own."

"Is that because your society needs labor to provide food and shelter, and killing oneself detracts from the greater good?"

"No. It's more about a prohibition to kill anyone, and executing yourself gets lumped into the same category. Some regions allow assisted suicide, but most times, when someone kills themselves, they do it alone. For example, they might take something poisonous or attack themselves with a razor, knife, or gun." *Suicide here, without a tool, could be challenging.* "What's the Sasquatch process for euthanasia?"

"We don't have poisons or weapons. Euthanasia is performed with a ceremony."

"Do you bore someone to death?"

Kalev cocked his head as if considering the statement. He smiled and shook his head. "I do not believe that method would succeed. At the appointed time, four Council members surround the petitioner. Each focuses on a separate quadrant of the body and lulls those parts into a permanent sleep. The body responds to the stimulus and shuts down. Within minutes the petitioner is dead."

"You put people to death with your thoughts?"

"Yes, you are correct."

"Can someone use this method for murder?"

Kalev rolled his eyes. "Leave it to a halvek to come up with a method to kill someone."

Dylan shrugged. "Just asking. Well?"

"There is no record in our collective knowledge about anyone who used this power to kill an unsuspecting Sasquatch. It would not happen. It takes four Sasquatches to complete the process. That level of violence is rampant in your world—not mine. We are not lawless gangsters with hit squads."

Kalev glanced past Dylan toward the entrance and smiled. Dylan turned to see Tiina with a fair-haired Sasquatch with doe-like eyes. "A shame the younger's hair is so light," Kalev transmitted before he nudged Dylan and gave full attention to the pair.

Dylan compared the approaching Sasquatches and considered whether lighter or darker fur seemed more attractive. They walked arm-in-arm with their heads nearly touching. Both strolled with straight athletic posture, shoulders back, and confident gait.

For the first time, he noticed faint lines at the corner of Tiina's eyes and the slightly hollowed cheeks that come with the decades beyond the 30s. Tiina's cheekbones seemed more pronounced, and her nose somewhat narrower than that of the younger Sasquatch, whose nose tipped provocatively upward at the end. *About the same*, he concluded and decided to call the younger one Kati.

He figured Kati had time to prepare for this first encounter. Why did she seem so frightened? She was taller and likely stronger than he.

When they approached the pool, Kati stopped short to stare at Dylan. She pulled away and attempted a full retreat, but Tiina firmly held her arm. Unable to penetrate their discussion, Dylan waited, with the pool's surface below his navel and his hairless chest exposed.

Kalev placed a hand on Dylan's shoulder and gently forced him down until only his neck and head remained above the blue liquid. "You might be showing a bit too much skin," transmitted Kalev.

Tiina and Kati stepped forward after many impenetrable transmissions. The younger Sasquatch tentatively nodded before she sat on the edge. Kati tugged a few blades of grass bordering the pool and watched them disintegrate when they absorbed into the surface.

Tiina gave Kati's shoulder a gentle push. The younger Sasquatch looked up at Tiina and shrugged before she delicately slipped into the pool with the grace of a nymph. Tiina slid beside her, and they linked arms. They moved as one, but Dylan suspected Tiina supplied the forward momentum.

When Dylan started toward them, Kalev grabbed his arm and transmitted, "Let her initiate this meeting."

Dylan relaxed and waited.

Kati grimaced. Dylan wondered if she felt skepticism or contempt. Clearly, this rendezvous was not her idea. They approached slowly, cautiously. Only an arm's length away, she turned to slip behind Tiina.

Dylan leaned around to see Kati shivering, visibly shaken by her proximity to him. *She's taller than me and has two bodyguards next to her. She can't believe I could hurt her. How can I let her know I'm harmless?*

Games might work. Dylan floated his hands toward her with his palms faced submissively downward. He waited for her to respond. Dylan sensed messages flying between Tiina and Kati. He noticed Tiina's raised hand but overheard nothing.

Kati gripped Tiina's waist with one hand and reached around the older Sasquatch toward Dylan. She tapped the thumb of his outstretched hand. Then yanked back as if she'd touched a moistened finger to a hot iron.

He did not react and left his hands to float on the surface. Kati tapped him again. This time, on a knuckle. Dylan did not move. On her third attempt, Dylan yanked both hands away and slapped her hand. He transmitted, "Gotcha."

She straightened, clearly startled. He slid his hand forward and sent the words, "Your turn." Dylan could hear Tiina's gasp and Kalev's chuckle.

Kati's eyes darted between Tiina and Kalev. Transmissions of still and motion pictures flew faster than Dylan could comprehend. He picked up a snippet from Kalev when he repeatedly sent visions of Dylan's extended hands and Sasquatch children playing something that vaguely resembled tag. Dylan assumed Kalev was asking her to hold out her hands the way Dylan had shown her.

She cocked her head, lips pursed. Kati stared directly at Dylan and complied with Kalev's suggestion. Dylan slipped his hands above hers. Kati tried to slap the top of Dylan's hands, but he pulled back before she could make contact.

Her mouth formed a determined line. She shot her hands forward, looking for a rematch. Dylan slowly placed his on top of hers. With the agility and speed of a mouse taking cheese from a trap, she slapped his hands and grinned at her success.

He responded with, "You win." Then he turned and pushed off from the bottom of the pool to stroke away.

Dylan caught a shred of their transmissions and noticed Kati's visions seemed faster and more urgent than the others. He heard a splash and glanced back to see Kati swimming toward him. Dylan quickened his pace to reach the far end. When he spun to face toward Kalev, Kati emerged in front of him and blocked his view. She mirrored his position with shoulders and head exposed. Her set jaw betrayed her misgivings.

Dylan transmitted, "I know Tiina explained how to communicate with me. I urge you to go more slowly than you can imagine."

She hurled a series of images, including visions of Tiina and Alevide and the words friends, hurt, and death. Dylan shook his head but motioned for her to try again. The second attempt showed Tiina and Alevide in their sleep site while they comforted Kati and held her while she fell asleep.

Dylan smiled. "I think you want to tell me that Tiina and Alevide are your friends. They're helping you to heal for the four weeks before the Council votes on your euthanasia petition."

Kati tilted her head to consider his message. Then nodded in agreement. Her next transmission came with slow precision. "Tiina explained that Kalev brought you to Reval to improve our understanding of the halveks. Do you consider yourself a good representation of your kind?"

Dylan laughed. "You're a quick study of English. I hope you can keep your transmissions slow. If not, my brain may explode."

She stared and bit the inside of her lip. "I do not believe our telepathy could harm you. But I will make my transmissions slow. Please, answer my question. Are you like all other halveks?"

"I'm not sure all humans would choose me to represent our race. But Kalev picked me, and here I am."

"I see that. What will you try to teach us?"

Dylan raised a brow. "I haven't thought about what I could teach you. Mostly I've learned how to communicate and exist in Reval without attracting attention."

"Why is Kalev keeping you a secret?"

"Good question. I thought he should take me to your leaders right away, but he believes we should wait until I've learned more about your customs."

Kati's lips pursed with skepticism. "Are you hoping with time you might fit in?"

Dylan chuckled. "Doubtful, but maybe I'd be less likely to offend everyone. I don't know what Tiina did to teach you how to communicate with me, but you've caught on a lot faster than Kalev or Tiina."

"We rely on our communal knowledge. With each new individual, the process will be faster."

"Isn't anyone an average student here?"

She gazed at him as if puzzling over his question. "I do not understand average. All Sasquatches have perfect memory. If we receive a transmission once, we never forget."

"Each moving or still image or, in my case, every word—you recall everything?"

Kati shrugged. "Yes. Halveks do not have the capacity to think as we do. Your language is slow and primitive, as are you."

Dylan scoffed and cupped his hands to splash Kati. "But we've built skyscrapers and rocket ships. What have you done with all of your knowledge?"

She turned an indifferent shoulder. "We do not need to manufacture things. You spend your time improving shelters and your food supply. We do not struggle for these necessities. Our time is spent in the company of those we care about. We continually evaluate and improve our society and learn from your mistakes."

Tiina approached and interrupted their conversation with a hand on Kati's shoulder. "That is enough for your first meeting. The winds will start soon. We will travel now, and Dylan and Kalev will go when the mist starts."

Kati nodded. When they left the pool, Kati turned to smile over her shoulder before they disappeared down the trail.

"Well?" Dylan asked Kalev.

"Well, what?"

"Did I do okay?"

"Tiina believes you will be a good distraction for Kati."

"That's what I am?"

Kalev sighed and rolled his eyes. "Many Sasquatches return from Porgu lean and traumatized from the solitude. We are social beings and need to engage at high levels of intellect. In our history, less than a dozen have suffered so severely they decided the only option was to ask for death. Tiina believes in the potential for Kati's rehabilitation."

"Is that what you believe, too?"

Kalev responded without delay. "This young Sasquatch is weak and should be eliminated from our breeding ranks."

Chapter 15

SALIDA, COLORADO
DESTINY STEWART, NÉE KUSIK

Over the shoulder of Salida's diminutive mayor, Destiny stared across the room at the front entrance of her recently inherited gallery. In walked a bronze-faced Rastafarian with dreads pulled into a loose tangle at the back of his head.

Mayor Rhoads rattled on about his re-election fundraiser Destiny's dead husband had committed to hosting on the twenty-eighth, only four days hence.

Her attention followed the stranger. The man scanned the room and unshouldered a duffle. His gaze fell upon Trip, her seven-year-old son, who had taken refuge on the couch away from the memorial service crowd.

The traveler crossed the room to sit on the sofa beside Trip. But the man allowed a respectful distance from the boy. Destiny nodded to the prattling mayor while she glanced past his silver combover at the scene unfolding with her typically unsocial son.

The stranger interrupted Trip's gaming with gentle persistence until the boy gave up the device and inched closer to deliver a tutorial. The man had captured her son's trust along with the toy.

She tucked a stray lock of her chin-length bob behind an ear and turned to the mayor. "You can cut the sales job. I'll keep Nate's promise to host your 'Re-elect Rhoads' gala on the twenty-eighth at the gallery." She laid a hand on the mayor's fleshy arm and continued. "If you'll forgive me, I'd like to speak with other guests and introduce myself to someone who's just arrived."

Destiny bee-lined to her son. When she approached, the man looked up from the game tablet and asked, "Trip, do you know this woman? I'd hate for you to start talking with a stranger."

Trip's eyes twinkled from behind black-framed glasses. He looked from his mother to the traveler. "Mom, this is Tom. He's Dylan's roommate from Chicago."

Destiny breathed a sigh of relief and held out a hand toward Tom. "Glad to meet you. Dylan's told us a lot about you."

Tom by-passed her hand. He stood, handed the device back to Trip, and took her into a warm embrace.

Unprepared for contact, Destiny stiffened. He pulled back and shifted his hands to her shoulders to run them down her upper arms. He looked at her eye-to-eye. "I'm not the enemy, but I can back off." She smiled in response. The sides of his mouth ticked upward. "You're taller than I expected."

"I'm nearly six feet and surprised Dylan didn't mention it. Most people do."

Tom turned to Trip, still seated on the couch, "If you take after your mom, you'll have offers to play basketball."

"Not interested," Trip responded without looking up from his toy.

Tom stepped back to release her arms and grasp each of her hands. "I'm truly sorry for your loss. Let me know if there's anything I can do."

"I appreciate your kind wishes." Destiny glanced at the door and asked, "Is Dylan with you? Augie said he planned to be out of town for a few days, but I assumed he'd be back in time for Nate's memorial service."

Tom squeezed Destiny's hands. "No, I don't think he'll make it. That's why I came from Chicago to see you. Do you mind if I hang out here until after the others are gone? We should talk."

Destiny straightened. "Did something happen to him? I heard he went to Colorado Springs to work on a case. Is he okay?"

"He's fine, and I don't want to keep you from your guests. Maybe I should come back in a couple of hours?"

"No, please stay. You can put your things in the back by the studio. Make yourself at home." She nodded toward Trip. "You've already made one friend here today. I can't imagine most folks will stay more than an hour or two."

Tom glanced at the crowd while they milled around with plates and wine glasses. He nodded. "They're not too scary. I can manage."

"I know you're from Chicago, but I don't know if you've ever met Dylan's aunt and uncle. They were Nate's parents, and they're here."

"I've not had the pleasure, but interestingly, I met *your* parents in North Carolina."

Destiny's brow creased, and she puzzled over this statement. "You have me at a loss."

"Dylan asked me to meet them to discuss Trip's disappearance and your suicide, which thankfully never happened. Your mother makes incredible cookies with chunks of peanut butter cups in them."

"I'm very familiar with those cookies." She took Tom's arm and pulled him out of Trip's earshot. "I'm sorry for my deceptions. At the time, Nate convinced me that leaving Salida and faking my death was the only way I could start a new life. I was wrong to think I'd be strong enough to leave Trip with his father."

"No need to explain. Dylan told me your friend Jen helped you to take Trip from Salida to Oregon."

Destiny nodded. "Trip was miserable here. Nate didn't want a better life for his son. He wanted to hurt me by keeping us apart. So Jen and our friend Augie helped me to snatch Trip and take him to Oregon. You probably learned about most of this when you talked with my parents."

"They never let on that Trip was with you, only that you were alive and had moved out west. Dylan found out Trip was with you from Augie. You realize once Dylan confirmed you and Trip were living out west, he kept your secret. He never told Nate or his aunt and uncle."

Destiny reached out to tap the arm of a passing waitress. When the server paused, Destiny took a glass of white wine from the tray. She motioned toward a collection of goblets, flutes, and rocks glasses. "Care for a drink, Tom?"

"I'd like some water, for now."

Destiny signaled the server with a head tilt, and the woman promised to return with a glass of water for Tom. Once she left, Destiny said, "Nate hired Dylan to find Trip, and Dylan could have collected a big reward for selling us out. I'm grateful he didn't."

Tom scoffed. "Dylan didn't take the job for the money. First off, he wanted to help find your son. Some part of him did it to gain Nate's respect. They had a complex relationship, with Nate drawing Dylan close only to turn around and crush his esteem. They had played that pattern since they were kids."

"Sounds familiar. Nate performed the same scenario with me until I finally left. I think Nate employed Dylan for the optics of hiring a detective but expected Dylan to fail."

"Why would he make that assumption?" Tom paused for a moment and backpedaled. "Don't get me wrong. We've had the detective agency for several years, and Dylan's great at what he does. But nearly all his work involves tailing spouses who cheat. When Dylan took this case last spring, *we* worried that finding a missing child might be out of his league."

"Well, he's a better detective than he thinks." Destiny scanned the room. "I look forward to talking with you more after the guests leave, but I need to make the rounds. Nate knew a lot of people in town. Unfortunately, some more intimately than he should have. I haven't seen any of his conquests today. At least, none that I know of."

Tom placed a hand on her shoulder. "I'm sure Nate's parents and Trip appreciate everything you're doing to honor Nate's memory. If you point me in the right direction, I'll introduce myself to Dylan's aunt and uncle."

Destiny extended a thin finger toward a discerningly dressed couple talking with a pair of uniformed men. She identified the officers as Merle and Erle Hodges from the Salida Police and Sheriff Departments, respectively. Destiny watched Tom pause in front of a garland-ringed poster photo of Nate blocking the opening to the studio. Nate's whiter than natural teeth and gel-spiked hair oozed self-assurance.

"Not anyone I'd like to meet," Destiny heard Tom utter when he moved his duffle into a corner behind an easel holding a partially finished oil painting. She watched Tom enter the cluster of Nate's parents and the officers with the ease of a politician preparing to kiss babies.

He's not what I expected. Dylan had described Tom as the house handyman, more comfortable working the business end of their detective agency. This guy could be a player. She'd fallen for his type before and had no plans to tumble into that trap again. But a familiar feeling tugged at her chest.

Chapter 16

TOM MORROW

Left alone in the great room of Destiny's top floor apartment above the gallery, Tom was drawn to the windows and the street below. He wondered how many people had stood in this spot to watch unsuspecting pedestrians. If their Chicago townhome had a view like this, he'd waste hours staring outside.

Tom shook his head to clear out rambling ideas. He needed to focus and did not relish talking with Destiny about his missing friend.

The click of the latch on the strike plate drew Tom's attention toward the door at the far end of the apartment. Destiny, still dressed in the black sheath she wore at the memorial service, softly closed the door to Trip's room and joined him.

They gazed out of the floor-to-ceiling windows at the front of the combined living and dining room, upstairs from the gallery. Lights from two boutiques and Salida's two-screen cinema shone from the street below.

"Long day." She crossed her arms in front of her chest. Tom nodded in agreement. They stared at a couple below who paused in front of the Coming Soon posters.

"I need to get into something more comfortable. Make yourself at home," Destiny motioned to an off-white Scandinavian-style sofa. "There's no beer, but white wine's in the fridge, red's in the rack on the counter, and Nate kept a fully stocked bar over there." She pointed before adding, "I'll be right back."

After Destiny left the room, Tom scanned the liquor cabinet and selected a bottle of bourbon. Cut crystal glasses were in an adjacent cupboard. He poured a drink and moved to the couch.

Tom ran a hand over the smooth leather cushion and wondered if Nate allowed Destiny any input in decorating the space. The white walls and austere lines screamed bachelor pad. Ceiling lights strategically illuminated each piece of art, likely Nate's masterpieces, rows of mountain landscapes with the perspective and color slightly off. Tom could not decide whether to blame his untrained eye or Nate's lack of talent.

Tom took a drink and let the liquor slip down the back of his tongue. He took a deep breath to relish the flavor. After he set down the glass, Tom leaned forward to run an index finger across the spines of a neatly aligned stack of coffee table books—Colorado scenery, French artists, and a white volume with no lettering to identify the book's content or author.

He pulled the unlabeled tome from the others and rested it on his knees. The word "Cunt" in pink script splashed across the otherwise pure white cover. Tom flipped pages flaunting nude and semi-nude models. He turned to the inscription. "Thinking of my favorite artist, and hoping you're thinking of me." The name Cynthia, in bold script, took up most of the page. He closed the book, walked to the kitchen, and stuffed it into the trash under a layer of wet food scraps.

Tom rubbed the back of his neck when Destiny returned in gray sweats and a nearly transparent white T-shirt that did little to hide her thin, athletic frame or the nipples centered on her small breasts. He sighed in relief as she walked to the kitchen and removed a fleece jacket from the back of a barstool.

Destiny zipped up and rubbed her eyes with the back of a hand before she placed a pair of dark-rimmed glasses on her face. "Contact lenses are a bitch." As she poured a glass of white wine, she asked, "Can I get you something to eat? There's a ton of leftovers from the memorial party." She stopped the pour but held the bottle over the glass. "I guess party isn't the right word."

"Maybe a celebration of life?" Tom marveled at Destiny's strength to honor the man who had treated her with little regard.

She crossed the room to sit next to Tom, slipped off her shoes, and raised her feet to the table. "Sounds more appropriate." Destiny took a sip. "Did you enjoy your talk with Nate's parents?"

Tom reached for his drink and held it in both hands. He sloshed the bourbon into a mini-whirlpool. "Seems like they're hurting, especially his mother. She lashed out at me for wearing a T-shirt and jeans. I figured she needed to vent about anything besides Nate's death. I can't imagine what losing a child must be like."

"I'd never considered her a warm mother-in-law, but I can forgive her for whatever she does now. Losing her only son must be horrific. Life without Nate is likely something she's never imagined. How could she prepare for this? I've given her wide discretion on arrangements for services and Nate's final resting place, which will be in their family plot in Chicago. They leave for home tomorrow and will host another service for family and friends back there." She paused. "They've asked to take Trip with them for a few days."

"Is that okay with you?" Tom's brow creased in concern.

Destiny sighed. "Not really, but they *are* his grandparents. And asking for Trip to attend the funeral in Chicago isn't unreasonable. They promised to drive him back in a week."

"A week's a long time for a seven-year-old."

Destiny nodded. "He has special needs, and I'm not sure they'll accommodate him. But Trip managed okay for the couple months he lived with Nate before I stole him off to Oregon. My son's tougher than you'd think."

Tom listened and assumed Destiny was attempting to convince herself.

"He'll miss six school days—not the end of the world. When I registered Trip to start second grade here, I asked his teacher about delaying his start until he comes back from Chicago. She put together a workbook for him to do while he's gone. I picked up a few books for him to take. He's got incredible self-discipline when it comes to school. Plus, we'll talk every night, and I can reinforce the importance of his assignments."

Destiny stood and walked to the kitchen. She unceremoniously emptied the partially filled wine bottle into her glass.

She plopped on the sofa and held the goblet forward to toast. "Here's to meeting new friends." They clinked glasses and sipped. Destiny tucked a leg underneath and turned toward Tom. "So tell me what's going on with Dylan in the Springs."

Tom reached forward to set his glass on the table. It was time to talk about why he'd come to Salida. He took one of Destiny's hands and said, "Dylan's not in Colorado Springs. I'm not sure where he is."

She straightened and pulled her hand away. "You told me he's fine."

"I'm confident he is. But I'm not sure *where* he is."

Destiny tilted her head. "What *do* you know?"

"I talked to Dylan on the phone about a week ago. He'd seen an animal at Jen's cabin and wanted to find out more about it. So he planned to follow it into the woods. Dylan said he'd call me the next day with information once he learned more, but I haven't heard from him."

"I don't understand. Dylan followed an animal into the woods a week ago, and you haven't contacted the authorities or started a search party?"

"It's not as simple as it sounds." He cleared his throat. "The animal was a Sasquatch."

Destiny stood, and her eyes scrunched with skepticism. "Are you crazy?"

Tom patted the sofa next to where he sat. He shook his head and stared at his hand, unwilling to make eye contact. Tom had to convince her, but he barely believed it himself. "You're going to have to trust me about this."

Destiny stooped forward and tipped Tom's chin with a knuckle to force him to look at her. He watched her face grip with determination as she said, "I don't have to do anything of the sort. Did Dylan put you up to this?"

He leaned back to free his chin and locked on to her eyes. "Sooner or later, you'll understand I'm telling the truth. Dylan communicated with the Sasquatch for a couple of days before he told me about it. Kalev twice saved Dylan's life."

"Dylan's Bigfoot is called Kalev?"

"Yeah, well, Dylan named him because he didn't have one already. Anyway, Dylan said Kalev stopped a mountain lion and a bear from attacking him."

"They came after Dylan, too? Sheriff Austin is convinced they killed

Jen in June and Nate a few weeks ago. How did this Kalev stop these creatures from killing Dylan?"

Tom stood and placed his hands on Destiny's arms. "Dylan was outside the cabin, retrieving firewood. The lion and bear came out from the trees without warning. If Kalev hadn't chased them away, they would have killed Dylan."

"Chased them off? How big is the Sasquatch?"

"He's big, but he didn't physically scare them away. Dylan said Kalev is telepathic and controlled them with his thoughts. But that's not all. He saved Dylan's life a second time. Later in the night, Kalev stomped out a fire that might have burned down the cabin while Dylan slept."

Destiny ran a hand across her brow. "You're not talking about an animal in the strictest sense. This is a conscious being. Maybe a dirty, hairy guy who lives a solitary life in the woods?"

"That's not what Dylan said. Kalev is over eight feet tall and covered with fur. He's telepathic, and also mute."

Destiny rolled her eyes. "Okay, you nearly had me, but really? What's the true story?"

Tom walked to the window to watch stragglers leave the movie theater and hurry to their cars. He needed her to believe him. If she turned him away, who could Tom enlist to help find Dylan? He swiveled back to Destiny. "I know this sounds incredible, but I believe Dylan told me the truth. Kalev was supposed to take Dylan to meet other Sasquatches on the night of October 18, and I haven't heard from him since."

"If he's missing, we should call the Sheriff."

Tom shook his head. "Absolutely not. First off, they'd never believe me. Secondly, I want to find out more before we get anyone else involved. Dylan said Kalev specifically contacted him—not the authorities, not a group of Believers, but Dylan. There must have been a reason for that. I'm afraid if we get a bunch of people out there searching, we'll never be able to find Dylan."

Destiny put her hands on her hips and tapped her foot, obviously weighing her options. Tom waited for her to respond. Finally, she said, Okay, I'll play along. How can I help?"

"Would you take me to Jen's cabin?"

"Tonight? Not a chance."

"Okay, how about tomorrow? We could go after Trip leaves with Nate's parents."

"I haven't been up there since Jen's death, and Nate's attack was only a week and a half ago. You've said a mountain lion and bear are still lurking around. That's in addition to an eight-foot-tall Sasquatch powerful enough to scare off those predators." She shook her head. "I don't think it's safe for either of us to go there. Not without weapons or backup."

"We don't need to stay long. I simply want to see if Dylan's rental car is still parked in the driveway. He and Kalev were supposed to travel on foot. The car should still be there if that were the case."

Destiny smirked. "Maybe Dylan's Bigfoot friend knows how to drive, and they've gone off on a road trip."

"I swear this isn't a joke."

She held up both hands in surrender. "Okay. I'll take you up there tomorrow morning after the Stewarts leave, but only to retrieve the car."

"Thank you for your faith in me." Tom breathed a sigh of relief. Even if she bailed on him after driving to the cabin, he'd know more than he did upon arriving in Salida.

"I'm not sure about this, but I'm willing to take a look. Maybe Dylan is pulling something over on both of us, but I don't know why he'd keep the gag going for a week. That doesn't sound like him. We should find out more at the cabin."

Destiny leaned forward to retrieve her wine and took a sip. She looked at Tom. "What about tonight?"

"What about tonight?" As soon as Tom said it, he wished he had not. Tom only meant to confirm her question. But it sounded like a come on.

Destiny huffed. "Have you made arrangements for someplace to stay?"

"No need to be concerned. I checked on-line before I left Chicago. There are a couple of hostels in Salida. I'll see if one has a vacancy."

"That's not happening. You'll stay here. I don't have a guestroom, but you can sleep on the couch." She turned to give him a narrow-eyed start. "Don't try anything you'll regret. Nate left a well-supplied arsenal in my bedroom."

"Thank you for the warning." Tom looked at the sofa. "You have me worried about the potential for an unwarranted shooting. I might have a better night's sleep at the hostel. Anyway, your sofa is pretty fancy."

Destiny shrugged. "This furniture is leaving soon. Consider this place as an apartment in transition. Currently, it's all about Nate—sterile and without warmth. In the coming months, I plan to remodel it into a home for Trip. Wait a sec while I find an extra set of sheets and a blanket."

Chapter 17

OCTOBER 25
DESTINY STEWART, NÉE KUSIK

Destiny pulled her worn but dependable Subaru off the dirt road and into the gravel driveway at the front of the cabin, next to Dylan's rental car. Desiccated aspen leaves in brilliant gold dotted with brown spots swirled under the vehicle and across the drive.

After they stepped from the car, Destiny paused to look at the log cabin's symmetric front with windows on each side of a sturdy wooden door. Taped cardboard blocked a pane on the left, a blemish from a hasty repair. Two wicker chairs sat next to each other on the porch.

Tom broke her concentration when he asked, "Do you think Dylan and Kalev talked while sitting in those seats?"

Destiny scoffed. "I'm not convinced Kalev even exists. So, no. I don't think they sat in those chairs sharing a beer or a conversation. Anyway, didn't you say Kalev is a deaf-mute?"

"Not deaf, just mute. He communicates telepathically."

Destiny stared at Tom, unsure if he was teasing. "How about we get what we came for? Any ideas about where the car keys might be?"

"Dylan said he'd leave them under the tire," Tom rounded the rental car and inspected the ground. "Found them."

Tom pulled a ring from the dirt and circled to the rear. He hit the trunk button and peered inside. "Looks like Dylan's stuff is still here."

Destiny joined him to stare inside the trunk at a duffle, leather messenger bag, and a partially filled white trash bag. "What's your plan?"

she asked, hands on hips.

Tom reached inside and opened the trash bag. He pulled out a Styrofoam container, pried off the lid, and sniffed. "Smells like chili. Could be a week old." He looked around the yard. "I'll bet it gets cold at night. It's not rancid." He held out the container and asked, "Want to smell it?"

"I'll take your word for it, Sherlock. What else is there?"

Tom rummaged through the contents. "A couple of empty water jugs and an empty package of this." He pulled out a brightly colored box with a hummingbird on the cover. "It's bird food. Dylan told me a story about a woman in Salida who thought she saw a Sasquatch eating out of her bird feeder last summer. Do you think Dylan made this nectar for Kalev?"

"If he's a big guy, I can't imagine that would give him enough nutrition to live on, much less what it might do to his teeth. Was Dylan into birds? I never saw a feeder when Jen lived in the cabin."

Tom returned the refuse to the bag. "Never had a bird feeder in Chicago. It seems unlikely for him to start here. Unless Kalev has a taste for hummingbirds."

"That's more likely than an eight-foot-tall hermit drinking sugar water to stay alive."

Tom nodded in agreement. "Why don't we put this stuff in the back of your car? If you bring it to your place, I can meet you there once I return the rental."

"How do you know where to take it?"

Tom opened the passenger door and leaned inside near the glove box. He held up the contract so Destiny could see it. She nodded affirmation, and he tossed it to the seat before he shut the door.

Destiny scanned the perimeter of the yard. A slight autumn breeze swayed the tops of the pines, but no movement or sounds came from birds or squirrels. She turned to Tom and asked, "Do we need to check inside while we're here?"

"Dylan's not here."

"How are you so sure?"

"I just am. If you want to go inside, I'll go with you."

Destiny stared at the door. "The last time I came here was after Nate asked me to leave. Jen was my best friend. I needed her perspective. Her advice was perfect—no judgment and a hundred percent supportive." Her eyes fell to the ground while she pushed a rock with the toe of her running shoe. "So much has changed since we had that talk. I miss her."

Tom stepped forward with his arms held wide, and Destiny stepped into his embrace. She sighed. "I don't want to go inside. She's not here either." They stood together with Destiny holding Tom around his waist.

He rubbed her back until she pulled away and said, "You were right to come here. I don't know where Dylan went or who he left with, but we'll figure it out."

Silently, they loaded Dylan's gear into the back of the Subaru. Destiny waited until Tom started the rental car and pulled forward in the drive. She looked through the windshield at the cabin and the yard. Neither seemed threatening or dangerous—simply a domicile built decades ago and lovingly updated by her dead friend and Jen's parents before her.

Destiny knew that Jen, an outdoorswoman, viewed her cabin as a staging ground for adventures in the woods. When she died, Jen had left the place to Augie, but he had no desire to come here. Destiny understood why. For him, it held memories of tragedy and loss. If Dylan encountered the mystical creature Tom described, she hoped Dylan viewed the cabin as Jen had.

Tom tapped the horn in the rental car, breaking Destiny free of her thoughts. She pulled the Subaru around the drive and followed him to the main road.

Chapter 18

Destiny stared out the picture window and tapped a trimmed nail against the double-paned glass. While early in the afternoon, long shadows darkened sidewalks, and shop lights spilled outwards. Despite Trip's proclivity for quiet study and earbud-compatible videogames, the apartment felt devastatingly empty without her son.

To support Nate's parents, Destiny buried her angst about the week she would be without her son. Trip seemed oblivious, still at an age when he allowed adults to make decisions without questions.

She forced herself from the window. Where in the world was Tom? Destiny checked her watch. They never discussed where Tom intended to return the car. Denver? Colorado Springs? Somewhere closer? She figured he knew where to go and would rendezvous at the apartment in an hour or two. Reluctant to leave for any length of time, Destiny came home to wait.

Why didn't I offer to give him a ride back?

Drawn to the allure of opening Dylan's things, she had placed them downstairs in Nate's studio to keep her distance. She had spent the day reviewing Nate's bills and books and cleaning the remnants from yesterday's event.

A bell chimed to notify Destiny that someone waited at the front door. She bounded down the stairs and crossed through the gallery to see Tom stamping his feet. Both his hands were stuffed in the pockets of his cargo shorts. She quickly went to the door to open the deadbolt and let him in.

"Man, it gets cold fast after midday." He entered the gallery and rubbed his hands across his ropey biceps. "Guess I should have brought my jacket."

"Come upstairs. I'll get you something warm to drink. I had no idea you'd be gone so long, or I would have suggested you take along a coat. Where did you take the car?"

Tom followed Destiny through the gallery and up to the apartment. "I stopped at the Salida library to look online for a place to return the car without a drop-off fee. Canyon City was the closest, so I got directions from the librarian and took the car there. There was a flaw in my plan."

She turned. "A flaw?"

Tom grinned. "Yeah. I planned to hitchhike back to Salida after dropping the car. It's only 60 miles away. Did you know there are 13 prisons in Canyon City? One of them is a Supermax. You can imagine how difficult it was to find someone to give me a ride. I hung out at the hardware store until I met an HVAC guy from Salida. He was in Canyon City to pick up some specialty parts and gave me a ride."

"Did you think about calling me to pick you up?"

Tom delivered a blank stare. "That did not cross my mind. You've already done so much."

"Coffee or hot tea?"

"Do you have herbal?"

Destiny removed four boxes of tea from the cabinet and placed them on the island in front of Tom. She filled a brown ceramic mug from the hot water dispenser and slid it next to the tea.

Tom examined the cup with the gallery's logo and pale blue letters. "Well, that's slick." The initials 'NS' overpowered shadowy lines presumably depicting the nearby mountain range. Tom turned to the tea and selected an infusion spiced with cinnamon, lemongrass, ginger, orange, and anise seeds.

"Nothing but the best for Nate."

"I meant the hot water dispenser."

Destiny chuckled. "That, too. Nate liked high-end stuff. I didn't have a clue about what type of appliances or furniture to buy for this place. Nate did it all. Well, maybe he had help from his mother. She's a brand-snob too."

"It must run in the family. Nate's mother was Dylan's dad's sister. Dylan's father had an eye for quality and passed the trait to Dylan."

"I thought Dylan was adopted."

Tom laughed. "Well, he didn't find out about it until Nate spilled the beans last summer. Dylan must have picked up habits from his dad despite a different set of genes." He paused. "Speaking of family connections, how are you doing without Trip here?"

"It's tough. This separation brings back bad memories from the months we were apart. That's when I was in Oregon and before I came back for Trip." Destiny shook her head. "He'll be fine with his grandparents, and it's only a week. I managed to find ways to distract myself today, but it wasn't easy with Dylan's bags downstairs."

Tom glanced toward the stairway leading down to the gallery. "Did you go through his stuff?"

"No. Why would you ask that?"

The ends of Tom's mouth curled into a smile. "Because I would have. Let's go check it out to see if there are any clues."

Destiny and Tom knelt on the floor with the duffle, leather messenger bag, and white trash bag between them. "You could have thrown away the trash. We already looked at it."

Destiny sniffed and raised her chin. "Not my decision to make. I didn't know if you wanted to trace where Dylan bought the groceries."

Tom gave her a blank stare. "Do you think that's important?"

"How should I know? You and Dylan are the detectives."

"Dylan is the detective. I take care of the books and his appointments."

"But you tracked down my folks in North Carolina."

Tom grinned. "My first assignment."

Destiny stood and grasped the trash with one hand. She spun the bag and tied a knot in the neck. When she stepped to the rear exit, she said, "I'll leave it by the back door. We can take it to the dumpster later. Don't blame me if you think of something we should have kept."

He raised a hand. "On my honor, I promise to assume all the responsibility for this decision." He turned, but she knew he hid a smile while he reached for the duffle.

Tom waited until she returned before he unzipped the nylon bag and removed three neatly folded Oxford shirts, two beige cotton trousers, five pairs of underwear, a swimsuit, three sets of socks, and a zippered pouch filled with laundry. A pocket of the duffle held Dylan's toiletries. Destiny watched him offload travel size containers of shave cream, deodorant, and toothpaste. From a side pocket, he removed a three-pack of condoms, with frayed edges and some letters wore off.

Tom looked at the condoms and then to Destiny. He shrugged and said, "Nothing out of the ordinary here." Destiny smiled. Had Tom referred to them being in the bag or looking like they were past their use-by date?

Destiny leaned forward to help Tom refold Dylan's clothes and return everything to the duffle. Once the bag was zipped and set aside, Tom tugged the messenger bag onto his crossed legs and lifted the flap. Destiny scooted next to Tom to gain a better view.

First, Tom pulled out a spiral notebook, filled with Dylan's chicken scratch about Trip's disappearance. Destiny leaned against Tom's arm while he flipped through the pages with a moistened finger. He stopped at the last entry, dated June 13, when Augie confessed to helping Jen kidnap Trip and deliver him to Destiny. The final pages were blank.

"Old stuff," said Tom. He set aside the notebook and retrieved a stack of loose papers, receipts, and business cards.

"Let's move to the conference table to sort through those," Destiny suggested.

Tom gathered up the documents while Destiny touched the switch for the gallery lights. Five hand-blown, teardrop-shaped lights skirted with brushed aluminum illuminated the polished round conference table. Destiny and Tom sat in adjacent chairs upholstered in rich, chocolate-colored leather. Tom rubbed the arms of his chair and said, "Nate *did* like fine things."

Destiny nodded, "Sometimes, it makes me want to buy a bucket of red paint and put polka dots on every surface."

"Plenty of paint here." Tom indicated toward the studio.

With a contemplative smirk, Destiny glanced at the racks of pigment. "You're a bad influence, but I like the way you think."

Tom examined each slip of paper and handed them to Destiny to sort into piles. Besides motel, food, and gas receipts from Dylan and Augie's recent trip to Oregon to visit Destiny and Trip, Dylan kept business cards from each establishment.

"Who are James and Joann Whited?" Tom held up a card with two smiling elderly faces, a phone number, and an address in Groverton, Oregon.

"She works at the church that handled Dylan's adoption. James is her husband. She gave Dylan an intake certificate from when he got dropped off at the church. I assume the document must be in this stack of papers. Dylan showed it to me while we were together in Oregon. The certificate didn't end up being much help, because the names were fictitious and tied to a Native American myth about a baby found in the forest."

Tom fanned the pile and stopped when he reached a frail yellowed certificate. "Dylan mentioned it to me, too. This must be it." He gently extracted the document and placed it in a separate stack. While Tom flipped through the remaining sheets, he added, "Most of the rest of these letter-sized documents are copies of photos and pages from books. Are you familiar with them?"

Destiny nodded. "Dylan got them from a professor. They relate to the myth I spoke about earlier. Frankly, I don't recall all the details. I've been focused on dealing with Nate's death."

"I wonder if Augie would remember more about them."

"He's practically got a photographic memory. I'm sure he would."

"I assume you're still in touch with Augie."

"We've been friends for years." Destiny had acquaintances in Salida. But with Jen gone, Augie might be her only close friend.

"Do you know his work schedule or if he might be home now?"

"He's up at the Matchless Mine in Leadville tonight. It's not an operating mine, only a tourist site. Augie's their night watchman for a couple of nights each week. He gets home early in the morning. We can drop by his place tomorrow and catch him before he goes to bed."

"Let's do that." Tom straightened when he reached the bottom of the stack. "What's this?" He pulled two sheets of lined paper from the pile. The pages had a ragged side as if hastily torn from a spiral notebook. Tom handed one to Destiny while he scrutinized the other.

"He's not much of an artist, but this might be a pencil sketch of Kalev," Destiny laid her sheet on the table and pushed it next to the one in front of

Tom.

Tom looked from one drawing to the other. "Yours captures a full body view, and mine's a headshot. I'm guessing they're both of Kalev."

"Probably, but I can't tell much from only two sketches." *Especially since Dylan, obviously, wasn't an art major in college.*

Tom pointed to the full body drawing. "Kalev's not an ape-like hunchback Sasquatch from the movies. He looks like a hairy human— more like a Viking than a gorilla."

Destiny nodded and placed a hand on Tom's bicep. "I still want to believe Kalev is a reclusive woodsman who contacted Dylan. But with all this hair, he can't be human."

Chapter 19

OCTOBER 26
TOM MORROW

Tom and Destiny stood on the rusting metal steps in front of Augie's single-wide, white-paneled trailer. When she knocked, the door opened to reveal a slender, middle-aged man, nearly a head shorter than his guests.

Augie peered at them with suspicion behind wire-rimmed glasses. "Destiny, who is this?"

"So because I brought a friend, you're not planning to let me in?" Destiny asked with a grin.

Augie opened the door wider. "Come in. But who are you?" he asked Tom.

Destiny spoke before Tom could introduce himself. "This is Tom, Dylan's roommate from Chicago."

Augie looked him up and down before offering a hand. "You're from Chicago. Why are you here?" He snapped to face Destiny. "Did something happen to Dylan?"

"Please don't worry, but we're not exactly sure where he is right now."

Augie stiffened. "He's in Colorado Springs, working a case. That's what he told me."

Destiny moved past Augie and into the living room, where she sat on the plaid couch. She motioned for Tom and Augie to join her.

Tom nearly took the recliner until Augie drew a sharp breath, shoulders rigid. When he sensed the chair was reserved for Augie, Tom joined

Destiny on the sofa and looked around the homey space decorated with dozens of porcelain figurines. "You have a great place here. I can tell you work hard to keep it looking nice."

Augie gave Tom a wary nod and lowered himself to the recliner. Augie nervously tapped his heels and made the chair shake. Jaw clenched, he asked, "Was it the mountain lion and the bear? They killed Jen and Nate."

Destiny crossed the room to kneel in front of Augie. "Please, don't assume he's hurt or worse. We know he's not in Colorado Springs, but we're not certain where he went. He might have gone into the woods with someone he met at the cabin."

"Who?" Augie stood and looked like he planned to search for Dylan.

Destiny jumped up and grabbed Augie by the arm. She urged him to sit. He reluctantly complied. Destiny knelt next to him and patted his hand. Tom recognized her attempts to calm him. But Augie's heels still tapped with nervous energy.

She stroked his forearm. "We're not sure, and we're trying to figure that out. We found some documents Dylan had. We're hoping you might know more about them." Destiny nodded at Tom to bring over the papers. "Some of them you saw while we were in Oregon. I've told Tom everything I recollect, but he'd like to know what you remember, too. Your memory is so much better than mine."

Tom first handed over a half dozen copies of photos and book pages. But he retained Dylan's drawings. Augie reviewed each one with slow deliberation before he placed them in a perfectly straight pile on an adjacent end table. Tom watched Augie's precise movements and hoped his attention to details might provide clues about how to find Dylan. He waited for Augie to begin.

"Dylan and I brought these from Oregon. They're from Dr. Breedlove at the university." Tom watched Augie glance up. But instead of looking at Tom, Augie stared at the refrigerator in the other room. "She is a professor of Native American Studies. She's very smart."

"I'll bet she is. Do you recall what she said?"

"Dr. Breedlove said the documents answered questions about the names on Dylan's birth certificate."

Augie placed a hand over the papers, but he still stared at the fridge. He said, "They weren't his parents' names. Hekewi means *making a joke,* and Desyelni means *baby found in the woods*. Dylan was sad because the names weren't real. He wants to find his parents."

"What about this one?" asked Tom while he reached forward to remove a sheet. Augie lifted his hand to hover over the papers. Tom slipped a photocopy from the pile. It looked like a color copy of a woodcut painting of two inky black evergreens with interwoven trunks. A pale sliver of moon poked through the branches. At the base of the connected trees sat an assortment of woodland animals focused on a swaddled baby with a toothless grin and almond-shaped eyes that glistened pale green.

Augie stared at the copy and nodded with crisp movements. Moments passed before he said, "That's a photo of a woodcarving that tells the story about a baby with magical parents. His father was an enchanted tree, and his mother was an Indian girl. The baby was born sick, so the girl agreed to become a tree, like the baby's father. When she changed, she saved the baby's life. The baby's name was Desyelni, and when he grew up, he became the tribe's chief."

Tom handed Augie the two sketches and waited for Augie's reaction. He stared at each and turned the pages at different angles as if to absorb every line. Silently he passed them back to Tom and left the room.

Tom looked at Destiny. "Did I do something wrong?"

She adjusted to sit cross-legged on the floor beside Augie's chair. "I'm sure he'll be back in a minute."

Shortly, Augie returned with a navy blue spiral notebook. He laid the book across his lap and clasped it tightly.

Destiny pointed toward the book. "I thought your drawings were in a red one. Is this new?"

Augie's eyes never left the notebook. "I started this one last summer. It's private." Augie ran a thumb over the spiral binding while his heels resumed tapping.

Destiny placed a palm over one of his hands. "You don't have to show us anything you're uncomfortable sharing."

Augie glanced at Destiny before he dropped his eyes toward the floor. In a whisper, he said, "Dylan's pictures don't look right." He slid the book from under Destiny's hand and gave it to Tom.

Tom opened the cover to the first page, and his jaw dropped. He looked at Destiny and said, "Augie's seen Kalev, too."

Chapter 20

REVAL
DYLAN COX

Dylan sat in the center of his and Kalev's sleep site and waited for his guests. Tiina planned to attend a Transfer Section meeting all day but would drop off Kati before she left for work.

He wondered how to prepare for a visitor. Dust? Buy wine? While he waited, Dylan stewed about Sasquatch etiquette.

Kati entered with the grace of a princess descending a staircase, head held high, perfectly erect. Dylan stood to greet her. She jumped with a start.

Dylan transmitted, "Don't Sasquatch men stand when a lady enters the room?"

"Why would they do that?"

"Polite manners? People stand to show respect and welcome an individual to a room."

"You halveks have strange customs." Kati pulled a half dozen large leaves from a bush and bundled them to form a pillow before she plopped on the ground in front of Dylan. She lay on her belly and perched her head on entwined fists. "Why do you think Tiina and Kalev have arranged for us to meet alone?"

Dylan sat crossed-legged in front of her. "You tell me."

"Tiina said I am more sociable after I meet with you. But I think they want me to talk about my experience in Porgu with you." Kati rolled on her back and fluffed the wad of leaves under her head. "Have they offered you an incentive to pry information from me?"

Dylan laughed. "Yeah. Tiina said I could have exclusive movie rights when I sell your memoir."

Kati's slack expression told Dylan his joke did not translate. He tried again. "They offered to double my time in the nutrient pool."

"Why would they do that?"

"You're right. What could they offer me as an incentive?"

"What do you want?"

"Eventually, I want to go home, but I don't think it can happen until the next full moon. For now, I'm satisfied to learn about your world. I'm fed and comfortable." Dylan tilted his head. "Since Sasquatches have all their basic needs fulfilled, how would anyone coerce a Sasquatch?"

She touched her chin, apparently to consider his question. "We exchange favors. Someone might speak in front of the Council on your behalf—on a transfer application or mating petition."

"It's good to know bribery is not lost on your society."

When Kati's jaw clenched, Dylan knew a harsh response would follow. It always did. She transmitted, "Bribery in your language implies corruption. We do not engage in dishonest activities. Our favors facilitate efficient decisions."

"Call it what you wish, but if the *favor* gives one Sasquatch priority over others, then it's a bribe." She huffed, and Dylan deflected. "Be assured, no one has asked me to find out why you left my world. But if you want to talk about it, you can feel safe with me. I won't tell anyone."

Kati turned toward Dylan and nervously pulled at the hair on the nape of her neck. "I have questions about what I saw. But nothing you say will change how I feel about my experience."

"I'm here to listen," he transmitted but assumed she would not confide in him.

She rose to sit in front of him. "If I tell you what happened, I want something in return."

"I don't know what I could possibly do for you."

She gave him a sly smile. "I do not have long to live and plan to die with my secrets. But you can give me a special gift no Sasquatch has ever tried."

Dylan moved closer. "Ask me."

"I want you to teach me how to use your language aloud."

"To speak?"

"Yes."

"I could try, but we don't know if you have the same equipment I do." *Since the Sasquatch evolved without speaking, do they have a voice box?*

Kati rolled her eyes. "Trust me. We have the same body parts as you. Anything you can do, we can do, too. I have never used my voice because talking is inefficient. I want to try it."

She sat up straight and placed two fingers against Dylan's throat. "Talk to me."

"What do you want me to say?"

She shushed him and touched her own throat. While her lips moved and air came out of her mouth, all Dylan heard was gurgly, incoherent noises. He said, "I don't think speaking will come to you as easily as picking up our language in transmissions."

She frowned, and Dylan continued. "But we can practice every day, and I promise not to tell Kalev about what we're doing." None of the other Sasquatches had taken an interest in what he might contribute to their knowledge of humans. Kati seemed different—genuinely open and curious.

Kati nodded before she closed her eyes and tucked her hands behind her head with her arms splayed out on either side of her neck. "I transferred to a place with unbearable heat and humidity. Insects swarmed everywhere, and the ground writhed with reptiles and rodents."

Surprised Kati felt comfortable to jump into her story, Dylan lay next to her. He crossed his legs and hoped a nonchalant demeanor would let her know she could trust him. "Sounds miserable, but Kalev can control animals. Weren't you able to do that, too?"

"Of course, but I would focus on controlling one set of pests, and another would start up. Buzzes and chirps never stopped. It filled my ears with noise, and I could not sleep."

"You could have been anywhere—maybe by the equator or inside the tropics. It would depend on the season."

"The halveks talked in your language." She paused. "The intonations were different, slower if you can believe that."

Dylan smiled. "Perhaps, in the U.S. South, but it could have been elsewhere. "What did you see?"

Kati took a long breath and rubbed her eyes before she clasped her hands across her tummy. "I wandered for a few months to learn the area. There were woods and plowed fields. I avoided roads and places with large populations. Most communities were small, and many lived in shelters away from other halveks."

"Did you see an ocean or big lakes?"

"No. There were small ponds, and many were choked with vegetation. Some were near a cluster of shelters, one for a halvek family and others for animals."

"Okay, a farmhouse and barn. I get the picture. Sounds pastoral."

"Farmland, home, domicile—the limits of your language continue to amuse me." She sent a vision of a ramshackle clapboard house with sporadic paint and a rickety porch with two louse-infested recliners.

"Maybe not so pastoral. How about a scene from *Deliverance*?"

Kati did not respond to the reference. Dylan knew she had no context but hoped she understood he was joking with her.

She continued. "The family only kept two dogs that I effortlessly encouraged to be silent. I easily observed the family's routines without being discovered. So I camped nearby and watched them at different times of the day and night."

"What were they like?"

"There was a family unit. I presume a father, mother, and three children, two females and one much younger male. There was another halvek who lived with them. I believe he and the father were friends or relatives."

"Maybe brothers like Alevide and Kalev?"

Kati's lips formed a straight line. "Maybe brothers, but not like Alevide and Kalev. These halveks were evil."

Dylan straightened. "What did you see?"

"They behaved in ways that would never happen in Reval." Kati paused to glance at the shrubs bordering the sleep site. Dylan wondered if she thought someone could monitor their telepathic conversation. After a moment, she continued. "They had sex with the daughters and struck the mother and son."

Dylan rose to sit cross-legged and shook his head in disbelief. "What?"

Kati nodded. "When it grew dark, the father and other older male dragged the two daughters from the house. The girls screamed, but their cries did not affect the males. They took the young females to the animal shelter and stayed there until I could no longer hear the daughters' calls. When they left the shelter, the males laughed and slapped each other with a fondness that signified their comradery in the crimes they committed on the girls. The females came out later, disheveled and cowering. They visited a mechanism to pull water from the ground."

"A pump?"

Kati thought for a moment before she responded. "Yes. They washed their arms and legs in the water, but the bruises remained. Often, before they had finished cleaning off whatever the males left on their bodies, the mother called to them from the door of the shelter, her voice coarse and full of anger."

"Angry with the girls or the men?"

"I do not know. Maybe with the mother's circumstances. They rushed to their mother. Perhaps they expected tenderness or security. But she tugged at their hair and pulled them into the shelter. I do not know what happened once they were inside."

Dylan moved toward Kati and touched her arm. He retracted his hand when she jerked away. He whispered, "This doesn't happen often, but I know it does. Bad people use others for pleasure, sometimes within the family and other times by abusing innocents. We have laws about these types of crimes, and if caught, the perpetrator suffers consequences. But the scars left on the victims may never heal."

Kati raised herself onto an elbow and asked, "Is it more pleasurable for a halvek to have sex with someone who does not want to participate?"

"No. This type of crime is not about sex or pleasure. It's about power over another."

"This behavior does not exist here. If two Sasquatches want to couple, they do. But if one does not want to engage, the other will seek pleasure with someone else."

"Sasquatches seem more enlightened than halveks. Thank you for sharing your story with me. I feel bad that watching this family's dysfunction caused you distress."

Kati shook her head. "I found the halvek males' behaviors troubling, but the story does not end with the mistreatment of the children."

"What else did they do?"

"It is not what they did. The worst part is what I did in response."

Dylan's eyes widened. "What did you do?"

Kati arose to face Dylan. Her crossed legs touched his at the knees. She placed her palms on his thighs and, without hesitation, transmitted, "I killed them."

Dylan recoiled. "All of them?"

Kati shook her head from side to side. "Just the males. There came a day when the men returned from killing an animal. The dead creature lay in the back of their vehicle, its head cocked sideways and antlers poked out. The males placed their weapons on the porch and started to drink. Soon they went into the house and retrieved the girls. Once they took them to the animal shelter, I walked to the yard and took one of their weapons."

"You shot them?"

"Only one. I followed them into the barn and saw a man force himself on a young girl. She cried and struggled to free herself, but her resistance prompted him to laugh and violate her more forcefully."

Kati tipped a defiant chin and continued. "He did not hear me approach, and when I drew close enough to aim the device directly at his head, I pulled the trigger. When the weapon discharged, the male fell upon the girl. Frightened that he would crush her, I set it down and pulled him away. The other man left his victim to see what caused the noise. When he saw me, his shock paralyzed him. His delay gave me time to retrieve a farm tool and bash in his head. They were slow, and I am strong."

Horrified by the brutality of Kati's actions and mystified by her nonchalant description, Dylan pressed for more information. "I assume the girls saw you."

"Yes. They went to the halvek shelter to find their mother."

"And you ran away?"

"No. The mother came out and saw me at the door of the barn. She passed by me to go inside and view the bodies. When she came out, she carried two shovels and handed one to me. The halvek grabbed my arm and pulled me back into the barn. When she started to yank the first male by his boot toward the door, she gave me a pleading look. I understood—she needed my help. We dragged the bodies into her yard and buried them in the soft dirt at the edge of her garden. When we finished, she took my hand in both of her frail ones. She uttered words I did not understand, but I believe she was grateful. Then, she pointed and nodded toward the woods."

Dylan's mouth gaped, unsure of how to react. Kati stared at him until he finally transmitted, "I want to say 'well done,' but I'm not sure how your intervention will be perceived here."

"That is the point. We are forbidden to engage with halveks, but sometimes we are caught unaware. These circumstances are unavoidable, and our kind can forgive a careless Sasquatch. There are no stories about a Sasquatch harming a halvek. If the Council finds out what happened, they will euthanize me whether I ask them to or not."

Chapter 21

SALIDA, COLORADO
KIRK STEADMAN

Kirk drove his peeling burgundy 1994 two-door hardtop Monte Carlo into the driveway and up toward Jen Rickard's old cabin. When he crossed over the landscape edging that marked the end of the dirt-packed drive, Kirk pressed on the gas to bump the car across rocks until he pulled up next to the porch.

Kirk opened the door and lifted his thigh to the left to secure firm footing for his arthritic joints. He rocked forward until he stood in a hunch and slowly inched upright. Kirk coughed to clear his lungs of a wad of phlegm and spat with authority onto the dirt next to his scuffed, secondhand work boots.

After Kirk rested a gnarled hand on the car to catch his breath, he limped toward the trunk to look past a row of trees toward the main road. "Good. Can't see any passing cars from here," he muttered in satisfaction. *I know this place will be perfect—just need to check out the inside.*

When he turned toward the porch, Kirk grabbed the handrail and pulled to ascend the two plank stairs. Out of breath from both the higher altitude and the limited capacity of his nicotine-coated lungs, he paused to sit on a wicker chair near the door. Not one to appreciate nature, Kirk scanned the perimeter for any signs of activity but saw none. The sky shone brilliant blue through the subtly swaying pines, but afternoon shadows stretched long across the yard.

"Time to get moving. I want to be home before nightfall," Kirk muttered while he pushed on the armrests to raise himself from the chair.

There were no flower pots or a welcome mat—the usual spots to hide a key. He stood on tiptoe and drummed his fingers across a ledge at the top of the door. "Bingo," he said. The key fell to the porch. *Good thing the little fucker didn't fall through the cracks.*

Kirk turned the key in the deadbolt and walked into the cabin. The air was dank and smelled of wood smoke. With limited light coming in from the remaining unboarded windows, Kirk barely made out the size of the common room that combined living, kitchen, and dining areas. Paintings and decorative blankets hung on the chinked log walls, but these held no interest for Kirk. He waited until his eyes grew accustomed to the semi-darkness. Then he paced off the room to estimate the size.

This should do. Kirk nodded.

After he inspected the bedroom with its stripped, iron bed and folded colorful quilts on a metal rack, Kirk opened the closet to find it empty except for a couple of wire hangers on the rod and a dime, centered in the doorway. He left the coin, as the value did not exceed his cost of energy needed to stoop to pick it up.

Kirk moved to the bathroom and slid the shower curtain across the rod with a vicious yank. A spider frantically crawled up the side of the tub, only to slide back down and start again. "Good luck gettin' out, ya loser," Kirk said to the insect while he turned toward the sink.

He tugged on the bottom of the metal-framed mirror to find an empty medicine cabinet. Kirk tried the sink faucet, but nothing came out. *Must have winterized the place.* He lifted the lid and urinated in the toilet.

Kirk limped his way back to the kitchen and opened each cabinet. Surprised they still held glasses and dishware, he kept opening doors until he discovered a half dozen liquor bottles. Kirk lifted them down from the shelf and inspected each one to evaluate the labels.

"Hot damn," he chuckled while he retrieved a coffee cup. After he poured a healthy drink, Kirk downed the contents and set the mug in the sink.

A hallway at the back of the cabin led to the rear door. When he walked down the hall, Kirk noticed a double row of hooks affixed to the wall. A single backpack hung on the last hook. He wondered what else had hung on the hooks. Maybe this is where she dried her home-grown weed, he guessed. Kirk yanked the handle of the backdoor to be sure it was locked before he lifted the pack off the wall. It felt nearly empty. But Kirk ran a hand through each pocket and down each seam to be sure someone had not left something easily pawnable. He discovered nothing of value.

He returned to the kitchen. With satisfaction, he nodded and surveyed the great room one more time.

Before he left, Kirk tucked the liquor bottles between his arm and his hollow chest. In a few trips, he transferred them, with considerable grunts and curses, to the back seat of his car. After a final agonizing climb up the front steps, he locked the front door. Kirk pocketed the key. He would replace it on the door frame once he'd made a copy.

Kirk rested once more on the wicker chair. He felt pleased with the size and seclusion of the cabin. A squirrel scurried across the yard with a pinecone in its mouth.

Kirk released a raspy laugh. "We got the same idea, little fella. I think this spot is the perfect place for winter storage."

Chapter 22

DESTINY STEWART, NÉE KUSIK

Destiny glanced up at Tom and noticed the way he rubbed his lower lip with the side of his finger while he concentrated. He sat at the kitchen island with Augie's closed sketchbook resting in front of him as Destiny prepared a dinner of salad topped with grilled chicken strips. She rock-chopped herbs and veggies with a professional chef knife.

"I'd cut off my finger if I tried that," Tom said with a smile.

"Takes practice. I've made a million salads, and this technique gets us faster to dinner time."

Tom was becoming a distraction. She needed to re-focus and set the knife on the countertop. "It's a good thing my technique is second nature. I keep thinking about Trip being with his grandparents."

Tom reached a hand across the counter and drummed his fingers. "Tell me what they did."

She looked at him over the top of her glasses. "I don't want to dwell on the details. But they keep calling to tell me how I've coddled Trip."

"Who are they to judge? Besides, I'm more worried about *his* reaction than what they think of your parenting. Did you speak with Trip?"

His redirect to what was more critical calmed her. "Yes. He's doing fine, in spite of their insistence for him to do everything their way. He's a great kid."

Destiny grabbed the knife and tipped the cutting board to scrape cilantro into an oversized ceramic bowl. "Let's talk about something else.

How was your day with Augie?"

"We spent most of the time at Max Garland's studio across the street. It's fun to watch them work. Max paints from his nature photos. They're from all over the Rocky Mountains. While Augie works from photos too, they're all in his mind. It made me think about how a professional photographer might take hundreds of shots to capture one with the right light or expression. Augie can hone in on an instant where his subject had the perfect expression or where the scene looked pristine." He paused. "I assume you did more today than talk with the Stewarts. What have you been up to?"

"I made all the arrangements for Mayor Rhoad's reelection fundraiser. I think everything is under control." Destiny nodded toward the notebook. "What do you make of Augie's drawings?"

Tom opened the book and turned the pages one at a time. "He's a talented artist. Each figure looks amazingly lifelike. It's like I can feel the person's emotions from their expressions."

Destiny sliced the plump, roasted chicken into strips. "I was referring to his subjects, not his talent."

He looked up from the first portrait. "I'm glad to see Kalev doesn't look like a monster from a horror movie."

"Or anything like the Bigfoot videos on the internet."

"I noticed that, too. Both Augie and Dylan's sketches give him a swimmer's body, only with loads of hair. Neither portrayed Kalev as a hunched over Neanderthal with a flat ape face."

"What do you think about Augie knowing Kalev's name? How is that possible?"

Tom ran a hand over the page with a sketch of two furry Sasquatches, one about a foot taller than the other. Destiny stopped her prep to look at the drawings. The Sasquatches smiled at each other, and the smaller one stroked the other's face. If they were humans, they'd be sharing a tender moment.

Tom looked up at Destiny and said, "Augie told us his last dream about Kalev happened seven nights ago. That would have been the 18th, the same night Dylan told me Kalev planned to introduce him to the Sasquatch group. I doubt it's a coincidence."

"That doesn't answer how Augie would know his name. Augie claims he didn't speak with Dylan about this, and Dylan *gave* Kalev his name. Supposedly, this guy didn't have one before Dylan and Kalev met."

"What if Kalev understood Dylan named him? If Augie somehow saw Kalev's thoughts or transmissions, the name may have been included."

"That makes sense. Augie said he didn't know the names of the other two Sasquatches in the sketches. If Dylan hadn't met them, then they wouldn't have had names."

Destiny sighed and shook her head. "Frankly, I would have thought there were only two of them. But Augie seemed clear there were three."

"They look similar, but after I looked closely at the sketches, I noticed subtle differences. The unnamed pair are in most of the drawings, and they're nearly always together. When Kalev appears, he's always alone."

Destiny rinsed her hands in the sink and dried them on a linen towel. She came around the island and leaned over the notebook to point at the open page. "That's the couple. Where's one of Kalev?"

Tom flipped to a sketch of a solo Sasquatch. "This is him. Despite not wearing a National Park Service hat, Augie believed Kalev was a ranger or some kind of law enforcement official."

"I guess he doesn't need to pack heat for his job."

Tom chuckled while he turned another page to a drawing of the pair. He pointed to the shorter one. "This one's like a doctor because she, as Augie put it, 'helps people who are sad.' So, maybe a psychiatrist would be more precise. Her buddy is a politician because 'he goes to meetings and tells people what to do.'"

"It's all so surreal. I can't believe the Sasquatch live in a culture with doctors and politicians. If they exist at all, they must spend their time hiding and rooting around for food like every other wild animal."

Tom shrugged. "Other animals live in societies and have roles like leaders or negotiators. I've read that about the great apes."

Destiny rolled her eyes. "Yes, but Augie's explanation seems a lot more sophisticated and makes them sound—well, human."

Destiny moved to a cabinet and took silverware and cotton napkins from a drawer to set places for them to eat at the island. After she put an oil and vinegar set and salt and pepper mills within arm's reach, she slid their heaping plates between the cutlery. Why did it seem so natural to play house with Tom?

She cleared her throat. "Even though Augie's sketches were in pencil, he seemed clear about their eye colors. Kalev and the politician both had blue eyes, and the doctor has green. I can't imagine why that's important, but Augie sensed it was."

Tom flipped through the notebook to the final pages. When he handed it to Destiny, he asked, "Do you recognize any of these places? Augie didn't know them, but they seem unique."

Destiny laid the open pages next to her meal. She speared a piece of chicken along with some lettuce and chewed while she reviewed the sketches. Abruptly she sat upright. "I know this one. It's the top of Church Mountain. I've hiked up there with Jen."

She pointed at the edge of a disk, barely in the scene. "See this curve? I think it's part of a radio tower on the top of the mountain. These boxes and lines in the background are buildings and roads down in Salida."

"That's a start. Can you take us there in the morning?"

Destiny shrugged. "Sure. We can park by the cabin and take a jog to the summit from there."

Tom placed the notebook to the side of his place setting. He pushed back his barstool to stand and draw Destiny into a hug. She leaned into him but felt awkward with her lettuce-spiked fork pointing out to her side. The unexpected intimacy of his embrace gave her conflicting emotions. Should she join his enthusiasm or close off the feelings he seemed to awaken?

She pulled back and nodded at her fork. "We should probably eat."

"Before the salad gets cold?" The corners of Tom's mouth ticked upward.

Destiny felt her face flush. Why did his smile make her tingle?

"You okay?" He brushed a stray lock of hair from her face.

Her breath caught in her throat, but she managed a strained response. "I'm fine. I swallowed the wrong way. About going up Church Mountain, it won't be fully light until close to eight a.m. So we can leave right after breakfast."

"I'm good with that. You can wake me anytime, and I'll be ready to go."

Destiny stood to refill her wine glass while she considered his offer. *I might be ready sooner than you think.*

Chapter 23

Misty rain sprinkled the windshield. The wipers slapped while Destiny's Subaru pulled off the main road and into the driveway next to the cabin. Tom closed the passenger door and stepped to the back of the car to open the hatchback and retrieve a borrowed rain jacket and purple Rockies baseball cap.

He breathed deeply and smelled the decaying pine needles overpowering the moist air. After he slipped on a pair of Dylan's merino wool running gloves, he yanked the cap's brim low and nodded at Destiny.

To warm their muscles, they started up the road at a slow jog. While the pair ran side by side, Tom pushed hard to keep up with Destiny's pace. His lungs ached in the oxygen-deficient air.

After a quarter hour, they reached a y-intersection where the main road continued toward a couple of cabins. They took the four-wheel-drive track to switch back toward the top of the mountain. Eventually, the trail narrowed and could not accommodate running abreast. Tom slowed and signaled with a nod for Destiny to take the lead. She continued up the path with gusto. Her running shoes skipped over loose stones and arms pumped like a locomotive's pistons.

Tom stopped to catch his breath. "Hey, I'm not going to be able to keep up this pace to the top. Can we walk for a while?"

Without coming to a full stop, she turned to look at him. "I'd cool down too much if we stop, but I can slow down until you catch your breath." He caught up with her, and they walked at a fast pace until he felt able to resume jogging.

While they continued uphill, Tom said, "I can't help but wonder how Augie had dreams of Kalev. Especially the backgrounds of Kalev's friends. Dylan told me Kalev was telepathic but didn't use a language as we do. He communicated with rapid-fire still and moving images. Visions included tons of data that gave context and emotions, as well as the overall message. Kalev tried to send Dylan a message in the way he'd normally communicate, but Dylan couldn't handle the volume of information and didn't understand the message. Kalev needed to slow everything down and send discrete visions for Dylan to get the gist."

Without slowing, Destiny removed her fogged glasses, wiped them on a cotton bandana, and tucked them in a jacket pocket. "I believe Augie has autism spectrum disorder. Traditional communication and language are laden with social nuances that, at times, escape him. But maybe somehow, he's able to consolidate information from Kalev's transmissions that appeared random to Dylan."

Tom nodded and started a slow jog. "Sounds feasible. I guess we'll know more when we talk with Dylan."

Despite the cold, moist air, sweat poured down Tom's face. He dragged an arm across his forehead to keep a stream of sweat and rain from dripping into his eyes. The nylon jacket did little to absorb the moisture.

Without warning, Destiny stopped short and bent over to look at the ground. Tom had been running too close and rammed her from behind. He grabbed her hips with both hands to keep her from tumbling forward.

She turned. "Well, that was unexpected, but not unpleasant."

Tom blushed, grateful for his already flushed cheeks. "I am so sorry, but you stopped without brake lights. What are you looking at?"

Destiny pointed, and Tom leaned around her to follow the direction. He saw two strands of desiccated animal waste on the trail. Destiny said, "I can't tell if these are from a coyote or something else, like maybe a fox."

Tom moved next to Destiny and strained forward to stare at the scat. "Why not a plain old domestic dog?"

Destiny scoffed and asked, "Can't you see the fur and bits of bone?

Unless someone is feeding rodents to Rover, I'm pretty sure this is from a wild animal."

Without changing his stance or taking his eyes from the ground, Tom asked, "When did you become interested in identifying shit?"

Destiny straightened. "I've raised a boy in these woods. Poop identification might have been the sole reason Trip hiked with me when he was between three and five."

Tom nodded. He imagined Destiny and a younger version of Trip while they stalked the trails in search of animal excrement. While the boy now chose to avoid any outdoor activities, he wondered if Trip might regain an appreciation later in life.

Tom glanced upslope. A bank of clouds encircled the summit like a smoke ring hovering over the top.

When they jogged up into the moisture layer, they lost sight of the road in front of them. Tom reached out to take hold of Destiny's arm. "I can barely see my feet, much less where I'm putting them."

Destiny turned to face Tom and jogged in place. "The road makes two more switchbacks before it reaches the top. We need to take it slow and not trip over any big rocks."

Before they broke through the top of the cloud, she stumbled once, but Tom snatched her arm to prevent a fall.

Once above the cloud, they saw clear blue skies and brilliant sunshine. Tom marveled at the solid layer of white forming a curtain between them and the valley below. He felt as if they could step out and walk across the puffy surface.

Destiny said, "This should all burn off soon, but it's incredible to be inside and then above a cloud without needing an airplane." She scanned the area and added, "There's a bunch of radio towers and antennas up here. Let's start looking."

They decided to begin at one corner of the summit ring and proceed in separate directions to meet up on the opposite side after they searched the ground and the bases of the towers.

A few minutes elapsed before Destiny called to Tom. "Hey, come here. I think I've found something."

Tom joined her. She huddled on the ground next to a stunted pine tree at the edge of the summit. Destiny pointed to a pile of fabric and a backpack. "Could this belong to Dylan?" she asked.

Tom glanced from Destiny to a patch of scorched earth only feet away. "I'll check it out in a sec. But what do you think of this huge burned spot?"

Destiny rose to look where Tom pointed. "It could have been a lightning strike, or maybe someone lit a campfire up here."

"I guess there's no telling how long ago it burned." Tom knelt to rub the charcoaled stems.

Destiny shrugged. "Not too long ago. There's no new growth between the charred plants." She turned to the pack. "But what do you think about this pile of stuff? Could it be Dylan's?"

They approached the stack, and Tom's heart beat faster. If the pack was Dylan's, they would know he'd been there.

A slow sigh escaped Tom's lips before he reached forward and opened the backpack. He unhooked a set of keys from a snap hook secured inside the top flap and dangled them on one finger. "This is Dylan's stuff. See this little braid on the ring? It's hair that he and Jen found on their first hike together. I'd know this anywhere."

He dug further into the pack and removed a stack of clothes, which he handed to Destiny. She snapped open a polypro shirt and refolded it before she placed the shirt on the ground. Next, she opened a pair of jeans. Steel-gray briefs dropped to the ground. Tom and Destiny stared in disbelief at the underwear and then at each other. Destiny broke the silence. "There's got to be a reason why Dylan ditched his clothes. It must have been freezing up here that night."

"You're assuming this was the only set of clothes he had. Maybe this was an extra set of clothes, or he changed into something warmer once they got to the summit."

Destiny nodded once while she stared at Dylan's underwear. "That's possible," she said hesitantly.

Tom smiled. "Once the others arrived, maybe they offered him a Bigfoot hide to wear."

"Not funny. What else is in the pack?" Destiny refolded the jeans and placed them on top of the shirt before she tucked the underwear between the layers. When she shook out a fleece jacket, she drew it closer to her nose. "Ugh. Tom, smell this. It's disgusting."

He lifted an eyebrow and said, "I'll take your word for it."

"If I didn't know better, I'd swear Dylan was living rough for a couple of weeks before he left with Kalev."

Tom shook his head. "Nope. But he might have picked up the fragrance from Kalev."

Destiny puzzled at the thought. "Do either of them sound like the cuddling type?"

"Maybe they became better friends than I would have thought."

Destiny gave his remark a tsk. After two quick folds, she laid the jacket on top of the pile. She moved from her knees to sit cross-legged on the rocky ground and watched Tom rummage deeper into the pack.

Tom lifted out a cell phone. He pushed the power button, and the screen illuminated with a selfie of Dylan and Jen in their hiking clothes with white-veined peaks framed in the background. Tom tapped in the password to access the phone.

"You know his password?" Destiny asked.

"I programmed it into his phone," Tom replied when he pressed the photo application.

"You don't own a cell phone, but you programmed Dylan's?"

Tom smiled. "Just because I don't want to rely on technology doesn't make me a Luddite."

"Point taken. What are you looking for?"

"Dylan is addicted to taking selfies. I want to see if any of his recent photos might give us a clue to where he is and if he took off his clothes."

Tom's jaw dropped. "What do you think of this one?" He passed the phone to Destiny.

Chapter 24

REVAL
KALEV

As Alevide and Tiina broke through the clearing and approached the bathing pool, Kalev could hear his brother ask, "You left them unsupervised?"

Tiina held the lead with Alevide a step behind, while Kalev waited for them at the far end. His eyes locked on Tiina, and he listened to their very public transmissions.

"Well, why not? I cannot believe he would hurt her." Tiina snapped.

"Kati is our responsibility, and we have no idea what he is capable of doing. Halveks are primitive and violent. They do not value our civilized traditions and culture. He could kidnap, rape, or murder her. They would do anything to enhance their advantage."

Kalev watched the drama unfold as Tiina stopped and spun to face her mate. She put a hand against his chest. "Kati is taller and stronger than him. Anyway, what does he have to gain here? He cannot escape or hide. He is totally under our control."

"While decisions related to Kati are yours, I am concerned for her well-being. We both know wild animals in Porgu do not like to be caged or frightened. Dylan is no different. He is not some docile beast bred for food or as a pet. He has greater intellect than lower animals in Porgu that react solely by instinct. He will seek to augment his leverage."

In a huff, Tiina plopped on the edge to dangle her feet while Alevide took a shallow dive. "This discussion is not finished," she transmitted.

He surfaced next to Kalev, where he embraced his brother and exchanged forehead rubs.

"You two always argue. Is there trouble in paradise?" Kalev sent the message to both of them.

Tiina kicked her feet to splash and send ripples their way. "We are not arguing. It is a discussion about whether we can trust Dylan not to harm Kati."

"Why would he harm her?" asked Kalev.

"My question exactly." Tiina slipped into the pool to breaststroke toward the males with her head held high above the surface. "Did you ever see him behave violently when you watched him in Porgu?"

"Never." Kalev looked at Alevide and tucked a strand of hair behind his brother's ear before he continued. "But I only observed him for a few months."

"Is this the evidence you are relying on?" Alevide asked Tiina.

Kalev raised a finger and continued. "When he opened his mind to me, I looked for more than his language skills. I searched his memories for any violent tendencies since childhood."

Tiina reacted with a start. "Your actions seem a bit intrusive on a sentient being. We would not allow deep thought penetration on another Sasquatch without their permission."

Alevide chimed in. "That is the point. He is *not* a Sasquatch." Alevide pulled himself from the pool and turned to sit on the edge. "There are no restrictions on how we can evaluate him." He turned to Kalev and asked, "What did you find? Is he prone to violence?"

Kalev saw Tiina purse her lips. He knew she wanted to barge into the discussion. But for some reason, she remained silent. Kalev considered Alevide's question and how his response might support Tiina's view. "There is nothing in Dylan's past to suggest he would harm Kati."

Tiina let out a deep sigh of relief while Kalev continued. "He has developed relationships with females and always acted with courtesy. However, there were instances of anger. He blamed a motorist who struck his parent's vehicle and killed them."

Tiina's brow creased with concern. "His parents were killed?"

Kalev placed a palm on Tiina's shoulder. "Their deaths were tragic. Dylan lived away from them at the time. He regrets not being closer."

"I had no idea he faced such adversity."

Alevide raised an eyebrow. "Do not assume their family bonds run as deep as ours. If he cared for them, he would not have left in the first place."

Tiina bristled. "We know little about their family connections. These relationships cannot be precisely understood simply with observation. To clearly know the extent of their attachments, we need to engage them. Dylan can help us in our initial research."

Alevide scoffed. "One set of observations does not prove a theory."

"But it is a start." Tiina ran a hand across the surface of the pool.

Kalev nodded in agreement. "Back to Dylan's predilection for anger and violence. He felt unfairly treated by a family member he called Nate Stewart. This halvek tormented Dylan and embarrassed him. Dylan's anger toward Nate Stewart seemed directed more toward himself and his inability to break free of the halvek's attraction. For many years, Dylan existed in a cycle with Nate Stewart drawing him close, followed by brutal rejection. To his credit, Dylan never blamed Nate Stewart for these taunts."

Alevide transmitted, "It seems like he misdirected his feelings. Why would he hold himself accountable for Nate Stewart's poor behavior?"

Kalev paused to contemplate. "I agree with Tiina, power struggles between halveks are complicated. We can start our research with Dylan's experiences. There may come a time when this information will foster a relationship between Sasquatches and the halveks."

Alevide laughed. "What makes you believe we want to advance our engagement beyond simple observations? It is intriguing to track their development, but there is nothing to be gained from direct engagement with this violent, desperate race."

Kalev held up a hand to Alevide and sent a message directly to Tiina. "You know Alevide is compassionate about Sasquatches, but he considers halveks inconsequential. Perhaps your divergent views come from your Council assignments. You are sensitive to these beings because you have debriefed transferees with positive experiences." To both, he transmitted, "Dylan never responded to Nate Stewart's behaviors with violence."

"Never?" Alevide asked.

Kalev shrugged. "Not directly. Once Dylan smashed a flimsy painting over Nate Stewart's head, but the act did not hurt him."

Tiina interjected, "See? I told you he has a higher intellect than other halveks. Now, do you agree I was right to let Kati and Dylan meet alone?"

Before Alevide could respond, Kalev interrupted. "What is your objective when you allow them privacy?"

"Kati refuses to tell me what happened during her transfer. I think she might communicate with Dylan about the circumstances. Since he does not know the rules of our society, he will not judge her and cannot influence her status here. I hope she will see him as a neutral confidant."

"Do you want me to probe his thoughts to see if she told him?" Kalev asked Tiina.

"Sure."

Alevide transmitted, "Aren't you being hypocritical?"

"How so?" She glared at Alevide.

"Not a minute ago, you accused Kalev of violating Dylan with a deep thought penetration, and now you ask him to do it again to gain information on Kati?"

"This is different. Our goal is to protect Kati and enhance our overall knowledge."

Alevide lifted both hands in surrender and shook his head. "I understand your objective and your commitment to our tribe, but I respectfully disagree with your motive and justification."

Tiina responded immediately. "You have taken this position to contradict my view."

"You know that is not true, but I know better than to argue when you have a strong opinion." Alevide sighed. "I will meet you later at our sleep site to take nourishment." After he nodded toward his mate, Tiina and Kalev watched him turn into the forest.

She turned toward Kalev. "He can be so stubborn."

Kalev took her into his arms and rubbed his body against hers. "Uncompromising positions are his specialty."

She raised her chin and looked directly into Kalev's eyes. "Alevide only sees the rules as prescribed. He cannot appreciate opportunities at the margins of what is right and wrong."

"He is still my brother. Let us not discuss him right now. There are other topics, more pleasant ones, to consider." He drew her close and moved his palm from her shoulder to rest on the small of her back.

Tiina breathed deeply and rubbed her chest against his. "Share these topics with me."

Kalev hesitated, then asked, "Are you outside of your conceiving time?"

"What do you think?" She reached up to grasp his shoulders and wrapped her legs around his hips.

Kalev accepted her offer and released months of loneliness from Porgu into her willing body. While Kalev stroked her back and transmitted thoughts of tenderness and intimacy, he sensed someone nearby. Kalev glanced toward the entrance path and saw Alevide. Tiina's husband stood stock still, his face frozen in a grimace.

When their eyes met, Alevide transferred, "I understand your attraction, but do not forget she chose to mate with me. You and Tiina are only casual lovers."

Kalev watched Alevide shake his head and retreat into the woods. Kalev hugged Tiina tighter, knowing she would someday be his in all respects.

Chapter 25

DYLAN COX

Dylan watched Kati pause at the site exit. She glanced over her shoulder and transmitted, "Tiina wants you to stay here until Kalev returns."

"I'll do my best to keep busy. But I can't get the TV to work."

She rolled her eyes and disappeared down the trail. Dylan knew she had wanted to leave before the early afternoon winds and mist.

Unsure when Kalev would return and with nothing to occupy his time, Dylan spent the next hours expanding the sleep site between naps.

"And Kalev believes Porgu is boring?" Dylan muttered aloud while he snatched a fistful of grass and threw it into the bushes.

When the gusts started in earnest, Dylan stared up at the swaying trees. They reminded him of videos he'd seen of Gulf palms in a hurricane. When the mist settled, Dylan lost sight of the treetops.

Time for a walk. Dylan tightened his leaf wrap and strode with assurance down the scant trail connecting their private space to the main path. When he reached the intersection, he paused to look in both directions. As an extra precaution, Dylan stepped back into the vegetation and opened his mind to detect any approaching Sasquatches. Kalev made him practice this technique each day. While not anywhere close to proficient, his ability to perceive subtle footfalls and faint transmissions of oncoming Sasquatches had grown stronger.

Dylan strained but heard nothing amiss before he eased on to the path.

Which direction to go? Their nutrition and soaking pools lay to the right. After a week in Reval, he knew that terrain well. Ready to see something new, he struck out to the left.

The flora on the unfamiliar route seemed identical to what Dylan had seen in the other direction. He paused to touch a crimson flower as big as his head. The blossom glistened with moisture from the mist. While the wind rattled the bush, it flung dewdrops onto his chest and wrap.

Dylan grasped the stem to shake off the water hidden between the tightly clustered petals and tipped the flower toward his nose. No scent. Dylan wondered why he kept checking—none of them had a fragrance. Did Sasquatches have an underdeveloped sense of smell from living in a world devoid of scents?

He thought back to his first encounter with Kalev and smiled. Dylan recalled Kalev's horrific body odor and made a mental note to ask Kalev about Sasquatches' ability to detect smells.

Before he started again, Dylan inched closer to the main trail to listen. His reaction was probably overkill because Kalev had assured him virtually no one traveled during the mists. But better safe than sorry. He did not sense anyone nearby.

Dylan strolled along the curvy path but suddenly stopped. While he had never traveled in this direction, something seemed out of place. He crossed to the right side and pushed leaves the size of platters out of his view. The Auk was here. But how could that be? It should have been in the other direction. Maybe there was more than one Auk, or perhaps the trails formed a circle around it? He stepped toward the edge and peered into the dense jungle of thrashing bushes and trees. Then, he *heard* them.

He froze. There was no time to run back to the sleep site. He must hide until they passed. *What was I thinking to come out alone?* Getting caught with Kalev would be bad, but being apprehended unaccompanied could be disastrous. There were no Sasquatch jails. Maybe they would kill him on the spot. Kati was an intelligent and generally peaceful Sasquatch, and she had killed humans. Why not the ones headed toward him?

Dylan concentrated on their faint transmissions to figure out where the Sasquatches were and how soon they might arrive. The overheard communications did not block his ability to see the trail and woods. But he sensed flashes of memories. Groups of Sasquatches floated in pools, sat huddled in circles, and walked along paths. He saw jagged peaks and a beach splashed with crashing waves. Some hesitated on faces with exaggerated emotions like fear or sadness, and Dylan assumed those messages transmitted concepts along with locations. While their high-speed visions no longer gave him a violent headache, he still could not puzzle together what they meant.

Despite the howling wind, he could sense more than one Sasquatch approaching. But how many?

Dylan's shallow breath came in short gasps. *Don't hyperventilate. Be calm and hide.* Dylan crouched and parted two massive bushes at the edge of the Auk. He peered over the edge and saw the ground steeply fall away. Trees and shrubs clung to the side of the precipice to block his view of how far the chasm dropped.

He took a breath and stepped forward into the thicket of vegetation. Dylan slid a trembling foot through the brush until he felt a sturdy branch that did not bend under his weight. He inched the other foot forward and clutched branches to maintain his balance.

Leaf-covered tree limbs cocooned his body when he twisted into the whipping mass of vegetation. Kalev had taught Dylan how to close off his mind to others while keeping open to their transmissions. With a clenched jaw, he focused and imagined a door to seal his thoughts.

Dylan shook with fear but peeked from his blind. Three caramel-colored Sasquatches reached his hiding spot. They engaged in a conversation Dylan perceived but did not understand.

From behind his thrashing screen, he guessed they were Kalev's size and age. They strode with confidence and purpose. One Sasquatch paused a few steps beyond where Dylan cowered. Had he heard Dylan over the sound of the wind?

Dylan's heart pounded as the Sasquatch tilted his head as if listening. Finally, he shrugged and moved on to catch up with his comrades. Dylan stole a glance from his blind to see them headed into the wind. Their long body fur streamed behind them.

Once their thoughts faded into the distance, Dylan glanced down at his trembling hand. He clenched and unclenched his fingers to steady his nerves. *I was reckless to come out on my own. I need to get back before Kalev finds out I left. What if he gets angry and leaves me to fend for myself? He's been my advocate so far, but that could change.*

He stepped forward and placed a foot squarely on a slick leaf. Before he could react, his leg shot forward. Dylan tumbled backward. His hands flailed and searched for something to grasp. Slender branches whipped across his arms. He twisted and fell. Leaves slapped his face and arms and tore off his wrap. The undergrowth's sharp edges sliced his skin while he toppled into the precipice.

Falling and falling, Dylan flopped against limbs and bumped down the cliffside. His torso slammed into a massive horizontal tree trunk. A millisecond later, the side of his face collided as well. Dylan felt his cheekbone crack when it drove a dent into the squishy, moss-covered bark. The abrupt stop forced all the air from his lungs.

He lay still and willed himself to breathe—grateful to be secure. Who knew how far he could have fallen?

Everything hurt. Dylan's chest had taken the full brunt of the collision. But his face tingled, and an eye started to swell shut. He tried to encircle the slick, spongy trunk with his arms and legs, but his reach made it only partway around. Desperate to assess his situation, Dylan slipped his arms under his chest to thrust himself upright. He gripped the slippery moss with both hands and pushed until he straddled the enormous log like an infant astride a Clydesdale.

Vegetation blocked much of the light and left Dylan in semi-darkness. Without releasing his hold, he looked up. Ferns and hanging plants clung to the chasm's walls, some with lily-like flowers and others with thick succulent leaves in blue-green and yellow. Bushes and trees sprouted from the dense undergrowth, including the life-saving tree he'd landed on.

Dylan leaned around his perch to gauge where the bottom might be. The wall continued downward—a never-ending pit that disappeared into blackness. "Fuck!" he yelled into the chasm.

He lay still and hoped no one had heard him. Dylan inhaled and then forced a great sigh. *Get ahold of yourself. No one knows where you are, and nobody is coming for you. Kalev wouldn't set foot in the Auk if his life depended on it.*

After he tightened his grip, Dylan tipped back and strained to see up the wall to guess how far he had fallen. It went up forever, but the distance was irrelevant. He would need to climb out of this hell-hole.

Dylan inventoried his limbs. He flexed fingers then toes and decided nothing felt broken, only bruised and cut. Dylan buried his fingers into the moss and leaned forward to balance on his hands and knees.

Ever so slowly, he placed a foot on the trunk. Without warning, it slipped and shot to the side. Dylan's heart raced. He collapsed his arms to grip the tree and keep from tumbling. Before he tried again, Dylan rested and waited for the trembling to subside. *I need a new technique.*

After taking a minute to breathe, Dylan pushed himself upright. He shook his shoulders to release tension and picked at the moss to toss bits into the abyss. *If only I could use this stuff to hold me to the tree, instead of slipping off.*

Dylan dug deeper until he reached the bark. It felt tacky. He pressed his finger and thumb together. They were stuck until he forced them apart. A tar-like goo coated the bark under the moss layer. *This could work.*

Dylan clawed the trunk with his fingernails until a piece of moss peeled away from the bark. He removed several more strategic strips to carve out a decent space. Once satisfied, Dylan slid a foot into the cleared area and wormed his toes under the edge of the moss. It felt secure like sticking his foot into a loafer glued to the tree trunk.

When he lifted his other foot to repeat the process, something caught his attention only a few feet in front of where he sat. A porcelain white object rested on his tree trunk—nearly covered with a limp leaf.

What could it be? Dylan strained in the dim light. Should he allow curiosity to trump his momentum to escape the Auk? He shrugged. *Things can't get any worse. Based on Kalev's tight lips about this place, it's not like he would tell me what it could be. And that's if I ever get out of here.*

Dylan leaned forward and stretched to reach the corner of the leaf-drape. He tapped the edge with an extended finger. The leaf flapped but fell back in place. Dylan clenched his jaws, determined to uncover the object.

He transferred more weight to his forward foot and strained until two fingers closed on the cover's edge. Dylan tugged—enough to compromise his balance. He thrust his arms out to either side like a tightrope walker to regain equilibrium. He stabilized and took a breath.

Once again, he regained a firm grip. Dylan strained forward with a free hand and stretched to pull the leaf sideways. It slipped away like a silk drape unveiling an object of art.

Dylan propelled back on his haunches. A tiny skeleton lay on the tree trunk. Had the baby fallen asleep on his belly and forgotten to live the rest of his life? Human or Sasquatch? Dylan could not be sure. He stretched forward but could not touch the minuscule feet bones.

How the hell did it get here? Dylan stared at the skeleton—tempted to carry the bones along with him. He had no satchel or bag. Maybe it should stay in the Auk, or perhaps it belonged in the Auk.

When Dylan ran a hand through his hair, remnant goo stuck to his waves. He cursed, and he tugged out a few hairs. Enough about the baby. He would think about it later. At that moment, he needed to focus on climbing out of the Auk.

Dylan readjusted his feet under the moss patch and strained to stand. While he balanced on the trunk, Dylan reached for the stoutest plants anchored into the wall above his head. He would not allow his bones to join the baby's.

Chapter 26

SALIDA, COLORADO
KIRK STEADMAN

Kirk Steadman slid into the booth at Molly's Pancake King on Highway 50, his back to the door. Across from him sat Mike Calvert, a brute with arms dotted with prison tattoos.

"You're late," said Mike, while he chewed a forkful of syrup-drenched waffle. He picked up a sausage link with fingers tipped with black-rimmed nails and took a bite before he put the stub back on his plate. Mike swallowed. With both elbows on the table, he stared at Kirk.

"I had another appointment before this one. Ran late," Kirk said.

"Whatever. You havin' breakfast?"

Kirk's mouth curled into a yellow-toothed grin, "Nah. I'm short of cash since my good-for-nothin' son left town. Unless it's your treat?" Mike released a snort and swiped his nose with the back of his hand. Kirk shrugged. "Never hurts to ask."

A waitress approached in a spotless white T-shirt with a purple Molly's Pancake King logo stenciled over her ample left breast. Both men stared at the logo when she asked, "Can I take your order?"

Kirk responded with a hacking laugh. "Honey, you can take more than that." She rolled her eyes and tapped a ballpoint pen on her order pad. "I'm kiddin' around with you, Doll. Bring me some coffee when you get a chance."

When she turned to retrieve a mug and coffee pot, Kirk and Mike watched her leave. In a stage whisper, Mike said, "Must wear a thong. I don't see any panty lines on her sweet ass."

"You got better eyes than I do. I'd have to feel my way under her jeans to be sure."

Mike shook his head. "Dream on, old man. You couldn't get near that with a fist full of hundreds."

"You'd be surprised at the action I get."

Mike scoffed. "You got that right."

The waitress returned with a full mug and a thermos of coffee. She said, "You guys let me know if you need anything else." When she tipped her head toward Kirk, she added, "From the restaurant that is."

Kirk sat tall in the booth. Arthritis in his hips kept him from finding a comfortable position. He added a creamer and three sugars to his coffee. After he slipped a half dozen packets into the pocket of his windbreaker, Kirk looked up at Mike. "Did you think about the deal we talked about at Tracy's last night?"

Tracy's Tavern sat on F Street and drew customers who looked for cheap beer and whiskey. No live music or bar food—simply booze and an occasional bar fight, likely started by a sparring married couple or a loner with anger management issues.

Mike looked around the restaurant as if checking whether other patrons were within earshot. He leaned forward, close enough for Kirk to smell the coffee on Mike's breath. "Like I told you, the U-Store-It between Salida and Buena Vista on Highway 285 got a new owner about a year ago. The guy's from Texas, and he's never around. I've been watching the place to see if he'd install cameras, new fencing, or lights, but there've been no upgrades. At this point, about half of the yard lights are out."

Kirk nodded, and Mike continued. "I got the tools and a truck, but no place to store the goods until we can sell 'em."

"For a 50/50 cut, I've got a location to store everything."

"You're not gettin' 50, and we don't take everything. There's tons of crap in storage. We take electronics or stuff that's new and still in the boxes. We'll hit about a dozen units unless we can fill the truck with less. Is your place dry? I don't want to turn over anything you'll put in a leaky garage or shed."

"I'm tellin' you, it's perfect, with lots of space, dry, and far enough out of town to not attract attention. You fill up the truck, and I can take you there to unload. If not 50, then I'd be willing to take 45 percent."

Mike wiped his sticky, sausage-grease coated fingers on a napkin and tossed it on his plate. "I'd be willing to give you ten percent of the take, but that's it. You're not the one in the yard with all the risk."

"Seems like you're just a guy with a truck and an idea. Without a place to drop the goods 'til they're sold, you got nothin'. How about 20?"

They fell silent when the waitress returned. She ripped a ticket from her pad, laid it face down on the table. "Not trying to rush you gentlemen along, but you can pay upfront when you're ready." The men briefly glanced at the check before simultaneously switching their focus to her retreating buttocks.

"They don't make 'em any nicer than that." Mike raised from the bench. "I'll set up everything in the next day or two. Can you take us to your perfect storage spot on the night of the thirtieth?"

"No problem. I'll be ready."

Mike looked from Kirk to the front door. Kirk knew his negotiating skills were working. He would have taken 10 percent, but 20 would cover his expenses for an extra month and maybe pay to get the heater fixed in his car—if he could keep from drinking away his share.

Mike gave Kirk a single nod. "Okay. We've got a deal at 15 percent. I've gotta hit the head. I'll be right back."

While Mike penguin-walked his bulk away from the table, Kirk emptied the thermos into a cup. The waitress passed, and he reached out to touch her arm. She jerked it away. "No touching, Gramps. Is there something else you need?"

"Yeah. I had a friend who worked here until last summer. Do you know Ariel Laurencell?"

"I had a couple of shifts with her but didn't know her. Ain't she in prison now?"

Kirk nodded with downcast eyes. "Yeah, I heard some snitch testified against her and Jason Gray. They were wrongfully incarcerated and didn't deserve that kind of treatment from a friend."

She shifted her weight to the other foot. "Word around here is some low-life named Kirk Steadman turned on them. Do you know him, too?"

"Nope. Never heard of him," Kirk said with a dismissive wave of a hand. He held up the thermos and jiggled the base. "Sugar, can you bring me more coffee. I still have business to discuss with my friend."

She glanced out the front window and pointed. "Looks like your friend had other business to attend to. Isn't that him pulling out of the drive?"

Kirk turned to watch Mike as he left in a panel truck. *The bastard is stiffing me.*

The waitress tapped the ticket with a black lacquer coated nail. "Be sure to take care of this bill before you leave."

Kirk shook his head. "He's a busy guy. Must have gotten an emergency call." He pulled a stash of bills from his front pocket. Kirk extracted a five and handed it to the waitress. "This is for you, Honey. Maybe one of these days, you'll stop by Tracy's and let me buy you a beer."

"Not a regular stomping ground for me, but thanks for the tip." She snatched the money from his hand and crossed to the servers' stand.

Kirk picked up the ticket and tapped the edge on the table. He looked out the window at Mike's empty parking spot and considered his options. He blew across his coffee and turned to scope out the cooks in the kitchen behind a window framed in stainless steel. A family of four youths and their parents walked through the front door. The tattooed hostess chatted with the adults and bantered with their offspring.

Kirk stood and walked to the men's room. He pushed on the hollow core door marked "Cowboys." Once he stepped inside, Kirk crushed Mike's breakfast ticket into a wad and tossed it into the trash.

He washed his hands before he retreated from the washroom. Then Kirk slipped out the restaurant's side door.

Chapter 27

TOM MORROW

After they repacked Dylan's belongings, Tom shouldered the backpack and followed Destiny down from the summit to the cabin. She paused only once to ask Tom if he needed a break for a clothing adjustment or bio break. On the return trip, the pair retreated into their thoughts.

Tom feared for Dylan's safety but assumed his roommate could rely on wits and charisma to create an alliance between himself, Kalev, and the Sasquatch colony—wherever they were.

When Tom reached the cabin, he stepped to the porch, where the building blocked the angled, late morning sun rays. He ran a hand over the door frame and searched the spot where Dylan said he would leave the key. Tom found it and turned the lock. While he held the door wide, Tom motioned for Destiny to enter first.

"Looks the same as when I was here before." Destiny stepped into the great room and appraised the space. She walked into the kitchen area and up to the island to open a drawer. "Jen's things are still here. Maybe Kate plans to sell the place furnished." She turned to look at Tom. "Since Augie doesn't want the cabin, Kate will help him list the property next spring."

Tom looked at the inviting rock-face fireplace, log furniture, and Native American rugs on the polished floor. "Wouldn't Augie prefer Jen's cabin to his trailer?"

"After I left Salida, Augie and Jen grew close. She taught him how to drive and took over all the things I did for him after his aunt died, like managing his savings, paying bills, and arranging maintenance on the trailer. When animals killed Jen outside of this cabin, Augie swore he'd never come here again."

She gave a dismissive wave. "Besides that, his trailer is close to downtown. He walks everywhere. I think the cabin might be too remote."

"I get what you're saying about why he'd stay clear of this place." He paused to smile. "It's funny. I'm a twenty-minute train ride from the center of Chicago, and I feel like I'm right downtown. Folks here think being a short drive from the epicenter of Salida is *way* out in the country."

Destiny smiled and moved to sit at the dining table. She ran the side of her index finger along a groove in the glossy split-log lacquered top. "Do you want to stay here to talk or head back into town? I could start a fire to get the chill out of the air."

Tom considered her suggestion. Nothing waited for his attention in Salida. He liked the idea of figuring out their next move in the place where Dylan spent time before his disappearance. Maybe they would find inspiration.

He said, "Let's stay for a while. I'll go to the car and get our warm jackets."

When Tom returned to the cabin, he found Destiny kneeling in front of the fireplace and lighting a firestarter cube she'd tucked under a stack of small logs. He draped a fleece jacket over her shoulders and pulled a throw from the back of the loveseat to sit on while the fire took hold.

While the little blaze grew, Destiny layered more sticks on top. They sat shoulder to shoulder on the floor in front of the fireplace. Both stared into the flames.

Tom broke the silence. "I feel like we're making headway on what happened to Dylan."

"Too bad he didn't turn on his flash when he took the selfie," Destiny mused.

Tom nodded. "I could make out he stood next to someone about two feet taller than him."

"How tall is Dylan, about six feet six?"

"Yeah. That would make Kalev well over eight feet tall. Based on what we could see from the photo, Augie's portrait did a good job of capturing what Kalev looks like."

Destiny turned to face Tom, brow creased. "If Augie's dreams come from what Kalev sees, then how could he have a picture of Kalev?"

Tom shrugged. "Maybe from reflections, like in a window or a lake?"

"I guess it's possible. More likely a window, though. A reflection in a lake would show Kalev looking down, with his hair flopped forward. Augie's sketch showed Kalev facing to the front." She paused. "What do you think about Dylan's caption for the photo?"

"He typed, 'I trust Kalev. Give me a few weeks.' I take it to mean he expected me to find the phone and wasn't in distress when he left." Tom puzzled over the message and added, "He's asking for time to learn about Kalev and what he wants."

Tom nodded toward the entrance. "I can't help but think this place is key to Dylan's return."

"Kalev and Dylan met here. So that seems logical."

"It's not just that. Before Dylan came to Salida, he had a vision of this place. It's almost like the cabin drew the two of them together."

Destiny opened her mouth to say something, paused, and then spoke. "Augie's drawings of Kalev included the cabin, too. If it's special to the Sasquatch, perhaps they'll come back here."

She leaned forward to add another log to the growing pile. Her jacket slipped from her shoulders, and she pulled it back up with a shiver. "I'm still cold from my wet running clothes. Jen kept extra quilts in her bedroom. I'll check to see if they're still there."

Tom pressed her arm. "You stay here, and I'll get them." He walked to the only interior door and into Jen's bedroom. At the end of the bed stood a quilt rack, heaped with meticulously folded quilts blocked in vibrant colors with intricate hand-stitching. Tom removed two and turned to go back into the living room.

His nose tickled from the ammonia scent of urine. Tom stepped into the bathroom and saw the toilet with a raised lid and splashed dried pee. "That's not like Dylan. Someone's been here," he said to himself. Should he alert Destiny? Better to ask Augie directly, he decided.

When Tom returned to the living room, he asked, "How long do you think we should wait to alert the Sheriff's Office about Dylan? I'm leery about telling anyone else about Kalev. We don't want to trigger a media shit-storm. But maybe we should tell *someone* about Dylan."

"There are benefits to telling the Sheriff. His office would start an official investigation. They'd organize search parties, bring in dogs, and do aerial surveillance." Destiny looked into Tom's eyes as if searching for answers. "Is that what Dylan would want us to do?"

"I feel like he'd want us to give him time. But how much?"

"It's hard to know what Dylan meant by a few weeks or whether his circumstances have changed. What do you think about two weeks?"

Tom dropped a small art quilt on the floor behind Destiny and wrapped the larger one across her shoulders. He stepped around to sit beside her and lifted one side of the blanket to join her underneath. She moved her hips to wiggle closer.

Tom pressed his thigh against hers. "I don't know. I keep thinking about Augie's other sketches. The ones that didn't include Kalev or his two buddies. I get the significance of Church Mountain. That's the place he took Dylan to meet up with other Sasquatches. I'm not sure where they ended up taking him, but I'm pretty sure they started at the summit of the mountain. There are a couple of drawings of a full moon. Augie didn't understand why they were relevant but knew the full moon was important to Kalev." Tom paused to adjust the quilt. "When Dylan went with Kalev, they left on a full moon."

"Do you think they only travel at that time?"

"Could be. Any idea when the moon is full again?"

Destiny escaped the blanket to cross to the kitchen. She pulled a calendar from the wall and returned to the warmth under the covers. Destiny rocked and snuggled closer to Tom.

She sighed and pointed to the month that the calendar last showed. "June was the month of Jen's attack."

Tom pulled her close while she flipped past scenic shots of Colorado's highest mountains until she reached October. After admiring the photo, a mountainside splashed with autumn colors, she turned to the next month. Destiny pointed to the box with a pale blue circle next to the 18th of November. "We're about three weeks out until the next one."

He rubbed her back and hoped to stop her shivers. "Maybe we should wait until then to see if Dylan comes back on his own?"

"I get your logic, but that feels too long for me. What if he's in trouble and hopes we're actively searching for him?"

Tom stared at the fire. "Seems like forever for me, too. But Dylan's street smart and a good judge of character. He could talk his way out of a difficult situation and find an ally if he needed one. He's told me about some cases where anyone else would have bailed, and Dylan not only got the information he needed, his target helped him get it." He paused. "Let's give him three weeks to figure things out.

Destiny sighed. "A lot can happen in three weeks. We don't know what he's up against."

"I think that's what Dylan would want us to do."

Destiny rocked back and forth. Tom knew she was considering his words. She stopped moving. "I can live with your idea. But how about taking hikes in the woods near Church Mountain every few days? Maybe we'll catch a break and find a clue from either Dylan or Kalev."

"Like what kind of clues?"

"In late October, we almost always have a day or two with light snow. You'd be surprised at the tracks I've seen along the trail after a dusting."

"As long as we don't see the bear or mountain lion," Tom said with a shudder.

"They've only attacked people who were alone. So maybe we should stick together."

Not a bad idea, thought Tom as Destiny continued. "But at one day past the full moon, I'm calling the Sheriff."

"Agreed."

They sat in silence until Tom said, "Besides joining you to hike, I'll have to keep busy here for the next three weeks. Or maybe I should go back to Chicago until closer to the date. You probably have other hiking friends in Salida who wouldn't need an excuse to hike with you."

Destiny turned toward Tom, her lips inches from his face. "I'd like for you to stay. If you need things to do, you could help me to de-Nateify the apartment." He could feel her breath against his cheek.

She would want a response, and Tom's heart started to pound. He stared forward to focus on the fire and try to suppress his attraction. "I'm happy to do what you need—either at the apartment or here at the cabin." He straightened and nodded toward the front wall. "I could fix the boarded up window and clean out the fireplace and chimney. That probably needs to be done before Kate puts it up for sale."

Destiny leaned closer. "There are other reasons why I want you to stay." She brushed Tom's cheek with a kiss. Not a brotherly-type kiss but one with a longing that sought something in return.

He turned to tilt her chin with a finger and kissed her lips. Tom pulled back to gaze into her eyes. "This is wrong, you know."

She stiffened. "In what way? Are you and Dylan more than roommates?"

Tom laughed and pulled her close. "He'd get a real chuckle out of that. I assure you, we're good friends and business partners."

"Then what? Aren't I good enough for you?"

"Believe me. I'm very attracted to you. But I don't want to start something when you're vulnerable."

In one motion, Destiny stood and left the quilt on Tom's shoulders. She tightened the fleece jacket around her torso.

"Who are you to tell me I'm vulnerable?" She wagged a finger at him. "Early this year, I kidnapped my son and restarted a pharmacy career in a new state. This summer, I made a home for Trip and mourned the loss of my best girlfriend. Then, I inherited a business that I'm completely unqualified to run and had to deal with a funeral and legacy issues from my cheating, narcissistic dead husband. And you think I'm too frail to handle you?"

Tom rose from the floor and pulled the quilt along with him. He gently placed it around Destiny's shoulders and drew her close. Tom pressed his lips to hers. She resisted and then relented.

Chapter 28

OCTOBER 28
DESTINY STEWART, NÉE KUSIK

After the previous day's dalliance at the cabin and an intimate dinner at a local bistro, Destiny did not have a good night's rest. All evening long, she imagined Tom sleeping on the couch in her living room. In her dreams, he would wake and pay her a welcome visit. In reality, he behaved like the perfect gentleman and did not knock on her door. Bummer.

Bleary-eyed, Destiny woke early to fix breakfast. While she ground coffee beans and transferred them into a French press, Tom poured over a topographic map of the area around Jen's cabin.

He looked up. "We've got the Rhoads reelection fundraiser tonight. But is there time for a short hike up near the cabin? Or if you'd rather, we could go in a day or two?"

Destiny searched her mind for any last-minute tasks—the gallery was spotless, and the caterer was coming at four o'clock with food, pub tables, and dishware. Better to be outdoors and busy than obsessed with her houseguest.

She pushed the plunger on the coffee. "Let's make it a short one, but I'm fine to start looking for any clues about where Dylan and Kalev might have gone.

Destiny pulled the Subaru in front of the cabin. The tires splashed across sporadic low spots where an evening shower had left shallow puddles.

Once Destiny and Tom secured their knapsacks, they stood next to the car and surveyed the drive and surrounding woods.

"Any idea where we should start?" asked Tom.

Destiny shrugged. "There's a trail next to the creek at the back of the cabin. Jen and I never walked it together, but she told me it connects to other trails across the face of Church Mountain."

"It's as good a start as any." Tom nodded for Destiny to take the lead.

She rounded the building and walked toward the back. But she paused at a massive pile of downed timber. "When on earth did this happen?" she asked.

Tom walked up next to her. "You haven't seen this before?"

Destiny approached the pile and leaned forward to rub a branch. "These trees have only been down for a couple of weeks."

"What could have caused them to fall over?"

"They didn't fall. I suspect a storm knocked them over."

Tom looked from the pile to the back of the house. "It's close to the cabin. I'm surprised the building escaped damage."

"Did Dylan say anything about being here when this happened?" If he experienced the storm, he would surely have told Tom.

"No. But that doesn't mean it didn't happen. We mostly talked about Dylan's relationship with Kalev and their plans to meet up with Kalev's friends." Tom touched Destiny's arm. "You don't think Kalev had anything to do with this, right?"

Destiny scoffed. "He'd have to be incredibly strong." She surveyed the pile of trees. Not just strong, but either angry or needing to burn off a lot of energy. Destiny chose to imagine a more docile Sasquatch. "My money's on the wind."

They circumnavigated the pile to walk into the woods. Destiny stopped in front of a creek beyond the back of the yard. While the stream was barely a trickle, the sides were muddy from the previous night's rain.

"If we head to the left, we'll be traveling uphill. I think we should start in that direction."

Destiny knelt to examine the ground. She cocked her head as she stared at the soft mud. "Come here and take a look at this."

Tom moved forward to peer over her shoulder. "Is that what I think it is?"

Destiny smiled and looked up at Tom. "Tell me what you think it is."

His eyes wide, Tom said, "You can see each toe and a full footprint. Don't tell me someone was out here last night in bare feet. Or maybe a jogger with those minimalist shoes that are more like a glove than a shoe."

"I think your imagination is carrying you away."

Tom placed both hands on his hips. "Okay. You tell me what could leave a print like a human?"

Destiny pointed to the tiny pinholes at the top of each toe. "Do you see these holes?" Without waiting for his response, she continued. "Those are claw marks."

"From a Sasquatch?"

She laughed. "No, silly. It's a print of a bear's back foot."

"It's got to be nearly a foot long."

"Closer to nine inches. But I expect it might be a big bear. Don't worry. It's probably a black bear. It doesn't want to see us any more than we want to see it."

"But the sheriff said a bear killed Jen and Nate near here." Tom scrutinized the woods. "Do you see evidence of the mountain lion?"

Destiny stood and turned to Tom. She placed both hands on the sides of his face and kissed him on the lips with a loud smack. "I don't see any evidence of a cat. But maybe we'd better cut short our hike."

Tom straightened. "Takes a lot to get me spooked, but I'd rather hike with some protection. Let's think about finding someone with a gun who could explore with us."

The studio and gallery, customarily filled with hushed voices and the fragrance of paint, clattered and clinked with dishes, glassware, and the sounds of people wanting to be heard.

"The gallery is packed with potential Rhoads contributors. It's amazing how many people will show up for free food and drinks," Tom whispered to Destiny while he slipped his palm onto the small of her back under her tailored suit jacket. He pulled her close. "You smell wonderful."

"Soap and shampoo." Destiny looked around at the sea of faces. "I've been away for less than a year, but there are loads of Rhoads supporters I don't know."

"Perfect time to make new friends. The caterer and bartender seem like they can handle the guests without our help. May I get you a drink?"

Destiny nodded. "White wine would be nice."

Tom left to visit the far end of the gallery where they had set up the bar. Destiny moved toward the crowd clustered around Mayor Rhoads, who could barely be seen from afar as he stood a foot shorter than his constituents. He made up for his height with a thunderous voice when he pontificated about affordable housing and population growth management. Destiny stood with the group for a few polite minutes, then grew weary of the rhetoric and moved on.

She threaded her way toward the buffet table and offered small talk. Tom arrived with her wine while she finished loading a plate with boiled shrimp and Asian-spiced kabobs.

When she turned to scope out a place to relax and eat, Deputy Sheriff Erle Hodges bumped her arm. "Nice of you to host this event for Mayor Rhoads. Based on the competition, he's not a shoo-in for re-election."

Destiny introduced Erle and Tom, then said, "The field is wide but not deep. The mayor is a proven commodity, and he's well liked."

"I hope you're right. He supports local law enforcement, which makes our work easier."

"Well then, it sounds like I'm supporting the best candidate." She paused to sip her wine. "I've seen fliers around town. It seems like you and your father are organizing a big event next month—a Bigfoot convention?"

Tom straightened, and Erle nodded. "It's Salida's first Sasquatch conference, and it's happening in about three weeks."

Tom interrupted. "Are Sasquatches from all over the country invited or only the Colorado ones?"

Erle cocked his head. "We have some highly renowned speakers lined up." With a smile, he added, "No Sasquatches have registered yet, but we're hopeful."

Tom gave Erle a friendly jab. "It'd make things more interesting if they came."

"I'd give my right arm to see one, but we'll have to settle for talking with the experts. Put it on your calendars. It'll be fun, and you might learn something new."

Tom said, "I wouldn't miss it. There's a lot I'd like to learn about these creatures."

Destiny looked from Erle to Tom. She sensed growing respect between them. Did Tom think Erle and his firearm should join them to search the woods? Or perhaps, Erle might have intelligence on the Sasquatch, and she and Tom could use it to find Dylan. Erle and his father Merle were Salida's brain trust in Bigfoot research. But telling Erle about Dylan's situation might bring notoriety to their search. Could they trust him?

Chapter 29

OCTOBER 30
KIRK STEADMAN

The panel truck backed into the drive and scraped low tree branches. The tires kicked up rocks before it stopped short of the porch. After Kirk slipped from the passenger seat, he clicked on a flashlight and limped up the steps.

Kirk pulled out the copied key from the front pocket of his jeans. He heard the rumble of a semi-truck engine downshifting on the highway, miles below. When it passed, Kirk broke the silence with a groan while he yanked open the front door. Kirk swung it wide and blocked the corner open with a small table holding a lamp.

"Let's get this show rollin'," Kirk called toward the truck.

Mike sat in the panel truck with a co-conspirator, who looked like a former NFL linebacker. After Mike stepped down from the driver's seat, the bruiser muscled his way from the back of the cab. Mike turned to his colleague and said, "Open the back, Roy, but let me make sure this place is okay before you start movin' boxes."

In the moonless darkness, Mike tripped on the porch steps and caught himself with one hand on the banister and the other on the decking. "Get over here with that light, Steadman," he yelled and righted himself. Mike wiped dirt from his hands to the front of his jeans. "You didn't tell me there ain't no lights."

Kirk straightened. "I brought a flashlight. Why didn't you? Aren't you the professional?"

Mike sneered, hands on hips. "Shine that thing this way, so I don't fall again. Who has a cabin without lights? Is this place abandoned?"

When Kirk did not respond, Mike turned to retreat. He huffed and shook his head.

Kirk shined his beam between the porch and the truck, while Mike lumbered to the driver's side door and reached inside to retrieve a military-grade camping lantern. When he clicked it, the light illuminated the entire front porch and into the open doorway.

"This'll work," Mike said when he walked past Kirk and through the entry. Mike held the light above his head. Slowly, he turned in a circle to scrutinize the great room. "This doesn't look abandoned. Who owns this place?"

Kirk joined Mike inside and placed a hand on Mike's arm. Mike pulled away with a jerk as if shaking off a fly. Kirk snorted and said, "The original owner died last summer and left it to a retard who lives in town. The building's winterized, and he never comes."

"Is it listed for sale? We can't risk anyone comin' up to look around."

"Nope. I checked with a broker in town. She knows the lady who watches over the retard. They won't list it until the spring."

Mike ran a hand over his stubbly chin, "I don't know. The place looks lived in."

"I've been up here every night for nearly a month. There's been no movement. I'm tellin' you—it's deserted. Anyway, how long do you need to store the goods?"

"My guy from Albuquerque can be up here to move it out within a week."

"Is that when I get paid?"

Mike lowered the light to glare at Kirk. "You'll get your share when I get mine."

Kirk shrugged. "Fair enough."

"Help us move some of this furniture to the sides, so we have more space." Mike pointed toward the loveseat taking up the lion's share of the living room.

"No way. I'm an old man. Not strong enough to move anything. My cut is for arrangin' storage and not to be your flunky."

"If you want your share, you'll help us get these boxes in the house.

We don't want to hang out in the driveway any longer than we need to." Mike scanned the room. "Start with pushin' the furniture to the walls. Roy'll bring in the boxes with a handcart."

Kirk snarled at Mike but acquiesced. At a snail's pace, he sought the lightest and smallest pieces and inched them toward the outside walls. Mike moved the loveseat and dining set while Roy hustled in load after load of boxed appliances and electronics.

"Sure seems like more stuff when it's inside the house," Kirk said while he moved a small box marked Dual-Band Wi-Fi 5 Router from the top of one pile to another.

"Keep your hands off the merchandise. I don't want you fallin' over or droppin' somethin'. My contact's payin' us top dollar, but he wants this shit to be in workin' condition. It's bad for business to send him damaged goods."

"Relax. I'm helpin' to even out the stacks."

"We got it. Hang out by the kitchen counter, 'til Roy's finished."

Roy pushed the handcart through the doorway and muscled a five-foot stack of boxes against the remaining wall space. "This is the last load, Boss."

"Let's go, Kirk. Don't leave anythin' of yours behind. The next time we're here, we're loadin' up for delivery." Mike grabbed the lantern and waited for Kirk on the porch.

Kirk followed Roy and Mike outside. He paused on the porch to watch Roy slide the handcart into the back of the truck and roll down the door. Mike stood on the porch and waited for Kirk to lock the door.

When Kirk turned the lock and started to return the key into his pocket, Mike said, "Don't even think about takin' the key. Gimme that." He grabbed Kirk's wrist and squeezed until the key fell to the porch. Mike stooped to retrieve it and slid it into the front pocket of his work pants.

"Suit yourself." Kirk ran his flashlight across the front of the cabin. He paused on the window to the right of the door and tilted his head, thinking. *Somethin's different. Wasn't the window boarded up the last time I was here?*

"What?" asked Mike. "Somethin' wrong?"

Kirk moved the beam toward the truck and stepped off the porch, "Nope. Everything's fine."

Chapter 30

REVAL—OCTOBER 31
KATI

Kati swam the length of the pool until her arms and legs ached from pushing against the sludgy liquid. She flipped on to her back when Dylan and Kalev broke through the bushes.

Kalev nodded toward Kati and squeezed Dylan's arm before he disappeared back down the trail. She pushed her feet into the soft bottom to stand but kept her body submerged to her shoulders.

When Dylan dropped his leaf cover and approached the pool, she stared at his body. *They look so vulnerable without fur. Everything is exposed— genitalia and imperfections in their skin. Fur provides mystique and sensuality. Hairless bodies are vulgar in their visibility. I understand why they clothe themselves. I would too if someone plucked me bare. How sad for them.*

Unaware of her judgment, Dylan slipped into the pool to join her. When he stopped in front of her, he pointed to his upraised arm. "Can you believe all my cuts and bruises are gone?"

"Why are you surprised? The pools have properties to heal bruises or bone breaks."

"Kalev told me, but I'm still surprised at these regenerative powers. Don't you ever become ill?"

"You mean like halveks with diseases that erode their bodies?"

"Yeah, like cancer or tuberculosis?"

She raised her eyes and released a sigh before she transmitted, "I do not know what those are, but we do not suffer from disease."

"What causes Sasquatches to die?"

"They grow old, or there might be an accident." Kati blinked as if considering his question further. "I'm surprised you did not suffer more from your tumble into the Auk."

"Took me hours to climb out of there. Kalev is still angry. He didn't send me any transmissions until the next morning." Dylan grew solemn. "I need to ask you about something I saw in the Auk."

Kati gave Dylan a playful splash. "This is not a day for serious discussions." Sometimes he posed thoughtful questions that made her think hard about her beliefs or Sasquatch customs. But mostly, he questioned rudimentary matters, things she took for granted. She wanted a break from his inquisition.

"That's what Kalev has said for the past four days. I want answers." Dylan reached forward to take her hands and looked straight into her with his captivating green eyes. This halvek had something that disarmed her. He continued. "Talk with me about this. There are things I want to know, and I need you to help me."

She pulled her hand away but stayed close. "Okay. What did you see?"

"After I fell and got hung up in the tree, I saw a full skeleton of a baby draped over the tree trunk. It wasn't in pieces. I would swear an infant must have been dead or asleep when it landed on the branch."

"It was dead before going into the Auk."

Dylan's jaw dropped. "How could you possibly know that?"

She shrugged. "There are many infant bones in the Auk. That is part of our tradition."

Dylan's eyes grew wide. When he did not question her further, she assumed the discussion was complete. Kati turned from him and started to swim toward the far end of the pool. He called after her. "Oh, no you don't. Unless you want me to believe you toss babies into an abyss as a form of birth control, you'd better get back here and tell me the whole story."

Disinclined to spoil her day with an elaborate discussion, Kati swam to lengthen the distance between them. Dylan splashed forward and stroked with force until he caught her heel. He yanked her foot to stop her momentum.

His playful pursuit triggered a tingle in her chest. She anchored her feet and turned to face him. Since the hair had filled in on his face, he looked healthier and, perhaps, desirable. Kati looked from his eyes to his lips. She shook off the highly inappropriate sensation and transmitted, "Why do you want to know? You will not understand."

"Try me."

Kati bit her lip. "Come closer."

"Please, tell me now."

"Whenever we discuss something that could prompt an emotional response, Sasquatches create an atmosphere of warmth and trust with an embrace. You have been in Reval long enough to have seen this behavior. Touching conveys our respect and tenderness for each other."

Dylan moved forward, but his raised eyebrows divulged his uncertainty. She embraced him and stroked his back before she slowly wrapped her legs around his waist.

Dylan pulled back and tugged at her legs to free himself. "This feels a bit intimate for me."

Grateful she had not acted on her earlier attraction, she laughed and released him. "Stop struggling. I am not initiating sexual pleasure with you."

"Well, I should hope not."

She snapped back as if struck. "Would that be unpleasant for you?"

"The thought has *not* crossed my mind."

"Do you find me unattractive?" Kati had taken a few lovers and refused several requests to mate. This halvek's rebuff came as a great surprise. When in Porgu, she had seen many females. They were dirty and unfit. How could he possibly not be attracted to her?

Dylan tilted his head. "Your question is not fair. I have no idea about your sexual customs. We've soaked and exchanged ideas. That sounds more like a friendship than a prelude to sex."

"You would only couple with a halvek you have just met or someone who you do not want to befriend?"

"That's not what I meant."

"Then you find me unattractive?"

He ran a hand across her cheek. "I think you are lovely. You have amazing eyes, and you walk with the grace of a fashion model." Kati received Dylan's transmitted visions—a series of tall, thin halvek women with perfect posture and commanding strides. They wore silky clothes that clung to their bodies when they walked.

"I do not know what models are, but I sense you find them attractive."

Dylan scoffed. "I'm probably not giving you the right impression. This is the last woman I loved." He sent a vision of a short, muscular female with blonde hair that fell to her shoulders. "Her name was Jen."

"Was she your mate?"

"If you mean were we married, our version of a committed relationship, then no. But I still loved her. Something killed her last summer."

"Was she brutalized by halvek males?"

Dylan gave her shoulder a playful shove. "You know us better than that. The vast majority of men aren't rapists or murderers. She was attacked by wild animals, probably a mountain lion and a bear. They tried to kill me too, but Kalev saved my life when he commanded them to leave me alone."

Tiina had not shared this information with her, and Kati decided to confirm the story later. Sasquatches were not supposed to interfere with natural events in Porgu. Perhaps Kalev's crimes went beyond bringing a halvek to Reval.

Dylan interrupted her thoughts with his transmission, "Are you going to tell me why there are dead babies in the Auk?"

"Yes." She moved forward again to take him in her arms and wrap her legs around his waist. "Please try to relax."

On her second attempt, he did not push her away but remained tense, his arms wooden. Kati ran a hand through his hair and tucked a lock behind his ear. "Halveks have a difficult time with trust, yes?"

"I trust you."

Kati smiled. "Not the way I interpret trust. If you told me to wait for a story, I would assume you have my best interest in mind, and I would let you decide when the time was right. I would not question your motives. This is the same for how we touch each other. Once we become friends, our touches are respectful. I would not do anything to harm you or take something you do not want to give. I assume you feel the same."

Dylan drew a breath and slowly let it out. "Humans are warier. It takes longer to develop a level of trust. We measure small actions that can be misinterpreted and collapse a relationship even before it begins."

"I am sad for you. You live in a world where suspicion runs rampant, and even those close to you are your competitors."

"If Sasquatches are fully benevolent, I would be surprised." While he spoke, she felt his body start to relax. He moved his hands to hold the sides of her thighs.

"You feel that way because you know nothing different than halveks who struggle for scarce resources or material goods. I am not surprised you are distrustful." Kati squeezed his shoulders. "You need to hear me. You can trust me."

"I know you are holding me because you think I'll be shocked about why there are skeletons in the Auk. Tell me why they're there."

She stroked his cheek with the back of her hand. "Yes. Don't judge our traditions, but listen and try to accept them."

Dylan nodded. "I can't promise I'll understand or not judge, but I'll try to be open-minded. What's this custom?"

"Not all babies are able to survive in Reval. Some have stunted intellect. They are barely able to learn telecommunication. They become malnourished because they cannot feed at the nutrient pools. These babies are brought to the Council and given the euthanasia ceremony."

"The same one you've asked for?" She nodded, and Dylan continued. "And then you toss their bodies into the Auk?"

"Yes."

"Are all dead Sasquatches thrown in the Auk?"

"It is not that simple. We normally revere our dead. Bodies of those who die from old age or by accident are treated with respect. They are dried in a sleep site until the flesh desiccates. Then, we bring the bones to the annual Festival and celebrate the deceased's life."

"I take it these infants do not receive the same respect?"

"They are considered waste, to be discarded unceremoniously. A birth of this kind usually means the mated couple will never try to have another child. There is a great risk for a second child also to be deformed."

"So any time a baby is born with a missing limb or misshapen head, you kill them?"

"I have never heard of any births with the deformities you describe."

"Then how do you know these infants deserve a death sentence?"

She shrugged. "It is obvious. They are born without fur."

Chapter 31

KALEV

Kalev fluffed leaves to prepare his bed for an afternoon nap, while Dylan did the same.

"I think Kati is coming on to me," said Dylan.

"Does that mean she wants to couple with you?" Kalev's lips curled into a slight smile.

"I get that impression, and I find her very attractive."

"You do?"

"You've told me of your preference for brunettes. But hair color isn't important to me. Anyway, I think Kati's incredibly attractive, smart, funny, and thoughtful."

Kalev snorted, then transmitted, "When she wants you, she will ask. Sasquatches are not shy about suggesting sex. If you are thinking about it, then ask her." Kalev rolled away from Dylan. *As if Kati could ever be attracted to this hairless, primitive being.*

Dylan would not let the subject drop. "You don't have a mating ritual with seduction?"

Kalev shrugged. "Once children reach maturity, they become curious and copulate. It is normal."

"It's not solely for married or *mated* couples?"

"Monogamy in our society is not valued. Even for a mated pair, Sasquatches couple with others who they care about."

"And nobody has a problem with that?"

Kalev turned his head to look over his shoulder at Dylan. "Why would they?"

"Ah, come on. There isn't an ounce of jealousy in your culture?"

"I have never felt jealous. I couple with those who desire me and avoid those who are not interested. If my partners seek pleasure with another, I do not care."

"What if you had a mate, and she wanted someone else?"

Kalev's lip ticked upward. "I cannot imagine she would need satisfaction from another."

"And if she did?"

"Impossible. She would be too exhausted to seek pleasure elsewhere."

"You sound pretty confident in your prowess. I'll have to take you at your word about that. Do mates stay together for their entire lives?"

"Sometimes yes and sometimes no. Mating is about a partnership to share space and raise children. If a couple is no longer compatible, they may separate and look for another mate. Or if they are unable to procreate, a new mate might be a solution for a Sasquatch who wants a family."

"Do they typically separate if they end up with a hairless baby?"

Kalev jolted and sat upright. He placed a hand on Dylan's bicep. "Who told you about that?"

"Since you wouldn't tell me about the Auk, Kati explained it to me."

Kalev snarled at Kati's inability to maintain discretion. "What did she tell you?"

"Kati said if a hairless child is born, the Council euthanizes it, and the body gets discarded in the Auk."

"That is all she told you?"

"Is there more?"

Kalev paused before he responded. Should he expand Dylan's knowledge on the topic? "No. That is our custom."

"What's your custom about mating or having sex between individuals with large age gaps?"

"You mean coupling with a child? Is this something you also discussed with Kati?"

"No. I wondered because Alevide and Tiina seem to be close in age, and the pairs of Sasquatches I've spied from the bushes seem to be age appropriate. I wonder if, like on Porgu, males tend to want a younger mate.

For example, if you were attracted to Kati and she was attracted to you, would you mate with her?"

Kalev shook his head. "There are many reasons I would not mate or even couple with Kati. Her hair color and features are not attractive to me. Also, she has few life experiences, and those she has had reflect her lack of character. Anyone who petitions for euthanasia is too weak for me to find attractive. But perhaps your question is broader—about cross-generation mating. It is not typical. We couple with those within our age group. Intimacy between individuals who have grown up together is the most desirable. Is this common in your society?"

"My cousin Nate used to go after women ten to fifteen years younger than himself. He's dead now, but if he lived into his sixties, I picture him hooking up with women a few generations younger."

"Why are female halveks interested in older males?"

"Good question. In my guess, power, protection, or money."

"Was your cousin a powerful man?"

"Not really, but he knew how to manipulate people. Perfectly sane folks would do things they normally wouldn't. Like he could charm information from cautious people." Dylan transferred an image of Nate. "He lived in Salida. This is what he looked like."

Kalev jerked with recognition. "I saw this halvek at your shelter in Porgu."

"The bear and mountain lion that nearly attacked me killed my cousin only a week before my encounter with them."

Kalev nodded stone-faced. He waited for Dylan to ask questions about Kalev's power over Porgu's lower animals or specifically about Nate Stewart's attack.

"Too bad you weren't around to save him like you saved me."

Kalev stared at the naive halvek lying next to him. He pulled the blanket leaf higher on Dylan's shoulder, which prompted him to snuggle under the covers and rest his head on the crook of his arm.

Kalev transmitted, "Yes. That is unfortunate."

Chapter 32

SALIDA, COLORADO
MERLE HODGES

E rle tapped his father Merle on the arm. "The meeting's scheduled to start in a few minutes. Do you want me to grab you a beer before you give the order to begin?"

Merle looked at his son. They used to be bookends—round-bellied, crewcut-sporting law enforcement officials. Merle served with the Salida Police and Erle with the Sheriff's Department. While Erle's uniform had not changed, over the last six months his physique evolved into the body of a biker and not the tattooed Harley riding kind—more like a Tour de France rider. *What's next, a ponytail?*

He accepted the offer for a fresh beer and moved to the front of the bar to address the members of Salida's Sasquatch Believers unofficial organization.

Without soft surfaces to absorb noise, the brewpub echoed every sound. Chairs scraped, bottles rattled, and patrons shouted. Merle clinked on an empty glass with a fork and waited for a semblance of silence before he started the meeting. "Welcome to Salida's newest brewpub, Ride the Chutes. Many thanks to our host for letting us hold our meeting here. There's a lot more space than at our last venue. So enjoy what the Chutes has to offer—both on the menu and on tap."

Merle cleared his throat and continued. "As you all know, Salida's first annual Sasquatch Conference weekend is a few weeks from now, on November 18. I plan to spend about fifteen minutes at the end of our meeting to talk about the speakers and workshops, but for the first part, we'll follow our normal program. I'm looking for volunteers who would like to talk about any Sasquatch sightings or other experiences they'd like to share with the group. If you want to speak, raise your hand." Four volunteers indicated they had stories, and Merle assigned each a number.

When the first speaker came forward, Merle stepped backward to give him space. As he let the speaker pass, Merle stumbled against an unfamiliar, dreads-wearing man about Erle's age. Merle apologized, and the stranger held out a hand. "Officer Hodges, I'm Tom Morrow. I hoped I'd run into you tonight. When you finish, maybe we can talk?"

"Sure, sure, sure. But we've got a lot going on. Can this wait until I'm at the station tomorrow?"

Tom smiled. "No need to be formal. You can call me Tom. Is there any way we can do this tonight? I can wait until after the meeting." Merle glanced at his watch but nodded in agreement.

He turned to lean against the bar when the first speaker started. The middle-aged man clapped his hands to get the full attention of the crowd. He laid his blaze orange baseball cap on an empty barstool and smoothed the sides of his salt-and-pepper hair with his palms. His creased, hat-hair remained.

"I've been a hunter all my life," he started. The crowd hushed. "I know the woods in Chaffee, Saguache, and Fremont counties like the back of my hand. For this season, I've got elk and deer tags and been out the last couple of weeks up near Dutchman Creek, along the east face of Mt. Cornell. In the morning, I'd been glassing open terrain to find a good shooting position, maybe at about 10,000 feet. So I was right below timberline."

"What were the weather conditions?" asked a reedy youth in a red and black Western State Colorado University ball cap.

Merle reached to grasp the speaker's arm and injected, "Chuck, I asked you not to interrupt the speakers. Please, hold your questions until the end."

The speaker held up a hand. "That's okay, Merle, I got this one. It was a cold morning, but no frost. I'd say in the upper 30s or low 40s with clear skies. So, I had a perfect view of everything. After an hour, I saw a movement between the trees. It was about as far away as this room is deep, maybe 60 feet. The animal was muscular and covered with dark fur, with long arms. It moved with a limp and had a hunched posture. Not as much as a gorilla, but it leaned over a bit."

A man in the back called out, "Could it have been a bear? I've heard of bear up around Church Mountain. That's not very far away."

Merle sent a piercing stare, and the speaker continued without missing a beat. "I've seen plenty of bears. This animal was near twice the height and not on all fours. Definitely not a bear. It moved down the slope with long strides and disappeared within seconds. I went to the spot where I saw him but didn't see anything related to the creature. No scat or marks on the trees."

The crowd asked a few questions about whether he had been drinking and why he did not take a photo. He claimed to be sober and without time to retrieve his cell phone for a snapshot.

After Merle thanked him and directed the hunter to return to his seat, he called the next speaker to the front. Each of the following three presenters had little to contribute. One heard unexplained whooping sounds around three in the morning by her ranch, and the other two talked about their otherwise well-behaved dogs that went crazy in the night. The final speakers commiserated about how to restrain their pets and recover lost sleep.

Merle thanked the volunteers and moved to the center of the bar when Cynthia Waters made her entrance. Petite and sporting a bouncing mass of red curls, Cynthia slammed the door.

All eyes turned toward her and did not leave while she peeled off her formfitting leather coat to expose alluring curves tucked into a beige, long-sleeved sheath dress. She turned away from the crowd to drop her massive purse on a chair. A full-length industrial-style zipper ran from her hem, over her perfectly rounded bottom, to the point of a V-neckline. Cynthia spun to face the group and delivered a perky cheerleader wave to Merle.

With difficulty, Merle shook his head and released a tsk while Cynthia settled into a chair. He cleared his throat before resuming his speech. "For the conference, we've signed three world-renowned speakers. Greg Taylor, our friend and columnist for the *Salida Sentinel*, has arranged for our opening night keynote speaker. He's a professor from a university in Oklahoma. He'll welcome everyone and talk about hair sample research."

He paused to scan the audience. "While hair research might sound like a yawner subject, you'll be pleasantly surprised. To find out what type of animal left hairs, scientists evaluate root structures and cuticle thickness. Besides that, they use scale casts to evaluate the scale patterns on the hairs. Believe it or not, hair isn't as smooth as you'd imagine. Don't worry, Dr. Mellon is a more enthusiastic speaker than I am."

He smiled. "Greg Taylor has seen this guy with an audience. I hear he'll keep your attention, and you'll beg him for more." The crowd politely smiled and clapped. Merle assumed they were not convinced, but knew they'd be there anyway.

"If weather permits, the opening event will be held at six o'clock in front of the bandshell in Riverside Park, right next to the Arkansas River. Concessionaires will be there with beer, hot and cold drinks, and brats. Sunset is around five, so dress warmly and come hungry." Merle paused to check the paper with his notes. "I'll be here for a while. If you have questions or want to volunteer to help for the conference, come up to talk with me after we finish tonight."

Merle closed the meeting, and Cynthia picked up her things to clack her six-inch heels toward him. She smiled and revealed her blindingly white teeth. "Hi, Merle. Sorry I missed the meeting. I've just gotten back in town from New York. It took a whole day to get here. You can't imagine what it's like to find a limo driver willing to come to Salida."

Merle blinked. "Denver's airport is three hours away."

"Oh, Merle." Cynthia gave his arm a playful slap. "One in ten commuters in *The City* travel at least an hour and a half to get to work every day."

"And ninety percent of all statistics are made up in the last five minutes."

"Including that one?" she asked with a tilt of her head.

Merle chuckled. "You got that right. Why are you back in Salida?"

Cynthia's mouth formed a pout. "Did you miss me?"

Merle recalled Cynthia's hasty departure from Salida about two weeks prior. She and Nate were shacking up when officers found Nate's mauled body near Jen Rickard's cabin. When Destiny and Trip returned to reclaim their lives and property, they discovered Cynthia living in Nate's apartment. Merle heard Destiny had given Cynthia an earful and tossed her out. Shortly after that, Cynthia returned home to New York. He asked, "You still writing articles about the Sasquatch movement?"

She took Merle's arm and pressed her ample breasts against him. "I am. That's what brought me to town. I plan to attend your Bigfoot symposium."

"It seems like there are others scheduled in larger cities. You might want to go to Texas, Washington, or Ohio. Why here?"

"I have a fondness for Salida."

Merle pried her fingers from his arm and stepped back. "Seems to me you've burned a few bridges. Your articles were less than complimentary of our law enforcement officials and city leaders."

"The press has a responsibility to report the truth. That shouldn't affect our professional relationship, right?"

"If you say so. Is there something I can help you with?"

"You can point me toward your son Erle. I've been in touch with him since I've been away."

Merle snorted. "Is that right? He didn't mention it. Didn't you recognize him when you came in? He's standing right there." Merle pointed to his son, next to the bar and talking with the camo-clad first speaker.

Cynthia gasped. "I guess I'm still used to the way he looked last summer. He's dropped a lot of weight over the past four months. He's not sick, is he?"

"Nope. He's on a heath-kick. He's dropped about sixty pounds."

"I'll say." Cynthia slung her purse over a shoulder, picked up her coat, and walked over to trace a blood-red acrylic nail across Erle's spine.

Merle watched his son turn with a start. When she cocked her head, curls slid in front of one eye. She raked fingers through the errant strands to tuck them behind her ear. To exaggerate the movement, Cynthia pulled her elbow outside and back to thrust her breasts forward. Merle watched Erle swallow hard.

"Not sure what she's up to, but I'm positive you're unprepared to deal with her," Merle muttered. He shook his head but turned when Tom approached.

"Do you have a minute?" Tom asked.

Merle scanned the crowd. "Looks like things are winding down. What can I help you with?"

"I'm a friend of Destiny Stewart. I saw you at Nate's memorial event at the gallery but didn't have a chance to introduce myself to you that night. Destiny has me doing some work to secure a cabin that belonged to Jen Rickard. We were there a few days ago, and I have reason to believe an unauthorized person may have been inside. After I replaced the broken window, I installed a wildlife camera in the yard. I'd like to go up to the cabin to check on the camera but wondered if I should take someone from the police with me. What do you think?"

Merle narrowed his eyes. He placed a hand on his soft hip, thinking. "The Rickard cabin is on county property, not within city limits. I don't have authority up there. But my son, Erle, is an Assistant Deputy with the Sheriff's Department. He could take a ride up there with you."

"I met Erle at the Rhoads fundraiser a few days ago, but we haven't spoken since."

Merle looked toward Erle right when Cynthia plucked a button on Erle's shirt with a fingernail and ran the tip up his sternum, throat, and under his chin. Mesmerized, Erle watched the finger approach but did not react. Merle wondered if Erle might be in a siren-induced trance. He turned to Tom and said, "You might want to give him a few minutes. How about I buy you a beer?"

Chapter 33

ERLE HODGES

Shortly before ten at night, the floodlights still illuminated the Chaffee County Courthouse, a few blocks away from downtown Salida. The white brick Art Deco style building faced Thornhoff Park, a neatly trimmed greenspace with lofty pines and deciduous trees that had lost their leaves months earlier.

Tom parked the Subaru in one of the many vacant spots out front. They took the granite steps two at a time, and Tom followed Erle inside.

Once the pair reached Erle's desk, the lawman pointed to a vacant white plastic chair on the side wall and said, "Stay right there." Erle tossed the SD card on his desk blotter and picked up the phone.

Tom dragged the chair from the wall to the front of Erle's desk. He leaned forward to place his elbows on the desktop and rested his chin on clasped fingers.

Before Erle poked the keypad, he said, "You and your roommate have a lot in common. Be sure to put the chair back against the wall before you leave."

Tom nodded in agreement when Erle tapped a number on the phone. While they waited for the call to connect, Tom touched the top of a Bigfoot bobblehead doll resting on the corner of Erle's desk. In one swift motion, Erle grabbed the nodding figurine and placed it out of Tom's reach.

Erle rolled his eyes and mouthed, "Answering machine," to Tom. "Sheriff Austin, this is Assistant Deputy Erle Hodges. I'm at the office and need to talk with you about a possible storage facility for stolen goods. Please, call me at the office when you receive this message." Erle hung up the phone.

"Now what?"

"We wait."

"Isn't there someone else we can call?"

"I need to call the Sheriff first."

Tom looked at the memory card on Erle's desk. "As long as we already brought it here, can't we take a look?"

Erle picked up the card. "We should probably wait."

"What's the harm? Sheriff Austin will want to see it when he gets here."

"The Sheriff can be a bit of a control freak. I don't want to piss him off."

Tom smiled and cocked his head. "You must be as curious as I am."

Erle thought about potential ramifications. Would letting a civilian see the photos compromise the evidence? Besides, over the past four months, the Sheriff had seemed less dismissive. Erle did not want to ruin any good rapport they had recently established. But Tom was right. The Sheriff would wish to see the photos immediately. Erle itched to see whether the camera caught a shot of a vehicle or the criminals.

Erle gave Tom a conspiratorial nod and turned on the computer. He inserted the card into the reader while Tom walked around to rest a hand on the back of Erle's chair. They both leaned in to view the monitor. The first few photos captured a mixture of daytime and nighttime scenes with deer, a rabbit, and a coyote crossing the yard.

The fifth caught the side of a white panel truck backed up to the front porch. Erle clicked through more photos. The pictures clearly showed three men while they delivered boxes to the cabin. Or, more specifically, one beefy guy hauled boxes from the truck, and two others hung out in the vicinity.

Near the end, Erle stopped on a shot of a skinny man holding a flashlight. "I know this guy." Erle pointed at the screen. "That's Kirk Steadman."

"Friend of yours?" asked Tom.

Erle's eyes narrowed. "You and Dylan—two peas *in a bowl*."

Confusion creased the space between Tom's brows. "I think you mean in a pod, but more importantly, I didn't intend sarcasm. How do you know the man in the photo?"

Erle's shoulders relaxed. "Sorry, I'm used to working with Dylan. He's a real smart-aleck."

He pointed at the screen. "Kirk Steadman is my best friend's father." He paused. "At least Jesse used to be my friend. Last summer, he moved to California."

"I assume his father stayed here?"

"Yeah. His dad's a piece of shit. He only cared about Jesse for the money he brought in. After Jesse left, his father got involved with two characters who ran a meth lab. I wouldn't be surprised if he's still up to no good."

"Based on this photo, it seems like he is."

Erle nodded in agreement and stared at the screen. Tom returned to his chair and pointed at the bobblehead doll. "Are you a Believer?"

Erle snapped to look at Tom. "I am. Do you have a problem with that?"

Tom held up both hands in surrender, "Don't be so sensitive. I'm only asking. We've got time until the Sheriff calls. I enjoyed tonight's Believer meeting, especially the hunter who saw a Bigfoot in the woods. Tell me about your experiences. Have you spotted one?"

"Not yet, but I'm optimistic. Last summer, we had tons of activity in Chaffee County."

"What kind of *activity*?"

Erle leaned forward with enthusiasm. "A dozen mountain goats were slaughtered in the spring. A rancher's steer got eviscerated a few weeks after the goat massacre. Finally, Sasquatch is a prime suspect in three otherwise unexplained deaths."

"I assume you mean Jen Rickard and Nate Stewart, but who's the third?"

"A college student from Kansas came out here to camp and hike. He got ripped to shreds in the middle of the night."

Tom swallowed hard. "Is there evidence that ties these killings to a Sasquatch? Or could it just as likely be another type of animal?"

Erle paused, and his shoulders slumped. "Why is everyone so ready to pin this on another animal?"

The edges of Tom's mouth curled upward. "Why are you so eager to say it was a Sasquatch?"

"Don't turn this around on me. For all three attacks, there were marks from both a bear and a mountain lion. These two don't work together."

"Maybe there's something wrong with this pair, and they've teamed up despite their *normal* behaviors?"

"Like you're a wildlife expert?"

Tom laughed. "Hardly. But that seems more probable than a killer Bigfoot. Have you considered maybe there *is* a real Sasquatch, but he's thoughtful and compassionate? Why do you automatically think he's a psycho-predator?"

"You think he's just misunderstood?" Erle scoffed.

"I'm keeping an open mind. Are all the experts at the conference convinced Sasquatch is a killer?"

"That's a good question. I guess we'll find out in a couple of weeks." Erle ended his statement with a definitive nod.

Tom glanced at the floor. Erle assumed he was wrestling with a decision. Finally, Tom asked, "Do you hike?"

This was Tom's big ask? Erle smiled. "When you're part of the Chaffee County Sheriff's Office, you hike whether you want to or not."

"I meant, do you hike for fun?"

"Occasionally." What was Tom getting at?

"Destiny and I want to do some hiking around Jen's cabin, but we're concerned about running into either the bear or the mountain lion that killed Jen and Nate. Or these thugs who stored stolen goods in the cabin for that matter. Any chance you and your firearm might join us?"

Were they interested in me or my Glock 17? "Why don't you carry bear spray?" he asked.

Tom tilted his head and smiled. "It might be more fun if you joined us. We could ask you questions about Sasquatch."

He had a day off coming up. But he was not sure about Destiny. Being social at the Rhoads fundraiser was one thing, but her actions from earlier in the year still pissed him off. She'd wasted official resources when she kidnapped her son and left the county. The search went on for weeks, and her only punishment was mandatory community service.

But still, after Jesse Steadman had left town in June, Erle was short on friends. Cynthia was taking up some of his spare time, but he would not call her a *friend*. Maybe Erle could hike with them one time to see how it would go.

"Okay. I'll go but just once. I'm off on Thursday. If that works for you, we can meet at the cabin at nine."

"Sounds like a plan. One more thing—I hear your dad is still looking for volunteers to help with the conference. Do you know what's needed?"

"There's lots of stuff to be done, like setting up chairs, registration, refreshment sales. Are you thinking of helping out?"

Erle's phone rang to interrupt the conversation and drew both Erle and Tom's eyes toward the handset. Erle answered. "Sheriff's Office. This is Hodges." A pause. "I didn't radio this in, because I wasn't in a cruiser when I saw the place. We retrieved a memory card from a security camera that might have recorded who left the stuff. We wanted to look at what's on the card." Another pause. "I'm with the civilian who planted the camera. His name is Tom Morrow. He's Dylan Cox's roommate from Chicago." A final pause. "Okay. I'll see you when you get here."

"Well?" asked Tom when Erle replaced the earpiece in the cradle.

"We probably should have left the camera in place for the Sheriff to handle as evidence. He'll be here soon."

Chapter 34

REVAL—NOVEMBER 2
KATI

Kati laced her fingers behind Dylan's neck and tightened her legs around his waist. Dylan glanced toward Kalev while the Sasquatch floated on his back at the other end of the pool. Dylan turned and said, "Do you think it's a good idea to do this with Kalev so close by?"

Kati shrugged and said in her hoarse whisper, "He does not have to watch if he does not want to."

Dylan grinned, likely at her attempt to speak. Every time they practiced, her diction improved. But her voice had no volume.

Kati leaned closer and giggled. Their relationship had turned intimate the day before, but she sensed Dylan's reluctance to repeat the act in front of Kalev.

She stroked his arm and recalled his barrage of questions when she suggested they couple. Dylan had asked, "I assume the basics are the same, but how do you feel about kisses and foreplay? What should I touch, for how long, and what amount of pressure?"

After a few clumsy movements, Kati had asked Dylan to slow down and do what his body told him to do. Once he pushed aside his anxiety, the act evoked pleasure and passion. At least that is what Dylan told her.

Afterward, he had asked if she viewed their coupling as another piece of halvek behavior to add to the Sasquatch collective knowledge. She understood his anxiety but could not admit most of her motivation rested squarely in curiosity. The act gave her pleasure, and his technique involved greater attentiveness to her body than her previous lovers. Perhaps the halveks' innate competitiveness drove them to impress their mates.

She hugged Dylan closer and felt his arousal between her legs. But before Kati could encourage Dylan to go further, Kalev flipped over to his stomach and, in a half dozen purposeful strokes, swam toward them.

"What is happening here?" Kalev crossed his muscular hairy arms across his chest.

Without loosening her embrace, Kati turned her head toward Kalev and boldly transmitted, "We enjoy each other and are having sex."

Dylan pulled her hands from his neck and propelled backward. "She doesn't mean we're doing it right at this moment."

Kalev took a hard look at Dylan and then Kati. "But you have coupled already?"

"Yes," Kati transmitted. She straightened her shoulders. Her body— her decision.

Kalev narrowed his eyes at Kati. "This is not natural. I am certain your parents would disapprove."

Dylan started to interrupt, but Kati held out a hand to silence him. To Kalev, she transmitted, "My parents are no longer part of my life. I can do as I please with whomever I please."

Dylan shoved Kalev's shoulder. "Do not have this discussion without me. I deserve to know what you are saying to Kati."

Kalev yanked Kati by the arm to pull her aside and left Dylan to helplessly scowl. Kalev raised a hand toward Dylan and transmitted solely to Kati. "You are under the supervision of Tiina and Alevide and have a pending petition for euthanasia. All of your actions will come under the scrutiny of the Council. We can keep a dozen clandestine meetings from the Council, but intimacy with a halvek is another story."

Kati tilted her head with defiance and sent an open transmission to both Kalev and Dylan. "My actions with Dylan are my choice, and the Council need never know. What happens in this four-week reprieve will extinguish with the rest of my secrets on the day they euthanize me."

Kalev responded, but only to her. "You do not know that. If the Council debriefs Dylan, he may be unable to keep your secrets."

Kati swung to look at Dylan. While she enjoyed his companionship, she could not deny his vulnerability and ignorance of the Sasquatch rules of behavior. Kalev squeezed her arm to gain her attention. "If you need physical attention, then I can provide it. Or, if not me, then ask Alevide."

"You're too old for me." Kati scoffed and transmitted to both.

Dylan stared hard at Kalev. "He's offering to service you?"

Kalev ignored Dylan and transmitted solely to Kati. "At least you would be having sex with your kind."

She pointed toward Dylan while his attention oscillated between them. Her next message went only to Kalev. "He *is* our kind—with less hair."

Kalev waved a finger at her. "This coupling is perverse. I forbid you to see each other again."

"You have no right to forbid anything. Your authority does not extend to me, and Dylan is a sentient being, not your pet," Kati responded.

Kalev released Kati and grabbed Dylan to pull him across the pool. Dylan squirmed and kicked, but Kalev managed to force him to the edge and out of the pond. Dylan nearly escaped to dive back in, but Kalev's iron grip held him back. Kati watched Dylan slip across the ground and struggle to stay upright as Kalev jerked the halvek toward the trail.

Kati pushed a transmission solely to Kalev. "I do not know how you plan to stop us from being together, but if you keep us apart, I will tell the Council about him."

Kalev paused before he pulled Dylan into the forest. "Your options are limited, weak child. Do not press me with idle threats."

Kati started to go after them but stopped. She wanted to help the halvek, but she'd already set a different course for herself. Her actions in Porgu had forever compromised her power in Reval. In some sense, she was already dead.

Chapter 35

KALEV

Kalev stormed into Alevide and Tiina's sleep site. He dropped Dylan in a heap at their feet and woke them from their nap. Was he angrier at Kati's smug attitude or at Tiina for introducing them? Perhaps he'd acted too hastily when he agreed with Tiina's plan. At the time, her short-term satisfaction seemed paramount. But Tiina's suggestion could compromise Dylan's usefulness. Kati's alliance with Dylan weakened Kalev's power over the halvek.

Tiina rubbed the sleep from her eyes with a delicate hand. She looked up at Kalev and gave him a smile that eased his fury. But one glance at Alevide, when he rose to sit cross-legged next to his mate, rekindled Kalev's rage. Alevide might assume his relationship with Tiina was secure. But not if Kalev's plan worked out.

Kalev pushed Dylan with his foot and transmitted to all three, "Tiina, *you* insisted Kati and Dylan should have unsupervised time. They have demonstrated they cannot be trusted."

Dylan brushed off the place on his thigh where Kalev had shoved him. He stood to pluck a towel-sized leaf from a bush and wrapped his body.

The halvek placed a hand on each hip and demanded, "What the hell happened back there? You told me to follow Kati's lead and do whatever she felt comfortable with."

Kalev shook with anger while he stared at Dylan. The Sasquatch's fists tightened into balls, and his jaws clenched. "In my wildest imagination, I did not believe she would agree to couple with you."

Tiina rose to sit but did not engage with the arguing pair. She nudged Alevide with an elbow.

Kalev poked a long finger into Dylan's chest. "She is damaged and fragile. Why would you take advantage of her? Your kind always puts their own needs before what is right."

"If I did something inappropriate, it's because you forgot to mention some important features of your culture and traditions." Dylan slapped away Kalev's hand. "I'm new to all of this. I rely on you to coach me. Anyway, she's the one who initiated having sex. Not me." Dylan scoffed. "I guess she's not as frail as you thought. It wouldn't have happened if Kati had waited for me to approach her."

Tiina stood and placed a hand on Kalev's arm. "I think we understand the gist of what happened, but why are you so upset? They have spent many days together. If she finds comfort with him, what is the harm in allowing them to couple?

Kalev left Dylan to scowl and sent his response solely to the Sasquatches. "What is the harm? Kati is having sex with a lower life form, and you ask, what is the harm? If the Council finds out, they may decide to euthanize them both for deviant behavior."

Tiina stroked the long hairs at the side of Kalev's face. "I understand your perspective, but I do not agree this act would automatically compromise Dylan's value with the Council. His ability to form a natural relationship with a Sasquatch may help the Council to see him as one of us."

"But he is not one of us. He is a halvek," Alevide injected. He stood to form a triangle of Sasquatches with Dylan on the outside.

Tiina looked from Alevide to Kalev. "You are both narrow-minded. He is less developed and crude, but he still deserves to be treated fairly. Anyway, if Kati finds him attractive, she is entitled to make her own decisions about sex. Perhaps experimenting with him will relax her, and he could convince her to share information about her transfer."

Alevide leaned his face inches away from Tiina's. "It is always about your objective with Kati. Anything to encourage her to share her story. Do you see that crossbreed relations are unlawful and vile?"

Dylan tugged at Kalev's arm and squinted as if he strained to breach the conversation. Tiina and Alevide leaned toward each other with foreheads nearly touching. Their transmissions had evolved into a private exchange. While Kalev could not penetrate their discussion, he understood their positions—Tiina patted her mate's arm in empathy, and Alevide flinched in defensiveness.

Kalev turned to Dylan. "Do not be concerned. They are talking about you and Kati but only in the most endearing terms."

"Yeah. I'll bet." Dylan retorted. "You make me feel like I'm five and got caught with a hand in the cookie jar."

"I assume you mean you feel like a child caught breaking a rule."

Dylan gave Kalev a single nod and crossed his arms in front of his chest. "On Earth, I'm considered an adult and can make my own decisions about my sex life."

"You *are* on Earth, and you sound like Kati."

"I suspect that means our cultures are not so different. Kati and I have rights, too."

Kalev moved to screen Dylan from where Alevide and Tiina stood arguing. He did not want Dylan to catch any of their discussion inadvertently. Kalev asked, "What would happen in Porgu if a male develops feelings for a sheep and decides to couple with it?"

"I'm guessing I'm the sheep in this scenario. Despite your bias about being the more developed race, you'd have to agree a sheep wouldn't have much say in the matter if some guy decided to prey on it. Kati and I are both higher-level beings who decided to make love. I hope you see a slight difference."

Kalev burst out laughing. "Love? Be assured emotions had nothing to do with Kati's behavior. She probably wanted physical pleasure and, considering her predicament, had few other options."

Dylan's jaw dropped, and Tiina stared at the ground. Kalev sensed her embarrassment for the halvek. If she became Dylan's champion, his plans could be compromised. He needed to find a way to keep Kati and Dylan apart.

Kalev held Dylan at arm's length and sent a transmission to all three, "I have a plan that is not open for discussion."

To Alevide and Tiina, Kalev transmitted, "This cannot continue. At the next windstorm, I am taking Dylan away."

Tiina stepped back from Alevide to look at Kalev. Her mouth fell slack. "Where will you go?"

"The Rangers are short-staffed, and the northwest quadrant has seen little attention since before I transferred to Porgu. I want you to notify the Council that I will take charge of the area. After we travel to the remote part of our territory, I will inventory unused sleep sites and check the status of remote pools. Dylan and I will move during the wind storms. I can find places to hide him when I conduct visits. We will return here before the Festival. I will introduce Dylan at the opening session of the Festival."

"Introduce him to whom?" Alevide asked.

Without hesitation, Kalev transmitted, "To everyone."

Chapter 36

SALIDA, COLORADO—NOVEMBER 4
DESTINY STEWART, NÉE KUSIK

Destiny closed the door to Trip's room and walked to the kitchen island. "It took two full stories before he was ready to call it quits," Destiny said while she pulled a wine glass from the rack and emptied the remainder of the bottle into her stemware.

She sat on the sofa next to Tom and elevated her feet to the coffee table. Destiny rubbed the side of her foot against his. She touched the faded lettering on his crimson t-shirt. "You have the most colorful shirts. What is Wrigleyville's TBOX?"

"It's a pub crawl they hold every December in Chicago, called The Twelve Bars of Christmas."

She cocked her head. "You've been there?'

Tom smiled. "Not my style, but I hear they have fun. I picked up the shirt at a resale shop."

"You're a good bargain hunter. Have you scoped out the resale shops in Salida?"

"It's my guilty pleasure. I'm on a first-name basis with all the owners." Tom clinked his glass with hers. "Enough about me. You must be excited to have Trip back home. I'm surprised you could hold him to two stories. He couldn't take his eyes off you at dinner. It must have been tough to be with his grandparents for over a week."

Destiny took a sip of wine and swallowed slowly. "They made him eat whatever they were having and forced him to talk with strangers. He can't handle that much change and engagement."

"At least you won't be getting daily calls from Nate's mother about Trip's meltdowns."

"It's not his fault. He needs a schedule and plenty of warning if things have to change. Even the car ride was a nightmare for them. Why would they try to force him to play games like *I spy with my little eye* or *I'm going on a picnic*? He doesn't think that way. Then, to get frustrated with his inability to play and tell me I'm a weak parent for not teaching him anything?"

"What did you guys do when you drove from Oregon to Salida?"

"Trip needs his space when he's in the car. He listens to music or plays games alone. He doesn't want to talk with me the whole way." She paused. "Why couldn't they take him on his terms?"

Tom slipped his arm around Destiny's shoulders. "Focus on getting him back on track and prepared to start school next week."

She slouched and rested her head against him. "Thank goodness you're here. You know what to say to help me. I should consider what needs to be done instead of rehashing the unchangeable past."

Tom pulled her toward him and kissed her deeply. Her pulse raced. He nuzzled her ear and whispered. "Some past events should not be changed."

Destiny smiled and playfully pushed his chest with a palm. "Don't get frisky before you tell me what happened with Sheriff Austin today."

Tom huffed. "Well, that was a bit disappointing. They cut a deal with Steadman to testify against the other two."

"What? He's not smart enough to be the mastermind, but I'm certain he played a big part in the plan. Wasn't he involved with a meth drug bust last summer?"

Tom nodded. "Yeah. He was a courier for their trash. But they didn't charge Steadman because he became a witness at their trial."

"And he's doing the same for this one?"

"Yep. Steadman claims they pressured him into finding a place to store the stuff, but he had nothing to do with the actual theft or arranging the ultimate sale of the goods. So, he'll get off if he testifies at the trial."

"Word will get out he's a terrible partner in crime."

"I'm not sure I care about that. I only wish Steadman would be held accountable for steering them to use the cabin."

"Was there any damage, or did they steal anything?"

"Not that I could tell. They moved furniture out of the way to stack boxes of stolen goods. They must have lifted thousands of dollars' worth of electronics. The place is a mess with fingerprint dust and crime scene tape. I'll go up there tomorrow and start cleaning up. The Sheriff's Office has Augie's key. I'll swing by there before I go."

"May I assume officers relocated all the stolen goods?"

"They cleared out all the boxes a few hours after Erle and I talked with Sheriff Austin. Too bad Austin is still pissed off at Erle for taking the SD card to the station. That might be why they cut a deal with Steadman—in case the photos get thrown out as evidence. Eventually, Austin will cool off. It's not like Erle got demoted or kicked out of his job."

"I hope everything works out." She paused to reach for her wine glass. "Erle sure has had a metamorphosis since I was away. He looks fantastic."

"Should I be jealous?"

Destiny rolled her eyes. "Hardly. Jen went to high school with Erle and his sidekick Jesse. She didn't have much good to say about them. What do you think of Erle?"

"He's an okay guy. Maybe a bit naive sometimes. Did you hear about who he's been spending time with?"

Ready for gossip, Destiny pulled back to look directly into Tom's eyes. "Tell me."

"Cynthia Waters."

Destiny leaped to her feet. She slammed her wineglass on the table and spun toward Tom. "No fricking way. That bitch is back in Salida?"

Tom patted the sofa with a calm, steady hand. "Sit back down. She's not here to give you any trouble. Erle said Cynthia is writing a story about the Sasquatch conference on the weekend of the 18th." Destiny stood stock still to think. Air pulsed through her nostrils like an anxious mare. Tom offered, "If she comes to the studio, tell her to leave."

Destiny picked up her glass and sipped. The wine sat in her mouth until she slowly released it down her throat. Tom was right—no need to get worked up about Cynthia being here. If the ambitious journalist kept her distance, they would get along fine. Destiny turned to sit.

She nudged her shoulder against his chest, her signal for him to put his arm around her. He complied, and she said, "I talked with Max Garland today. Max and his wife share the gallery across the street. I don't know if you met her, but you were there with Augie and Max last week."

"Sure. Max is helping Augie work on his technique.

"He and his wife pay ridiculous rent for their gallery and workshop. So I made him a low-ball offer to work and sell their paintings from here."

"What are you planning to do with all of Nate's work?"

"Throw it in a dumpster out back."

Tom tilted his head. "Is that what Trip would want?"

Destiny rolled her eyes. "You're too easy. Max will keep a section of my gallery for Nate's paintings. Once they're gone, Max will use the space for his work. His wife's stuff is good, too. Her style is graphic and whimsical, while Max's reminds me of Van Gogh with landscapes and lots of paint. He's a master at capturing light in his paintings. Putting Max's work next to Nate's will reinforce that Nate cranked out shit."

"Seems like that won't trouble you." Tom massaged Destiny's shoulder. "Speaking of people who don't have your respect, have you thought any more about whether you want to help out at the Sasquatch conference?"

"In case Dylan is with one, it might be a way to hear what the experts say about them. Maybe they'll talk about techniques to track them. We sure haven't seen any sign of Dylan or Kalev on our hikes."

"No, but I'm okay with continuing to look for clues." He paused to smile. "Anyway, if we go to the conference, we might meet a handful of Believers who don't think Sasquatches are fierce carnivores."

Destiny wanted to believe Kalev would protect Dylan. "But what if Dylan has it wrong, and the majority is right?"

Chapter 37

REVAL—NOVEMBER 5
KALEV

Right after the afternoon mists subsided, Kalev glanced at the tips of snow-covered peaks, which barely poked above the trees. He announced they had arrived at a new destination.

When Dylan caught up to the Sasquatch, the halvek transmitted, "We've been walking for hours, and this place doesn't look much different than any other place. How do you know we're where we need to be?"

While the halvek's short legs could not keep pace with Kalev's stride, Dylan was probably doing his best. He glistened with sweat and panted hard to catch his breath.

Kalev frowned. "For three days, we have traveled together, and every afternoon I tell you when our journey should end. I find undisturbed relaxation pools and secluded nutrient ponds. I have identified isolated places for you to rest while I engage with those who live in these remote parts of our region. What makes you question my knowledge of this territory?"

Dylan shrugged. "Instead of arguing, can't you tell me how you know one trail from another?"

Kalev sighed and pointed toward the distant peaks. "You can see the position of those mountains, right?"

Dylan looked toward where Kalev pointed but shook his head. "I don't see anything up there—not a single airplane or a far-off satellite—only the tops of trees and your murky pink sky."

Kalev looked from the view to Dylan and back. Then he smiled. "Your height puts you at a distinct disadvantage."

Before Dylan could protest, Kalev leaned over to grab Dylan by the thighs and lifted him into the air so he could see the peaks on the horizon.

To keep his balance, Dylan grabbed fistfuls of hair on the top of Kalev's head and chuckled. "I see them now. Are the mountains part of your region, or do they mark the end of your territory?"

"The ones you see are still within our region, but they border another tribal area. So, we could meet up with Sasquatches from either group."

"Are there turf battles between those who reside in this commingled territory?"

"Arguments about who can live here?"

"Yes. Do Sasquatches want the best pools for their own families?"

Kalev scoffed. "You are such a halvek—always focused on competition for resources."

Dylan tugged at Kalev's ear. "Put me down and answer my question."

Kalev set Dylan back on the path. "There is no reason to argue or compete. Nutrient pools are continually regenerating themselves, and there are infinite possibilities for sleep sites."

"Not *infinite*."

"Any part of the forest can be used to create an adequate private space. While abandoned ones are faster to prepare, a pair of Sasquatches could clear one of sufficient size within a day."

"Okay. What would happen if someone moved into a nearby site and was loud or made unsettling noises?"

"How would this happen when we can control who receives our messages?"

"Doesn't anyone make sounds when they sleep?" Dylan punctuated the question with a rattling snore.

Kalev sniffed and transmitted a simple, "No." After a pause, he added, "If we have finished with your questions, I would like to establish a camp and engage with some families."

"May I come along and listen? I can hang out on the trail when you do your visit. I wouldn't transmit anything."

Kalev sighed. "What if you are detected? Anyway, you would never be able to comprehend our discussion. The transmissions are too fast, and you have no context to understand."

"I'm getting good at hearing when someone approaches, and I can hide in the undergrowth. Besides, I'm fairly certain there aren't any forty-foot pythons in the brush waiting to make a meal out of me."

"Your paranoia never ceases to amaze me." Kalev weighed the danger of allowing Dylan to eavesdrop on his visits. Risk of detection seemed remote, but what if Dylan learned something he could use to his advantage?

Except for the unfortunate incident with Kati, Kalev had, thus far, remained in complete control of what Dylan knew about Reval and its residents.

If Dylan expanded his ability to communicate, perhaps Kalev's domination would diminish. However, insisting Dylan remain in their private space could present another assortment of challenges. If the halvek grew bored and wandered out unescorted, who knows what he might uncover? While primitive, all halveks were curious creatures.

"Well?" asked Dylan.

Kalev nodded. "You may accompany me, but you must be vigilant to remain undetected."

Dylan broke into a broad grin. "Great. I can't wait to see what you do for a living."

Kalev took hold of Dylan's arm and leaned down to look directly in his face. "Do not expect me to translate every vision you see. I have work to do and will need my rest when we return to our camp."

Dylan saluted and clicked his heels.

Kalev raised a brow and shook his head. *Silly creature.*

Kalev directed Dylan to a deserted sleep site where they cleared the encroaching vegetation. Side by side, they rubbed leaves until the space seemed large enough to accommodate their two bodies.

Once satisfied, Kalev stood at the center with his hands on his hips. He transmitted, "It is time to go. The first family is a short distance from here. I sent them a message yesterday, and they will expect me."

"You never said you could send messages without being nearby."

"You have never asked."

"Are the messages like a full conversation? Do you receive a response in return?

Kalev assessed how much to reveal before sending his next transmission. "These communications can travel great distances. They are targeted at specific individuals and not captured by others. We use them to notify someone that we intend to visit or to broadcast a topic they might find interesting. For example, my father might send a message to me about my mother's health or a decision handed down by their High Council. There is no response needed for these messages."

"How do you know they were received? Or how does the recipient say they appreciate the message?"

"Usually, we sit down and carefully craft a written thank you note, apply a postage stamp, and bring it to the post office that will deliver it in a week."

Dylan huffed. "If you're going to make fun of our traditions and infrastructure, you should stop poking around in my head. You have the innate ability to take a time-honored courtesy and trivialize it by focusing on the process rather than the sentiment. Tell me *how* do you know they received the message."

Kalev shrugged. "The recognition and appreciation of the message will be part of the initial communication at their next meeting. We have infallible memories."

"Have you ever sent a message to me?"

"Why would I? You are always nearby."

"What about before we met?"

Kalev sighed and rubbed his chin. He considered how much to disclose. When Kalev had arrived in Porgu in the spring, he sent many messages to Dylan. Some contained images of the location where they would ultimately meet—Jen's remote mountain cabin. Others, Kalev designed to entice the halvek to look for him.

As far as Kalev knew, most of the transmissions ended up being a painful explosion of scenes in Dylan's mind. When he probed Dylan's memories, Kalev discovered the only image in these early messages Dylan could clearly see was a vision of Jen's cabin. That image was partially responsible for Dylan's decision to come to Colorado.

To avoid a more in-depth discussion of the topic, Kalev transmitted,

"None I recall. Come. It is time to engage with the family."

With Dylan securely hidden off the main trail and a short distance from the opening to a relaxation pool, Kalev strode into the pool's clearing and nodded to the four Sasquatches who soaked in the turquoise liquid. He sent a greeting and slipped in to join them.

After he rubbed the heads of the two offspring, Kalev leaned toward the adults and transmitted a flurry of visions to update them with news from the tribe. Births, recent Council decisions, and transfer updates flew from Kalev's mind, and the adults absorbed each nugget.

The two youngsters quickly lost interest and drifted to the far end of the pool to resume a game of tag. When their splashing became overly rambunctious, their mother raised an open hand to the adults and glared at her children. Kalev did not intercept her message but knew she had admonished them. They moved to a secluded corner to drape their arms on each other's shoulders and touch foreheads.

Kalev smiled when he recalled he and Alevide received similar rebukes and would drift into their own world to create stories of adventure with scraps of images.

"I apologize for their behavior. We are overly permissive with them since we are frequently just the four of us." The mother glanced up while she transmitted but quickly looked back at her children and grimaced.

"They are young and need time to test boundaries." Kalev transmitted after their father nodded his agreement. "Your offspring look much taller than the last time we shared a soak. It has been too long."

The female Sasquatch replied, "Your rounds do not take you near our site often enough. I think it has been several years since we have seen you. We have news of our own. The Council will want to know we are expecting another child." She stood to proudly rub her extended belly.

Kalev looked from the male to the female. *This is another example of how our society is more civilized than the halveks. Since Sasquatch females know precisely when their bodies can conceive, they do not leave procreation to chance encounters.*

To the couple, he transmitted, "I will notify the Council and the Family Section about your third. There are many families within our tribe with one or less, and everyone appreciates you will keep our population in balance. They will be as pleased as I am."

Kalev turned to the taller youngster and transmitted, "You are approaching the age to consider your future. Do you plan to stay remote or move closer to the center where you can participate in one of the sections or learn to transfer?"

The wiry young female pulled away from her younger brother to look at Kalev. She swam closer before she transmitted, "I would like to be a Ranger."

Kalev smiled. "It can be a lonely life. Why do you want to be a Ranger?"

"I want to see the ends of our territory and meet new Sasquatches along the way." The older youth stopped in front of Kalev while the younger followed shortly behind.

"If you desire adventure and seeing new places, you might consider transferring to Porgu."

The young female's brow furrowed. "I would be frightened to be so far from home and my family. Porgu is a violent place. Our knowledge of their development is important, but I do not want to go."

Kalev nodded and turned to her parents. "Soon, you must decide as a family whether she will come to the tribal center to train with one of the Council sections or join a seasoned Ranger on rounds. She could always go on a few rounds and then decide whether she appreciates the Ranger lifestyle or would rather contribute to the tribe in other ways."

The father asked, "Can you be the one to take her on rounds?"

"Your request flatters me. I have taken only a few protégés, but your daughter's inquisitiveness and intelligence show she would make a good Ranger. If you want me to suggest to the High Council that I be her mentor, I would gladly tell them." Kalev paused. "May I assume your family will attend the Festival this year?"

The mother looked at her mate before she responded. "We have not attended for many years, but our children should be exposed to other tribes. Maybe we will make the journey this year." Her husband nodded in agreement.

Kalev transmitted, "This will be an important Festival. Besides the typical tribal exchanges, I understand there will be remarkable discoveries discussed."

"From Porgu transfers?"

Kalev nodded solemnly. "Yes. You will want to be there to understand the magnitude of the discovery, and how it will exponentially advance our knowledge of life and culture in Porgu." When Kalev saw the excitement in their eyes, he continued. "We were born into an age when breakthroughs in Porgu occurred very slowly. By the time your next child is born, we will understand halvek behavior, like why they cherish their primitive customs and what incites them to be violent and uncivilized."

The male put his arm around his mate and nodded eagerly. "We will be there," he transmitted.

Chapter 38

SALIDA, COLORADO—NOVEMBER 10
KIRK STEADMAN

Glass shattered and fell to the floor. The shards twinkled in the low beams of afternoon sunlight. Kirk reached a leather work glove inside the broken pane and flipped the backdoor deadbolt.

"This place is cursed," he said when he bumped a shoulder against a backpack hanging from a hook on the wall adjacent to the door. He yanked the pack free and tossed it on the floor. Empty water bottles, a camp stove, and a zippered pouch in red and white marked First Aid clattered from the pack to the floor. Like an over-the-hill soccer star, Kirk kicked a bottle. It spun down the hallway until it stopped next to a bag of charcoal at the end of the mudroom.

When he entered the great room, Kirk put the lantern on the kitchen island and explored the cabinets. He hoped to find another stash of booze.

"Score," he rasped when he found a plastic liter bottle of vodka behind a row of canned goods. Kirk snatched a coffee mug from a rack and filled the cup before he staggered to the loveseat he and Mike had pushed against the wall days earlier. He took several large gulps and coughed. The alcohol burned his tongue and throat.

He set the mug on the floor next to his mud-covered work boot and partially unzipped his hoodie. Kirk slid a pack of cigarettes and his Zippo out of the front pocket of his flannel shirt. He rested them on his knee and stared into space. "Why can't I catch a break?" he said to no one.

His last two sets of business partners ended up in prison. While he remained free, their incarceration left him without an income source. Over the past weeks, he had worked hard to surveil the cabin and build trust with Mike.

"All that work for nothin'," muttered Kirk. He pulled a cigarette from the pack and tapped it on his scrawny, blue-jean clad thigh to pack the tobacco.

"I wouldn't be in this mess if Jesse hadn't left town. Worthless kid. He's got no respect for his father. He should be *here* taking care of me and the house. I'm too old to handle all this on my own."

He lit the cigarette and blew smoke out of his lungs with enough force to prompt a coughing fit. A sip of vodka burned his throat but stopped the cough. "This stress will probably give me cancer and kill me. That'll make Jesse wish he'd treated me better."

Kirk thought about the unpaid bills for electricity, cable, and phone that sat unopened on his kitchen table. Kirk couldn't afford to eat out, but the fridge stayed perpetually empty. Visits to the food pantries in Salida were demeaning. Twice he drove thirty miles to the Buena Vista food bank. The volunteers smiled and helped him to load boxes of noodle dishes and soup cans into his car, but he knew they judged him for accepting charity. What did they want him to do? Take a job as a store greeter or work as a laborer? At forty-eight, his body couldn't handle standing all day long, much less learning a skill.

"Maybe I should move to California. I could move in with Jesse and his fag boyfriend." Kirk snorted when he imagined living in the same house with Axel Fountain, the man who turned Jesse away from Kirk's view on morality. He considered bringing home whores for Jesse to lure him back to the other side. He'd heard California women were hot—with their suntans and bikinis. Perhaps a move out west was not such a bad idea.

Kirk rose from the couch to pour more vodka into his mug. He stood next to the counter and finished his cigarette before he tamped it out on the granite top. "I'm not leavin' Colorado. I got friends in town, and my house is here." He waved a hand to emphasize his point and whacked into the bottle, nearly knocking it off the counter. He caught the neck before it tumbled sideways and slammed it upright.

"That boy'll come to his senses and crawl back to me. He can't leave me here forever."

He poured another drink and stumbled to the bookcase. "What the fuck is all this outdoorsy crap?" Kirk returned to the counter to retrieve the lantern and placed it on the top shelf next to his mug.

He slid a finger over the spine edge of a guide book and pulled *Lake Hikes in the Sangre de Cristo Range* from the shelf. Kirk flipped open the book. Glossy pages gave driving and hiking directions with photos of topaz blue lakes nestled below jagged mountain peaks.

"Who gives a shit?" Kirk sneered. He tossed the book to the floor in front of the fireplace. A dozen more followed—bird identification, trails to summit Colorado's highest peaks, and fun flower hikes to do with children.

Kirk paused at a shelf filled with novels, their spines neatly arranged from tallest in the middle and the shortest at either end. He touched the top of the books and glanced at the titles. Mostly hardcovers, Kirk knew they focused on words rather than photos and maps.

He opened a thick one with a gray-blue cloth cover and walked over to the lantern to read the inscription. "Robert—You understand more than your age suggests. Thank you for coming to my lecture, Ayn Rand." Kirk shrugged and pitched the book onto the growing stack on the floor.

Book after book hit the pile until the shelves were empty. Kirk filled his mug with the last of the vodka and plopped on the loveseat, exhausted. He stared at the mound, indifferent to the jumble of volumes once stored in order of topic and size.

His thoughts returned to Jesse and his financial predicament. Kirk reached into his pocket for the lighter and flipped the lid open and closed, a nervous habit that afflicted him all of his life. The sound amplified into the hollow room. Click, click, click.

A grin spread across Kirk's face. He pushed off the sofa and grabbed the lantern on his way to limp into the narrow mudroom where he nearly tripped over the discarded backpack.

Kirk waved the light above his head and scanned the room. "There it is," he said and picked up a quart-sized plastic bottle from next to the bag of charcoal.

Back in the great room, Kirk twisted open the scarlet cap, and with great fanfare squeezed lighter fluid over the books. He laughed while he doused the thick dusty ones and kicked the pile to consolidate the heap.

Kirk picked up a couple of paperbacks and laid them across the loveseat. He squirted the rest of the fluid across the cushions with broad strokes before he stuck the empty bottle into a crack between the cushions.

Kirk admired his handiwork. "One more detail," he said while he unzipped his pants and peed his initials on the floor in front of the pile.

Kirk grabbed a paperback and, with a snicker, splayed the book open. When the lighter's spark wheel responded to the flick of his thumb, Kirk waved the flame underneath the pages. Once they caught fire, he flung the burning book to the loveseat. The fluid-soaked cushions ignited with a whoomp.

Kirk inched backward toward the exit while he watched the flames grow and spread. When he reached for the handle, he spat a wad of phlegm on the backpack still on the floor.

Once outside, he turned to face the cabin. "You refused to be a place *I* could count on. Now you won't be here for anyone else."

Chapter 39

Tom caught Destiny's arm to steer her around the mud puddles from residual firefighting water, not yet absorbed into the dry soil.

He said, "Fire Chief Brian Goodman told me by the time they got up here with the water trucks, the fire had engulfed the front of the cabin. He could see flames coming through the windows and around the roofline. The team started by containing the fire in the woods because they had to wait for the power company to turn off the electricity. The Chief worried lines might burn through and drop to the ground. It'd be too much risk for the firefighters."

"How long did that take?" asked Destiny when she approached the blackened, boot-marred porch. Some roof beams remained and stuck out at awkward angles from the stout sides of the log cabin.

"The power was off within minutes. They contained the fire both in the woods and the cabin in less than two hours. Yesterday they were up here to look for any hot spots. The Sheriff's deputies came, too. They searched for evidence of arson."

The pungent, acrid stench from the recently extinguished fire stung Tom's nose and forced him to rub the side of a finger across his nostrils. "Smells like a campfire."

"Yeah, but the fragrance doesn't give me an image of Scouts singing *Kumbayah* and roasting marshmallows."

From what used to be the doorway, Tom saw the blackened remains of appliances next to a leaning granite-covered, stacked-rock kitchen island. The stone fireplace stood charred but erect at the end of the room. Piles of saturated debris covered the floors and trailed out into the yard.

Destiny sighed. "Jen would be devastated. She lived her whole life here."

Tom took Destiny's hand. "You'll always remember her spirit and friendship. The cabin doesn't need to be here for her memories to stay strong."

Destiny drew him close. "Thank goodness you're here to help me through this."

"I wouldn't want to be anywhere else. "Tom kissed her neck and held her tight against his chest. He hoped she felt protected from any more tragedy.

Tom looked over Destiny's shoulder and into the charred remains. "The most intense part of the fire seems to have been in the front of the cabin. Let's go around back and see if there's anything recoverable there."

After they stepped to the side yard, Destiny pointed to what was once a jumbled pile of downed timber. "Look at what's left."

Tom paused to look at the charred limbs and logs. No needles remained, and the branches were charcoal sticks, with cracks reminiscent of recently cooled lava.

They approached the back door, and Tom said, "This is what the Sheriff talked about. See the smashed window?"

"It's pretty clear to me someone broke in to set the fire. But why? I'd blame Nate, but he's got a rock-solid alibi."

Tom raised an eyebrow. "Don't say that anywhere near Trip."

"I won't, but I figured you wouldn't mind me saying it."

"I don't." He nodded toward the open doorway. "Do you think kids may have broken in and set the fire by accident?"

"That's possible. But it's more likely Steadman was involved."

Tom recalled Kirk's photo from the paper. Probably not his best photo shoot, but the man looked rough with week-old stubble and chipped front teeth. "Do you think he was pissed off and retaliated for our call to the Sheriff? We were the ones who reported him for storing stolen merchandise at the cabin."

"But burning down the cabin doesn't affect us. It belongs to Augie."

"You're right. Anyway, would Steadman be stupid enough to come back here after cutting the deal that got him released?"

Destiny frowned. "You're asking me about a man who used to beat his ex-wife and kid, hasn't worked for years because his boy supported him, and got tangled up with a meth ring last summer? Do *you* think Kirk Steadman is dumb enough to retaliate against an innocent person?"

"Great points. He's at the top of my suspect list. At any rate, I'm glad my wildlife camera was in place with the new SD card. Sheriff Austin took it to see if there are any photos of people entering the cabin."

Tom stepped through the open doorway. Leery to advance beyond the threshold, he glanced upward to decide whether the ceiling might collapse. Destiny followed his lead and stopped short of the entry.

A moan came from the woods and snapped their attention. Tom's breath caught, and he pulled Destiny behind him and away from the door.

Destiny whispered, "What the hell was that?"

His heart pounded in his ears. Tom slowly pivoted toward the open doorway and strained to listen.

The moan repeated, followed by a clucking sound like a person sucking his tongue against the roof of his mouth. Destiny whispered, "Do you think it's Kalev or one of his buddies?"

Tom leaned forward. He strained to spot anything moving in the forest. *Why didn't we ask Erle to meet us up here today?* "If it's Kalev, I hope Dylan is with him." He cupped hands around his mouth and called out. "Dylan? Are you there?"

No response.

He turned and placed his hands on Destiny's shoulders before he mouthed, "Stay here. I'm stepping outside. If nothing comes after me, then follow. If something does, see if you can make it through the front of the cabin to the car. But be careful, the floor and ceiling might not be stable."

Destiny's chin lifted. "I'm going with you."

Tom smiled and nodded. He knew she'd made up her mind, and nothing he said would change it.

He took Destiny's hand and led her forward beyond the door frame. They paused outside to stare at the line of scorched pines bordering dense woods. For the first few feet, cinders and ash covered the forest floor where grasses and shrubs should have been. The ink-black pines looked like perverse pencil sketches of their former selves.

Tom moved sideways, his back to the cabin. His eyes darted across the trees. Another moan, followed by the clucking. Tom paused until the sounds stopped. The noise didn't sound closer, just more often. He inched toward the front with slow side-steps.

They were halfway between the building and the car when Tom stopped in his tracks. He pointed up at a bushy twenty-foot spruce beyond the fire line. "What's that?"

Destiny strained to see, when another moan released. "I can't be sure, but I think there might be a bear up in that tree."

"A bear?"

She nodded. "Yes. It's shaggy and bulky. Can you see it?"

Tom took a step forward to stand between Destiny and the trees. "It's not moving very much, but the sound seems to be from over there. If you can make it out, I'll take your word for it."

"Do you think we should check it out?" asked Destiny. She peeked from behind his shoulder.

Bug-eyed, Tom yanked her hand and pulled her toward the car. "Are you nuts? We're locking ourselves in the car and calling the Sheriff."

Chapter 40

REVAL—NOVEMBER
DYLAN COX

More than a week had passed since Dylan and Kalev left to patrol the far reaches of the territory. In Dylan's perspective, Ranger duty combined the grueling physical challenges of boot camp with the intellectual stimulus of a semester abroad.

They had traveled exclusively under cover of the winds and mist and met no others along the trails. While plant life remained dense, full of multicolored flowers and lush undergrowth, paths traversed craggy cliffs and mountains.

With each passing day, Dylan felt his thighs grow stronger until they no longer ached and cramped from overuse. While Dylan was not strong enough to keep up with Kalev's massive stride, a day earlier Kalev had finally ceased his offers to carry Dylan.

Kalev continued to allow Dylan to eavesdrop on visits but dodged Dylan's requests for full-on debriefs. Dylan assumed Kalev wanted him to improve his telepathic skills. But why all the secrecy?

The first meetings seemed a blur of visions, without any order or theme. But after a few encounters, Dylan noticed the first couple minutes included identical images. With considerable thought, Dylan managed to group the visions into concepts related to expanding families and visualizations of Porgu. The rest seemed hopeless, but Dylan persevered. He insisted Kalev allow him to spy from the outskirts.

When they lay side by side in their sleep site each night, Kalev listed each turned pool and family modification they learned each day. Despite his exhaustion, Dylan forced himself to stay awake for Kalev's mundane updates, because after the news, Kalev gave Dylan a special treat. He told fables traditionally used by Sasquatch parents to teach their young. All were about the halvek's life in Porgu, and Dylan found them irresistible.

Early in their trip, Kalev narrated his professed *favorite* tale. "We transmit our stories with visions, but I will translate them into your words to help you understand."

Dylan rolled his eyes. "Thank you for dumbing them down for my deficient intellect."

Kalev patted his arm. "I am pleased to help you understand."

Dylan smiled but did not respond.

"Sasquatch ancestors tell the tale of the halveks growing food. A family arrived at a dusty crossroads where fields of grasses flourished and harbored wild animals such as rabbits and foxes. The halveks settled into a shelter made of cloth and wood. They spent years fortifying the family shelter and adding refuges to protect animals."

"Barns," Dylan injected.

Kalev paused, then continued. "Yes, barns. They brought the first cows by vehicle, most likely from one of the areas with clusters of mature frightened cattle held captive for sale. While the family cared for the cows by feeding them and providing fenced land to wander, they encouraged them to overbreed and either enslaved or slaughtered their offspring."

"Sounds like a profitable farm."

Kalev turned to look at Dylan. "Profits are not the point of the story."

Dylan waved a hand. "I'm sorry. Please continue."

"The halveks destroyed the lush grasses and planted seeds that took essential nutrients from the soil to feed the family and the cattle. There came a time when nature fought back to reclaim the land the halveks tragically desecrated. Moisture came sporadically and finally ceased altogether. Winds whipped up the depleted soil and piled it like snowdrifts against the halvek-made shelters and equipment. In desperation, the family killed the remaining cows to prevent their starvation and ultimate annihilation."

"This sounds like something from the Dust Bowl in the 1930s."

Kalev leaned forward with his elbow wedged against the ground. "I do not know how this story relates to your specific years. Let me finish."

Dylan pretended to zip his lips.

Kalev lay back and fluffed the soft leaf under his head. "After the halvek baby died, the family struck out in a windstorm to abandon their shelter and the land they had depleted. Nearly a century has passed, but the fields remain barren except for a few hearty seedlings taking hold on the surface. Maybe in a thousand more years, the grasses will again reclaim what the halveks destroyed."

"That's your favorite story?" asked Dylan.

"Yes."

"Is there a moral to the story?"

Kalev nodded. "Those who misuse resources do not thrive and can impair the longevity of a society."

"Anything besides the obvious? Any chance there's a positive message about halveks growing food?" Dylan transmitted in a huff.

"These are our narratives. If you have a different one, feel free to share."

On the next night, Kalev told a story of halveks taking decades to create shelters only to ultimately destroy them and pollute lifegiving resources. Three nights into their trip, Kalev began another, but Dylan interrupted. "How about I take a turn?"

Kalev lay on his back with legs crossed at the ankles. He waved an inviting hand to ask Dylan to proceed.

Dylan told the fable of the shepherd boy who cried wolf. When the story finished, Kalev remained stoically silent.

"Don't you want to know the moral of the story?" Dylan assumed Kalev might be interested in hearing how human parents might teach their children not to lie.

"I already know it."

Dylan suppressed a laugh. "I'm interested in your interpretation."

"Animals who behave outside of the halveks' rules should be removed from the breeding pool by methods consistent with their faults."

Dylan thought about the wolf eating the dishonest shepherd after the townspeople did not come to the boy's rescue. He tapped a finger on his clasped hands resting across his belly. *We'll probably be out here a few more weeks. Maybe it's not the time to challenge Kalev's perceptions of human behavior.* "Yep. You got it. Now tell me another one of yours."

After nearly a week and their third new sleep site, Kalev started a story with, "Our ancestors tell the story of the halveks resolving disputes."

Dylan responded. "Oh, this one will be good."

Kalev ignored his comment and started the legend. "In a land where the halveks built clusters of shelters protected by earthen walls, most halveks lived in squalor."

"Do you mean castles? I get the feeling this may have happened long ago."

After a moment of silence, Kalev nodded. "Yes, they were castles surrounded by a moat with wild beasts like crocodiles and snakes. Outside the castle walls, a family scratched the earth to grow plants. They ate and enslaved animals for food and labor. There was a significant disparity between the halveks in the tribe. Some slept in poorly constructed shelters, and their hygiene-deficient offspring were more likely to die young than live to old age."

"May I assume a Sasquatch, who did the transfer, observed these behaviors?"

Kalev shrugged. "Of course. We have watched halveks for centuries. Let me continue."

"Please do."

"While many of the halveks lived outside, some lived inside the castle. They were hidden from view unless they chose to leave. When they did, an entourage of servants and harnessed animals accompanied them. One day, a group of male halveks came from far away. They wore matching clothes and carried weapons designed to maim or kill."

"Sounds like a war party." Dylan rolled over and lay his head on a bent arm.

Kalev squinted. "Your use of party confuses me."

"Don't worry about it. Let's assume they were foreigners coming to cause trouble."

"Indeed. Those with shelters outside of the moat ran into the entrance and sought safety behind the walls. The leader of the foreign group called to the halveks who hid inside, but their statements were met with hurled rocks, arrows, and heated oil. Despite the approaching tribe's efforts to initiate conversation, those in the shelter refused to come out. Eventually, the tribe outside grew angry and attacked the fortress with armaments to breach the earthen walls. They entered the castle and enslaved or killed the residents. These foreigners took control of the tribe's territory until the next tribe of halveks came to talk."

"Is that the end?"

"Yes."

Dylan smiled. "Is the moral to this story—dialogue and not violence is the solution to settle all disputes?"

"Yes. It is good to know you can understand these stories. Before we met, I assumed your primitive upbringing would not allow you to comprehend our complex views on these matters."

"I'm glad you believe I'm capable of higher thought." Dylan cleared his throat. "Why are halveks at the center of your fables?"

"We highlight the failures of a primitive civilization and contrast them with sound values of our society."

"Would it trouble you to know your stories are inaccurate?"

"They come from factual observations." Kalev pursed his lips.

"Perhaps you've misunderstood what you saw."

Kalev gave Dylan a pat on the head and a knowing smile. "Again, these are *our* stories."

"Will the Sasquatches pass along stories about your experiences in Porgu?"

"Of course. When the time is right, I will share my experiences, and my memories will become part of our collective knowledge."

"I know you weren't supposed to interfere with humans, yet you twice saved my life. What will the Sasquatches make of that?"

Kalev stroked Dylan's arm. "Once they meet you, they will forgive my transgression. If I had not saved you, you would not have made the transfer."

"But why did you pick me? I'm sure you've seen plenty of other humans in remote places. You could have befriended any of them."

"There were others I considered. But I was fortunate to select you. You are willing to learn about our customs. While you are still incredibly slow, you have shown remarkable progress at telepathy. Others may not have had the aptitude. Also, another halvek may not have lived through the transfer."

"I'm grateful for that, too. And when will I be able to go back to my home?"

"The next full moon is a few days after the Festival. You can transfer home then." Kalev smiled and tweaked Dylan's cheek.

Dylan pulled back as if a patronizing grandparent had touched him. He tried to shake off the feeling and rolled over.

Kalev's explanation seemed reasonable about why the transfer worked out, but he didn't answer my question about why he picked me. There must be something Kalev doesn't want me to know. At least not yet.

Chapter 41

Tiina left the Amphitheater in a rush. She wanted to distance herself from the day's discussions and sought an audience with Kati without distractions from Alevide. While the vote on the young Sasquatch's euthanasia petition was still a week away, the Transfer Section had discussed the matter at length.

Members had pelted Tiina with questions about Kati's mental state. They wanted details about any progress she and Alevide had made to discover what prompted Kati's request. Tiina's answers had stayed sufficiently vague and dodged any reference to Dylan.

Tiina fumed that the section members had asked her about Alevide's influence on Kati. Maybe they wanted to understand better how the couple worked in concert to heal Kati and discover her secret. But Alevide's input was irrelevant. After all, she was the one who comforted the damaged Sasquatch and encouraged full disclosure about the events in Porgu. But Tiina wanted the section to assume she and Alevide worked as a family to heal Kati. In response to the section's questions, Tiina embellished the relationship between Alevide and Kati and said Kati basked in his counsel.

In truth, he had not engaged with Kati in more than a week, not since they uncovered the intimacy incident. Alevide shunned Kati like a pariah and continually affirmed his opinion about Kati's dalliance with an inferior being.

The young Sasquatch had firmly stood by her convictions. Despite

Dylan's stunted communication skills, his intellect and compassion were on par with Sasquatches. Thus, he should be allowed consistent respect and status.

Tiina ignored their impasse. She understood both points of view and tried to maintain neutral ground between the two warring factions.

While she walked toward her sleep site, Tiina heard footsteps approach from down the trail. She turned to see Alevide hurrying to meet her.

He grasped her arm and pulled her close. Alevide petted the fur along her neck with the back of his fingers. Her tension started to fade when he transmitted, "I tried to catch you when the meeting ended. I hope we have time to soak before the afternoon winds start."

With a sigh, Tiina stepped forward to embrace his waist and lay a cheek against his chest. Of late, he had put in long days with the Family Section. "This is a nice surprise. Your section meeting discussions have distracted you most afternoons for the past week. I suspect couples are anxious to make last-minute mating commitments before the Festival."

Alevide smiled. "Those close to a decision would not want to risk losing their intended mate to someone from another tribe. The Festival tends to bring out the romance in everyone."

"It did for me. I still find you irresistible." Tiina stroked Alevide's back. "But time is short to finalize mating decisions. Was your roster manageable today?"

"No, but I asked to be released from the end of the meeting. I wanted to spend time with you alone." Alevide cradled the back of her head in his palm and combed her long hairs with his fingers. "Every evening, we are with Kati. I feel our relationship suffers from a lack of attention."

Tiina stood on tiptoes and stretched upward to kiss him—first the way a sister kisses her brother and then with the longing and passion shared by lovers.

He tightened his embrace. "I missed you."

"I missed you, too. Caring for Kati has put a strain on our relationship. She takes the energy we should use to attend to *our* needs."

Alevide responded with a faint moan. As she felt his body express his interest, Tiina continued her transmission. "I find her issues exacerbate our philosophical differences."

He pulled back to look at her. "How so?"

"I know we have similar values about respect for each other and our mating vows, but we have different perspectives about how to raise children or how much latitude to give young adults. These issues seemed irrelevant before Kati entered our lives. For well over twenty years, these contrasts were irrelevant. Now they are all-consuming." She sighed. "Maybe we were never equipped to be parents."

Alevide tilted her chin with a knuckle. "That's not a fair evaluation of our ability to parent. We acquired Kati as a young adult. Someone else raised her with their ideals. She has independent experiences and strong opinions I do not share. Raising a child from infancy allows parents to imprint their beliefs."

"I am not sure all children adopt their parents' values. But having a child since birth could be helpful." Tiina swallowed before she transmitted, "Kati's situation was the primary topic at the meeting today. The members are pressuring me to find out what happened in Porgu. The vote on her petition is only a week away. When you caught up with me, I was headed to our sleep site. I hoped to convince her to confide in me."

Alevide stiffened. "This cannot wait until tonight?"

"You will be with us later, and I want to be alone to discuss this with her." Tiina pressed his chest with her palms. "I would rather deal with this now."

"Perhaps it is not simply our different perspectives on Kati's issue that is causing our disharmony. Maybe you place greater priority on her and ignore our needs?"

"You mean *your* needs?" She asked and took a step backward.

"I am not ashamed to admit we have ignored my needs of late. But Kati is a symptom of our problems and not the cause."

"Are you saying you are disappointed with our relationship? And not just of late, but for some time?" Tiina placed her hands on her hips. Alevide reached forward to stroke her arm, but she shook off his touch.

"You exaggerate what I meant."

Tiina allowed him to take hold of her arms but remained stiff. She tilted her head and waited for him to continue.

"For now, we can focus on how to get through this commitment with Kati. I know you have a duty to the Transfer Section to seek information, and I respect your commitment to that end. But I disagree with your methods." He gently squeezed her arms. "I will give you the space you need to deal with her until the Festival. Hopefully, all will be resolved in one way or the other by then. After the Festival, we will have time to rekindle our relationship. But do not expect me to help you with Kati. She is your project."

Fine with me. You have not seen fit to help me thus far, Tiina thought with a scowl when Alevide turned and stalked away.

Tiina entered the sleep site and woke the napping Kati. She placed a gentle hand on Kati's shoulder. "I need to speak with you about your plans for the coming week."

Kati rolled over and rubbed her eyes with the back of a hand. "What happened? Have Dylan and Kalev returned?"

Tiina shook her head. "No. They will not come back until right before the Festival. Kalev wanted you to have time to consider your options without Dylan as a distraction."

Kati smiled. "He is a nice distraction."

Tiina pulled four bulky leaves from a bush. After she wadded them into a bunch for a pillow, she settled in for a discussion.

"Do you trust me?" Tiina asked. Kati nodded, and the older Sasquatch continued. "Then I would like to share a story with you about a decision I made over twenty-five years ago. It was the toughest of my life. I do not tell anyone outside of our family about these circumstances, but I feel you have become part of our family."

Kati pulled closer to Tiina. Their knees touched, and Kati hunched forward to accept Tiina's transmission. "When I mated with Alevide, I chose him for his dependability, predictability, and loyalty. I knew his strength and support were the qualities I needed in my mate."

"I have observed his unwavering sentiments." Kati's transmission included images of smirking faces.

"Please do not disparage him. He is my mate, and I love him."

Kati shrugged, and Tiina continued. "Early in our relationship, we assumed we would raise a family. That was never up for debate—we simply knew. When I was about your age, we received permission from the Council, and I became pregnant. Alevide and I both were blissfully happy. We could not wait to welcome a child."

"I did not know you had a child." Kati's brows drew together and made small creases above her nose.

"When my day came to deliver, Alevide and my mother were both there to help me. I was fit, and the birth was easy. But when our son came out, I did not hear what I expected. I waited for the praise about my beautiful child, but all I heard was my mother's gasp and Alevide's groan. I knew right away the baby was defective."

Kati placed a hand on Tiina's shoulder and sent images of compassion while Tiina continued. "There was no other explanation. They handed my son to me. He was beautiful, with his father's pale green eyes. My boy smiled at me with an innocence I will never forget. A crop of brown hair covered the top of his head, but everywhere else was just pink skin. I looked at Alevide and saw tears track down his cheeks. Our coupling had failed, and our child was cursed."

"I had no idea."

Tiina drew a long breath. "The baby would soon want nourishment and comfort, so Alevide and I needed to decide what to do with my boy. My mother took the child to her sleep site and left us alone to talk."

"What did you decide to do?"

"I was inconsolable, and Alevide insisted we decide right away before the baby started to bond with us. I knew my choices. We could either send him to the Council for euthanasia or transfer him to Porgu. Alevide told me it was my decision. I could not bear to have my child raised by the halveks. He looked so innocent. They would imprint their violent ways and crude culture on him."

"I can understand why you would want to spare him that life. Porgu is a brutal place."

Tiina nodded. "So I asked Alevide to take him to the Council. Alevide started to disagree, but I would not change my mind. If I sent him to Porgu, I would banish my child to a life in hell. So Alevide and my mother brought my baby to the Council."

"Did you perform the ceremony?" Kati asked.

Tiina groomed the hairs on Kati's arm. "No. I could not be part of my son's death. The Council appointed my parents, Alevide, and Kalev. They performed the ceremony right away. Afterward, Alevide took our son to the Auk."

Kati took Tiina's hands in hers and squeezed. "I cannot imagine your pain. Did you and Alevide decide not to try again?"

"The chances of having another deformed child is high. I could not risk needing to make such a decision again. Even though we have the Council's authorization, we abstain when I am in my time to conceive."

"You would have been a good mother. I have appreciated your tenderness and counsel."

"I am afraid I have failed you. I hoped you could reconsider your decision and perhaps think about other options."

Kati patted the older Sasquatch's hand with the authority of someone beyond her age. "There are no options. I have petitioned, and they should confirm my request for euthanasia."

Tiina pulled free a hand and laid it above Kati's breastbone. "Why do you feel there are no options? You could tell the Council about what happened in Porgu and retract your petition."

"That is not possible. Disclosure of my circumstances in Porgu would end in the same result. I am willing to accept euthanasia without the embarrassment of the disclosure."

"You cannot be blamed for any horrific events you observed. Halveks are cruel creatures."

"They can be brutal and depraved. But that does not release us from being responsible observers."

Tiina's head tilted. She puzzled over Kati's statement.

"I will tell you what happened, but I expect you never to disclose my crime." Kati stared into Tiina's eyes. "During my transfer, I killed two halveks because they tortured their family members." Kati hunched forward and covered her face with her hands.

Tiina sat speechlessly. She took Kati's head in both hands and kissed the top of her head.

Tiina searched for alternatives but found none. The young Sasquatch had acted far beyond the bounds of a forgivable offense. Even the most liberal Council members would find her transgressions abhorrent.

She took Kati in her arms and rocked her. "I understand why you feel there are no options. I want to tell you something hopeful, but the Council will look harshly on your actions in Porgu."

Kati shuddered. "I tried to tell you—knowing my story would not make any difference."

Tiina considered the facts and imagined every possible outcome from the Council. "Influencing any halvek's life is punishable by banishment. Causing the death of a halvek would advance to punishment by euthanasia, but it has been hundreds of years since the Council has meted out such a penalty. Maybe you are right to ask for euthanasia rather than forcing them to hear your crimes and sentence you to death."

Chapter 42

Augie unloaded the bag and said, "Thank you for the bagels." He motioned toward the marred, linoleum-topped table. "Sit down."

Tom knew an invasion of Augie's space or process could prompt stress. So he waited until Augie arranged plates, silverware, and precisely folded napkins for two place settings. Tom had not mentioned the bear at the cabin either. Since he and Destiny had driven away without mishap and saw no sign of the bear on their next trip to the cabin, they saw no point in reporting the incident to Augie.

Once Augie selected a chair, Tom sat in the other and popped the lid on his black coffee.

"How are your art lessons with Max Garland?" Tom asked.

Augie chewed slowly and swallowed before he answered. "Fine."

"Learn anything new?"

"We're working on light."

"Seems like your pencil sketches already have a realistic sense of light and dark."

"He's helping me to make it better."

Tom nodded. "Understood. Irrespective of how good we are, perfecting our craft is a lofty goal. Glad you enjoy working with him. Does it bother you to work in what used to be Nate's studio?"

Augie tilted his head as if he puzzled over the question. "Nate's dead. The studio belongs to Destiny now. I like being around Destiny."

Tom smiled. "You got that right." With a clean, cheese-free finger, he dragged the notebook with Augie's Sasquatch sketches toward the center of the table. "I've got a few questions for you about your drawings."

Augie nodded and worked on another bite of bagel. Tom opened the cover and pointed to a sketch of Kalev. "Do you remember anything more about this image? Like what Kalev was doing when he saw himself?"

"Kalev liked to look at himself."

"Does he own a mirror?"

Augie tilted his head as if he wondered why Tom would ask such an absurd question. "Kalev lives outside. He doesn't have a mirror."

"Then, how does he see himself?"

"Every time he walks by a window, he stops to see his reflection."

"Each and every time?"

"Yes. He likes to see himself."

"Sounds a bit vain." After a pause, Tom asked, "You said Kalev didn't talk in your visions and dreams. So how do you know what Kalev thought about seeing himself?"

Augie tugged the book forward and flipped the pages with a moistened finger, thinking. "They were flashes of movies and pictures, all mixed up but in the right order. I could tell how he felt from what I saw."

"What kind of emotions did Kalev feel?"

Augie squinted. Clearly, he did not understand the question. Tom tried again. "You said Kalev liked to look at himself. So you know when he likes things. Did he like Dylan?"

Augie looked at Tom, took a sip of hot chocolate, and wiped his lips with a napkin. Tom waited while Augie worked through the question. After a few moments, Augie said, "Kalev didn't like him, and he didn't hate him. He doesn't want to hurt Dylan. Kalev needs him."

"For what?"

Augie repeated his routine—sip and wipe.

While the silence weighed on Tom, he pushed the chair forward and rested his elbows on the table, chin perched on his clasped hands.

Finally, Augie said, "I don't know. Dylan is important to Kalev. He will protect him."

"From what or whom?"

Augie smiled. "You ask a lot of questions. I don't know all the answers.

When Kalev thinks about him, he makes Dylan seem important. Sometimes, he thinks about Dylan when he pictures the doctor. But not so much when he thinks about the politician."

"What about these drawings of the full moon? Do you know how Kalev felt about them?"

Augie bit his lip while he concentrated on a picture. Moonbeams illuminated the tops of clustered pines and shone on the gentle waves of an alpine lake. A gray night sky dotted with frayed clouds encircled the full white orb.

Augie pointed at the moon and said, "This is important."

"You've said that, but do you know why?" If Augie could expand on Kalev's purpose for taking Dylan, Tom might have a clue about where they went.

"It's the key."

"Okay. I appreciate it's important. Take a look at this one." Tom opened to the page with the two Sasquatches in an embrace. "This is the politician and the doctor, right?"

Augie glanced at the sketch before he nodded in the affirmative.

"If I recall correctly, the smaller one is female and a doctor. The larger is male and a politician. Right?" Tom asked.

"Yeah. They're married."

"Married, like they had a wedding and children?"

Augie grinned. "I don't know about their wedding. They're married like Nate and Destiny were." He paused. "Like you and Destiny are now."

"Very perceptive, Augie. I thought we were discrete." Tom cleared his throat. "Do you have a problem with me being in a relationship with Destiny?"

"No. Destiny's happy now. She wasn't happy with Nate." Augie took the final bite of his bagel and washed it down with hot chocolate.

Tom looked at the drawing and sensed the tenderness of the Sasquatches' embrace. The male looked down at the female with a longing that comes from unbridled love. She leaned into his arms as if she would collapse without his support. Their attraction seemed obvious. Tom wondered why he had not noticed before.

"How does Kalev know these two?"

Augie answered immediately. "The politician is Kalev's brother."

Surprised, Tom scooted his chair around the table to see the drawings from Augie's angle. Tom pointed to the taller Sasquatch and asked, "Is this Kalev's only brother, or does he have more brothers and sisters?"

"He's the only one."

Tom puzzled over the revelation. "Could you tell from your visions if Kalev and his brother are friends?"

"Kalev hates his brother."

"Why would Kalev hate his own brother?" Tom straightened.

"Because Kalev loves his brother's wife."

Chapter 43

ERLE HODGES

Cynthia ran her bare foot against Erle's leg under the table. On her third margarita, she licked flecks of salt off the rim before she pursed her lips and sucked through the straw.

Erle tugged at the front of his slacks to give himself more room. He hoped Cynthia did not notice.

His life had changed over the last two weeks. While Cynthia sipped her drink, Erle reminisced about how Cynthia had taken over his life.

Back in June, Erle had remained in sporadic contact with her, when he fed her information about everything happening at the Sheriff's Office, including investigations into a meth lab sting and the slaughter of a hiker, mountain goats, and farm animals.

When Destiny Stewart threw Cynthia out of Nate's apartment in October, Cynthia began to send him daily emails. Her questions had ranged from investigations to personal inquiries about local gossip—especially about Destiny's activities.

Each email had slathered Erle with compliments about his commitment to the search for Bigfoot. They also asked him about any new sightings. Erle could not resist the allure of Cynthia's attention or her interest in the Sasquatch search.

Until the Sasquatch Believer meeting a few weeks prior, he had believed her sole interest in him rested with whatever information he could provide. Before Erle left the Believer meeting to go to the cabin with Tom, Cynthia had slipped a business card into his pocket and whispered to call her when he finished for the night. Terrified to contact her after midnight, Erle had delayed until a respectable nine o'clock the next morning.

"Did you find a better offer last night?" she had asked after picking up on the first ring.

"I didn't finish work until late and didn't want to wake you." Erle had replied timidly.

"Do I seem like the type who would fall asleep after I made you an offer? I stayed up until after three, expecting you to call or stop by."

Unsure of how to respond, Erle had said nothing.

"Hello? If you're not planning to come over and make things right, then I at least want an apology."

"I'm sorry," was all Erle could stammer.

"So let me get this straight. You've turned me down twice in less than 24 hours?"

"No, ma'am."

"Ooh. Now you're batting a thousand. If you ever call me that again, there'll be hell to pay. What are you doing right now?"

"I'm at work."

"If you're not saving Salida from a drug cartel or nuclear destruction, I expect you to be at the Palace within the half-hour. First, you're taking me out for breakfast. Then, you'll bring me up to my room and stay with me until I'm satisfied." She had abruptly hung up.

Erle had always imagined his first experience would be with a girlfriend and not an experienced woman ten years his senior. For a nanosecond, he wondered if Cynthia's proposal would bother him afterward. Nah. Erle had made a hasty excuse to the Sheriff and left the office.

That morning, Erle rode to the Palace Hotel on his bike and parked it on the rack at the front. He entered the lobby to find Cynthia on an overstuffed sofa, feigning interest in the *Salida Sentinel.* She'd replaced her skin tone dress from the previous night with leopard-spotted yoga pants and a matching sports bra that barely contained her ample breasts.

When he approached, she glanced up from the paper with indifference.

"You look a bit sweaty, Erle. But I'm pleased you could get away. Where are you taking me? Hopefully, somewhere nearby. I'm not planning to ride on the back of your bike."

"How hungry are you? We can go to a coffee place or a restaurant."

Cynthia smiled. "We're going to a restaurant, and I will order a full breakfast. My level of hunger and how much I eat is irrelevant."

Upon arrival, Erle watched while Cynthia evaluated the table placement and selected the seat with the most favorable view. She charmed the waitress with the skill of a cobra mesmerizing its prey. After Cynthia received her bacon, eggs, waffles, and a cappuccino, she picked at the food and talked nonstop about her journalistic acumen. Erle hung on every word and nodded when he felt Cynthia expected it.

When she decided breakfast was over, Erle had paid the bill and followed her back to the hotel, where she sat him down and peppered him with questions about Sasquatch lore.

He'd been embarrassed about his misunderstanding of where Cynthia's interests lay. But he would never let on how much he adored her. If he kept feeding her hunger for information, maybe she'd someday discover his importance.

Cynthia brought Erle back into their Mexican dinner when she tapped his hand. "Baby, you're a million miles away. You'd better be thinking about me,"

"You know I'm always thinking about you."

"I know you are. That's why I adore you." She paused to pucker her lips—the sign Erle knew preceded a request. "I hope you can help me with something."

"Anything," he said and meant it.

"I want a list of all the speakers and vendors coming to the Bigfoot conference. I want headshots of each one, so I can recognize them in a crowd. Once I see the list, I'll pick out the people you'll contact for my interviews." She reached across the table to place a hand on his. "As an organizer, they'll do whatever you ask."

"When do you want all that?"

Cynthia's head cocked. "Tomorrow would be fine."

Erle nodded agreement and figured it would take him most of the night to complete the task.

When Erle paid the bill, the restaurant's door chime rang. He stood and turned to the front to see who had come in. Tom and Destiny approached the hostess stand. Erle wanted to avoid a confrontation between Cynthia and Destiny. He said, "Let's wait a minute before we leave."

She followed his gaze. "Baby, I'd love to say hello. I haven't seen Destiny in weeks. I'm sure she's missed me."

Cynthia scooted out of the booth and steadied herself on the table. When she walked past Erle, she said, "Grab my shoes and my purse, won't you?"

Erle's mind wandered to his secret hikes with Tom and Destiny. He had not told Cynthia about his outings because he enjoyed them and worried Cynthia would forbid him to keep company with Destiny. After all, Destiny was the widow of Cynthia's former boyfriend. Erle had heard the women's last meeting was less than civil.

Cynthia staggered toward Tom and Destiny's booth. She muscled the server aside to lean on their table when Erle showed up with her purse and shoes. Destiny's eyes never left her menu, but Tom's amusement shone in the uptick at the corner of his mouth.

"We haven't seen you in ages." Cynthia looked from Tom to Destiny. "Are you a couple now? A bit soon to be finished with your mourning period, Destiny. What's it been? A month since Nate died?"

Tightlipped, Destiny looked up from her menu to stare at Cynthia. "My personal life is absolutely none of your business. I'd appreciate it if you'd leave us alone." She returned to the menu.

Tom reached across the table and stroked the back of Destiny's hand. He turned toward Erle. "Great to see you. I hope you had a nice dinner."

Cynthia blurted, "I wouldn't be back in Salida, but I have readers who are desperate for my Bigfoot coverage."

After a glance at Destiny, Tom replied, "Sounds like you'll be around for the Sasquatch convention next weekend. Maybe we'll have time to catch up at one of the events."

Tom turned back toward Destiny. "What looks good to you tonight?"

She shrugged while they both focused on the menus.

Erle hoped to deescalate the confrontation and tugged Cynthia's arm toward the exit. But she held firm. "Have either of you seen Dylan around?"

Tom glanced at Cynthia with a look lacking emotion or interest. "Nope. You?"

"I have not. Do you know where he is?"

Tom nodded as if measuring his response. "He's away, working on a case. Would you like me to pass along a message if I hear from him?"

Her lips pressed into a line, and Erle wondered why she seemed interested in Dylan's whereabouts.

"I find it curious you're here. Why would Dylan's roommate come all the way from Chicago to Salida when Dylan isn't even here?"

Tom smiled. "I'm enjoying the wonderful fall weather in Salida."

Cynthia scoffed. "Not likely. I'm surprised Dylan would land a case close enough to Salida for his roommate to come here."

"I didn't say Dylan's case was nearby."

"No, you didn't." She narrowed her eyes at Tom, and Erle took her hand. He wanted to extract her from the conversation.

She shook his grasp away with a snap of her hand and leaned against the table. Cynthia tucked one leg behind the other and slowly swiveled back and forth. "I can't imagine what would bring you here."

"Have you considered this is none of your concern?" Destiny interjected.

Cynthia tilted her head and smiled. "How naive you are, my darling Destiny. When you're a member of the press, everything is of concern and a potential story."

Chapter 44

NOVEMBER 15

After Erle removed the final bound, color copy of the weekend program from the copy machine, he put it into a cardboard carton and carried the box from the supply room to the front office.

"If the Sheriff caught me, he'd have my head," Erle muttered. "Seems like we could have billed the participants a bit extra and had these done professionally." Erle shoved the illicit copies under his desk when the Sheriff walked through the front door.

"You look guilty," Sheriff Austin said while he passed Erle's desk. Austin strode toward the inner sanctum with the straight shoulders and assertive gait of a U.S. Marine.

Erle pushed the carton farther under his desk with his foot. His sweaty hands clasped firmly on the cleared desktop. "I probably am, but it's not worth your time to find out what for."

Austin paused and rested a hand on the door frame. "Do I need to ask?"

"You don't want to know. I'm adding fifty of my own money into the coffee fund, so I think we're close to even."

With a nod to Erle, the Sheriff turned and walked to his office. Erle released a stressful sigh. *Dad better get here soon. I'm not leaving my desk until the programs are gone.*

He unlocked his desk and pulled a stack of envelopes from a lower drawer. He ran a letter opener into the first correspondence as Tom entered the office.

After he delivered a warm smile to Erle, Tom said, "Merle called and asked me to pick up the programs. He's dealing with the release of a couple of miscreants charged with public intoxication and outraging public decency."

"Let me guess. They peed outside of Tracy's Tavern?"

"He didn't say, but I suspect so. That alley smells like a urinal."

"The only place on the planet where the five-second rule would not apply."

Tom choked out a laugh. "You got that right." He paused. "Based on your dining companion from last night, I assume you had an interesting evening. But how's your morning?"

Erle rolled his eyes. "Sorry about the confrontation with Cynthia last night. I begged her to leave without dropping by your table. But when she decides to do something, there's no way to stop her."

"Don't give it another thought. Destiny knows how to handle Cynthia."

Erle glanced toward the inner offices. "It's a slow morning, and I could use a decent cup of coffee. Do you have time to walk over to Café Dawn?"

Tom agreed. Erle forwarded his phone to another deputy and locked his desk. After he lifted the carton of conference materials, Erle followed Tom out the door and down the wide granite stairs of the courthouse.

As he lifted the hatch of the Subaru, Tom said, "I can store these at Destiny's gallery until you need them."

"If you could bring them to Riverside Park for the opening night event, I'd be grateful. Our keynote starts at six o'clock, and registration opens at five. Can you be there at about four-thirty?"

"I told your dad I'd work on the set-up crew. So I'll be there anyway."

"Thanks. One of these days, I'll get my license and a car." Erle slid the box into the back next to a plastic carton filled with cloth tote bags advertising drug companies and pharma conferences. The swag made Erle wonder whether Destiny planned to return to her pharmacist career or run the gallery.

Tom put a hand on Erle's shoulder. "Driving is over-rated. Stick with your bike." He nodded toward the street. "Let's get some coffee."

They strolled past homes and small businesses toward Café Dawn's new location on 1st Street and enjoyed the crisp morning air and clear, bluebird skies. Dried leaves skittered down the street, and Erle made a mental note to clean out the gutters before the snow fell in earnest and clogged up his drains with a soggy mess.

Tom stopped to pick up a candy wrapper from the sidewalk and slipped it into his pocket. "I'm excited to attend the conference. I didn't know much about it at the beginning, but now I realize it's a big deal—for the town and the Believers. Merle tells me people have registered not only from Denver but also from Kansas and Wyoming."

"I'm not surprised. We've advertised it for nearly a year."

"You and your dad have done a great job with promotion." He paused to look at Erle. "What are you hoping to learn at the conference?"

Erle stopped in front of a stucco-covered, two-story Tudor home. After considering the question, he said, "Breakthroughs. The rumor mills are full of fake news about sightings. It's hard to know what to believe."

"You make a great point. But I still don't understand why these creatures have a reputation for malicious mischief. According to websites, they mutilate livestock, kidnap children, and molest women. Doesn't anyone think they're peaceful and from family-centered societies?"

Erle scoffed while they crossed the street and turned toward the café. "They don't make movies about nice sharks. People like to hear about the horrors that come with attacks."

"Isn't it a disservice to the creatures? To assume they're all vicious?"

Erle nodded. "In reality, most Sasquatch sightings are glimpses from a car or in the woods. Once it's spotted, the animal leaves and doesn't stick around to hurt humans. They have a reputation for being loners but not violent."

"Then why the horrific reputation?"

"Why all the questions?" Erle placed a hand on his hip.

"I'd like to let you in on a secret. Destiny, Augie, and I are the only ones who know, and we'd like to get insight from someone familiar with the research. Before I tell you, you have to swear you won't tell anyone else, especially people from the press or involved with the Sasquatch conference. That includes your dad or Cynthia."

Erle's heart started to race. "Have you seen one around here?"

"No, I haven't."

"Then what are you getting at?"

Tom pulled Erle to the edge of the sidewalk to wait for an elderly pair of window shoppers to pass. When they were out of earshot, he said, "I'm not telling you until I hear you commit to keeping this quiet."

Erle was confident he could keep a secret from his dad but was less optimistic about leaving Cynthia in the dark. Despite his apprehension, Erle gave his promise.

Tom laid a hand on Erle's shoulder. "We believe Dylan made contact with a Sasquatch and followed it to a colony."

Unable to respond, Erle simply stared. Tom continued. "Dylan's been gone for a few weeks. Before he left, he directed us to give him time before we would start to look for him. We've decided to wait until the morning after the full moon on the 18th."

"How is Augie involved with all of this?"

"It's complicated, but Destiny and I believe Augie has received messages from this Sasquatch."

Tom's story was groundbreaking. Erle wanted to be front and center for the discovery. He asked, "What kind of messages?"

"Nothing in detail. Only that he wanted to meet with Dylan, and there are more of them. Augie doesn't believe they're violent—just very private."

"What does the full moon have to do with this?" Erle asked.

"Dylan and the Sasquatch left on October 19th, the last full moon. Augie believes there's significance about them traveling that night. We'll go to where Dylan met them and hope he might be back."

"I've never heard of any link between Sasquatch sightings and the lunar calendar, but I haven't looked into it either. Maybe my dad or Greg Taylor would know something."

Tom grasped Erle's arm. "No way. We're not expanding the circle. I came to you specifically. You can join Destiny and me when we head up to Church Mountain on the 19th, but you can't tell anyone about this until after *we* decide our idea didn't pan out."

Erle nodded thoughtfully. "I've got dozens of books and clippings at home about research and sightings. Can you come over tonight to look through what I have? I'm supposed to meet Cynthia at the Palace, but I can push it until later."

"You have the power to direct Cynthia?" asked Tom as he lifted an eyebrow.

Laughing, Erle said, "Not really. But I can come up with an excuse she'll buy."

Chapter 45

REVAL
TIINA

Tiina tried to focus on the two pending petitions for transfer that came before the Transfer Section.

The first involved a twenty-one-year-old male who had trained for the past three years. His mentors believed him qualified and prepared. He sought a transfer to observe deforestation in a tropical climate with an emphasis on the effects of wildlife extinction. With pre-approval by three mentors, she knew the application would sail through the review process with little debate. It did.

The second transfer application came from a female interested in tribal activities in a high mountain zone. While her dark coloring would normally preclude this assignment, she planned to transfer to the area below the tree line and promised only to enter the glaciated regions after nightfall. Tiina voted affirmative as did the other section members.

Tiina scanned the circle. With both applications approved without controversy, she felt the members were primed to be openminded. She glanced at her father and sent him a transmission to ask permission to speak. He agreed and gave her the floor.

Tiina looked at each member and took a deep breath. "Several days ago, this section spent the better part of our meeting discussing the status of Kati's petition for euthanasia. At that time, I could not announce meaningful progress to calm her or sense whether she would come before us to describe the events that occurred in Porgu. I felt I had failed you."

Several colleagues sent consoling messages. They did not blame her for the lack of progress. She continued. "Since that day, Kati shared with me the circumstances she had endured." Congratulatory messages came forward, which boosted Tiina's confidence. "I agree the conditions of her transfer were horrific. She suffered from trauma, the likes of which I have never heard. She believes there is no way to recover from her exposure to these events. If placed under these same circumstances, I fear I would come to the same conclusion."

A senior member interrupted. "Can you tell us more about these events?"

"I cannot."

The member persisted. "Based on her circumstances, there may be ways to prevent a similar situation in the future. While she could not operate under this level of distress, a Sasquatch with training on how to deal with comparable circumstances might be better prepared."

Tiina nodded. "I agree with your point. But, in my view, these events were isolated from the observations she made during her transfer. The likelihood of identical incidents occurring is extremely remote."

Tiina's father intervened. "When you asked this section to postpone our decision, you based your argument on two premises. Initially, you wanted Kati to heal so she might withdraw her petition. Secondarily, you suggested our collective research of the halveks would suffer without her contribution about the details surrounding her transfer. Is this correct?"

"Yes."

"Today, you are telling us there is no hope for her recovery, and you and Kati will be the sole confidants of what happened in Porgu. That is, until her death. Then you will be the only individual who knows the truth about what occurred. I would like to know why you have changed your position on the two criteria that supported your original proposal."

Tiina swallowed hard. Leave it to her father to call her out. "When I spoke to the section on Kati's behalf, I did not understand the depth of her resolve and her mission preparation. She is younger than most who transfer, and I assumed she suffered from a lack of preparation. Now that I have grown to know her, I see she is mature beyond her years. I was foolish to assume her age hampered her ability to understand the magnitude of this decision. Her family, who knew her far better than I, accepted her choice and started their bereavement for her. They understood she did not come to her decision lightly."

Her father nodded. "And what about diminishing our collective knowledge of halveks?"

"What she experienced was gruesome beyond our comprehension. She pleaded with me not to disclose the circumstances. I hope this section and the High Council will allow me to keep her secret. Once she is deceased, the Council could reconsider her request. I promise to comply with any decision rendered about subsequent disclosure."

"But how do you promise to use this experience to modify *your* future contributions to the Transfer Section?" her father transmitted openly for all section members to receive.

Tiina had not considered the section might retaliate for her failed plan. Would they hold her responsible for any undue grief she had caused Kati's family? Maybe they would deem her unworthy of a position in the section.

She straightened and held her chin high. "It is easy to take the conservative path. We could have accepted Kati's petition and respected her and her family's wishes. If we had, the High Council would have euthanized her weeks ago. For the rest of my life, I would have wondered if we had acted too quickly. Since Kati has lived with Alevide and me, I have gained much respect for our younger tribal members. Additionally, I have developed a stronger understanding of the conditions and residents of Porgu."

"Will you open your mind and share that knowledge with the section so we can all benefit from your experiences?" her father asked.

Tiina wanted him to stop pushing but knew the request was reasonable. "I will, but only after Kati is no longer part of our tribe. She deserves privacy before her death."

"What else have you learned through this process?"

"No issue brought to this section has a clear-cut answer. We must weigh each matter by the merits of arguments on both sides. Even if the section makes an error, we can still learn from the experience."

Her father nodded and sent her a private transmission acknowledging his respect and admiration. To the group, he transmitted, "Do you have a proposal for us to vote upon?"

Tiina responded. "I recommend we accept Kati's petition for

euthanasia in five days. But she will remain in my care until then. We will take her to the Festival, and she will stay with our family to avoid distress from meeting with her own. The section and the High Council will agree to not request or require specifics about events that occurred during her transfer. After her death, I will disclose these events to the Council, if asked."

The proposal passed unanimously. Tiina breathed a sigh of relief. She would never tell Kati about her plans to disclose the younger Sasquatch's secret after Kati died.

Chapter 46

KALEV

Dylan and Kalev entered their sleep site while the afternoon wind storm faded into a blustery memory. The mist disbursed and revealed a rose-colored sky that glowed between the uppermost branches. The final remnants of moisture plopped from leaf to leaf and disappeared into the tangle of stalks, leaves, and flowers in the dense bottom layer of vegetation.

Kalev notified Tiina of their return, and within minutes she appeared at the entrance with hugs for both adventurers.

To both Kalev and Tiina, Dylan transmitted a flurry of visions and words about what they saw. Tiina nodded while Dylan flashed images of a dozen sleep sites, snow-covered peaks, Kalev's daily updates, and remote pools in a range of colors to reflect either abandonment or overuse.

"Your ability to communicate through telepathy has vastly improved since when you left." Tiina tucked long hairs behind Dylan's ears.

Kalev watched her attentiveness to Dylan. *She's charmed by the halvek.*

Dylan nodded toward his mentor. "Kalev has been sharing Sasquatch history and myths. That's helped me to improve."

"Myths?" Kalev raised an eyebrow.

"Yeah. Stories designed to transmit a moral without being based on reality."

Tiina smiled. "Seems like the two of you developed a strong bond in the few weeks you have been away."

Dylan laughed. "I don't know about a bond, but I've learned he's a narrow-minded control freak."

Kalev waved a dismissive hand. "At least I do not create excessive noise or question everything."

"I wouldn't question what you say if you'd base your perspectives on logic or facts rather than prejudice." Dylan gave Kalev a playful slap across the arm. Kalev raised a brow.

Tiina moved to stand between the pair. She turned to Dylan. "When I received Kalev's message about your return, I sent Kati to wait for you at the relaxation pool where you used to meet. Do you feel comfortable going there on your own?"

Dylan glanced at Kalev. "I've had plenty of practice to sense approaching Sasquatches and block out my thoughts to avoid detection. I'll be fine." He turned to Kalev and asked, "Can you handle things without me for a while?"

Kalev smirked. "I will meet you there shortly. So, don't start something I will not let you finish."

Once Dylan left, Kalev embraced Tiina and kissed her long and deep. She responded and transferred visions of longing and passion. "When you returned from Porgu, I had hoped you would never leave. Yet you left me again. Will you ever become more dependable?"

Kalev deflected. "Why did you send Dylan off to see Kati? What is her status?"

Tiina sighed and tugged Kalev's arm to encourage him to sit with her. He sat cross-legged, and she climbed on his lap to rest her head on his chest. "Kati will be euthanized two days after the Festival. I assume she will tell Dylan her decision when he meets her at the pool."

"In all this time, you did not manage to change her mind?"

"I have not told Alevide or the Transfer Section, but I will tell you. She committed a crime while she was in Porgu."

"What type of crime?" Maybe the young female had more spirit than he gave her credit for.

"One that would require a death sentence. She will die whether she asks for euthanasia or confesses. If she takes the punishment without disclosure, the Council does not need to condemn her, and her misdeeds will not become part of our history. I think it is best that way. She faced terrible circumstances and dealt with them fairly."

"If her actions were fair, then she committed no crime."

"*I* feel Kati took morally appropriate action, but neither my section nor the High Council will see it that way. I am glad the Council will allow her to attend the Festival. Her last days should include amusement and good company."

"So, we should allow them to couple?"

Tiina's transmissions included faces carved with exasperation. "That again? Let them have pleasure. Kati only has a few more days of life. Anyway, we have no idea of the Joint High Council's response when you present Dylan at the Festival."

"What do you think they will do?"

"Hopefully, they will let you keep him as a pet."

"Do you plan to begin a halvek custom in Reval?"

She shrugged. "We could start it here. If not, then maybe they will have you transfer Dylan back. Although I cannot imagine they would allow a halvek to go back to Porgu. The risk of him talking about what he experienced here is too high. If the other halveks became aware, they would look for us or attempt to transfer. So much for our *observation* principle. The Council's likely choice is to euthanize him—if the technique works on him."

"You've summed it up well. It seems you have decided to accept Dylan as a lower animal." He nodded, pleased with her change of perspective. "It is consistent with Alevide's view."

"If you heard Kati's story, you would think badly of the entire species, too. Porgu forces them to struggle for survival. It distorts their attention to serve the greater good. They are primitive and, while a few might have an ability to learn our ways, the majority are a violent, disgusting breed."

Kalev wrapped his arms around Tiina and stroked her arms. "I have something to ask you."

He tipped her chin with a finger. She smiled in response. Fortified, he continued. "Since I have been away from you, I realize how much I need you in my life. I know why you chose Alevide over me. He is dependable and stable."

"He has been a good mate for me."

"I love our physical time together, but that is not enough for me. I want you to give up Alevide and become my mate."

Tiina pulled away, seemingly to take in the full measure of Kalev's suggestion. "I enjoy our time together, but Alevide is my mate. We do not always agree, but he is the one I go to when I am confused or need to make a life decision. I could never turn him aside. Not even for you."

Kalev straightened, unsure of how to react to her rejection. "Tell me there is room for discussion. I want to tell you why I would be a better mate than Alevide."

"I do not want you to talk ill of him. He is your brother. He and I have dealt with matters other mates never needed to face. You helped us to euthanize our deformed son. Our relationship could be better but has strengthened with everything we have endured."

"If the way he deals with adversity and his honesty are your main reasons for not turning him aside, then I need to tell you something. You will find this difficult to hear."

"Then do not tell me. Alevide and I have committed to strengthening our relationship after the Festival when the Council resolves Kati's issue."

"You should make that decision with your eyes open. Alevide lives a lie."

Kalev could feel her resolve start to fade while she scanned his face. Her brows drew together. "Okay. How?"

"Alevide did not have your son euthanized."

Tiina tensed and pushed a palm against Kalev's chest. She twisted from his lap and knelt before him. "What? That is not possible. He took our son to the Council. My parents, you, and Alevide did the ceremony. My son is in the Auk. I recognize his death each day with thoughts and flowers."

Kalev shook his head. He rested a hand on Tiina's shoulder and traced a finger along her arm. "You should finally know the truth. Alevide lacked the courage to bring your son to the Council. He found someone transferring to Porgu, who agreed to take the baby along."

Tiina jutted out her chin. "Alevide would never lie to me. My baby is in the Auk."

"No. Your baby is relaxing in a pool with Kati."

Chapter 47

SALIDA, COLORADO
ERLE HODGES

Cynthia opened the door and clasped a fistful of Erle's down jacket to yank him into the hotel room and slam the door. She slid a hand behind his neck and pulled his face toward hers.

"You were supposed to meet me right after work. Who do you think you are coming here at this hour?" Her warm breath heated his already hot cheeks.

Erle glanced at his watch. "It's only eight-thirty. I told you I needed to work late, and I'd be here as soon as I finished."

Flushed with rage, she tightened her grip before she released him with a shove and sent him stumbling backward against the wall. "You weren't at work. I saw Sheriff Austin on the street, not a half-hour ago. He said you left the office on time today. Where the fuck did you go? And don't even think about dishing out another lie."

She moved toward him to press a stiletto-clad foot on Erle's shoe.

"If you stop pushing me around, I'll tell you all about it," Erle said with a grimace.

Cynthia strutted to a marred antique table next to the windows at the front of the suite. Lights from Riverside Park shone through the wavy, century-old glass. She lifted a wine glass from the table and took a long drink. Cynthia glared at him with a look Erle took as disgust and contempt.

She pointed toward one of the two armchairs next to the table. "Sit there and tell me what happened."

Erle slunk to the chair. Timidly, he asked, "Can I have a drink, too?"

Cynthia grabbed the open wine bottle and moved it farther out of Erle's reach. "I'll let you have some when you've told me where you were."

Erle considered how much to disclose. If he opened the door to Tom's theories about Dylan, there would be no stopping her. She would dash out of the hotel and into Destiny's studio in a heartbeat. He would need to be truthful but discrete. Maybe she wouldn't ask too many questions.

He said, "I was with Tom Morrow."

"Tell me what you mean by *with*," she demanded. Cynthia shifted her weight to the other foot, and her breasts jiggled from the transfer.

Erle felt his self-control eroding. "I met him at my house after work. Well, it's really my dad's house, but you know where I live."

"What did he want? Does he know where Dylan is?"

Unsure of how to proceed, Erle simply said, "He wanted to look at my Sasquatch research. We spent a couple of hours going through my clippings and books."

Cynthia squinted at Erle and shook her head. Her auburn curls flung into frenzied motion. "Hanging out with Tom to talk about Bigfoot took precedence over meeting me?"

"He seemed desperate to learn more before the conference."

"You could have taken a few hours off work instead of cutting into our time."

"I'm truly sorry. It won't happen again." Maybe she wouldn't press him for more. His friendship with Tom and Destiny could remain under wraps. Erle started to relax.

He rose to stand in front of Cynthia and placed his hands on her shoulders. She responded with a deep breath. Her eyes closed, and Erle read her reaction as positive. He added, "Next time, I'll put you first. Can you forgive me?"

He expected her to lean forward or give him a suggestive look. But instead of teasing him, she stepped back.

Cynthia swaggered away. "Why is Tom suddenly interested in Sasquatch?"

Erle retreated to slump into the chair. He grasped the upholstered arms with a death grip. He was losing ground, but maybe not defeated. "Tom's been helping us to organize for the conference. Maybe he's curious?"

"Maybe?" She moved forward to lean against Erle's armrest. Her thigh pinched his hand against the furniture. Cynthia extended a finger under Erle's chin and tipped his face upwards. "From what I've observed, Tom's pragmatic. He wouldn't waste time on research without an objective. Tell me what he's up to."

Erle struggled to swallow with his neck extended. Then the words came flooding out before he could stop them. "He thinks a bunch of Sasquatches took Dylan."

Cynthia moved back to glare at him. Her face transformed from incredulity to mirth. She laughed out loud and plopped into the opposite chair. Cynthia threw one spray-tanned leg over the other and swung her foot like a human metronome. "So, Dylan's missing. That's why Tom is in Salida."

Erle nudged his chair forward and asked, "Can I have a glass of wine now?"

She flung a dismissive hand in his direction. "Sure. Why not?"

Erle stood to fetch another glass while she continued. "Why hasn't Tom gone to the police?"

After he returned with a piece of bulbous blown stemware, Erle picked up the bottle. First, he refilled Cynthia's glass with most of the remaining wine. Then, he dumped the remnants into his own. No point in holding back. He knew Cynthia would squeeze out every detail. "When Dylan went with the Sasquatch, he left a message."

She straightened. "You mean Tom believes Dylan left with one of them?"

Erle spilled everything. He outlined Tom's description of conversations with Dylan before leaving with the Sasquatch—followed by the message on Dylan's cellphone. Finally, Erle told her about Augie's sketches. When finished, he looked for Cynthia's reaction.

She took another sip of wine and rolled it in her mouth before she swallowed. Cynthia uncrossed her legs and placed her glass on the table before she folded her hands on the tabletop. When she leaned forward, Cynthia pursed her lips. "I know what we need to do."

"Are we going to Destiny's studio?

Her head snapped upright, and confusion crossed her face. "Why on earth would we go there?"

"I thought you'd want to interrogate them."

"I can't imagine what they could add to what you've told me." She paused to smile. "No, you've given me exactly what I need. I don't want them to know what I know."

"Fill me in."

"We're spending the night of November 18ᵗʰ on the summit of Church Mountain."

"Outside?"

She scoffed. "No. You will arrange for us to camp out. I want to be warm and comfortable."

"An RV?"

"Absolutely not. If you rented one, the locals would hear about it." She tapped a finger on her chin. "Surely you have access to camping equipment."

Erle nodded. "Between what my dad and I have, I can put together what we'll need."

His dad? How could he forget? Erle backpedaled. "Wait a minute. November 18ᵗʰ is the first night of the conference. I'll be downtown helping my dad."

She tipped her chin downward, a silent reprimand. "We've had this discussion once today. I'll not have you managing your time in conflict with my needs. You must come with me and protect me from whatever might be out there. I'll rent a four-wheel-drive Jeep for the night. You can arrange whatever we'll need to spend the night in the fucking freezing cold. Bring plenty of booze and guns."

"Guns?"

"Of course. We don't know what these beasts are capable of."

Erle shrugged while he worked up a plan. "Okay. I'll help out at Riverside Park in the afternoon until we need to leave. I can tell my dad I'm coming down with a cold. He'll be so busy with the conference, he won't care if I beg off." He paused. "We've got tons of camping gear. It'll be cold up on the mountain, but I can make sure you're comfortable."

Calculatingly, Cynthia stood, turning her back toward Erle. She bent over and inched the hem of her dress up the back of her legs, feet wide apart and inviting. Erle set his wine on the table and nearly toppled the glass, mesmerized by the unveiling.

"Baby, just think about the rewards I might give you once you help me win a Pulitzer."

Chapter 48

REVAL
TIINA

Tiina stormed into the sleep site and kicked Alevide before she dropped to her knees and pounded on his chest with her fists. "How could you send our baby to Porgu?"

Alevide rose slowly. He shielded his body with his arms to take the brunt of the blows.

"You cannot continue your lies." Tiina stopped her attack and crumbled into his blanket leaves—spent and lost in conflicted emotions. Did she despise him for the deceit or admire him for shielding her from an ugly truth?

Alevide cradled his wife and rocked her. He petted her back while she trembled. "I knew this day would come. Kalev must have told you. I admire your strength because I am weak."

Without raising her head, she transmitted, "You are not weak. You are a liar."

"When you sent me to take our son to the Council, I could not do it. His only crime was to be born without fur. He did not deserve to die. Please forgive."

Tiina sat up. "Forgive you? For more than a quarter-century of lies? The decision to euthanize our son was mutual and binding. But you, Kalev, and your parents have mocked me with this deception. I did not want to sentence our child to a life of want and greed."

Alevide wiped the tears from her cheek. "They did not mock you. Your parents and Kalev agreed to spare you from my failure. At first, they all tried to convince me your desire was all that mattered."

"You started the process?" Tiina could not bear to hear the details but knew she must understand Alevide's role in deceiving her.

He nodded. "My parents persuaded me to conduct the ceremony. We gathered in their sleep site to perform the thought control, but it does not work unless everyone contributes. I could not will him dead. He was our son, a perfect and healthy child. "

"Not perfect. A deformed baby who could not survive in Reval." She pictured Dylan in her private thoughts but did not transfer the image to Alevide. The halvek had grown hairier since he had come to Reval, but he would never fully take on the features of the Sasquatch. He was short— probably because Porgu's food lacked nutrient-infused pools, and smoke and pollution plagued Porgu's air.

Alevide's transmission interrupted her thoughts. "He deserved a chance to thrive in Porgu. I found a Sasquatch from my former tribe who planned to transfer that evening. He agreed to take along our son. I have not contacted him since he left. I did not want news of whether a halvek found our boy or if he perished after the transfer." Alevide bowed his head. "In my dreams, our son was raised by a kind family. They taught him to appreciate nature and not harm animals or other halveks."

"I understand he became a meat-eater."

Alevide straightened and cocked his head. "How do you know?"

"You have met him. Dylan is our son. Kalev brought him from Porgu."

Alevide stood. He looked toward the exit, then to her, and back. She knew he struggled to process the news. Finally, he turned to leave the site. "Stop!" She jumped up to grab his arm and hold him fast.

He jerked his arm free. "What are you doing? He is our son. I must go to him."

Tiina's eyes narrowed. "To what end? Do you intend to tell him I decided to kill him? Or perhaps you will inform him he is one of many discarded, deformed infants that now struggle to populate Porgu?"

Alevide's shoulders dropped. He stared at her. "But he is our child, from our bodies."

"He is our child no longer. Our claim to Dylan ended the day you sent him to Porgu. He is of a different world with separate beliefs and values.

He could not survive here."

"You do not intend to acknowledge your relationship with him?"

"Until moments ago, when Kalev told me of your deception, my son's spirit lived in my heart. The halvek Kalev brought from Porgu is evidence of your betrayal but does not diminish my memories of the baby we decided to shield from a life of misery. We cannot tell Dylan who we are or that our society transfers malformed babies to Porgu."

"Why? How could that knowledge affect him?"

She scoffed. "If Dylan knows about our sacred traditions, the Council may reach a more perilous decision on what to do with him once Kalev unveils him at the Festival. If there is any chance for him to return to Porgu, he cannot know the origins of his species."

"What if we forbid Kalev to show Dylan to the Council? Maybe we could move to a remote territory and take Dylan with us."

"Your attitude about halveks has taken a paradigm shift. Before I told you about Dylan, you believed Kati had coupled with a feral animal, and now you want to run away from everything we hold dear and make a home with him?" She knew Alevide searched for a positive way forward. But she was not so naive. "You can try to convince Kalev to keep Dylan a secret, but he will not listen to you."

"My brother can be reasonable."

"You know as well as I do that Kalev has planned Dylan's capture for years. Above all else, he desires the accolades that would come from his announcement."

"Did he tell you about these plans?'

Tiina raised a brow. "He did not need to. Kalev never does anything on a whim. Think about it. Years ago, he joined the Transfer Section to gain knowledge about how to make the transfer to Porgu. Kalev transferred to find Dylan and brought him to Reval. Now he is keeping the halvek a secret until the Festival—where Kalev can make a grand presentation with Dylan."

"Kalev does not always get what he wants." Alevide ran a hand through his hair.

She recognized the movement, but not from years of Alevide's oblivious actions. She had seen Dylan do it, too. Why was she noticing it now? Tiina stared at her mate and wondered whether to respond to his statement about Kalev's ambitions.

Tiina agreed Kalev did not always obtain what he wanted in traditional ways. But eventually, he acquired everything he desired.

Chapter 49

NOVEMBER 17
DYLAN COX

Most Sasquatches had traveled to the Festival a day earlier and left their private spaces and pools abandoned with Dylan free to roam and explore. He poked around their sites but discovered little diversity. How could they look different without artwork or chachka?

Dylan joined Kalev, Alevide, Tiina, and Kati shortly after Kalev transmitted for them to gather before the wind storms fired up in earnest. After they organized into a line, Dylan took the rear spot in the little convoy. He wanted to get lost in his thoughts.

Over the past two days, Tiina had barely spoken with him. She still sat with him in pools but watched him with the concentration of a hawk on a mouse. The lighthearted banter from before his journey with Kalev was gone. He wondered what he might have done to drive her away. At least there was no change in Alevide. He remained stoic—consistent with the indifference he had shown before.

On the other hand, Kati never left his side since she made her disturbing announcement. That day, he had broken through the trees and dove into the pool to surface beside her. She giggled when Dylan plucked her from the liquid and swung her in circles. He had nuzzled her neck with his bristly beard and mustache.

"Finally, the great adventurer has returned." She had returned his embrace and squeezed his waist between her thighs.

"Have you missed me?" he asked.

Kati traced down his neck and into the crevice defining the muscles on his chest. "I have, and I've considered my predicament during your absence."

"I hope you've changed your mind about accepting the ceremony."

She lowered her eyes. "I have reviewed every possible course of action. The only appropriate alternative is to accept punishment for my crime."

Dylan started to protest, but Kati placed two fingertips across his lips. "Let us enjoy the next day and the Festival. Your life will change once Kalev introduces you. After that, you will not notice my absence."

Dylan scoffed. "That's not true."

Kati had pressed further. "Do not spoil our remaining time together in a futile attempt to change my mind."

Despite Dylan's reluctance, he had agreed to honor her request. Each day since then, he had regretted his decision. He needed to figure out a way to save her from herself and the Council.

Kalev interrupted his thoughts when the Sasquatch joined Dylan at the rear of the column. "You have not asked about the Festival. Has Kati told you why we gather?"

Dylan shook his head. "No details. I know all of the contiguous tribes come together once a year. They honor the dead and look for mates."

"When someone dies in the time between Festivals, we prepare the body by covering it with special plants with properties to enhance dehydration. Within days, the body shrivels. The leaves dissolve flesh and organs to leave clean bones. Families store skeletons until the Festival, where we bury them in a communal grave. We hold services to praise the deceased."

While Kalev transmitted to Dylan, his eyes never strayed from the trail and the waving trees.

Dylan glanced from his protector to the line of towering trunks that bent and creaked far above their heads. Kalev knew these forests better than any of them. As a Ranger, he saw the trails in all levels of light and weather. He would protect them.

"Do you know anyone they will honor this year?" Dylan asked.

"No, but Alevide told me a friend of my father has died. He was old and died a natural and peaceful death. Stories about his transfer and service on the Council will be shared. He had two children, three grandchildren, and seven great-grandchildren."

"How long will the service last?"

Kalev smiled. "Not a service like in your culture. Those who knew him will gather and sit in a circle to transmit stories and visions. The contributions will be made simultaneously with each Sasquatch giving and receiving messages. For someone with a long and full life, this sharing may take an entire night."

"They replay every significant moment of his life?"

"Exactly." Kalev grabbed Dylan's arm and pulled him sideways when a branch dropped from above.

The limb fell at Dylan's feet, and he looked skyward to see from where it had fallen. All the swaying trees looked the same. Dylan stepped around the branch and thanked Kalev for the warning.

Without acknowledging the event, Kalev continued his tutorial. "The Festival mating activities are less organized. We understand the need to breed outside family circles. The Festival provides opportunities for younger Sasquatches to meet others from neighboring tribes." He glanced at Dylan, "Alevide and I met Tiina at a Festival several decades ago."

"And she picked Alevide over you?" Dylan's lip curled at the corner.

Kalev raised a brow. "Actually, she preferred me, but Alevide snuck behind my back and approached her family after the Festival. He emboldened himself to them and courted her. She could not resist his relentless pursuit."

"Must have flattered her."

"Indeed."

Once the wind storm dissipated, Kalev directed the group to a seldom-used nutrient pool. They fed without shared transmissions. Each dove into the green sludge to gain nourishment by swallowing and absorbing.

Dylan and Kati clustered with Kalev at one end, while Alevide and Tiina fed at the other. When the couple stepped from the pool, Alevide pointed toward Dylan and tilted his head toward Tiina. He raised a hand to indicate they were holding a private conversation. Without hearing their thoughts, Dylan knew the discussion centered on him.

Kati snuck a glance in their direction, but to Dylan she transmitted, "You and I need to talk privately."

After they fed, Kalev directed them to a relaxation pool to wait until the afternoon winds would give them cover to complete their journey. Once in the pond, Kati pulled Dylan away from the older adults and into a secluded corner.

She asked, "What is happening between Alevide and Tiina? I could not catch their transmissions, but they are stressed and angry with each other."

Dylan glanced at the far end of the pool. Tiina directed a cold shoulder toward Alevide. She clung to Kalev and touched his face and arms—obviously only transmitting to him. "Not a clue. They must be fighting. It's a big one this time." He turned to Kati. "Have you overheard anything when you're with them at night?"

She shook her head. "They have barely communicated in days. Before you and Kalev returned, they always placed me between them. But last night and the night before, Tiina told Alevide to sleep at a different site."

"Kalev has been walking with me at the back. I'll see what I can get out of him. It seems like there are usually no secrets between the three of them."

Kati agreed and offered to see if Tiina might open up to her.

When the afternoon wound down and the light changed from bright to dim, the winds started again. Kalev approached Dylan and suggested they continue the journey. After they paused at the main path to detect other stragglers headed to the Festival, Kalev nodded toward Alevide to lead the group. As before, Kalev stayed back with Dylan to scan the uppermost boughs of the trees. The branches snapped and whipped in the storm.

Minutes later, Kalev yanked on Dylan's arm to pull him away from the others. Dylan heard a pop like an exploding firework. While he stumbled to keep up with Kalev, Dylan kept looking over his shoulder at their companions and an ancient tree that stood thirty yards ahead—where the path made a sharp turn. The tree had a trunk as wide as a minivan.

"Run!" Kalev transmitted. He pulled again, harder. They rushed down the path and away from Alevide, Tiina, and Kati.

When Dylan realized they were not following, he dug his heels into the path's soft surface. "We have to warn them."

But before Dylan could formulate a message to Kati and the others, the mighty tree cracked at its midpoint. Limbs and leaves hurtled to the ground to bury the trail and anything near it. When the massive tree trunk hit the ground, its branches collapsed, rebounded, and settled.

Kalev and Dylan dashed toward the fallen tree. They tugged at the tangle of limbs to search for the others. Near the edge of the rubble, Dylan heard Kati and Tiina as they transmitted pleas for help. Kalev grasped Dylan's forearm. "Help the females. I will look for Alevide."

Dylan pushed aside debris until he found their extended hands. He tore at leaves and levered apart branches to give Tiina and Kati an opening large enough to squirm free. Once huddled outside of the rubble, he examined their injuries. They assured him they'd broken no bones—only scratches and missing patches of fur.

Tiina rocked Kati and asked, "Where is Alevide?"

Dylan looked to the dense end of the pile where Kalev balanced on top and bent branches out of his way. Dylan overheard Kalev's transmissions calling to his brother.

Dylan turned to Tiina. Her eyes were wide with shock and fear. He transmitted, "Stay with Kati. I will help Kalev. Don't worry. We'll get him out."

She nodded and patted Kati's back while Dylan turned and decided how best to reach Kalev.

The trail was covered from edge to edge with the fallen tree. Dylan looked to the side. *It's too dense to make any time bushwhacking through the forest. Kalev had scrambled over the top. That must be the fastest way.*

Like a child on a jungle gym, Dylan crabbed over the springy branches to inch his way forward. Each foot placement and handhold shifted under his weight, but he made steady progress.

"Can you hear anything from Alevide?" Dylan asked. He approached Kalev, who sprawled over the branches at the thickest part of the pile.

"His transmissions are weak and growing fainter. I am right over where he is trapped."

While Dylan balanced on the massive boughs, he glanced back at Tiina. She still held Kati and stroked her back. But the younger Sasquatch pulled away and motioned for Tiina to help Alevide. After a quick squeeze and kiss on the forehead, she rushed to the mound. Tiina maneuvered up the heap with the agility of a spider.

She reached Dylan and laid a hand on his shoulder. Her chest heaved, and worry creased her forehead. "Do not tell me if you cannot hear him. I am not prepared to know that."

"He's below us. I can barely hear him, but Kalev is receiving his transmissions." Dylan broke a fistful of small branches and flung them into the forest. Saving Tiina's mate would be a Sisyphean task considering the amount of debris between them. Alevide was pinned below the boughs beneath them.

Kalev pressed a shoulder against a massive branch. It shuddered but fell back into place. With a nod to Tiina, he pushed on the rubble and thrust an arm between the branches. Dylan could hear his transmission. "I can feel your hand, my brother. Keep pushing to reach us. We can pull you out."

Alevide's response came slow and faint. "I am caught and cannot move farther. There are tears in my body that the pools cannot heal. I am dying, but your presence calms me to accept what will come next."

"No!" Tiina transmitted. "You must not stop trying." She wiggled headfirst between the boughs and progressed until only her calves and feet stuck out of the pile.

"If you bury yourself any more, we will lose you, too," Dylan said and grasped her ankle. She stopped forward momentum. Her legs trembled, and sobs racked her body.

Dylan watched visions flash between Tiina, Alevide, and Kalev. Pictures of youth and vitality combined with tender moments of sensuality and love. They came too fast for Dylan to be sure which Sasquatch originated each transmission, but he understood they were sharing the memories of times together.

Since Dylan had focused on Alevide's predicament, he had not realized Kati joined them. Her transmission came when he felt her hand on his leg. "Nothing further can be done here. Let us leave them alone."

Dylan looked from Kalev to Tiina, buried in the boughs and comforting Alevide in his final moments. Dylan released his hold on Tiina's ankle and followed Kati to solid ground. They huddled before the mound, shoulder to shoulder, and watched the final exchanges with Alevide while his transmissions grew feeble and finally stopped.

Dylan drew Kati into his arms. "You may believe Reval has everything you need, but I'd sell my soul right now for a chain saw. We could help him if we just had the tools."

Chapter 50

SALIDA, COLORADO—NOVEMBER 18
DESTINY STEWART, NÉE KUSIK

Riverside Park teemed with activity. Vendors set up canopies, and volunteers arranged barriers to manage lines and pedestrian flows. Destiny connected cable ties between the metal fence panels while Tom muscled the barricade sections into place.

Despite expected evening temperatures in the high forties, Destiny had heard the crowd for the opening event would be unprecedented. Fans had fully booked all hotels within a fifty-mile radius of Salida. Organizers asked hometown Believers to rent out spare rooms in their homes for those unable to find accommodations.

"Merle did a good job ordering these." Destiny pointed to the graphic design on the left breast of Tom's gunmetal gray sweatshirt. A circle enclosed a stalking Sasquatch's silhouette superimposed over the outline of ragged, snow-covered peaks. "Whose idea was the full moon?"

Tom grinned. "I asked Merle to add it when I saw the thumbnails. Since the first day of the conference starts on a full moon, he liked the concept. He hasn't a clue about why the moon is significant for us and our search for Dylan."

Destiny chuckled. "No need for him to know. This is our secret." She surveyed their work. "Now that the barricade is up, Merle wants us to help arrange chairs in front of the bandshell."

Tom and Destiny tromped across the lawn. They nodded at the other volunteers, and Destiny inhaled the fragrance of wood smoke. The scent brought back memories of grilled meat—not unpleasant but unfamiliar since she had changed her diet over a decade ago. Tom paused in front of a commercial charcoal grill laced with smoldering bits of woodchips. While the vendor had not yet added meat to his station, his wares were apparent. The front of his canopy held a banner saying, "Gosar Sausage, A Taste of the Old Country."

Destiny saw Tom's expression. She smiled, knowing his mouth must be watering.

He turned toward her and said, "I hope there's time to eat before registration starts. I'm famished—didn't have a chance to stop for lunch today."

Destiny moved between Tom and the smoking grill. "I'd like to have a quick dinner at home with Trip before I come back to work at the registration table. Do you want to join us, or do they need you here?"

He glanced up at the banner before he answered. "Maybe they need me here."

Destiny grinned. "While it would be better for your body to eat my meatless spinach lasagna, I get what you're thinking. The gallery is a five-minute walk. Why don't you pick up a couple of brats and bring them home? Trip might like the change of pace, too."

Tom chuckled. "You're the best. Now let's get to those chairs."

They pulled white, plastic folding chairs from a rack and placed them in evenly spaced rows on the grass. A couple of other volunteers noticed them and joined to help.

Destiny eyed the stage. Merle Hodges had traded in his police uniform for jeans and a quilted hunting jacket. He stood at the front and talked with two other men in a tight cluster. One of them she recognized—the gnome-like Mayor Rhoads. But the tall, silver-haired man seemed unfamiliar. She nudged Tom and pointed to the men.

Tom suggested, "That must be tonight's speaker. He looks like a college professor."

Destiny appraised the group. "Nope. He can't be. The guy's wearing a down vest and flannel shirt. The standard issue for a college professor is a tweed jacket with patches on the elbows."

"Only in old movies." He paused. "I'd like to meet him. Let's go introduce ourselves." Tom took her hand and led her down a set of concrete steps to the stage.

When they approached, Merle stepped aside to widen their circle. He introduced Dr. Bryan Mellon to Destiny and Tom, reportedly his most hard-working volunteers.

After handshakes all around, Tom turned to Dr. Mellon. "I hear you're talking about hair analysis this evening. It should be compelling."

Dr. Mellon released a deep chuckle, reminiscent of a seasoned radio personality. "Only to those who find the search for Sasquatch persuasive. I'm afraid talking about microscopic and infrared fluorescence examination can put a lot of people to sleep."

Destiny chimed in. "Merle has heard your lectures before. He says you can invigorate an otherwise mundane topic. I'm looking forward to your speech."

The professor looked at Merle. "You've set the bar pretty high. I hope I can live up to your expectations."

Tom touched Dr. Mellon's arm. "I hope this is an appropriate time. I'd like to share something with you."

"A sighting story?" The professor gave Tom his full attention.

Destiny wondered what Tom might ask. Without hesitation, he laughed and pulled Dylan's keyring braid from his pocket. "A friend of mine found these hairs. The analysis came back anomalous primate, but I'm hoping you might have a look."

The professor took the braid and held it at eye level to benefit from the proximity to the stage lights. He pulled a pair of readers from a breast pocket and examined the strand. "Where did your friend find this specimen?"

"In the woods, a few miles from here."

"The texture is consistent with human hair, but you say the findings didn't come back as Homo sapien?"

"Nope."

"Any chance you'd let me take this for further testing?"

"It's not mine to give, but I'll talk with my friend and ask if we can send it to you."

Dr. Mellon pulled a business card from his pocket and handed it to Tom. He passed it to Destiny. She smiled and asked, "Does the university mind you've added a Bigfoot print to your card?"

He leaned toward her with a conspiratorial nod. "That's the nice thing about tenure. They can't kick me out for my outrageous beliefs." He turned back to Tom. "Contact me as soon as you talk with your friend."

"You'll be one of the first calls I make."

Destiny hoped that call would be soon.

Once the seats, barricades, and banners were in place, Tom and Destiny stopped at the Gosar Sausage booth before they left the park. Tom ordered two brats—one loaded with grilled onions and peppers for himself and a plain one for Trip.

Destiny gave Tom a knowing smile. He'd been a part of their routines for only a few weeks, but he understood Trip preferred his meals with easily separable components and no condiments.

When they reached the sidewalk, Destiny spotted Erle leaving the park a few yards ahead.

"Hey Erle, wait up," she called. Erle turned, but his eyes darted between the couple and the Palace Hotel immediately across the street. Destiny thought he looked like a trapped animal.

Once they reached him, Tom said, "Registration starts in about fifteen minutes. I thought you planned to help check people in and hand out wrist bands. Where are you headed?"

With a voice nearly an octave higher than usual, Erle said, "Gotta do a quick errand. Then I'll be back."

Destiny injected, "If you're running out for a quick dinner, you can join us at my place. I have loads of extra lasagna."

She noticed Tom chuckle. He held the brat-filled bag close to his chest as if to protect it from Destiny's offer.

Erle stuffed his hands into the front pockets of his jacket. He stared at the ground in front of his feet. "No, not dinner. I'll be back at the park in a bit."

Tom nodded toward the hotel and asked, "Booty call?"

Erle looked at Tom and then Destiny. She thought he seemed conflicted and wondered if Cynthia had summoned.

Erle shrugged. "I might see you later." He glanced toward the hotel. "I'll be away as long as I'm needed."

Chapter 51

ERLE HODGES

Cynthia jerked the steering wheel. Their rented Jeep bounced violently and tossed both her and Erle against the doors despite their seatbelts. With a white-knuckled death grip, Erle held the roll bar with one hand and the seat bottom with the other to counteract the force of each jolt.

When she turned on to a switchback, Cynthia hit the accelerator right before the right front tire fell into a mini-crater. Erle tasted blood when his tongue wedged between his colliding teeth.

He wanted to ask if she had ever driven on mountain roads. While Erle played the scenario in his head, he figured the question would not be well received and likely encourage her to go faster. Instead, Erle turned his head toward her and offered an encouraging smile. "This road sucks, but you're doing great."

Cynthia glanced at him, all flouncing curls and spandex. Her maniacal grin told him adrenaline pounded through her body like the water over Niagara Falls. Getting her to slow the vehicle was not an option. He gritted his teeth to avoid further self-inflicted cannibalism—only three more miles to go.

When they reached the flat summit, Cynthia pulled the Jeep close to a cement barricade encircling a radio tower. Erle unclasped his seatbelt and gratefully exited the Jeep. He stood and stretched his beaten muscles. The lights of Salida twinkled below with the large illuminated "S" on Tenderfoot Hill glowing above the town but well below his vantage point.

Every few minutes, the "S" disappeared, replaced by bright beige LED lights in the shape of a huge footprint. The Chamber of Commerce had paid for the lights to commemorate the first annual Believer Conference.

Erle rubbed his arms to generate warmth while a breeze chilled the evening air. To the west, the sky still glowed dark gray from the recent sunset, a jagged reminder that the summit of Church Mountain was several thousand feet lower than many other peaks in the vicinity. Patchy black clouds congealed above them and threatened to block out the stars and the moon as it rose from the east.

Cynthia's voice broke the silence. "I got you up here. Now it's time for you to take over. Let's get our camp set up. I'm freezing my ass off."

Erle unloaded a ground cloth and tent from the back of the Jeep to create a mini-mountain of plastic and nylon. He struggled to assemble the tent and shoved poles through grommets. Erle forced stakes into the rocky earth. Every few minutes, he blew on to his freezing hands to keep his fingers pliable.

Cynthia sat on the driver's side of the Jeep and tapped her hand on the wheel while she listened to the radio. Erle figured she had the blower and seat heaters on high. Between pounding stakes with his rubber mallet, he watched her suck on an open bottle of wine. By the time the tent stood erect, with a slightly cockeyed lean where Erle had forgotten to square up the fabric, Cynthia had finished the first bottle.

The breeze grew more ferocious and made the sides of the tent pucker. After Erle shoved two sleeping bags through the opening, he went inside to lay out their gear. When Erle finished smoothing out the corners of the bags to meet the tent sides, Cynthia poked her head through the open zipper.

"What? No cots or air mattresses? How do you expect me to sleep?" She shook her head in disgust. "Camping is staying in a hotel with a number in its name. I don't know what to call this."

Erle switched on a tiny battery-powered lantern and hung it from a strap at the apex of the domed roof. He patted a fluffy, down-filled sleeping bag. "It's more comfortable than you think. Give it a try."

Cynthia bent to enter the tent and slid to recline on the bag. She shoved her hands into the pockets of her overstuffed puffy down jacket and lay with her feet mannequin-straight. "This sucks. How can people make a hobby out of this?"

"It's one night, and if Dylan shows up with his new friends by midnight, we won't even have to stay until morning." Erle zipped the tent closure. Once their refuge seemed secure, Erle mimicked Cynthia's position on the other sleeping bag.

Plop. Something splattered on the top of the tent.

"What the hell was that?" Cynthia bolted upright to stare at the spot.

When another spray of moisture hit, Cynthia rose to her feet and scanned the ceiling with her fists raised. *As if she could do battle with whatever attacked the shelter?*

Erle laid a tentative hand on her ankle. "I'm pretty sure it's snowing."

She turned to stare down at Erle, who lay stoically on his sleeping bag. "You can't be serious. The weather service mentioned the possibility of rain but no indication of snow."

"Did you listen to the forecast in town?"

"Of course, but it should be the same, we're only a couple of miles away."

Erle rubbed a hand across her bag. "Come and relax. We're about 4,500 feet higher than downtown. At this time of year, if there's rain in Salida, there will be snow up here."

A gust of wind shook the tent, and snow slapped against the sides. Cynthia dropped to her butt, legs outstretched like a molded plastic baby doll. She turned to Erle and asked, "Are we going to get snowed in? How deep will it get? I've heard of people who suffocated on Everest when their tents got buried in snow." She punched his arm. "How did I ever let you convince me to come up here?"

Erle sighed and sat up. While he'd left Tom and Destiny in the dark, they would appreciate his being here if Dylan did show up. And if Dylan and his Sasquatch buddies did not appear, Erle could be back in town before Tom and Destiny left to search around the cabin ruins.

To Cynthia, he said, "This was *your* idea, and it's brilliant. There could be a few inches of snow by morning. That's all. Anyway, it might help us to track a Sasquatch if it brings Dylan here and then takes off."

Cynthia straightened. Her mouth spread into a grin. "I like that idea. I packed camera equipment in the Jeep, but we should probably have it here. We may need quick access to take photos." She ran a long, lacquered nail across the sleeve of Erle's down jacket. "Baby, would you please fetch my camera bag? It's behind the front seat."

Erle pulled a knit cap over his head and unzipped the tent opening while Cynthia reached up to rub her hand against his calf. She asked, "What shall we do while we're waiting for Dylan?"

Erle turned before leaving the tent to say, "You know I'll do anything to make you comfortable."

Chapter 52

REVAL
KALEV

Kalev entered the clearing on an emotional high reserved for the High Council elite. He had accomplished his objectives and laid a foundation for success. Now, he needed to parlay his hard work into the rewards he had sought for many years.

While he scanned the crowd, Kalev absorbed the din of hundreds of transmissions. He recognized many of the Sasquatches, including those of his tribe. They were males and females with whom he'd learned life's early lessons. They had played and satiated desires—mostly his own but theirs, too.

He watched while Sasquatches from other regions, some familiar from his Ranger walks and others unfamiliar, networked in small clusters or pairs. Their heads respectfully bowed to each other while visions flew in a flurry. He navigated the throng and absorbed their transmissions about family matters and news from the far reaches of their territories.

An exceptionally tall male jostled Kalev's shoulder when they passed. While disturbed at the Sasquatch's clumsiness, Kalev paused to touch his arm and smile a greeting. This was not the time to stimulate disharmony.

Kalev recognized him. He was a member of the Ranger Section in Kalev's parents' tribe. The Sasquatch sent a burst of images of Alevide, tragedy, and suffering. Kalev accepted his sympathy and returned a message asking for information about recent Porgu transfers from their tribe.

"Two have returned recently. One added significantly to our body of knowledge on halvek ice sports."

"I can see by your transmission he would be well suited for a cold climate. He could stay hidden in snow-covered environs and easily acclimatize to a frigid environment. How did this white-haired Sasquatch become a part of our tribe?"

"We accepted him a few years ago. After he was excommunicated, the white Sasquatch wandered for years. He crossed through many regions before he stopped here to share stories from his journeys."

"What prompted his excommunication?"

"He trained for transfer but decided, at the last minute, not to go. His tribe's Judicial Section decided he had misused training resources and taken an opportunity from a worthier transferee. So they banished him until he might gain respect for our common goals. While he misses his family, he has found a new home with us. In gratitude for the information he brought across these many regions, we accepted him into our Transfer program."

Kalev straightened in shock. "Our tribe gave him a second opportunity to transfer?"

The Ranger nodded. "Seems unprecedented, but yes. He had matured while he traveled and came to understand the importance of our collective goals. He already understood much of the training. But he worked with senior Transfer members to fine-tune his knowledge of what transferees should know, like protocol for chance interaction with a halvek or how to deal with the harsh environment and control lower animals."

"Yes, yes, yes. I know the training program."

"You've transferred? I understood you had applied and were denied. Congratulations. Share with me what you learned."

Kalev paused for a moment to gather his thoughts. He smiled. "I only meant I took a short leave of absence from our Ranger team and sat on my new tribe's Transfer Section. While with them, I became familiar with the instruction topics and objectives. Tell me more about this celebrity from your tribe."

The Ranger gently grasped Kalev's arm and gazed into the Sasquatch's eyes with pity.

Kalev shuddered at the offer of consolation and placed an authoritative hand on the Ranger's shoulder. Kalev transmitted, "Not everyone aspires to follow the High Council's cherished path to enlightenment. There are other ways to advance our knowledge and serve the tribe. Now tell me more about this resurrected soul whom you idolize. Has he chosen a mate from within your tribe?"

"Not yet, but there are a few females who have indicated an interest in him." The Ranger gazed across the crowd and pointed toward a large group gathered around a central figure. He stood a few inches taller than the rest and had snow-white hair that cascaded down his body.

The white Sasquatch's audience stroked his body and laughed while he seemingly transmitted stories worthy of their apt attention. The Ranger continued. "He's probably telling them about the halvek ice sports. After months of observation, he grew to understand they recreate by competing against each other."

"Understandable, as everything halveks do is about dominance over others. They would not be satisfied with our games of collaboration." Kalev paused to watch the group gathered around the white traveler. "I'm surprised your females indicate any interest, considering his coloring."

The Ranger straightened. "He is one of us. Why would his color matter to anyone?"

Kalev backpedaled. "I certainly do not find him unattractive. I only meant some prospective mates might wonder if mixing with someone from such a distant tribe might affect offspring viability."

He cocked his head. "I had not considered there could be differences beyond appearances. Do you have information from your travels about mating between members of remote tribes and failure to produce healthy children?"

"None I can specifically recall, but our communications are limited by whom we have contacted. There could be cases we do not know about."

"I will make a point to seek information on this topic during my future travels to the outskirts of our territory. Maybe someone has experiences to share."

"Yes, it would be good to understand more about this issue before your Family Section authorizes a mating for him." Kalev turned his back on the white Sasquatch and his admirers. "May I assume you will be at the ceremonies this evening?"

"I will. Our High Council has asked our white friend to present his gaming discoveries to the full collective."

"I look forward to his presentation. I also would like to make a presentation for the full audience, but I have not discussed the topic with the High Council or asked to have it added to the main agenda."

The Ranger nodded toward a group of Sasquatches who stood near the far entrance of the clearing. "Those members of the High Council are greeting newly arriving members. Perhaps you should ask them whether your topic should be on the agenda or added to the list of ancillary announcements at the end of the ceremony?"

Kalev bristled at the slight—ancillary indeed. He stared at the cluster of Sasquatches with contempt over their power and authority. He took a deep breath and bid farewell to the Ranger before he made his way toward the High Council members. With each step forward, he gained strength and momentum.

When he reached the group, he muscled into their tight circle and forced them to give way. He placed himself next to a female High Council member with a reputation for liberal views.

He joined the group's jumbled transmissions. Kalev first took in the squall of visions and concepts and eventually caught up with the pace of communication. Their discussions focused on sadness over Kati's situation, enthusiasm about a mating pair from adjacent tribes, and anticipation over the white-haired Sasquatch's upcoming presentation.

Kalev injected a set of transmissions to introduce himself and to broach the subject of adding a topic to the agenda.

The adjacent female Council member leaned toward him. "Kalev, it is good to see you here. I heard about the death of your brother. You have my sympathy. How is your family dealing with his demise?"

He nodded with feigned sadness. "Your compassion is appreciated. Alevide's widow and my mother are taking this situation the worst, but they will heal with our family's support and the passage of time."

"Will we honor him at this Festival or next year?"

"My father intends to mention his passing tomorrow when we honor the dead. But Alevide will not be officially honored until we have time to prepare his body. So next year will be more appropriate."

"Since you and Alevide left our tribe for Tiina's, we have missed you.

Your Ranger contributions here were legendary, and I am certain her tribe is reaping great benefits from having you there."

"You are most kind. I only do my part to help fulfill the collective objectives of the tribe."

"Surveying resources and communication with the farthest ends of the region are important. Your services are appreciated. What news do you have that rises to the level of interest for the full Festival audience?"

Kalev paused for effect, then transmitted, "I have discovered a resource that will move forward our Porgu research well beyond what we can learn in dozens of transfers."

She straightened and raised an open hand to the others before she leaned toward Kalev to engage with intimacy. "You have my attention. What is this resource?"

"The method of acquiring this source is unconventional. So to avoid pushback from more conservative members of our leadership, I prefer to announce my discovery to the entire group."

"Are you concerned some High Council members will find your resource or the methods to engage it outside of our protocols?" She grasped Kalev's arm and pulled him aside, away from the others.

Kalev nodded. "While the source is unconventional, our knowledge of Porgu's history and expectations for its future will be immeasurably clearer. The halveks' own rationale for their violent and primitive behaviors will be unveiled to all of us."

"How?" She glanced at nearby Sasquatches to ensure their conversation stayed private.

"Through understanding their language and thus their motivation and justification for actions."

Eyes narrowed with suspicion, she stepped back and surveyed his face. "We did not approve your application for transfer, and no one is authorized to engage with halveks. So tell me, how did you come across a way to translate their language?"

"I will not tell you more. A discovery of this magnitude deserves to be revealed to everyone at once. We must not risk burying the resource without taking full advantage of what is possible."

She stood staring at him without comment. "I understand your concerns. There are those among us who focus on the method rather than on the return. They hold us back. Your suggestion to notify the masses before leadership can stifle our knowledge has merit. Unfortunately, our agenda is already quite full."

"You could eliminate the session by the white Sasquatch. How could a deeper understanding of the halveks' games provide substantial gains in our knowledge base?"

She laughed at his suggestion. "While I agree his presentation will be entertainment rather than informative, many look forward to his session. He is a popular member of our society. Don't dismiss his contributions so quickly. His trajectory within our leadership ranks is remarkable."

"When I divulge my discovery, his meager contributions will become a faded memory."

"I can ensure your time on the agenda without minimizing his allotment. I will need you to be present from the onset of the opening festivities, but your presentation will occur about midway through the session."

"I can attend the full session but may need to leave for a short period before my announcement."

"Stay near me during the event. I will send you a transmission shortly before your presentation is called."

Kalev agreed and bid farewell to the Council member. While Kalev threaded his way through the crowd, his eyes never left the white Sasquatch and his admiring throng. This new anomalous newcomer did not deserve attention or adulation—after all, his former tribe has cast him out.

Kalev searched his bank of Dylan's memories to decide on a name for his new nemesis. He smiled. *If Dylan had an opportunity to name the white traveler, he would call him Olev.*

Chapter 53

DYLAN COX

While everyone else spent the day at the Festival, Dylan split his time either in a pool or in the dense brush to hide from passing Sasquatches. Kalev had directed him to several ponds located far from the Festival grounds. He had assured Dylan anyone who attended the event would want to be close to the center to exchange thoughts with extended family and friends.

Despite Kalev's confidence, Dylan continually scanned for anyone coming near.

Suddenly, he heard someone's subtle footfalls and indistinct thoughts. Without waiting to see who approached, Dylan leaped from the pool and jumped headfirst into the bushes. He righted himself to peer above a chest-high shrub, between velvety round leaves and turquoise blossoms that opened and closed like an oyster shell exposing a pearl.

Kati entered the clearing and scanned the brush to find him. "Why are you hiding?" she asked in her hoarse whisper.

"Why didn't you send me a personal message when you approached?"

Kati shrugged. "I guess a warning would have been good. Sorry about that. I have been distracted and forgot."

Dylan indicated toward the pool. "Come and relax with me. I want to hear what's happening, and I can barely hear you when you speak aloud from over there."

They submerged in the liquid, and Dylan moved behind her. He slid his arms around her waist and slowly pulled to lower them until their shoulders were covered. He asked, "How's Tiina?"

Kati moved to rest her head against his shoulder. "Inconsolable. She did not attend the start of our celebration of lives this morning. Instead, Alevide's mother brought her and Tiina's parents to a soaking pool to relax."

"What about Kalev?"

"Strangely stoic. Kalev and his father attended the Festival events. It seems like they are unaffected."

"Do male and female Sasquatches deal with grief differently?"

Kati slipped around to face Dylan. "Everyone is different. When I told my parents about my decision to euthanize, my father broke down. He relied on my mother's strength to get beyond his emotions and start the mourning process."

Dylan took Kati's hands in his. "I need to share something with you. But I hope you will convince me I'm wrong."

Kati's forehead creased with concern. "I am not sure I like where this is headed, but try me."

"I suspect Kalev may have played a part in Alevide's death."

Kati stiffened. "How could you say that?"

"I know he loved his brother and can't imagine he could hurt him, but I heard the tree crack and start to fall."

"We all did. It happened very quickly."

Dylan nodded and considered his next message carefully. "Kalev is a Ranger. He can read the forests and trees better than anyone. I'm certain he must have known what was going to happen long before I did. He never raised the alarm."

"What good would a warning have done?"

"I've played that day over and over in my head. We weren't very far apart on the trail. With some notice, Alevide may have been able to run back to us or maybe gotten past the tree and avoided it altogether."

"This is a serious accusation. Are you certain?"

Dylan shook his head. "Not certain, but suspicious. Almost before it happened, Kalev pulled me away from the danger. But he didn't transmit a warning to Alevide or to you and Tiina for that matter. Do you think I'm crazy to think Kalev might be capable of killing his brother?"

Kati drew a sharp breath. "There is more going on than what you realize." She held his shoulders. "I think you are in danger, too."

"Okay. You're frightening me. What do you know?"

"Kalev made an announcement at the Festival. He told everyone he discovered a way to advance our knowledge of halveks beyond anyone's imagination. He plans to 'show' them tonight."

"He's talked about his plans to introduce me to the High Council tonight for weeks. So I'm not surprised. How did they react to his announcement?"

"Obviously, they are intrigued. Discussions are circulating within the Festival. Everyone is guessing about what he knows. He talks like he plans to unveil an oddity to everyone. If he intended to arrange a private meeting with only Council members for the potential of dialogue, there would not be a public announcement. Showing you to a crowd limits the Council's options. In your terms, the display would be a circus act with Kalev playing the ringmaster and you as the freak show. The Sasquatches would label you as something to be observed with no potential for true engagement."

"Why do you think Kalev would do this? I expected something small to avoid sensationalism. I'd be fine to meet the High Council of both tribes to talk about my civilization. It might be a good way to destroy some misunderstandings and find a path toward a relationship between Sasquatches and humans."

Kati grabbed his face with both hands and planted a kiss on his mouth. "You are so naive. You do not understand the depth of our feelings toward halveks. We place your kind in the ranks with lower animals. Before I met you, I believed halveks were something to be studied."

"Just because our forefathers evolved differently than yours doesn't mean we are lower creatures."

Kati tilted her head. "Has Kalev never told you how halveks came to populate Porgu?"

Dylan laughed. "Humans have raised that question for centuries. And Kalev knows the answer?"

"All Sasquatches know. Hairless babies who are not sent to the Auk are taken to Porgu to live among their own kind."

Dylan examined her expression, hoping to find a hint of humor or sarcasm. He found neither. Could beings from a world with all their needs met kill or banish their unwanted children to a place rife with wild animals and disease? "This can't be true."

"But it is. For millennia, we have watched while halveks struggled to exploit their world. We have observed you develop tools and harness energy to make more food and to build stronger and more comfortable habitats. You have come a long way from when we left the first halveks there. But your struggles have made your kind competitive and power-seeking."

"Some might say ambitious."

"You have many words for it, but I refer to when someone seeks power to the detriment of another."

"This is too much for me to work out now. We need to decide what to do about Kalev's announcement. If you've been watching humans all this time, why wouldn't the High Council want to meet with me?"

"You are not hearing me. We do not hold you on the same level as the Sasquatch. The High Council would not decide to schedule a few casual discussions and allow you to live among us. They would interrogate you and keep you restrained. I am afraid once they know enough, they would discard you in the Auk like a halvek baby. I do not have faith that my peers would grant you the respect of an equal."

"Kati, I trust your judgment. But if Kalev plans to expose me tonight, what can we do? It's not like I can go into hiding. He will come for me, and he knows this territory better than anyone."

Kati glanced at the sky. "I have an idea. Tonight is the full moon."

"No." Dylan vigorously shook his head. "It's not. Kalev told me the next full moon isn't until after the Festival."

Kati raised an eyebrow. "More of his half-truths. The full moon is tonight, and I know others who are transferring. I can take you to a transfer site and help you journey back to Porgu. But we must leave now before Kalev comes to retrieve you."

"This feels like a snap decision. Shouldn't I talk with Kalev to discuss options?"

Kati placed a hand on his shoulder. "A moment ago, you accused him of playing a role in his brother's death. He lied to you about the next transfer opening and is using you to gain status with the High Council, irrespective of consequences for you. Why would you trust him?"

If Kalev was capable of orchestrating Alevide's death, then what else had he done to trick Dylan into coming here? Kalev needed Dylan to be alone at the cabin. Could he have summoned the mountain lion and bear to kill Jen and, months later, Nate? Perhaps the Sasquatch was not Dylan's guardian angel. Maybe the opposite.

"You're right. There's a big part of me that wants to give Kalev the benefit of the doubt. Nate could charm me in the same way. I need to get away." Dylan glanced up toward the unmoving treetops. "Is it wise for us to leave for a transfer site before the wind storms?"

"He wants to unveil you at the start of the next Festival gathering. I suspect he will fetch you at the next storm. We should leave now before he comes for you."

Kati's logic made sense. If he had an opportunity to return to Porgu, he should take it.

Dylan and Kati left the security of the pool and took the scant trail that led from the clearing to the main path. When they reached the intersection, they waited for a pair of Sasquatches to pass. Once all was clear, they alternated between running and hiding in the bushes.

The pair snaked their way back to the territory of Tiina's tribe in half the time of their initial journey. Once they reached the sleep site Dylan had occupied with Kalev, they rested.

When they lay on the ground and caught their breath, Kati briefed Dylan on how to clear his mind to allow the transfer to take hold of his body and hurl him into Porgu.

"How long did you train for making a transfer?" Dylan asked.

"Months."

"Then how can you expect me to succeed with only a few hours of instruction? I liken this idea to a model plane builder being encouraged to fly a jumbo jet." Dylan had grown used to Kati's blank stare. "Take my word for it. I don't have the skills to pull this off."

"A successful transfer is implemented by allowing thoughts to take you to Porgu. You are adept at telecommunication. I have faith you can transfer."

"What happens if I can't transfer?"

Kati shrugged. "You will still be here."

"So, no danger of disappearing from here and not showing up there? Or appearing somewhere other than Porgu?"

"Like where? There are only two places—Reval and Porgu."

"I'd feel better if you assured me that if it doesn't work, I won't be stuck in some weird purgatory or with half my body in each place."

"Halveks have ridiculous imaginations. If not there, then you will be here—end of story. But you need to be confident about harnessing the power to transfer. Can you do that?"

"Considering I don't want to become Reval's first zoo animal, I'll do my best. Can we practice, or do we only have one shot at this?"

"Just one, but I will be here to help you."

Dylan took Kati by both arms and said, "Why can't you come with me? You've transferred before, and Kalev did it with me. Others have transferred with babies."

Kati peeled away Dylan's fingers. "I need to face my punishment for what I did in Porgu. I must stay here."

"Come with me."

"Can you promise I would not face the same fate in Porgu that you would have here? You have explained that Porgu has well-established zoos and laboratories. They would love to add me to their collections."

"I could hide you."

"I have been to Porgu. Life there is impossibly harsh with imminent risk of detection. I could not live that way." Kati looked skyward, and Dylan followed her gaze to see a brilliant full moon start to rise above the tree branches. "There is no reason to discuss this further. I cannot leave." She paused, then added, "I must tell you something before you go."

Dylan held her close and whispered, "I am in love with you, too."

Kati stepped back, smiling. "I am fond of you, but for Sasquatches, love is an emotion reserved for those who mate. Is that what you would suggest? You would like to become my mate?"

Dylan blushed. His emotions were on overdrive. If she were human, she'd be out of his league. Apparently, Dylan did not measure up in the Sasquatch world either. "Sorry, I called that wrong. I suspect you planned to tell me something else?"

"Yes. We do not have much time. I need to tell you—Alevide and Tiina are your parents."

Dylan's jaw dropped. "My parents are Sasquatches?" *Hold on a minute.* "They sent me to Porgu?"

"When you were born hairless, they decided to invoke the euthanasia ceremony and deliver you to the Auk. But Alevide could not go through with the decision. He gave you to a researcher transferring to Porgu. You are their son."

Dylan released Kati's hand and turned toward the sleep site exit. He fully intended to return to Kalev's tribal home and the scene of the Festival. "I need to go to Tiina. Does she know?"

Kati grabbed his arm. When Dylan pulled to free himself, she held fast. Kati whispered, "Kalev told Tiina only a few days ago."

"She knew but didn't tell me?"

"Both Alevide and Tiina were working through their feelings before they would approach you. Before Alevide died, she told me of her plan to talk with you before the Festival started. Now she can only focus on mourning Alevide's death."

Again, Dylan tried to pull free, but Kati did not let go.

He transmitted, "I can't leave until I see her." Dylan thought about the myth surrounding his abandonment to a church in Oregon—only days or hours afterward, someone from an Indian tribe found him. They had called him a *foundling in the woods.* What if that were true?

Kati pulled Dylan's arm and pointed to the darkening sky. "This is our only chance. If you don't leave in the next few minutes, you will not have an opportunity until the next full moon."

"It doesn't matter. You can help me to stay hidden for another month."

"In two days, I will be gone. Who can you rely on to hide you? Tiina, a wife in mourning? Kalev?"

Dylan stood in the center of the sleep site and considered his limited options. Kati drew him closer. She folded her arms around his shoulders and whispered to be calm and relax. He felt her raising her arms to the sky.

A streak of lightning blasted into the clearing, and Dylan collapsed into a heap.

Chapter 54

WHEREABOUTS UNCLEAR

Dylan woke to find his cheek pressed against pebbled earth. He maneuvered each palm against the ground next to his head and lifted his face from dirt.

The fragrance of decaying pine needles assaulted his senses. Had the transfer worked? A bitter wind tore at his battered body. He pushed up to sit. Dylan raised a hand and stared at sleet and flakes of snow striking his skin. *This must be Porgu.* He smiled when he realized he'd lived through another transfer.

While his eyes grew accustomed to the darkness, the precipitation grew sparse and stopped. But clouds blocked the sky and any hope of moon or starlight to brighten his way.

Dylan stood and turned in a circle. He made out shadowy pine trees, but the undergrowth was sparse—either from a lack of light to filter through the canopy of branches or because freezing temperatures of late autumn shriveled leaves and low-lying plants.

He wondered if Kati had followed him. Maybe she lay nearby. "Kati?" he called into the darkness. Only the howling wind responded. *Better get moving, or I'll freeze to death out here.*

Dylan needed a plan. He could be in Colorado or anywhere else on the planet. Well, maybe not on the equator or at the poles, and based on the weather, perhaps not in the southern hemisphere—it would be summer there now. But he might be near civilization or, as likely, a thousand miles from help in the Canadian wilderness.

What would Jen tell me to do? He imagined her standing before him with her smirk and a cocked head full of self-assurance. She would say to stay calm and find a way to get warm. "Fat chance of that without matches or clothes," he said.

He needed to find a road. But which way should he go? Any direction could be equally right or wrong. After he puzzled through alternatives, Dylan decided to make a marker of sticks and branches—something he would recognize if he saw it again.

Once satisfied with his stack of rocks and limbs propped into a teepee, Dylan turned his back to the marker and stepped off one hundred paces. He stopped and listened for any sign of human development.

Nothing. Dylan returned to try another direction. Dylan believed Kalev's lessons on telepathy had enhanced his hearing. Using those skills might help him to find his way home.

He took several series of steps along the spokes of his marker without discovering anything. But sharp rocks cut his bare feet, and a binding vine tripped him and forced a tumble to the root-laced ground.

When he glanced skyward, Dylan watched the clouds part. The full moon filtered through the branches and illuminated the trees to cast shadows across the forest floor. The light lifted his spirits while he started on his fifth attempt.

After he walked one hundred paces, Dylan stopped to lean a shoulder against a thin tree trunk. It bent when he pressed forward to hear any evidence of humankind.

When Dylan first heard the sound, he wondered if his imagination was playing tricks. Dylan held his breath and listened harder while he grasped the tree and leaned into the wind. There it was—the rattle of a truck engine climbing a mountain road.

He stumbled through the forest toward the fading sound, grasping at tree trunks to stay upright. Dylan did not care whether he might ultimately be able to flag down the truck. He knew there was a road nearby—and it was improved enough for semi-trucks.

After he thrashed for twenty minutes, at times erect and others on all fours, Dylan crashed through a line of trees and tripped over a berm that sent him tumbling to a paved road. Despite his cuts and bruises, Dylan leaped to his feet and danced on the blacktop to cheer for joy. With little thought about which direction to go, he stomped down the middle of the road to head somewhere.

Time passed, but the snow did not return, and the wind subsided. Dylan maintained a slow jog to keep himself warm and to continue moving forward. All the hours spent walking through Reval with Kalev had toned his legs. His stamina helped keep his consistent pace.

Suddenly, Dylan stopped to listen. A car engine rumbled from far away. Dylan swiveled, trying to detect from which direction it would appear. Soon he saw the glow of approaching headlights. As they grew nearer, Dylan hoped they would stop.

They *must*, he decided but wondered if he was in an English-speaking country. The lights grew in size and intensity, and Dylan stood on the centerline to wave his arms in a frantic plea for help.

The car slowed, and the driver switched on the brights. They blinded Dylan but did not diminish his panicked, flailing arms. As the car braked to a stop and the front bumper was only feet away, Dylan moved toward the driver's side door. The driver stared at Dylan with mouth agape, as if the man had frozen in time.

When Dylan motioned to roll down the window, the driver snapped forward to rev the engine and accelerate away. The car left a trail of exhaust and bits of road grit where it used to be. Dylan stood slump-shouldered and deflated while he watched the taillights grow faint and finally disappear into the distance.

"Fuck!" he screamed after the car. "Come back and help me, you bastard!"

Dylan stood with his hands on his naked hips. *You didn't stop. But based on your plate, I know I'm in Oregon.* After a series of additional expletives, Dylan resumed his jog along the pavement.

When the moon receded behind the trees, shadows crossed the road. But the iridescent lane lines guided Dylan's progress. All at once, flashing shapes crept across Dylan's vision. He slowed, then stopped.

A migraine? A message? Dylan could not determine what it was. When Dylan had met Kalev, the Sasquatch sent him messages that caused visions like a migraine. But that was long ago—before Kalev learned how to send slower images Dylan could comprehend.

The gray night faded, replaced by angular lines dancing across an inky background. Dylan strained to clear his vision, but the shapes became a barrage of images at a pace that dispersed them into a mass of flashing lines and colors that were at once vivid and simultaneously stark. Amid the chaos, Dylan saw himself in Reval's pools. Some images showed him clean-shaven and others with hair down to his shoulders.

"Kati?" he called into the darkness. Had she made the transfer and landed somewhere nearby? He called again and again but received no response.

Did my transfer trigger remnant memories? He rubbed his eyes, and the images faded. The moonlit stretch of road reappeared.

Before long, Dylan detected the far away sound of another engine. He spotted a glimmer in the distance coming toward him. While the light approached, Dylan wondered if he should try a new approach from his last vehicle encounter.

"What can I do to make you stop?" he asked the advancing car. "Maybe you'd like me to take a shower or get a haircut." He stared at his hands in the darkness and called out, "I must look a sight."

Dylan stood his ground in the center of the road and waved his arms, not with wild exuberance, but with the gentle rhythm of windshield wipers. He yelled, "I'm not a crazy man. Don't hold my nakedness against me."

The car stopped fifty feet from where Dylan stood. A beam from a spotlight snapped on from the side of the vehicle. Two armed men exited from each side and leveled their weapons at Dylan. Before he could explain the situation, one called out, "Keep your hands raised and stay where you are."

His partner followed with a scoff and said, "What makes you think it understands us? Maybe we should wound it so he can't run away."

They think I'm an animal—probably a Sasquatch. Dylan smiled at the irony. Hands still firmly in the air, Dylan yelled, "I'm not an animal. I'm human. I've been lost for a month. If I had clothes, I'd be wearing them. Please, help me!"

Chapter 55

SALIDA, COLORADO
TOM MORROW

Promptly at six p.m., Tom heard Merle Hodge's voice rise from the stage. "I want to give a big welcome to everyone who's joined us tonight for this first annual Sasquatch conference in Salida, Colorado."

Hundreds of down-clad audience members took their chairs or pushed forward from the edges of the seating area.

While Merle went on to thank sponsors and recognize those who traveled from far-away states and overseas, Destiny and Tom threaded their way through the crowds to their assigned posts.

At the last minute, Merle had roped Tom into the registration desk duty to watch for latecomers. Destiny joined the drink ticket sales team under a canopy directly in front but fifty feet from the amphitheater.

If the straggler crowd slowed, Tom hoped to hear parts of the lectures over the loudspeakers. As he greeted the few latecomers, he nodded at the bespectacled woman who worked in the booth with him. When she glanced toward Tom but did not return his nod, he wondered if she would rather be somewhere else.

Merle's booming voice introduced Dr. Mellon, who began his speech by saying, "I'd like to take a poll before we start. Please applaud if you'd respond in the affirmative. How many people here have actually seen a Sasquatch?" A polite few clapped. "Sounds like a couple of dozen. How many people here know someone who has seen a Sasquatch?" Significantly more applause. "Finally, if Merle Hodges could arrange for a Sasquatch to come to tonight's welcoming ceremonies, who would like to meet one?"

The crowd exploded into thunderous claps, eardrum-splitting whistles, and whooping. When the din died down, Dr. Mellon continued. "I can't promise you'll meet one tonight, but I hope there'll come a day when we can convince them to come out of their solitude and engage with us. Our research does more than attest these magnificent creatures walk our earth. Tracking their movements and learning about their physical makeup prepares us for when we gain the opportunity to have more than a chance encounter with them."

Tom turned to his not-so-friendly colleague. "Mellon is good at working up the crowd." She nodded in agreement, and Tom continued. "I like his premise about meeting them rather than trying to capture one."

His coworker drew herself up to her full height. "Just because he's a college professor doesn't mean he knows anything about the real world. I wish I could get paid to conduct make-believe research, sell fairy-tail books touted as truth, and rake in thousands for speaker fees to talk about bullshit."

Tom smiled. "I'm guessing you're not a Believer?"

"Not a believer in his pagan mythology."

"Hmm," said Tom. Maybe some of the workers were not unpaid volunteers.

Before Dr. Mellon finished his opening remarks, the wind gusted and rattled canopies, sending plastic cups down the lawn. Tom leaned to the side to peer around the vinyl roof. The sky boiled with black and gray clouds, some with streaks of virga, falling rain that evaporated into the dry atmosphere before it reached the ground.

Tom and his cohorts scurried to lower the sides of their shelter. Only a handful of people in the audience left their seats in response to the impending rain. Most simply pulled up hoods and tucked hands into gloves.

The storm front passed as fast as it had come and scattered remnant clouds to allow stars to shimmer across the night sky.

When Tom glanced down the street to spot any late registrants headed his way, he noticed Merle Hodges approaching. Tom asked, "Where are you coming from? You were on the stage not fifteen minutes ago."

Merle nodded to the exit. "Needed to take a call away from the din. Erle phoned right before Dr. Mellon spoke. He must have picked up a flu bug. Said he didn't want to start spreading anything around. He plans to start fresh in the morning with the panel discussion at the Steamplant."

"In the morning?" Tom puzzled about Merle's implication. Erle had committed to join Tom and Destiny to search for Dylan the next day.

"That's what Erle said."

Merle raised a hand in a brisk farewell wave and headed toward the vendor tents. Moments later, Destiny came up behind Tom and wrapped her arms around his waist.

She said, "It's me. We had too many volunteers at the ticket booth, so I'm taking a break. Did you hear any of Dr. Mellon's talk from here?"

"I did. He's a great speaker." Tom glanced at the woman next to him before he whispered, "Makes me think not all Believers want to kill or capture a Sasquatch."

Destiny nodded. "I think Dylan would be squarely in that camp, too."

Tom excused himself from the table and pulled Destiny to the back of the booth. "Merle told me Erle called in sick tonight."

Destiny cocked her head. "Didn't he tell us he planned to come back here after meeting up with Cynthia?"

"Merle said Erle's not coming tonight but plans to help out at the morning sessions." He paused. "Maybe he's not planning to join us to check out Church Mountain."

"Do you think he and Cynthia are up to something?"

"Up to something personal?" Tom paused to consider alternatives. "Or do you think he told her about what's going on with Dylan?" Of all people, Tom did not want a journalist involved.

"He swore he wouldn't, but Cynthia can be persuasive." She paused. "Particularly to someone as naive as Erle. Should we call him?"

"Couldn't hurt." Tom pulled Dylan's phone from his pocket and pressed Erle's number. After a moment, Tom mouthed, "Right into voice mail." He left a short message to call. An instant later, the phone rang.

"Is it Erle?" asked Destiny.

"No. I don't know who it is. Do you recognize the number?" He showed her the screen.

She responded immediately. "The area code is definitely in Oregon."

The noise from the grandstand and the crowd was deafening. Tom stepped away from the booth and walked toward the sidewalk, and Destiny followed.

Tom held a finger to one ear and pressed the phone to the other. "This is Tom Morrow. Who's calling?"

"Joann Whited," said a faint voice. Tom tapped the volume button on the phone. He moved farther from the crowd as Joann continued. "I'm a friend of Dylan's from Oregon. He asked me to call and tell you he's okay."

Tom nodded at Destiny and mouthed, "They found Dylan."

They rushed to cross the street, and Tom put the phone on speaker so they both could hear.

Tom gave Destiny's shoulder an enthusiastic squeeze. Into the phone, he asked, "Are you calling from Oregon? Where's Dylan now?"

"I'm at the regional hospital in Groverton, Oregon. Dylan's in the ER but will be released to a standard room soon. They're giving him fluids for dehydration and slowly warming him to reduce hypothermia. He's fortunate. Despite being found jogging naked at night along a country road, his symptoms were mild."

Tom's jaw dropped. He barely noticed Destiny's grip tighten on his forearm. "Jogging naked at night? Is he delirious?"

"I don't want to scare you, but he looks completely different than when I met him a month ago. He hasn't shaved, and his hair is down to his shoulders. It looks like he's been living in the woods for a year. I don't know how he got this way. He won't say what happened to him. The county sheriff received a call about a naked man flagging down cars along the highway. When they went to investigate, they found Dylan."

"Is he coherent?" Tom asked.

Destiny raised a hand to her mouth, and concern creased her brows. Tom patiently waited for Joann to respond. Finally, she said, "The officers said Dylan had no idea where he was. Once they told him he was in Oregon, he asked them to contact me. James and I came right away."

"Can you give him the phone?"

She paused, and Tom imagined her checking to see if Dylan was able to speak.

In less than a minute, Tom heard Dylan's voice say, "Tom? I'm okay."

Tom breathed a heavy sigh of relief. "I'm with Destiny in Salida. We've been worried sick about you. How did you end up in Oregon?"

Dylan's speech came slow and halting. "I didn't have a lot of say about where I ended up. But there are too many people around to get into details right now. I'll give you more information when you come here to pick me up."

"We're just happy you're safe." Tom looked at Destiny before adding, "I'll come to get you, or maybe we'll both come. You must have learned a lot while you were away. We'll want a full play-by-play."

"By the time you get here, I might be questioning my sense of reality. I already doubt what happened, and I was there. Suffice it to say, I finally know where I came from." Dylan paused. "Incredibly, I know where everyone else came from, too."

READ ON FOR AN EXCERPT FROM

PASSAGE

of the

Sasquatch

BY L.V. DITCHKUS

Book IV of The Sasquatch Series

Available soon on Amazon.com

Chapter 1

Oregon—November 18
Kati

I stood erect and braced my body against the storm. Sideways sleet and snow whipped my fur and obscured my view. But I knew what lay beyond. Between the raging gusts, I could make out the shapes of towering pines. Last season's needles confirmed the trees' existence with an unmistakable scent aroused by the moisture.

My gut clenched. I was not supposed to make this trip. We intended for only Dylan to travel back to Porgu—his dimension. Since he had never instigated a transfer, I needed to help him attract a lightning bolt. When Sasquatches journeyed between Reval, our home world, and Porgu, we focused on the destination. I had instructed Dylan to visualize a spot in Porgu where he would be welcomed and safe.

Conditions in Reval had been perfect with the moon at its fullest. When I raised my arms to capture the energy from a bolt, I imagined blue nutrient pools, bushes filled with flowers as big as my head, and my soft sleep site. Logically, I should have stayed in Reval.

But no one had ever tried to send someone forward and remain behind. Most of us went alone. Or Sasquatches might travel in pairs if they were bringing a newborn baby. I considered all possible scenarios of what had happened before and what might have occurred. Then my situation became clear. When a close pair attracted a bolt, they both left—irrespective of their intended destination.

I needed to return to Reval immediately. I faced severe charges back home and felt obliged to accept the consequences. Representatives of the

Council would start looking for me and might imagine I had transferred to avoid my death sentence.

Despite my thick fur, I shivered when a gust nearly blew me sideways. The wind storms of Reval might be more intense but lacked precipitation and never came with plummeting temperatures. My world remained at a constant temperature—never too hot or cold. Porgu's weather was as insufferable as the halveks who lived here.

If I considered the conditions distressing, how did Dylan feel? I cursed myself for thinking of only my predicament. Had he lived through the transfer? Was his naked body capable of surviving in these conditions?

"Dylan?" I called in my hoarse whisper of a voice.

No response.

Telepathy, the Sasquatch way to communicate, might work better. Dylan had spent a month in Reval and learned how to send, receive, and block messages. Despite my higher intellect, his progress to communicate in our way far exceeded my meager attempts to speak out loud in his language.

I sent a broadcast mixture of images and words, including Dylan, as he looked when he arrived in Reval, with little body fur and his head hair cut short. I followed with visions of how he looked before we left, with hair down to his shoulders and the shadow of fine fur starting to grow across his chest and arms. I sighed as I recalled the hours we had spent in intimacy and sharing details of our very different lives.

With a forceful crack, a branch broke under the strain of newly fallen snow and snapped me back to reality. There was no time for reminiscing. I focused on my transmission. Our way of talking was remarkably faster and rarely gave a false message. Halveks needed words to describe emotions, places, and beings. With a few rapid-fire visions, a Sasquatch could convey an idea in an instant.

I knelt to the ground and hoped to gain a better view of what lay nearby. Nothing moved except the boughs and desiccated autumn grasses bowing against the wind and snow. If we transferred together, surely, he must be close at hand. I crawled on all fours in a circle but could not make out a prone body.

I stopped my search to sit cross-legged, my back propped against a rough tree. Where could Dylan be? Then I realized the worst of all possible scenarios. I leaped to my feet. What if I transferred, and he did not?

If Dylan had remained in Reval, he was in grave danger. Until I had convinced Dylan that Kalev planned to use him as collateral to gain influence with our High Council and curry favor with his brother's wife, the naive halvek believed Kalev to be a friend and mentor.

Our hasty effort to transfer Dylan back to Porgu was meant to get him out of Kalev's clutches. My attempt to save Dylan from Kalev may have put us both in the wrong place.

I looked upwards and wondered if the moon might be close enough to its fullest point to allow my transfer back to Reval. Blowing snow impaired my ability to make any accurate assessment. I rifled through my memories of Sasquatch transfers and could not think of a single attempt at an immediate return passage. Others had waited until the next full moon or, more commonly, a year or two later. Sasquatches had come to Porgu for thousands of years to silently observe the flawed race and track their decisions and development. My perfect memory recalled them all.

Without the luxury of time, I needed to face my sentence and confirm whether Dylan had successfully left Reval. If he had not, I might delay my execution and help him find a safe hiding place, away from Kalev and those who would search for him. With another month of practice, Dylan could try the transfer on his own at the next lunar cycle.

I stood to raise my arms toward the moon I could not see. Despite the unrelenting gale, I envisioned Reval. Mild temperatures and faint fragrances of home came to envelop my body. I could almost feel Porgu's atrocious storm start to dissipate. An electric pulse tingled my fingertips to track down my torso. My hair stood on end. I willed myself to leave Porgu behind.

Time slowed to a crawl, and I watched a serrated lightning bolt spike from the sky and detonate the towering pine standing next to me. My muscles collapsed as splinters of wood shot in every direction. The blast threw me to the ground. Just before I blacked out, my head snapped against a boulder. I heard the crunching collision of my skull against granite. Then the world went black.

ACKNOWLEDGMENTS

I must start by thanking my writing partner Susan Bavaria. From reading early drafts to giving me suggestions on character development and scene-setting, she was vital in my journey to complete this book. Two special beta readers, my sister Tina Pickell and brother-in-law Bruce Ianuzzi provided in-depth comments that resulted in this book's complexity and consistency. Sherry Richardson, Laurel McHargue, Matt Cushing, and other beta readers spent countless hours reviewing drafts and providing helpful suggestions.

From their detailed technical edits to broad content recommendations, I very much appreciate the feedback from the Rocky Mountain Fiction Writers Speculative Fiction critique group members.

Thank you to my neighbor Jim Finn, a friend and devout Sasquatch believer, for planting the seeds that grew into this series. This project started as a joint effort with my nephew Cody Tracy. Without his infectious passion for writing and confidence that I could complete this series on my own, it would still be an outline of an idea.

While none of the events in this book happened, I thank business owners in Salida for allowing me to use names of their establishments, including Phillip Benningfield fellow-author and co-owner of Café Dawn and owners of the Palace Hotel.

My final thanks are to my loving husband, David. His line edits helped to create consistency and clarity. For all the times we've been hiking, and I've asked you to remove my phone from my pack so I could record an idea and taken hours away from our vacations and at home-time to write and edit—I give you my sincere thanks.

If you are familiar with Salida, Colorado, you will know some of the places in this book are real. However, none of the places where 'bad things happen' are real. That includes Reval (obviously), Jen's cabin, Nate's gallery, and a few others. Absolutely all of the people in this book are fictional.

L.V. DITCHKUS is the author of *Legacy of the Sasquatch: Book III of The Sasquatch Series*. While writing these three books, she's led adventure travel trips, hiked and snowshoed hundreds of miles, and volunteered for wilderness advocacy and writing organizations. She and her husband live in a rural mountain community in central Colorado, where she gains inspiration from the five 14,000+ foot tall peaks viewable from her window.

Watch for her new series *The Chrom Y Chronicles*—with an expected release in 2021.

Check out her blog at LVDitchkus.com

Made in the USA
Columbia, SC
26 September 2020